IT CAME FROM BEYOND . . . AND WITHIN!

Tendrils. Little vine things. A few, at first. But Jeffy opened his mouth wider, and wider still—the lips rolling away from his open mouth—until a whole forest of them wormed their way out of his gullet. Thin, white, maggoty things, waving their way towards Ed.

Now Ed jerked and went into a spasm like a madman, yelling, then gibbering, the drool pouring out of his mouth . . .

And the sound they made as they slithered out of Jeffy! The same tearing sound made by pulling the skin off a chicken. The sound he once heard when he stepped on a dead flounder and made its eyes pop out like marbles.

They touched his face . . .

Midsummer

A novel of soul-shattering terror by the acclaimed author of *Beneath Still Waters*

D0920071

MIDSUMMER

MATTHEW J. COSTELLO

CHARTER/DIAMOND BOOKS, NEW YORK

MIDSUMMER

A Charter/Diamond Book / published by arrangement with
the author

PRINTING HISTORY
Charter/Diamond edition / September 1990

ISBN: 1-55773-383-X

Charter/Diamond Books are published by The Berkley Publishing
Group, 200 Madison Avenue, New York, New York 10016.
The name "CHARTER/DIAMOND" and its logo are trademarks
belonging to Charter Communications, Inc.

PRINTED IN THE UNITED STATES OF AMERICA

10 9 8 7 6 5 4 3 2 1

For Devon Costello . . .
for so many reasons . . .

MIDSUMMER

Prologue

FEBRUARY FUCKING ELEVENTH, Alan Ward thought, rolling his squeaky chair to the one decent-sized window in the stuffy, cramped building that was part lab, part dormitory, and all pisshole.

February eleventh.

Midsummer.

Down here, that is, here, right near the anus of the planet. Midsummer, and the sleek digital thermometers said it was five below outside, and falling fast.

Of course it was to be expected. He knew that when he volunteered for the assignment. Two and a half months at a Naval Research Station at latitude 89 degrees south.

A dream come true, he thought at the time.

Ever since he could read he had loved the stories about the poles, and the strange men who were compelled to go there. From tubby old Sir John Franklin, who completely disappeared in the no-man's-land of the Arctic Ocean (and whose wife spent their entire fortune trying to find him) . . . to poor, foolish stiff-lipped Robert Falcon Scott, the very epitome of the British asshole, leading his men on a 1000-mile jaunt to the South Pole, man-hauling their cumbersome sleds, only to discover that crafty Amundsen—on skis!—had beat them by weeks.

Yes, Scott probably was glad it all ended with his dwindled party freezing in a tent eleven miles from all the food and fuel they would ever need. His one shot at being a hero.

Alan Ward grew up thinking—no, *knowing*—that he'd go to

Antarctica. He took all the right courses at the State University at Albany, learning everything he could about weather and geology. In the winter, he cross-country skied. In summer, he climbed mountains. He subscribed to *The South Polar Times* and the National Science Foundation's quarterly newsletters on polar research. And he joined Navy ROTC.

After graduation he got his choice of assignments. To the beleaguered modern Navy, he was a godsend. They were all too glad to post him to polar duty.

And here he was. . . . Sometimes, if you aren't lucky, you get what you want.

He leaned closer to the triple-paned window. According to the manufacturer it shouldn't ever frost up. Still, Alan had to run his hand over it scraping a thin sheen of ice off its surface if he wanted to look out.

Too damn moist in here, he thought. Too many pots of tea, too many showers.

When you came in from outside—so cold and dry—your whole body just screamed out for moisture. If you weren't careful, your lips would start to crack, and ugly little tears would begin to grow.

And they just never healed down here.

He looked outside.

In the distance he could see—barely—one of the smaller peaks of the Queen Maud Mountains, half-hidden by all the swirling snow that beat against the window.

Not that it was snowing.

It *was* summer, after all. Beach weather. No, that wasn't snow he was looking at. It was the wind, incredible winds that blew across the great southern ice cap, picking up speed before ramming into the mountains. The wind blew the icy granules into the air, sending them up and around, making tiny white Kansas twisters.

It was all topsy-turvy. Snowing from the ground. And some of the granules were years old . . . maybe decades.

Alan saw that the wind, and the snow storm, were picking up strength.

"Damn," he said. He was all alone. They slept in shifts, and while one group worked at the fissures off to the east, the other two Navy lieutenants and two NSF scientists were in the back, sleeping like babies.

He pushed his chair across the gritty floor, towards the computer console.

He hit the keyboard with practiced ease—if nothing else his typing sure had improved—and the screen flashed the current satellite weather information. First the active storm systems, if any, were displayed. As he suspected, there was nothing, except for some small ocean squalls off the Ross Ice Shelf. Another chart displayed polar wind speed and direction.

Not good.

The temperature was dropping all across the shelf, and fast, as the winds started turning back to South America. The wind speed would create blizzard conditions all across the polar ice cap.

3:15 A.M.

The men weren't due back for another four hours.

By then, they would be in deep shit.

He put on his headphones and began calling.

The transmitter in the small station was powerful enough to reach all the way to the Amazon.

"Emperor Two, this is Ice Box calling. Come in, Emperor."

Within seconds he heard an answer, as clear as a call to the local Dominos.

"Yes, Alan, we're here. What's up?"

It was Dr. Wynan, civilian leader of the project, a man openly disdainful of any procedure that smacked of the military. Alan found him arrogant, obnoxious, and, after six weeks, totally insufferable.

"We've got some bad weather coming in, Doc. Winds, snow, and temperatures that may make the cats give up and die."

Wynan said nothing for a moment.

The snowcats were almost impervious to any kind of terrain, or weather. They used a special oil that remained viscous no matter what, and in the engines were completely insulated. The plastic treads were harder and more durable than any metal. They were practically submersible.

Space-age snowmobiles.

Still, an Antarctic blizzard was nothing to fuck around with.

"We've just broken through," Wynan said, as if explaining his hesitation.

Ward knew what that meant. After weeks of working on a tantalizing fissure at the first exposed hills of the Queen Maud range—a fissure that might lead to parts of the Antarctica continent that hadn't seen light in over 40 million years—somehow they had broken through.

And now he was telling them to leave.

"I understand," Alan said. "But it looks real bad, sir. I'd hate to—"

He felt a bit nervous now. Computers or no computers, if the winds petered out, and Wynan lost track of their opening, it would be a major gaffe on Ward's part.

He wished one of the scientists would hear him and wake up. Let *him* come over and make the decision.

"All right," Wynan interrupted. "We'll just mark our position. We can still see the sun. . . . We'll get some reading on it, and head back. Let me know if there's any change."

"Yes, sir," Alan said, and the line went dead.

At best, they should be back in forty, maybe fifty minutes. Enough time, he thought, looking at the weather charts, to miss the worst of it.

He stood up. His muscles were all cramped from sitting through the night. He stretched in the electronic gloom of the data screens that surrounded him.

All this technology. Polar suits designed by NASA that kept you toasty warm. High-tech transportation from Japan. A hefty video-tape library. And a microwave cuisine that would put some restaurants to shame.

All that, and it still felt like he was on another planet.

Wynan had four men with him. Two Navy scientists—generally left out of the interesting discussions—and two scientists under Wynan.

No women, much to everyone's chagrin. There *were* limits to self-control. At least, the Navy thought so.

The research project had a 50-50 chance of making history. It would either produce some major discoveries about the early history of the continent—when it was warm and crawling with who-knows-what prehistoric animals . . .

Or it wouldn't.

Even armed with the best satellite infrared photos, it still required trained geologists stomping around, looking for some opening in the ice cap that would lead to a land buried under millennia of ice.

As if he gave a damn anymore.

Four more weeks, and it was all over.

'Cause nobody wintered in the center of Antarctica.

He poured the hot water into his cup, all sticky and lined with the stains of the half dozen cups of coffee consumed during his watch. This time, though, he fixed himself some herbal tea, from a box featuring a bear in a red flannel nightgown. Disgusting stuff, but at least it was hot and without caffeine. He wanted to sleep when Wynan's crew came back.

Tomorrow it was his turn to go out with Wynan, and it sounded like there might be something to see.

He was jiggling the rose-colored tea bag up and down, smelling the unappetizing brew, when a single, high-pitched buzzer went off.

It was a message from McMurdo, the main Navy station on the continent. It had probably been sent from NOAA, the National Oceanic and Atmospheric Administration, in Washington.

He walked quickly over to the keyboard and hit ENTER, silencing the beeper before it woke anyone. (Wishing immediately that he had let it ring on. Some company would be nice.)

The message was two lines long. Terse and direct.

"Suspend all out-of-base activities for the next twenty-four hours," he read aloud. "High winds and extreme lows expected."

"I know," he said to the screen.

Supporting information—the maps, with curving lines indicating the direction of the wind—were available. But he didn't need them.

What he needed to do was have Wynan get his ass back here. Prontissimo.

He slipped on his headphones.

"Emperor Two," he called. "This is Ice Box."

He waited.

"Dr. Wynan. Come in, please."

Even if they were already on the snowcats, barreling over the frozen waves of ice, they still would have their earphones on. They should hear his voice no matter what racket was going on.

"Dr. Wynan. Come in."

Alan waited. Listening to the silence.

"Shit," he said aloud.

Pat Murphy, one of the Navy's men and the closest Alan had

to a friend at the Ice Box, gulped at some air in his sleep. Alan thought about going over and shaking him awake.

What for? he thought.

He tried the radio again, but there was no answer.

Now what the fuck do I do? he wondered.

Chances were they were making their way back right now. Wynan *said* he was on his way. They had four snowcats, so if there was a problem, they could easily double up. Even triple up, if they had to . . .

There was only one cat left, just outside the station.

It didn't make any sense to think about launching a rescue party. None at all.

"Damn," he said. He went over to the keyboard and typed a message for transmission to McMurdo.

"Off-base team notified to return. No answer."

He hit ENTER.

And waited.

Well, he thought with grim satisfaction. *I've just given someone on the night shift there a little problem to deal with.*

He looked up at the clock over the radio: 3:55 A.M.

Almost four.

And he remembered an old Ingmar Bergman flick, murky, confusing, but compelling just the same. . . .

Hour of the Wolf, it was called . . . the hour, one of Bergman's cheery characters explained, between four and five. More people die in that hour than in any other, claimed by heart attacks, seizures, or God-knows-what.

For Bergman it was a chance to face the darkest, bleakest regions of a man's soul.

Well, there was no bleaker place than right here . . . right now. . . .

He went back to the window, scraping again at a new paper-thin layer of ice. It was like looking into one of those goofy paperweights with the billowing swirls of styrofoam snow.

No. It was thicker than that. The mountains, the sky (which if it could be seen would be a bright, blinding blue), were all gone.

If Wynan was on his way, Alan wouldn't even be able to see him.

Instead, he'd hear him. Some faint sound, at first, just a tad louder than the tiny pings of a thousand crystalline pieces of snow scratching at the window.

The sound of the snowcats—a deep, throaty rumble—that was one of the sweetest sounds on the frozen ice cap. That sound *was* civilization.

Still, he stared out the window and listened.

Ten minutes, he told himself.

Ten minutes, and if I don't hear anything, I'll wake everyone up and share the grief.

4:00 A.M. the digital clock said.

(In the Bergman flick some old man came into this guy's shack . . . grinning, toothless at four in the morning. He then proceeded to peel his face off, like it was just some clever Halloween mask. Then he popped his eyes out. Go figure. . . .)

4:01 . . . 4:02 . . . 4:03 . . .

He thought he heard something then. Very faint. Maybe more in his head than anywhere else. He leaned closer to the icy glass, almost reluctant to get closer to the snow.

There! Yes, it was a rumble, tiny, but definitely *there*. He took a deep breath, glad that the crisis was over, that soon Wynan and his crew would come barreling into the heated prefab palace, cook up some dehydrated eggs, and talk about what a bitch it was outside.

The sound grew.

And Alan Ward felt his heart sink.

It was a snowcat engine, all right. Big and noisy, easily louder now than the storm itself.

But there was only one engine.

Alan scraped at the window, rubbing at it, searching for the first slight darkening of the jet-black cat.

One fucking cat . . .

What the hell had happened to the other three? Did they break down? Was everybody crowded onto the one cat?

That was impossible. There was no way it could hold five people. Two, maybe three . . . but not five.

Had there been an accident? Were the others hurt, or trapped somewhere? Was Wynan stupid enough to leave them behind? And why hadn't anyone answered the radio?

The roar of the engine grew and grew, but still no shape appeared from out of the white shroud of snow.

Then it was right there! Right next to the hut, but he still couldn't see it.

He heard the engine cough once, and then die as it was shut off.

Alan had his face right next to the glass, his eyes pressed right up to it, struggling to peer right and left.

"What the fu—" he started to say.

The main entrance to the compound was only about ten feet from him. It was a system of double doors, with a small insulated tunnel leading to the outside door. In between was a place for storing gear.

It was the way everyone always entered the hut. Always.

Alan heard a sound from his right, back in the darkness where all the beds were.

There was another entrance. A back entrance. Rarely used. Another setup of two doors, a smaller corridor. No place to stash your parka.

Alan heard the rear door open.

Someone was coming in. The cat had been brought around to the back . . . out of sight.

The lieutenant turned in his chair, his heart suddenly beginning to race, a funny feeling growing in his gut, like he had to take a crap or something.

He didn't move though, waiting for the other door to open, the one that led to the sleeping area of the hut.

(One of the sleeping scientists seemed to stir . . . as if sensing the sudden gust of cooler air.)

The door opened.

It was Wynan, his hood pulled tight, his red-tinted goggles almost glowing.

His face was covered with a crystalline hoarfrost.

In five minutes, when his face thawed out, the pain would be unbearable.

Alan stood up.

"Dr. Wynan . . . Where are the others . . . ? Why didn't you answer?"

Wynan took a step—only one step—and Alan saw a detail he had missed at first.

In Wynan's right hand, held almost casually, dangling like some small, unimportant object, was an ice axe.

It had a small shaft, with a thick, almost unbreakable blade made of tungsten, iron, and some new, very strong alloy. Ice, no matter how cold, would yield to it . . . as would most rock.

But the head of Wynan's axe was covered with a dry reddish crust.

Wynan took another step.

Alan licked his lips.

He took a step back. Back to the computer consoles, to the radio, to the multicolored glow of all the data screens.

Not so reassuring now.

Wynan pushed his hood back off his head.

For a moment, Alan didn't expect it to be him.

"Wh—what happened?" Alan stammered, unable to take his eyes off the axe head. "Should we notify McMurdo? Let them know . . ."

Wynan's face changed. For a moment Alan thought he saw something flash across the scientist's features, some cloud that sent the facial skin rippling, distorting it. His mouth opened, as if he was about to say something.

Instead Wynan gasped, uncomfortably, as if laboring to breathe.

And he raised his axe.

"Jesus," Alan screamed.

And his mind scrambled, trying to remember where the weapons were and just what the fuck the procedure was for getting at them.

They were in a cabinet, off the cooking area. A lock, with two keys.

Two fucking keys! So no cabin-feverish maniac could take it upon himself to end the research expedition.

Alan stumbled back to the cabinet. Maybe the lock could be broken off.

Wynan gasped at the air, choking at the door.

Pat Murphy woke up. He rubbed his face and looked up at Wynan.

"What the—"

Wynan brought the axe down, right into Murphy's tousled hair.

Alan, his eyes fixed on Wynan, who stared right back at him, reached down and fingered the lock.

It might just be pried off, he thought. Maybe. He looked around, and saw a metal rod hanging on the wall near the tools.

Wynan gasped again, and brought the axe down on the other sleeping lieutenant.

Alan grabbed the rod and brought it over to the gun cabinet.

Now the two scientists were awake. Alan barely heard their screaming; his own brain was pounding.

"Dr. Wynan," one of them began, "What is going on—"

Then . . . *thwack!* A sick, moist sound.

Wynan buried the blade in the scientist's chest, pushing the man's thermal pajamas, tucking the top taut into the hole he'd just made.

Alan wedged the rod between the lock and the heavy metal latch, and he pulled at it with his entire weight.

The other scientist . . . the last of the four sleepers left alive, was up, kneeling on the bed, crying, begging, praying to Wynan as he pulled the axe blade loose.

"Run, for Chrissakes!" Alan screamed at him.

The pleading man looked at Alan, looked right at him as if he could somehow stop all this.

He didn't see the blade come flying right at him, covered now with a bright filmy red, didn't see it as it quickly severed his head and sent it flying to Alan's feet.

Please, God, Alan prayed, as he tugged on the bar.

Please, and he gave it one more pull.

The latch and the lock went flying.

Wynan took a step towards him. Hard, as if he were laboring to move. And another.

Then, just as Alan was awkwardly digging out a rifle, Wynan let the axe slip to the ground . . .

As he kept on walking towards Alan Ward. . . .

I

Before
the
Carnival

One

JOSH CAME UP to his grandmother's elbow and perched there, watching her fingers smooth the pie crust to fit the pan. Then she pinched the lip of the crust, over and over, using her thumb to create a rippling pattern.

"Never seen someone make an apple pie before?" she asked him.

He grinned and shook his head.

She frowned—all in fun, he knew. "It never fails to amaze me the things children don't see anymore."

Josh watched her rub her large, wrinkled hands on her apron.

"Well, I guess that's why your mom wanted you to spend the summer here. At least"—she sighed—"I certainly hope that's the reason."

Josh followed her to the old, yellowish-white refrigerator. He was pretty sure that it, and everything else in the kitchen, was the same as it had been when his mother was his age . . . standing around, watching a pie being made.

"Is it for dinner?" he asked.

"No . . . not this one." She reached into the refrigerator and brought out a great brown ceramic bowl. She plopped its contents into the pie shell and Josh could see the glistening chunks of apple tumbling haphazardly. "It's for a friend," she said. "But I'll make another one, just for us. Want to help?" she asked, arching her eyebrows.

"Sure," Josh said.

His grandmother quickly fixed him up with some dough and

instructions on how to knead it. And, while he worked, she talked to him.

"You're happy here, aren't you Josh? I mean, it's still new and all—"

He nodded. "Sure," he said again.

"That's good. 'Cause if you weren't, there's camp and things—"

"No!" he said strongly, surprising himself. "I'm fine here."

"Yes," his grandmother said quietly. "I suppose you are."

He kneaded the dough some more, until it felt smooth and silky. He grabbed at it, enjoying the way it squeezed through his clenched fingers.

"That's ready, sweetheart," she said gently. "You can spread it in the pan."

This was a trickier part, Josh saw. Soon his smooth crust had tears and holes, until it looked like a piece of Swiss cheese. But his grandmother came over, and after a few almost invisible presses and pinches with her thumb, the damage was all gone.

He smiled, thinking, *There's magic in those fingers.*

"Will Mom call today?" he asked, trying to sound offhand.

"Don't know," the woman answered, going to get the bowl of apple filling. "You can call her, you know, if there's something—"

"No. I wouldn't want to bother her. She's busy and—"

And that's the real reason he was here, wasn't it? She had responsibilities . . . a career. All by herself. She couldn't have Josh around . . . distracting her . . . reminding her.

"Listen," his grandmother said, turning quickly and placing her strong hands on his shoulders. He was almost tall enough that he could look at her face to face. But *her* hands were like a lumberjack's. He wouldn't want to go one-on-one with her.

"She's your mother, Josh, and she'll never be too busy to speak with you. And I don't want you to forget that."

"If I promise not to forget, will you," he said, glancing left and right at her hands, "let me go?" He grinned and she laughed.

"Okay," she said, still chuckling. "This time."

He went to the sink and started washing his doughy hands.

"What are you going to do today?"

"I thought I'd go exploring . . . near Barrow's Hill. Maybe bring my sketch pad."

These days just about everywhere he went Josh brought his

sketch pad. He never could play soccer worth a damn, and he was barely able to hang in the middle math group. And writing was about the hardest thing in the world for him . . . the words just never came.

But he could draw.

At first he copied cartoon characters, gradually learning how to create a perfect Smurf or Fraggle. But he quickly moved on to sketching anything that wasn't moving. His remote control Godzilla. Their Audi station wagon. And, for months at a time, trees. Hundreds of them. Never satisfied, he threw away ten sketches for every one he let stay in his battered sketch book.

He had found his thing.

Josh had high hopes for his art classes next year, when he went to high school. It *had* to be better than the moronic projects the klutzy middle school art teacher had him do.

"Well, don't go too far afield, Josh. And don't go up near the gorge. Rocks fall all the time there." He started for the door, snatching up his small spiral pad and a pencil. "And be back for lunch," he heard her call out to him as he left the kitchen.

"Right." He yelled back.

And then he was out.

Moving away from his grandmother's small house, past her small, neat tract of land with just a few rows of corn—just starting to get tall—and past the small barn with two mottled cows, two grizzly furred sheep, and the old horse, Mister.

This was his summer. Here.

He trooped up the gently sloping hill, almost able to look back now and see the town of Stoneywood. The very tops of its buildings peeked up from behind the dense stand of trees that cut his grandmother's house off from the rest of the world.

A whole summer, he thought.

It had been his choice. His mother had explained that. He could live with his grandmother . . . help her with the corn when it came in . . . live a different kind of life.

"Like City Mouse becoming Country Mouse," she'd said, grinning at him.

"Or," she'd gone on, all too casually now, trying to keep the threatening tone out of her voice, "you could spend the summer in camp."

His eyes went wide with that one. She knew that his social skills weren't the greatest. There had been more than one conference on Josh's inability to get along with his peers.

He shrugged.

It was no contest, he thought, breathing hard now, as he climbed up to the top of the hill. Here, at least, he'd be free.

Bored, maybe. Lonely. Probably.

But there were worse places.

He reached the crest of the hill and looked at the town. The crisp white church steeple seemed to hang protectively over the town. The main road was bustling, filled with what his grandma called 'the summer people,' a brainless species that made her shiver in disgust.

They were all down there, buying ice chests and cheapo fishing rods and cases of Genesee beer, while the locals tried to grab every dime possible.

He turned away from the town. Just ahead, past the hill, was an honest-to-God mountain. Covered in green, with bits of blackish-gray rock sticking out.

He sat down on the grassy hill. Some crickets and leaf hoppers scattered away.

Josh dug out his pencil and pad, and started sketching the mountain. He quickly outlined the bumpy, irregular lines, erasing a bit here and there, until what he saw on his paper began to resemble what was standing before him.

Then he began putting in the details. He had a good eye for the small bits. The way a certain tree leaned out and away from the slope. A gathering of boulders piled precariously near the top. The mixture of shadow and light that made the mountain so secret . . . so interesting to look at.

And then—for the first time that day—he thought about his father.

(His pencil faltered. His hand drew a stray line that belonged nowhere. He erased it angrily.)

Each day it was the same thing: How long could he go before he'd think about him? How long before he'd have to replay the whole scene over in his mind?

He kept on drawing, clutching his pencil tighter, hoping it would pass. *Please*, he wanted to say. *It's so beautiful here. The sky is so blue, and the clouds are pure white. And the air—God, it smells so good.*

Not now. Not here.

But it came anyway.

And like a prisoner, he was forced to sit there and watch the show that his mind had on permanent rerun. . . .

* * *

A school day. Like hundreds of others. All equally horrible.

He found himself wondering, as he did every day, *Why do we have to go through this? It's no different than yesterday, is it?* His mother was rushing between the bathroom and the bedroom, now with just a slip on, now a dress, then her hairbrush in hand, then her lipstick . . . just like, he once told her—laughing so hard that he collapsed onto the hallway floor—just like Frankenstein's monster coming to life.

"Let's see you, buster," she said, "when *you're* pushing forty."

"I seriously doubt, Mother dear," he said, laughing, "that I'll be dashing around with lipstick in hand, wearing just a slip."

And she smiled, one of the great sights on the planet.

"Let's hope not," she said, laughing now. "For your father's sake."

As usual, his dad was well behind them, unable to get out of bed until some mental alarm told him that another minute's delay would make him impossibly late. Then it was whirlwind time, like he was the Flash. The same bit as his mother, only three times faster, running around, gulping coffee, his tie undone, combing his thinning hair (a forbidden subject), acting as if it was their fault he was running late.

But on that day, he hurried even more.

Catching a shuttle, he explained to Josh . . . to D.C.

"Be back for dinner?" Josh asked.

"That depends," he said, smiling as his mother came into the room. "What's for dinner?"

"Just be back for dinner," she said, laughing, leaning her head on his shoulder. And Josh smiled. Then his cheeks reddened as he saw his father grab at her, holding her close as she giggled.

"Just be back for dinner," she said.

Then his dad, the last one up, was the first one gone.

So quickly. Just a few quick kisses, hurried goodbyes, and then gone.

And as soon as Josh heard the door slam he felt funny.

His mother was still running around, getting ready for her departure.

But it all felt different. The sounds, the air . . . as if there were some kind of void . . . just outside the door.

Something made Josh run to the window, to see if his father was down at his car.

He watched him get into the Audi, hoping he'd turn and look up at the window. Wave at him.

Instead, his dad just drove away, joining the press of cars making their way to the cluttered highways of suburban New York.

Then his mother left . . . another quick peck on the cheek, another door slamming, and Josh was left there, spooning down his cereal, searching for the source of his strange feelings.

Finally he left, riding a crowded bus to the middle school, sitting alone, looking out the window.

All day the funny feeling grew until his English teacher, a young woman named Miss Walker, who wasn't afraid of stirring the minds, and the fantasies, of her young students asked him what was wrong.

"Nothing," he said. "I just don't feel all that well."

But he didn't want to see the nurse.

Going home was even worse. The sky had clouded over, and everyone on the bus wore an expression like they all knew some bad news that they just couldn't bear to tell him.

The world had never seemed a friendly place to Josh.

On that day, it seemed hostile. An enemy.

He got to their apartment, poured some milk, and made a show of doing his homework.

But all he was really doing was waiting.

Then, at four thirty, he heard the front door being opened, its twin locks giving way in sequence. Four thirty. Too early for anyone to be coming home. On a normal day.

He had a pencil in his hand then too . . . and a piece of paper in front of him. . . .

He heard her steps, coming into the kitchen, slow, measured. Then, just before she reached him, she said his name.

"Josh."

He heard her voice. The strained way it sounded. Like she was lost in some dismal forest.

"Josh," she said again, louder, clearing her throat.

"Mom," he said, just to let her know where he was.

She stepped into the kitchen.

Her eye makeup had gone all weird. It was all smudgy, and her eyes glistened in the light of the kitchen.

She took a step.

"Josh," she said quietly, wringing her hands back and forth (and he looked to see if she held anything in them . . . but it was just her fingers, trying to tie impossible knots).

"Josh, your father—"

She stepped closer to him.

No, he wanted to say. *Don't come closer. If you stay away, I won't hear it. I won't hear it.*

But it was too late.

"His plane," she said, ". . . it . . . somehow . . . it . . ."

And then it all fell apart, and she dropped into a chair and her hands—suddenly freed—came up to her face, trying to stop the tears.

He sat there, angry. Scared. Lost.

She had said the words. If only she hadn't *said* the words. Then it would have been okay. Then everything would have been fine. . . .

No. It wouldn't have.

'Cause he had known all along, hadn't he?

He looked at his pencil. Then the paper. The heading said 'Josh Tyler, Math, Room 210.'

But the only other thing on the paper was a detailed sketch of a small plane crashing into some murky swamp.

His mother moaned, bellowed in their small kitchen.

And Josh stood up and made his way over to her.

Trying to see.

'Cause, for some reason, everything looked so blurry. . . .

Josh put his pencil down.

The sketch was done. Perhaps the mountain in his picture didn't look as big and fierce as it really did, sitting before him. Perhaps it looked darker, filled with more shadows and hidden places.

He stood up, stretched, reaching up to the deep blue sky. And as he stood, he saw, just at the base of the mountain, the gorge.

It wasn't far, just down the hill, and past a few fields.

It was hard to make out just how far away it was, or even how big the gorge was. But he could see the great yawning, full of mystery and the promise of secrets.

He looked back at his grandmother's house.

He had promised her he'd stay away from the gorge.

But it would be a mighty long summer if he spent the whole time baking pies and doing exactly what his grandmother asked.

That was something she'd have to learn about boys, he thought. They have their own business to be about.

And his, now, was to get a look at that gorge . . . up close.

The sun was warm. The air too-rich with the smell of grass gone to seed. And ahead, down the hill, lay adventure.

He put his pad and pencil in his back pocket, and started down the hill, towards the mountain.

TWO

THE CAR COUGHED, lurching off the Massachusetts Turnpike—an ominous warning as it braved the endless loop of traffic that girded Boston.

I hate Boston, Brian McShane thought. *It's some damn theme park for college kids, with its coffeehouses and red-brick walks, and the whole air of intellectual snobbery.*

Of course, he knew that his feeling could simply be sour grapes that Harvard had passed on admitting him to its hallowed halls.

Their loss.

They probably had their quota of Roman Catholic kids from the wilds of Flatbush.

So what? Who said the State University at Albany wasn't just as good a school?

Sure.

At least everyone there wasn't walking around with cashmere scarves and Geoffrey Beene corduroy jackets, with dogeared copies of the *Harvard Law Journal* tucked under their arm.

Someone honked at Brian's rent-a-heap, an obnoxious noise that summed up the total inadequacy of Brian's chosen mode of transportation. And then—on cue—the Reliant K sluggishly sputtered ahead, into the maelstrom.

A Black Trans Am did an end run, screaming past Brian's left.

I'm like some little old lady, Brian thought. *Don't mind me, sonny. Heh-heh . . . just can't seem to get the lead out anymore.*

But the Reliant adopted a more confident pose once it joined the slow lane. Brian took a quick look at the street map, trying to glance at the circled street without sending his car right up someone else's butt. God only knew the state of this heap's brakes.

To the right, he saw the Harbor and the Boston Aquarium, surrounded by the cobblestoned marketplace, a yuppified restoration with expensive restaurants and shops that specialized in semi-genuine scrimshaw bought by the bushel and sold at the salty-aired boutiques.

Of course, there were other reasons he hated Boston.

Like Susan.

(And he'd never be that vulnerable or stupid or whatever again. . . . Just like he'd never be twenty-five again . . . or thirty or . . .)

He saw a sign for Massachusetts Avenue, and even though his destination was still much farther south, he decided to get off the loop. Another such opportunity to escape might not present itself.

The midday Monday traffic was incredibly dense. It made rush hour in Washington look restful.

He passed a few down and dirty blocks, less ugly than D.C.'s ghetto wonderland but all the more visible surrounded by the wealth of Beantown. His car wheezed again, and he hoped that it lived long enough to get him to a more desirable breakdown location.

A traffic light let him study the map carefully.

The Naval Judicial Office had arranged a room for him near Boylston . . . within sight of the subject's house. He'd be able to settle in, sort of get to know the neighborhood . . . maybe ask a few questions.

"Looking for what?" he had asked his boss, Commander Charlie Alexander. "Just what the hell am I supposed to be looking for?"

Grins, smiles, all around the table. "We're not too sure, McShane. Not too damn sure.

"Just this," Alexander said. "No uniform. No Government car. If you're going to find out anything at all, it will be as a private citizen."

So now, here he was—Lieutenant Commander Brian Mc-

Shane, Assistant Navy Prosecutor and counting the days till he hit his twentieth year. Then goodbye Navy.

And hello what?

Private practice?

Unlikely. He had heard enough stories from other Navy attorneys. Not only were the various state bar exams bitches to take, after years away from the old law books, Naval law was an incestuous little world all its own. He knew that world, its code and rules, real well. But once outside, he'd be an over-the-hill, out-of-touch lawyer. Maybe he could bag a few clients from the service, guys who wanted a civilian representative who knew Naval law.

And, there was always the occasional will and house-closing.

Another light, and he glanced at the map. The next right should bring him close to the tenement-cum-stakeout that was to be his field position.

He looked at the backseat. Two boxes of material. Important stuff, they had told him. Statements, medical records, maps, everything that they had been able to find out.

Everything, except who killed whom . . . and why . . .

That was his job.

He licked his lips. Boy, a Marlboro would sure hit the spot now. Nothing like plowing through city traffic, destroying your lungs with the wonderful burnt-shit flavor of an honest-to-God cigarette. Quitting had been easy. Who wants to die?

Staying off them was boring.

Then the block was there. Federal Street.

Looking not unlike the lower-middle-class houses that sprawled around Flatbush, nice houses that were once all of the American Dream that people wanted. All, that is, until suburbia was invented.

He slowed . . . an easy task in his heap . . . and scanned the numbers of the houses. . . .

The woman, if in fact it was a woman and not some gynandromorphic creature from another, more unusual universe, shuffled up the splintery steps. Her body odor, a dizzying mix of beer, coffee, and a dozen sloppily eaten meals, trailed behind her.

It all blended, Brian thought, with the almost overpowering stench of the staircase. Garbage, urine, and who-knew-what-else, all coming together to create a decidedly special ambience.

What did I do to get so lucky? he thought.

The woman's legs, encased in sagging stockings that bunched up around her ankles, shuffled steadily up—two, then three flights, before arriving at the prize, the Grail.

"A nice room," the landlady announced. "Nice view . . . good refrigerator."

"Nice and hot," Brian commented. "The windows"—he gestured hooking a thumb in the direction of the single window, solemnly shut—"They open?"

"Sure . . . whatever you want." Then she turned. Every jewel has its price. "Four hundred fifty security and annuder four hundred fifty the first month." Her mouth hung open, froglike.

Brian dug out his wallet. *If I'm here a month I'll kill myself, lady, and you can take my four fifty and buy a new wardrobe.*

He handed her nine crisp hundred-dollar bills. Fresh from the good old Government Accounting Office.

She counted them slowly—who says trust is dead?—nodded, and shuffled out, giving Brian a few last-minute pointers.

"No noise . . . the neighbors don't like it."

This—even as she had to raise her voice to be heard above the crazy din emanating from the building's other quiet tenants. "And no drugs . . . I call the cops. . . ." She stopped at the top of the stairs. "You can have all the women you want"—she grinned—"but—"

"I know." Brian smiled back. "No noise."

She nodded, and he closed the door on this Ancient Mariner of tenements as her worn flip-flops rapped their repetitive tattoo on the stairs.

Brian turned. The smell of roach powder—a massive batter probably launched that morning to give the six-legged boys warning to stay out of sight until the sucker was landed—stung his nostrils. *Who knows?* Brian thought. *Maybe you can get high from it.*

He put down his attaché case on the bed, noting how even the light weight of the case made the decrepit mattress sag. He walked over to the grimy window. It looked as if it had been painted with scum . . . something new to decorate your windows with.

He reached down, grunted, and pulled on the window.

As he expected, the window wouldn't budge. The last paint job had sealed it tight.

He walked back to the bed, worked the attaché's combination, and popped open the twin clasps.

File folders sat on the top, a notebook, and a phone directory.

He lifted them up, and grabbed a service revolver, a small Colt. Brian had laughed when Alexander told him to bring it. Laughed.

His Commander didn't laugh. He just smiled, and said, "Bring it."

And Brian thought . . . *maybe he knows something I don't*.

He brought the gun over to the window and rapped with the butt at the molding, splintering the paint, sending eggshell flakes flying to the floor. In a minute, the window looked like mice had been chewing at the edges. The smell of the room—the mix of roach killer and the smell of the insects themselves—had him dizzy. His clothes, khaki slacks and pale-yellow short-sleeved shirt were plastered to his body with sweat. His hair, blond but thinning, was glued to his forehead.

The fucking room was an oven.

After some more sharp bangs, he was ready to give the window another shot. He reached down and dug his hand into the finger holds. Nothing happened, no matter how purple he turned.

And then, as if the window were giving up at last, it suddenly released its hold on the surrounding frame, and shot up a foot or so, before quickly digging in once again. As if to say, "I go this far, and no further."

But it was enough.

The air outside, almost as hot but just a tad fresher, didn't exactly rush in. But now he could stick his head out, sniff, and for the first time, look at the small brownstone just down the street.

Pretty innocuous-looking. Nobody up and about.

Brian pulled a plain wooden chair—the single one in the room—close to the window. He also picked up a manila file.

Though he'd read it before.

But now, with the subject of the dossier so close, it might make even more interesting reading.

The letter carrier, a young black woman in grayish-blue shorts and skirt, was working her way up the block.

Brian looked at the folder, labeled:

UNITED STATES NAVY—JUDICIAL DEPARTMENT, WASHINGTON D.C.

He opened the folder.

The deposition, dated March 10, 1990, of Lieutenant Alan Ward, U.S.N.

Salsa rhythms magically filled the hallway, the booming music easily penetrating Brian's door.

And he read just what Alan Ward had told the Navy . . . about Antarctica . . . about crazy Dr. Wynan . . . and all those chopped-up dead bodies. . . .

Josh had it all wrong.

He could see that. The shadows on the mountain hid twisted, stunted trees that clawed at the mountain, trying to hold on.

And the blackish gray rock hid tiny bits that sparkled and twinkled as he got closer. And the wind! It constantly ruffled the bushes and shook the trees, making the old lumpy mountain seem alive.

He'd have to sketch it again and again, he knew. It would take more than one drawing to nail down this baby.

The gorge remained hidden as he came closer. He hurried now, running down the small hill, leaping over tufts of grass, narrowly avoiding rabbit holes, while dozens of nervous insects darted away.

His grandmother's farm was gone now, as was the town, hidden by the small hill.

He was alone.

The hill ended, tumbling into a scoop-shaped depression cut by a narrow stream. The water was clear and icy-looking, bouncing slowly left and right. He slowed down. And there, to the right, was the gorge.

It was like someone had taken a shovel and dug away a jagged chunk of the mountain. The stream went right down the middle, and the walls on either side were gigantic.

Josh stepped down to the stream and looked at the dark corridor of the gorge. But he could see only a few feet before it veered sharply to the left.

It was cool here. Josh felt the goose flesh rise on his bare arms. Gusts of wind rushed out of the gorge, blowing his sandy-blond hair off his forehead.

He thought of going back then. It had to be lunchtime by now. The apple pie would be baked.

The boy leaned down, picked up a stone, and chucked it into the gorge. It ricocheted off one of the walls, and plopped down into the stream.

He took some steps closer to it, walking on the stream, the tops of his sneakers darkening as they became wet.

Josh was completely in the shadows now, just before the entrance of the gorge. It seemed to run right into the mountain itself.

A crow screeched, or maybe, he thought, it was a raven. It flew out of the gorge opening, a smudgy black shape, and then it soared back over the hill.

Josh started walking.

He came to the elbow, and he turned, all the time looking at the walls of the gorge. He knew what a gorge was . . . knew it from countless visits to the American Museum of Natural History.

(And he thought, then, of how his father used to tease him about his love of dinosaurs.)

"A gorge is like a time machine," his father had lectured him . . . the Professor . . . "It's hundreds of thousands of years of history, split open, like a brittle book."

There'd be fossils here, Josh knew . . . some right at the surface. Others, hidden, just below the surface.

It smelled dank, like a basement. All the rock was dotted with greenish clumps of moss and lichen. His steps echoed off the walls, and the small stream sounded as loud as a rushing river.

The gorge narrowed, then cut to the right.

Like it led someplace . . . some hidden underworld kingdom.

Suddenly it was darker here. He looked up. A scrubby pine tree arched over the opening, cutting down the light.

He stopped. He could hear his own breathing.

I should go now, he told himself. *Enough exploring for today. It's a pretty neat place. Lots to sketch. Fossils to be dug up. Pretty neat.*

He started to turn.

When he saw it.

Lying in the stream bed, just ahead, near another elbow.
Something big, and lumpy.

He licked his lips.

Just an old bag, or some other garbage. That's all.

But the more he looked at it, the more he knew it wasn't just an old bag. His eyes became used to the shadows. And he thought he saw some kind of shape to the darkish lump.

It was an animal.

He went closer, and with each step the shape became clearer, more defined, sitting there on the shiny stones of the stream bed.

Then he was close enough to see it.

It was a deer. A big doe, he guessed. All curled up on itself. He took another step. Its mouth was half in, half out of the water, the eddies of water swirling around the still nostrils.

He walked around to the other side of the deer. Its eyes were wide open, looking deeper into the gorge.

What killed it? Josh wondered.

Did it come to drink the water? Is the water poisoned?

He looked around, and saw a twisted branch leaning against one of the gorge walls. Josh went over and picked it up. He brought the stick back and wedged it under the deer. He tried to move the deer up and out of the stream.

But the deer was heavy, and he only succeeded in making the deer's lifeless legs kick up at the air and then plop down into the water.

Josh just wanted the deer out of the stream.

He could imagine it sitting there, the skin rotting away as the crows—

Or ravens—

Came to chew at it.

He could see it, months from now, a skeleton, still standing guard in the stream bed.

He'd never be able to come to the gorge again. Not with the body just sitting there.

Josh kept pushing at it, sweating in the chilly air, hearing strange lifeless gasps coming from the deer as he worked on it.

Forget it, man, he was telling himself. And just then, with one last heave, the deer flopped over, and around. It now lay on its back, mostly on the rocky bank.

And Josh saw what killed it.

It was a wound. A thin, metallic shaft was buried in the

deer's right side. Dried blood and scab surrounded the entry hole. But the shaft was still there, buried in the deer.

He knelt down, fascinated, and looked closely at it.

How long had it been running around like that? The small metal arrow stuck there, half-in, half-out, digging around in its insides.

Josh reached out to touch the shaft.

And as he did, he heard the voices, laughing, echoing, from behind him.

Three

ERICA TYLER PICKED up the phone.

For the third day in a row she almost said the hell with the call.

Someone knocked at her office door, and then let themselves in.

"Busy?" It was Tom, the art director.

She shook her head, smiled, gladdened by the sudden reprieve.

"Good," he said, closing the door behind him. "I have a proposition for you."

"Tom, you know—"

He smiled, open, friendly, ready to counter whatever she might say. "Yes, I *know* that you're concentrating on your work. And," he said, raising his eyes, "I know how much you want—and deserve—that VP sign on your door. But that doesn't mean that you can't take some time out for a quick dinner tonight with a lowly art director, now does it?"

Erica smiled, pushing her dark hair off her forehead. Tom was harmless. Terribly flattering, horribly persistent, but ultimately harmless. When she was ready to finally reenter the world, he might very well be the first candidate. Certainly not some of the other heavy hitters in the office who did everything but suggest how hard it must be, physically, "you know, when you're used to having a man in bed beside you . . . and he goes and gets himself killed in a plane crash."

Thoughtless.

But there was a grain of truth in what the creeps had to say.

The time for keeping herself locked up was coming to an end. Not tonight . . . not this week . . .

But soon.

"I'm sorry, Tom, but I'm just—"

"I know. Too busy. Well, sweetheart," he said, in a bad imitation of Bogart, "don't forget us creative peons as you claw your way to the top of the Warfield and Burns executive pyramid."

"Don't worry about me forgetting you, Tom. You're first on my hit list."

He laughed, and grabbed at the door handle. Another divorced man used to handling rejection, she thought.

"And when I'm ready, I'll treat you to dinner," Erica said quietly.

"You're such a tease," he hissed, slipping out of her office with wide-eyed furtive glances left and right.

She was still laughing when she looked at the phone.

I have a son, she told herself. *I can't just forget that.*

As much as I want to.

She picked up the phone and dialed.

The phone rang just as the pie, all bubbling and brown, was ready to come out of the oven.

Josh's grandmother gave her hands a quick swipe across her apron and picked up the phone.

"Erica . . ." she said quietly. "I expected you to call yesterday."

She listened to her daughter's glib explanations—the pressure of work, the demands of a career, the need to make a living.

And Elizabeth Stoller felt angry, listening to it all again. But she decided not to deliver another lecture. Her daughter would work it all out. Somehow. She was sure of that. Sooner or later.

Erica asked for her son.

"Josh's not here. He's out—Yes, Erica, I do keep tabs on him. The boy hasn't run away to join the circus. He's just out sketching and—"

Her daughter sounded almost relieved.

She'll have to get over this, Elizabeth thought. Her daughter couldn't go on looking at Josh and seeing his father. Somehow, it would all have to end.

"I'll have him call . . . when he gets back. You'll be

there?" She waited, hearing her daughter check her appointment book. "Well, Erica . . . take care of yourself."

She put the phone back on the hook.

Where was Josh? She had told him to be back for lunch, and it was already past one.

She walked to the back door, to the yard where the afternoon heat was building. A hot, summery stillness settled here, with no movement, no sounds of birds.

She squinted, staring up at the hill, up where Josh should be perched, sketching who-knows-what.

But he wasn't there.

In the distance, she saw the mountain, an old ugly thing that seemed to squat on the horizon like some sleeping animal.

Boys are different, she reminded herself, not ever having had the experience of raising one. *They like adventure. They like to explore.*

Maybe they even like danger.

She called out for him, timidly at first, then louder, till her voice sailed across the fields.

"Josh!"

But there was no answer.

"And just what the fuck do you think you're doing here?"

Josh stood up slowly. A cool breeze whipped through the cleft of the gorge. His fingers went cold, like they had been digging into the icy water of the stream.

"Yeah," another voice said. "Who the hell do you think you are?"

Then there were giggles, tinkling noises that scared him even more than the voices.

"I was just looking around. . . . I—"

As he turned, he saw them, in the shadows. Five kids. One tall teen-ager standing near the front, legs apart, shaking his head. There were two more boys, one a runty-looking kid, and another about Josh's size. And two girls, giggling, leaning into each other.

"I was just—"

The big kid took a step closer to Josh. The teen-ager's heavy work boots plopped right into the stream. He kept his eyes fixed on Josh, and they glowed even in the cool darkness of the gorge.

The teen-ager wore a sick, nasty grin. He looked mad. *Mad*,

Josh thought, *and ready to kick my ass from here to Stoney-wood*.

What the hell did I do? he wondered.

The boy stood close to Josh, as if daring him to go on—to take a step backwards, back to the deer. He was tall, almost a man, with a dusting of black hairs on his upper lip. His black T-shirt showed some long-haired heavy-metal wailer, mouth open, tongue licking the air. *Dokken . . . Hell to Pay . . .* was all it said.

The teen-ager had to look down at Josh. Josh could smell his breath, the stale-sweet smell of beer, a smell he knew from his father. The memory jarred him.

"This"—the boy gestured at the cavern of the gorge—"is our place." The boy's face came even closer. "No one comes here without us inviting them." He looked over his shoulder. "Isn't that right?" he asked the others.

The two girls—just shapes in the darkness—giggled some more. But the other two boys came closer, contributing to the fear created by the tall kid.

Three of them, Josh thought. The smaller kid came up right alongside the first boy. But one of the kids stepped to the side, splashing in the water, moving to the side.

Josh turned to watch him.

A finger was suddenly jammed into his midsection.

"No, you still don't understand, do you?"

"What?" Josh said, his attention returned. "What do you mean? I just hiked here and—"

"You don't hike here!" the teen-ager bellowed. "Not ever! Do you"—*jab*—"understand"—*jab*—"that?"

The last jab sent Josh stumbling back.

"Where the fuck is he from?" the voice behind Josh said.

"Just a fuckin' tourist, ain't that right?" the big kid sneered. "A summer asshole."

"I—I'm staying with my grandmother. . . ." Josh stammered. "The Stoller place."

But the kid just shook his head, and Josh saw a sick smile bloom on his face.

"Oh, well, in that case—"

The punk lunged at him, shoving Josh backwards. The other kid was there, just behind him, his leg catching Josh, sending him into the icy water.

They laughed. But they weren't done with him.

He had hoped they were. Yes, maybe they'd just get him wet and that would be it.

Josh tried to get up, his face red. "Hey, cut—"

But the big kid jumped on him and smashed Josh's head hard against the rubble in the stream. The teen-ager's long, muscular body was dead weight on him. Josh wriggled an arm free, and tried to punch his attacker. But with practiced ease, the kid slapped away Josh's fist and quickly pinned it under his knee.

And now Josh was helpless, completely pinned by the kid. The stream swirled around him, icy water swirling against his cheek. He saw the blue sky above him . . . a brilliant blue, then all blurry, out of focus.

I'm crying, goddammit, crying! The big kid started slapping at Josh.

"Hey, Bobby . . . c'mon, that's enough. Let's—"

One of the girls had come close . . . and looked down at Josh.

But her appeal to Bobby was ignored.

"Drag it here, man. Quick before he squirms away!"

Drag what? Josh thought. And all the time, Bobby was slapping him—light, taunting taps, back and forth, from one cheek to the other.

"What's amatter, baby? Getting the idea now, huh?"

There was a sound from just behind Josh. Something being moved through the water. And the two other boys were grunting, pulling at something.

"Bobby, come on. I've got to go. My mom—"

"She doesn't know where the hell you are, Clara. So keep your panties on."

The other girl laughed at that.

"Get off me!" Josh screamed. "Get off me!"

"Fuck you, buddy. We're going to welcome you real nice to Stoneywood. So you don't forget . . ."

The sound was right there, close to his ears. Josh tried to twist his head, left and right, trying to see what was coming at him. And all the time, Bobby kept slapping him, laughing, grinning. . . .

"Yeah, Jacko, bring it right up to him. Yeah. . . ."

Bring what? Josh thought. *What*—

Bobby reached down and grabbed Josh's hair. Bobby tugged at it, pulling Josh's head up. "That's it. . . ." Bobby laughed.

Then the teen-ager let his hair go and Josh's head flopped back down . . .

Onto the deer's body.

"Oh, man . . . look at that. Hungry, kid? Lunchtime!"

"Bobby!" the girl called Clara said.

And Josh twisted against it, turning left and right, smelling the animal, feeling its wet fur against his skin. He was inches away from the arrow wound; the long shaft of the arrow looked like a telephone pole.

His face slapped against the deer's carcass like a flounder.

"No!" Josh yelled.

Then, from the wound opening, there was movement.

Just the slightest bulge at first, right along the edge of the wound. But then the torn skin seemed to lift. Josh's mouth fell open. *What's going on?* he wondered. . . . *What's happening?*

Let me wake up, he prayed, hoping that this was some sick dream . . . that he was still in New York . . . living with his mom.

The wound rippled, and then these worm-things crawled out. All puffy and white, big plump things that wriggled free of the wound.

"Oh, Jesus!" Bobby screamed.

Then Josh felt the teen-ager pull back, watching the maggots squirm out of the hole.

I'm pushing them out, Josh thought. *My head . . . my body . . . squeezing them out of the dead animal.*

He was screaming, wild now, shaking his head violently, leaping up when the teen-ager was finally off him.

And he stood there . . .

As the other kids backed away, looking at the deer . . . looking at Josh, his clothes soaked through.

Josh thought about picking up rocks—big, heavy chunks— and throwing them.

The one called Bobby grinned.

"Fucking A, man. Fucking A! And welcome to Stoney-wood."

Then they turned, running away, leaving Josh alone, cold and crying in the shadow of the gorge.

Josh tried to sneak back into his grandmother's house . . . checking through the window to see that she was in the kitchen. Then he darted into the house, dashing up the stairs two at a time.

But he didn't reckon with the preternatural speed and senses of the old woman.

"Josh . . . is that you?"

She appeared in the hallway, wiping her hands on her apron, looking up at Josh, still moving straight up.

"Josh!" she called out. "What's wrong, honey? What happened?"

And he knew that if he didn't stop, she would just follow him up, right into his room.

He stopped and turned on the stairs.

"Hi, Grandma . . . I . . . I—"

She took one step up.

"—had an accident."

"I guess so, Josh." Another step, until he was sure she not only saw his soaking-wet clothes and the blackish clumps of mud, but also the trails of his tears.

Tears! Jesus, he felt like an eight-year-old.

"I slipped . . ."

"You were at the gorge," she said, her eyes narrowing, her lips gone all straight, tightly pressed together. She said *gorge* like it was a bad word.

"I—"

"You shouldn't have gone to the gorge, Josh. I'm responsible for you. . . . Your mom expects me to—"

She stopped—right next to him. He felt her studying his face. She raised a hand to his right cheek. "You're all red—there and"—she gently turned his chin—"and there too. What happened, Josh? What did you get into out there?"

He was about to say "nothing," to just shrug off her concern.

But he knew her well enough to know that she wouldn't give up until she had an answer.

"It was a fight," he said quietly. "Some kids . . . I guess"—he smiled—"they had nothing better to do."

She shook her head.

"Go up and change, son. Then come down. You can have a piece of pie and tell me all about it."

His smile opened a bit, and he nodded. "Sure," he said.

And he felt her watching him as he went up to his room, his sneakers making squeaky wet sounds on the wood stairs.

* * *

Brian crunched down on what looked like a fishburger, some pasty filet of sea creature served on a doughy burger bun with the inevitable secret sauce.

(And this was one sauce that should be kept secret, he thought.)

But Captain John's, one of a dozen such salty establishments in the Boston area, served their food as promised. Fast, and with enough fries to tile your bathroom floor.

It also had the added advantage of being just down the block from Alan Ward's home. The Navy files didn't say too much about Ward's home. All Brian knew was that after Alan's father died, when he was seven, his mother turned all but a few rooms on the first floor into small apartments. The rent money helped her raise her son.

Brian chewed away at his sandwich, marveling at the amazing lack of taste. A gulp of almost fizzy Coke helped wash it down. He nibbled a few fries before deciding to call it a meal.

He carried his tray over to one of Captain John's garbage cans (emblazoned with a jaunty picture of the one-eyed, one-legged Cap offering a cheery, Thank you, matey, for helping swab the deck).

Then, with the early evening air taking the edge off the heat, Brian walked slowly back toward the tenement and, farther down the street, the Ward house.

The neighborhood had long since given up the ghost.

Brian guessed that come dark it would be a nasty place to stroll through. Already there were people lounging on the stoops, looking grateful for anything resembling a gust of air. Brown bags hid unknown beverages, and boom boxes poured out an incessant jumble of Latin rhythms and a barrage of rap music.

Everyone checked Brian out as he walked down the street.

He decided it was best to keep his eyes ahead.

Should have brought my gun, he thought.

He reached the Ward house, a three-story brownstone, with a separate entrance leading to the basement. The first-floor windows were covered with bars, and the front door sported three heavy-duty locks.

Brian walked up the steps, the reddish stone dotted with candy wrappers, ice-cream sticks, and other garbage.

He stood at the door, looking at a half-dozen buttons. He found one that said 'Ward.'

He rang it, and waited, while he silently rehearsed his story: *I'm looking for a room. Nothing fancy. Just a place to stay.*

Maybe he'd try to get inside the apartment. Get a look at Ward.

And see what?

See if he looks crazy? Out of his mind? Crazy enough to— Nothing happened.

He rang the bell again, and he heard some steps from inside. Someone was coming down the stairs.

An old man opened the door. Bald at the top, wearing glasses. A rumpled brown suit that was pockmarked with shiny grease stains. His tie was a brilliant striped thing that emblazoned his entire frail chest.

He seemed to be startled to see someone at the door.

"Oh, hi," Brian said cheerily. "I was looking for Mrs. Ward."

The old man looked up, and shook his head as if Brian had just said something incredibly stupid. "I'm looking for a room," Brian said, and smiled.

"She's not here. Ach, she's been gone for a week . . . maybe more. And everything looks like shit now. . . . Shit."

Brian's smile faded as the old man squeezed past him. Brian turned to the man as he passed, and he reached back with one hand to catch the door before it closed.

"Gone?" Brian asked affably. "Where'd she go?"

The man kept moving down the front steps, shrugging. "How should I know. She left . . . with her son. . . ." The old gnome kicked a wrapper off a step. "Look at this!"

"Well, thanks," Brian called after him. But the man went on, muttering to the pavement, shaking his head.

There goes one unhappy dude, Brian thought.

Then he pushed back against the door. No one seemed to be looking at him.

He took another step backwards, pushing the door open wide enough for his body.

He slid in, as the door slowly wheezed shut.

Brian turned around. He could see that it had been a great house, the deep dark wood floor was covered with a threadbare carpet, and the staircase sported a handrail polished to a brilliant patina by thousands of hands steadying themselves.

To the left, there was a door.

If the Navy was right (and boy, could they ever fuck up) that was Ward's apartment.

He walked up to the door.

It had only a single lock, a Yale that should give way to the tiny wire he'd bought. He dug out the thin piece of metal and stuck it into the hole.

There was sudden burst of music as a car with a nuclear-powered sound system slowly cruised by. Brian froze for a moment, and then went back to working at the lock.

It seemed stuck.

"Damn," he said. He tried twisting the wire to the left, and he felt the lock mechanism jiggle a bit.

Upstairs, someone flushed a toilet and Brian heard the water follow a trail inside the walls of the building.

"Come on," he hissed at the lock. Then, responding at last to his impatient coaxing, the lock popped open.

And he walked inside the home of Mrs. Mary Ward and her son, Alan.

Four

A CLOCK TICKED in the corner. The only sound, save for the street noises that fought their way through the modern storm windows.

In here, it was 1948. A mixture of cheapo modern furniture and genuine antiques, Ward heirlooms. A kidney-shaped coffee table served a claw-footed easy chair, with embroidered upholstery guarded by long-faded antimacassars.

But Brian didn't linger in the living room. They might be gone, but they could come back. It would be tough explaining his prowling around their house. The Boston police would be interested in his lack of a search warrant.

The Navy might let his ass just hang there.

The kitchen was small, but the cupboards were glistening white, freshly painted. Blue gingham curtains did their best to keep the sun out. A shiny toaster looked pert and ready for breakfast.

Brian took another turn, and was in a bedroom. Mrs. Ward's, from the look of it. A simple post bed, two night tables. Brian gave the table tops a quick check for any notes, some clue as to where they had gone.

But there was nothing.

He found another bedroom, a smaller, dingy place. One wall had a great map of Antarctica, with three small pushpins. Brian leaned forward and saw that one of them marked the Naval Research Station.

Alan's last posting.

And wouldn't that be a cold little sucker today, Brian

thought. Nothing like winter at the poles to take the edge off the heat.

As it was, though, he was trailing droplets of sweat through the house.

Ward's bed was crisply made, ready to bounce a quarter if some wayward captain should want to inspect it.

But still, no notes, nothing to indicate where Mrs. Ward and Alan might have vanished.

A flurry of voices—loud, drunken sounds—echoed from the street.

And Brian figured it was best to get out.

He walked to the front door of the apartment, turned and checked that he hadn't missed anything.

Then he opened the door and stepped out into the hall.

"Can I help you?"

The voice startled him, and he spun around. The woman stood at the top of the hall stairs, looking at him, suspicion and fear in her eyes.

"I was just looking for—"

Then, there was someone else on the stairs. A man. His hand in his pocket.

And Brian didn't have to let his imagination go too wild to imagine what he might be hiding in his pocket.

He smiled as disarmingly as he could. "I was looking for Mrs. Ward. . . . Someone recommended—"

"How'd you get in?" the man barked from the top of the stairs.

"An old man . . . little guy upstairs . . . he—"

But Brian saw the couple shake their heads and exchange knowing looks. Obviously they were familiar with the old gent's preoccupied ways.

The man came down the stairs . . . slowly. . . .

"They're not here," he said. "Gone to their summer place."

Brian kept the smile on his face.

He knew nothing about any summer place.

"Summer place? I didn't know she had—"

"She's rented it out mostly, at least after her Alan went in the Navy," the woman explained, coming down to join her husband.

"Oh." Brian nodded. "I see. And when did they go there?"

The two people hesitated, now standing side-by-side. But Brian could feel that they no longer saw him as a threat.

"They left last week. Just after she picked up her son."

Brian nodded. "Yes," he said knowingly, "I heard he'd been in the hospital."

The woman took a step closer to him. "You know him?"

"Alan? Oh, sure. That's why I came here."

"Poor boy," the woman said. "His mother was so upset. Couldn't imagine how he could be the same, I mean, after that."

"Last week," the man repeated. "Last Sunday. And we don't have a clue when they're coming back."

"And where's the summer place?"

"It's just a cottage," the woman explained. "His father had bought it. All by itself on a hill . . . in the Catskills. A town called—"

The man stiffened, his grizzled beard catching the dull light in the hall. He shook his head . . . reached out for his wife . . . trying to quiet her.

But she didn't see.

"Stoneywood. Just across the state line."

Brian smiled.

"What?" the woman said, feeling the man's hand close around her wrist. "Oh, it's okay, John. He obviously knows them."

"Right," Brian said. "Well, I have to get going. But thank you. I'll have to look Alan up."

Brian walked to the front door and fiddled with the battery of locks that kept a strange and hostile world away.

He felt the old man looking at him.

"And who are you?" the man said belligerently. "If they ask who came to see them."

The last lock clicked open and Brian opened the door, and then he just turned slightly.

"Just tell them an old Navy buddy stopped by."

The man nodded.

And Brian stepped out into the dark, noisy world of Federal Street.

Erica Tyler worked late, even though she really didn't have much to do. Her big account, Tempus Tissues, was still in its third go-around in the art department, and there were rumblings that the company's execs might be ready to start shopping around for another agency.

All her other accounts, ranging from the Brazilian Beer Libre (Taste the Freedom) to Wilson's Nuts (Go Crazy for Wilson's) were all pretty much wrapped up, with firm commitments for print and video budgets. Throw in a half-dozen hot prospects just one power lunch away from signing with Cooke and Collier, and, well, things couldn't be rosier.

So why didn't she go home?

Cause Josh wasn't there?

No, she admitted to herself, filling her yellow pad with aimless doodles, that wasn't the reason. If anything, she was glad Josh wasn't there.

She loved him. But after Jack's death—Jack, who had been more like an older brother to him—well, it was hard to be with Josh. He looked so much like Jack . . . dear, sweet Jack . . . the way he tilted his head when he talked, as if figuring out the way everything worked.

And his sense of humor. It didn't take much to make Josh laugh . . . just like his father.

She worried that Josh felt the change in her . . . felt how difficult it was for her to look at him, hunched over his homework or his drawing pad, listening to his day, the tests at school, the other kids. . . .

When all she wanted to do was scream and say, "I want my husband back! That's all . . . don't you see? I love you. But I love him more."

The point of her pencil broke, sending a tiny piece of graphite shrapnel flying onto the plush blue carpet. The cleaning service would soon descend upon the offices of Cooke and Collier Advertising, and she'd have to leave.

She was checking her calendar for the next day—hoping it was full—when there was a rap at her door. It was Tom.

"Still here?"

She looked up and smiled, glad to be saved from her thoughts. "Yes, just taking care of some odds and ends."

"Well," Tom said stepping into her office, "I just caught sight of Elsa and Jaws. You've got five minutes to get out of here safely."

She grinned. Jaws was their nickname for Elsa's vacuum cleaner that did everything but suck the color out of the rug.

"You wouldn't be the first promising young account executive lost to her demon machine."

Erica laughed. Tom was funny. He'd been great during the horrible weeks after the accident. Supportive, always ready with a smile. Some of the people in the office avoided her like the plague, as if they were waiting to see if she were going to implode under the stress.

And she'd remember who they were . . . in case she ever got the VP slot.

"C'mon . . . what say you and I retire to Georges Ray for escallope de veau and Fumé blanc."

She shook her head. "No, Tom. Thank you. But I'll just—" He came close to her, and touched her shoulder.

"And you'll just what?"

She looked up at him, her smile halfhearted.

She paused, and Tom leaped into the opening. "A drink, then. Chase away those midsummer blues. After a martini or two, who needs the Hamptons?"

She laughed. *Why not?* she thought.

"Okay, but just one drink. I've got a bitch of a day tomorrow."

"Tell me about it. My department can't come up with anything to please your goddam tissue czar." Tom grinned. "I'll meet you at the elevators in five, okay?"

Erica nodded.

She had made his night.

And maybe her own.

Her one drink turned into three, until they were sitting in a corner booth, nibbling at a matched pair of club steaks.

Tom had avoided asking her about anything that touched on recent history, and she feigned some interest in his background, nodding when he went on about his days at NYU, then a teaching stint at the School of Visual Arts.

After one Tom Collins, she had switched to wine coolers, while Tom worked on his third martini, very dry.

She didn't realize how close they were sitting until he reached over and rested his hand on hers.

For a moment she thought about quickly pulling it away, perhaps on some feigned mission inside her purse, or to jab at the steak fries.

But she let it sit there.

Encouraged, he closed his fingers around hers.

Why not? she thought at last, almost angry with herself. *Can't I just say the hell with everything?*

Why the fuck not?

It was an awkward moment. They were at her apartment, at least.

She wasn't quite ready.

Until she let herself imagine, yes, pretend, it was Jack.

Tom said something.

She asked him to please just not talk.

Not while they made love.

(And later, she'd think it so terribly rude.)

But it didn't matter then, not really. The room was dark, the hum of the air conditioner soothing and familiar. The alcohol hadn't yet turned into the splitting headache she knew was coming.

She bit her lip, wanting to call out Jack's name, to say it, to make the magic even more alive.

Jack, she wanted to whisper in his ear, biting him there, gently, just the way he liked her to.

Instead, she kissed this phantom lover on the mouth, letting him enter her and begin his rhythm as she moaned . . . and pulled him close, trying to control his movements.

Oh, Jack . . . my husband . . .
Why the hell did you have to leave me?

The phantom moaned and tightened against her. She hurried, feeling him leaving her. And then she was there, lost in the darkness.

She gasped, her nails digging into his shoulder.

Then it was over.

(And Tom sat up on the bed, lighting a cigarette.)

She cried—a gentle, sad heaving, her cheeks dotted with tiny, pearly tears.

Sometime later Tom pulled on his clothes . . . kissed her good night . . . and left her.

With him knowing, she was sure, exactly what had happened.

Ann Mayhew ignored the pair of truckers, perched on stools, watching her lean over to scoop up the two Hamburger DeLuxe Platters.

She heard a faint snicker (and she could imagine them arching their eyebrows on their broad, beetle-faced heads).

Smirking, tub-bodied idiots.

I'd love, she thought, turning with the platters and a smile, *to send their greasy burgers flying right into their faces.*

Instead she put the plates down and, brushing the straggling brown curls off her forehead, she asked them if there'd be anything else.

Always a tricky question with these assholes.

One of the truckers, wearing the regulation red plaid shirt and quilted, sleeveless jacket, looked up in mock surprise. "Hey, babe, no ketchup."

"Oh." She nodded. "Coming right up."

She reached under the counter, where a squadron of red bottles stood posted, ready to do battle with the Mohawk's legendary strong-stomached customers.

"Here you go."

"Thanks, babe," the trucker said, his hand almost too large as he unscrewed the top.

What a dream hunk, she thought. *Going to bed with that bozo would be like sleeping with the missing link. His idea of foreplay is probably having you suck on his dick for an hour or two.*

"Enjoy," Ann said brightly.

And checking that no other of the Mohawk's distinguished clientele needed anything, she hurried back into the kitchen, past Eduardo, the shifty-eyed cook who chewed his toothpick to a droopy pulp and said *nada*. Back to the employees' washroom, a foul cubicle that made even the customers restrooms look pristine.

She went in and locked the door.

Her outfit, a dark blue suit with a cream-colored blouse, hung on the door. She had her heels in her car.

Ann started stripping out of her waitress gear.

She was about to take a shot at getting out of here. She had started working at the Mohawk as something to help with the car payments . . . to pay for her apartment over Gelson's Hardware. To help her . . . after she got out of the hospital . . . No big deal. Just a job. Near Stoneywood. Until she got back on her feet, maybe back to Cobleskill Community College . . . get her Associate Degree in Nursing.

Right. Except one year had turned into two, then three. And the idea of college, let alone the cost, scared her. She had zero savings, and more often than not her father hit her up for a spare ten bucks.

But this, yes, was the first step out. An interview with Wallace Porter, general manager of the Miller Inn. The Inn was an oversized castle, three large buildings built over the past hundred years right at the foot of Mount Shadow, on a cliff overlooking Miller Lake.

It was elegant. Every weekend brought a special group to the Inn. There were conferences for everyone from psychologists to fitness nuts.

And, if Porter liked her, she could work in the Inn's dining hall. No more fifty-cent tips for counter service. No more leering baboons staring at her legs and ass.

Instead, there would be intelligent, polished people who tipped—in a big way—at the end of their stay.

She zipped up the skirt of the blue suit, feeling it a bit more snug than the last time she wore it. There was a tiny coffee stain on the blouse, but if she buttoned the jacket it should stay out of sight.

She put some makeup on . . . not a lot, just some color on her cheeks . . . some pale lipstick. The Miller Inn used to be a pretty straight place . . . started by a Quaker named Miller. Used to be you couldn't even get a drink in the Inn.

She turned her head left and right in the spattered mirror.

Good, she thought, pleased with the way she looked.

Slipping back into her white, rubber-soled waitress shoes, she walked out, smiling as first Eduardo, then the other girls, commented on her looks.

"Enjoy your shift," she called out to them.

And she strolled out of the Mohawk, with its big neon Indian sign that grimly, but wisely, looked away from the diner.

With luck, she thought, *I'll never be back.*

Jeffy Post stuck the fucking gas nozzle into the pickup truck. He brushed his thin brown hair off his smudgy forehead and leaned his lanky body against the gas pump.

And he watched Ann come out of the Mohawk.

Lookin' good, mama . . .

Bob O's Service Center was just up Route 122 from the

diner, and Jeffy enjoyed checking out the comings and goings of Ann Mayhew.

She was a tight little bitch. And old Jeffy enjoyed stopping into the diner, ordering a cup of coffee, maybe a slice of pie, and watching her move . . . up close.

Real cute . . . real tight . . .

He even joked with her about going out . . . or something. . . .

Head up Mountain Drive with a couple of six-packs. Watch the sun go down.

(And he always grinned at this point, unable to keep his face from revealing his real plans.)

And she smiled, real nice, but always had something else to do.

Like now.

He watched her get into her squat gray Toyota.

Where was she going, all dolled up like that? Like she was going to some party or something.

I'll party with you, baby, he thought. *Yeah, I'll show you a real bitchin' party.*

Of course, he knew why she wouldn't go out with him. She must've heard the story. In a small town like this, people grabbed onto a story and passed it on, like some freakin' treasure.

You hear? That new kid at Bob O's is an ex-con. Yeah, did some time for dealing a little blow.

Big effin' deal.

Thirteen months in Attica. Pumping iron, and dodging the black boys with twenty-inch biceps and ten-inch schlongs.

Not always successfully.

But the good folks of Stoneywood gave Jeffy Post a lot of room on the street. It felt real good, walking downtown, and watching everybody step just a little bit to the side.

Everyone just a tad nervous.

The gray Toyota pulled past the gas station, just as the gas pump clicked off.

Jeffy pulled out the nozzle, and watched Ann Mayhew drive by. He saw her look over and catch him staring.

Oh, yeah.

I'm a watchin' you, baby. Real close.

Um, um, ummm!

He jabbed the nozzle back into the pump.

Five

"BYE!" JOSH SHOUTED, pedaling his bike up the small hill that led to the dirt road and, beyond, to Stoneywood.

It had been cool this morning when he had finished feeding his grandmother's livestock, the old horse named Mister, and two dopey-eyed sheep. But by the time he finished cleaning the barn, it was getting hot. Maybe after he got back from town, he'd go over to Miller Lake for a swim at the town beach.

When he went back inside his grandmother didn't look so good. She gave him a list of a few things she needed from town. Some flour, a gallon of milk—nothing he couldn't carry in his backpack.

Her eyes had been all foggy this morning, and she hadn't joked with him the way she usually did.

And he felt the tiniest bit of fear.

He loved the old woman. More now than ever. And today she seemed so fragile.

He mentioned the doctor, but she quickly, almost angrily, shushed him.

"Just need some rest," she snapped. "Now, don't you get to worrying about me, Joshua. I'm just a little tired today," she said.

He nodded, swallowing his worried feeling.

He reached the crest of the steep hill, pumping hard, and then he went flying over it. His ten-speed had a tough time in the ruts and furrows of the dirt path. But its gears would help him get up all these hills without splitting a gut.

The path ended in a country road, lined with lush oak and

maple trees in full leaf. A small breeze rustled the brilliant green leaves, and he soared down the road, taking care to avoid the deep gouges in the packed dirt and the stray rocks that could send his bike tumbling over.

The country road led to Highway 22, a two-lane blacktop. But he saw no cars.

Josh stopped, and looked behind him.

His grandmother's farm was completely hidden now, and Mount Shadow filled the western horizon.

At the end of the day the mountain would send its jagged shadow creeping over the town, robbing it of the last hour of sunlight.

Josh began pedaling.

He heard the drone of an engine behind him.

The boy turned around and saw a black Chevrolet pickup coming close. Some old pickup, a dinosaur from before 4x4's became the hot vehicle . . .

He edged his bike towards the nonexistent shoulder, branches and bushes almost touching his spokes.

And he pedaled slowly, waiting for the truck to pass.

But it seemed to hang back, just behind him.

Come on, he thought. *Pass me. Go ahead.*

The truck gunned its engine and came even closer. Right on Josh's tail.

"Damn it," Josh said to himself. "What the heck is he doing?"

The truck lurched forward another few feet. Then it started to pass Josh. Slowly, creeping past him. Right next to him.

He felt the driver staring at him.

Josh turned and looked.

It was just an instant.

A quick glance.

He turned, and looked again.

The man's eyes were locked on Josh.

The eyes looked dead.

(Like the deer's . . . just like the deer . . .)

Josh's chain seemed to sputter, rattling. He reached down and played with the gears. He felt the chain lock, caught between gears. The bike screeched, followed by a wrenching sound that made Josh's stomach tighten. The rear wheel of his bike locked, and then started sliding to the left, towards the truck.

"Oh, Jesus," he moaned.

(And he could see himself then, sliding under the truck, right between the front and rear wheels, as the driver's face finally came to life and he gunned the engine and rode over him.)

But Josh was also trained by years of boyhood tumbles and spills. He threw himself into space, off the bike. He landed, rolling onto the grassy shoulder, into bramble bushes and rough-edged grasses. His bike seemed to slide after him.

And the truck roared past him.

Josh quickly stood up, breathing heavily, half expecting the driver to stop, back up, and try to run him over.

But the pickup continued along the road, the engine's hum fading as it swerved out of sight.

Josh stood there, his breathing slowly becoming normal. He heard a few birds chirping. Some cicadas rattled in the grass.

The hum disappeared.

And he wondered . . .

What happened? The driver passed me—looked at me . . . then my bike's chain got screwed up. Isn't the first time it happened. Yeah, maybe it was nothing. I'm just jittery, that's all. Still rattled after yesterday.

"Yeah," he said, "it was nothing."

He picked up his bike, checking the derailleur. The chain was caught up between two gears. Probably got banged around too much on the way down.

He dug his hand under the chain and tugged at it until it popped onto one of the smaller gears.

I need a mountain bike, he thought. *Something with chunky wheels and straight-out handlebars.*

He got on his ten-speed. His knee throbbed from his landing.

And he started pedaling down the road, down to Stoney-wood.

All the while trying to forget the sick way the man had looked at him.

He was coming out of the Grand Market—a small, inaccurately named grocery store—when he saw her.

The girl from the gorge.

The teen-ager had called her Clara.

She had seen Josh first, obviously, since she stood there, on the sidewalk, just watching him.

He decided to ignore her and keep on walking to his bike.

Josh went right past her, over to his bike, which was chained to the curbside parking meter.

Then he felt her tapping his shoulder.

"Hey, you okay?" she said.

He didn't turn, just busied himself undoing his lock, wrapping it around his seat.

"Yeah, great. Always feel great the day after being beat up by a gang."

"Hey, look," she said, working her way around him so that he had to look at her. "I'm sorry. I tried to get them to stop. They're just animals, especially Bobby Tamm. He's always in—"

"Well, they're your friends—not mine." He hoisted himself on the bike.

The main street, called Faith Avenue, was quiet. Only a few cars were parked in the many metered spaces, most in front of the bank, a few down by what looked like a bar. The first thing Josh had noticed when he came into town was the names of the streets. Felicity. Charity. Faith.

Boy, did they have this town wrong.

He inched his bike forward.

But the girl grabbed his handlebars.

"Hey, I feel bad about what happened. I just want to, I don't know—"

"Yeah, I don't know either. And I feel bad about it too. I guess I just gotta avoid the gorge with the goons."

He looked at her now, at last. She had short brown hair and wide blue eyes. She was easily as tall as he was, maybe a fraction taller. But he guessed she was younger than he was.

"Maybe—" Clara said, "Maybe we could be friends. This ain't such a bad town."

"Well, so far I haven't been too impressed."

She grinned. A broad, open smile that seemed to catch every bit of the brilliant sunlight that filled the main street. "Oh, there's lots of neat stuff." She let go of the handlebars.

And Josh didn't pull away.

"There's caves, great dark tunnels filled with bats and pits that go down forever."

"Just what I need."

"No," she said. "I know where they are. I could get you through them. If you went with me, you'd be fine. Honest. No problem. And there's the lake. I know where there are rocks, under the water, that nobody knows about. Big rocks that you can stand on, way out in the middle of the lake."

Josh looked at her, and shook his head. This townie seemed to be in real need of impressing Josh with the wonders of Stoneywood.

"And back at the gorge—" she went on.

Josh held up his hand. "I don't think I need to go there again, thank you."

She grabbed his bare arm and squeezed it. It seemed like a natural gesture. "The Tamm brothers don't hardly ever go there. And they always ask me and Sammi Reilly. Usually it's just to drink some beers they snatched from their folks."

Josh nodded. "I've seen the gorge."

Now the girl shook her head.

"No you haven't. Not the best places. Not the falls, or the great pool where you can swim in ice cold water. And not all the fossils."

He stopped his bike.

"Did you say fossils?"

"Sure. Hundreds of them, thousands. Things I can't even find in books."

They have books in this *town*? Josh thought. *Hard to believe* . . .

He looked at her.

"Okay," Josh said with new appreciation. "You know all the hot spots. So what are you saying?"

Her grin turned shy. "I don't know. We could hang out . . . do stuff."

"And your friends?"

She looked around.

"I'm not too crazy about them. I mean, they seem to be heading for trouble."

"That's obvious." Josh looked at her smile, as big and bright as the day. Then he grinned back at her. "Okay, you're on. You can show me the wonders of Stoneywood."

"Great!" And she tilted her head to the side. "I'm Clara Skye."

She stuck out her hand.

"Josh Tyler."

Then some movement down Faith Avenue caught his eye.

Josh saw someone come out of the bank and slowly walk down the steps, over to an old black Chevrolet pickup.

The same pickup.

His hand slipped away from Clara's.

Josh walked towards the bank, while Clara went on talking a mile a minute.

It was nothing, he told himself again. Just some upstate hick in an old Chevy.

Nothing.

"So big Bobby Tamm wouldn't go in, even though I told him and his brother that it wasn't a real haunted house, not really. Just a creepy old building. I'll show it to you; it's down by the paper mill. They were like babies, I mean, really, how punk can you—Hey, what's wrong, Josh? You look—"

The man stepped up to the cab and slammed the door after him. Josh tapped Clara's arm.

"Who's that?" he said.

Clara turned, squinting in the sun, looking around. "Who are you talking about?"

"That guy there . . . in the black pickup!"

The truck backed up, and then slowly turned, heading out of town.

"Who was it?" Josh demanded, his breathing getting all funny again.

Clara shrugged.

"I don't know," she said. "Never saw him before in my life. Probably just some dumb-ass tourist. Probably."

But Josh barely heard her as he watched the pickup disappear.

Brian McShane, nursing a back that felt permanently creased into a U-shape, pulled off the Stoneywood/Hudson Hills exit of the Taconic Parkway.

This was, he guessed, about as close to nowhere-land as you could get. The Big Apple was a good two hours away. And the nearest big city, Albany, was almost an equal distance north.

But, as he curved around, heading west on Route 133, he had to admit that it was beautiful country. Lots of lush green rolling hills and, further west, the old tree-covered mountains of the Catskills.

There were worse places on the planet to live.

Stoneywood was still twenty miles west of here, right in the middle of a valley nearly surrounded by those mountains.

Pretty secluded spot . . . Damn near isolated. One road in. And the nearest highway was a half hour's drive away.

Must be lots of fun come winter.

He saw a diner right off the Taconic. The Mohawk, with a big neon Indian looking sternly north. *Him like paleface's fried egg sandwich, you betchum.* And, across the street, a gas station. The area around the station was littered with rusting heaps in various stages of disrepair.

Some gas wouldn't hurt, Brian figured, and maybe some suggestions of a place to stay.

He pulled the car over to Bob O's, with its Certified Mechanic and a brand of gas that he'd never heard of. An attendant, wearing a blackened shirt embroidered with the name Jeffy strolled languorously over.

"Yeah . . . what'll it be?"

"Fill it," Brian said. He watched the attendant pull out the pump and then, not without difficulty, work it into the narrow, no-lead opening of the Reliant. If this was the certified mechanic, Brian thought, that explained the collection of decaying cars outside good old Bob O's.

The attendant stared off into space, as if waiting for someone to beam him out of there.

Brian got out of his car.

"Excuse me . . . but I'm headed to Stoneywood. Any idea where I could stay?"

But Jeffy kept on looking away, disinterested in the question. He scratched his head.

A great mind at work.

Finally, he spoke.

"There's the Miller Inn. Real fancy . . . real expensive, you know what I mean?" Jeffy was eyeing Brian and his car as if to say: *I know you can't afford that joint.* Aloud, he said, "B'sides, they're usually filled up this time of year. Lots of old people with money."

"Anything else?"

Jeffy rubbed his chin, his powers of recall being put severely to the test.

"There's a Day's Inn up the Taconic . . . oh, fifteen miles or so."

Brian shook his head.

"I wanted something in Stoneywood . . . or at least close to it."

"Gotcha. There's a guest house. Yeah, right in town. Run by an old black lady." He grinned. "Only one in town. It's across from the church. She'll even feed you . . . if you like soul food."

The gas jockey snickered at his bon mot.

Christ, Brian thought, *it's going to be a long week here.*

The gas pump clicked off.

Jeffy coaxed some more gas into the car, topping off the tank at $10.50. Brian paid, and got back into his car.

And he pulled away, hoping he wouldn't have any need of Bob O's service facilities while visiting Stoneywood.

Mary Ward sat at the small kitchen table. Her fingers worried a frayed piece of paper towel, stringing it through her red, crippled hands.

Over and over.

I didn't want to come here, she thought. She shook her head. *I didn't want to come here*.

And now her son was gone, off in his father's old pick-up, driving who-knows-where. When he should be here, resting . . . getting better.

She stood up and walked to the tiny refrigerator.

Mary wished she was back in Boston. Her friends were there, all the people who still could say Good Morning in English, and her tenants, most of them good people.

She opened the refrigerator door. The pale yellow light lit her lined and wrinkled face.

There was some milk, a loaf of bread, a tub of I Can't Believe It's Not Butter.

Her son had told her he'd run out and just pick up some things, some food, some tea. That would be nice. "Maybe some of those nice Pepperidge Farm cookies," she had urged him. "You know, the ones with chocolate on both sides . . . and chocolate inside . . .

"Like your father used to buy me . . ."

But where was he?

Where was Alan?

She walked over to the sink. The last person to the cottage had left two weeks ago. But the sink drain still held bits and pieces of their last meal. A few sickly pale brown crumbs of chopped meat. A snaky strand of spaghetti.

"Pigs," she said aloud.

A note—neatly written—right over the sink told guests what was expected of them. Broom clean. Dishes washed. Sink empty. Not . . . not like this.

She reached down and clawed away the debris. It felt old and slimy. She scooped it out and threw it into the brown garbage bag.

And then she went back to looking out the window.

Josh stopped walking, right across from the bank. There was a ladder on each side of the street, and two men, each on one ladder, were stringing a sign to stretch right across Faith Avenue.

"What are they doing?" he asked Clara.

She looked up and shrugged.

"I don't know. Let's wait and read it."

The sun was hot on his face. He looked over at Clara, who was squinting at the white banner with brilliant red letters as it was unfurled.

She turned, catching him, and he quickly looked away.

The men shouted to each other from atop their ladders, and the sign was pulled across the street:

STONEY . . . WOOD . . . VOLUNTEER FIREMEN'S 1990 CAR—

"The carnival!" Clara yelled, finishing it for him. "That's right . . . it's this weekend. It's great! You're going to love it!"

Josh marveled at Clara's enthusiasm. It was completely overpowering.

But there was something about it, something he couldn't put his finger on, something that worried him.

The men finished unfurling the sign. Small crescent moons had been cut into the material. The wind blew, filling it like a sail. The sign wasn't new. Last year's date had just been painted over with bright white paint, then replaced with '1990' in bright red.

"I've been to carnivals before," he said. "They're kinda goofy."

Clara shook her head. "Not this one, Josh. They get the greatest carnival to come. People don't just go one night, they go to it *every* night, all three nights."

Josh turned to her, interested despite his memories of creepy church carnivals held in towns outside New York City.

"It's got the neatest rides, not baby stuff. There's one where you spin around and around—you think that you're going to barf—then the floor drops away. It's great. I mean, as long as you don't barf."

Josh grinned at Clara's wild-eyed impression of someone about to toss their cookies.

"And there's the coolest games. I won a giant Snoopy last year. And there's a bozo—"

"Bozo?" Josh laughed. "What's a bozo?"

"You know, a guy who sits in a chair dressed like a clown and goofs on people . . . calls 'em 'nerds' and 'jerks,' trying to get them to pay just to knock him in the water. They got the coolest bozo. He's real gnarly."

"Shit," one of the men on the ladder said. Josh looked up.

One of the strings holding the sign had flapped loose. It whipped through the air wildly. Josh watched one of the men lean out, trying to snag it. He made a grab at it, and missed. Then he tried again.

He leaned a bit farther. And he started falling off the ladder.

"Shit!" Josh heard him cry.

The man started to pitch forward . . .

When his friend, standing just below him, grabbed his belt.

The tumbling fireman reached frantically around and grabbed at a rung of the ladder. He just barely caught it, stopping his fall. He pulled himself back on, wearing a sick grin while his friend asked if he was okay.

But Josh watched the sign . . .

While the loose line went on flapping, whipping this way and that, wild in the strong wind.

Six

"PLEASE COME IN, Miss Mayhew."

Ann Mayhew took a breath and stood up. Wallace Porter stood in the doorway, filling it. But he smiled warmly at her, holding the door open, still smiling as she passed him.

His office was as wonderful as the Inn itself.

Everywhere there was wonderful dark wood, a rich, deep brown mahogany that just asked to be touched. His desk filled one side of the office, with an enormous color photo of the Inn behind it, showing an aerial view of the lake and the Inn's three buildings.

"Please," he said, following her, moving back to his chair. "Have a seat."

She sat down, returning his smile, taking care to keep her knees together.

And she worried that her blue suit was too short, or too out of fashion. When she wasn't waitressing, she lived in her jeans.

"Well," Porter said, looking down at his desk, "I see you've lived in Stoneywood all your life?"

"Yes." She smiled.

He nodded. "A good place to grow up, I bet."

"Oh, yes, it's—"

"And some college. Just one year?" he said, looking up at her, his eyes squinting just the tiniest bit, the rolls of fat on his face crowding the sockets. "Why just one year?"

"I was—ill." The lie, rehearsed many times, still came

uneasily. *It's not his business*, she thought. *It had nothing to do with anything*.

"Oh, too bad. And never got back?"

She shook her head. "I started working . . . bought a car. I might start taking some night classes."

The General Manager smiled.

"Good. Education is very important." He looked down at the papers on his desk. "All your references are good . . . very good. Yes, and"—he looked up at her, carefully now, appraising her—"I think you'd fit in very well at the Inn."

She smiled a bit more . . .

As she pictured the Mohawk disappearing, fading into a bad memory, some old nightmare. No more truckers. No more Eduardo ruling the kitchen with his toothpick.

Porter stood up and came around to her. He sat on his desk, perching there like Humpty Dumpty. "We have guests from all over, you know. Lots of nice older folks, looking for the peace and quiet of the mountains. And of course our special weekends have become very popular. This weekend we're having our fifth annual Miller Murder Mystery. Patrick Cabot—the writer—is the guest author. Have you read any of his mysteries?"

"Yes," she lied, hoping he wouldn't ask her which books.

"Yes," he said, nodding. "It's very exciting. The important thing, for a Miller employee, is to remember that the guest's needs come above everything else." He stood up. "You may have bad days, you may have good days. But every day for our guests should be wonderful."

She nodded eagerly.

Porter stopped talking, and just sat there—interminably, it seemed to Ann—as he perched and studied her.

Then, slowly, as if making some deeply pondered pronouncement—

"And I think you'll do just fine."

He smiled warmly.

"Oh, thank you," Ann said. Porter hurried back to his desk. "I'll buzz Miss Wilcox . . . she's our Head of Staff. She'll get you all set up." Porter smiled again. "And you can start tomorrow."

"Thank you, Mr. Porter. Thank you very much. . . ."

Then Porter nodded one more time, dismissing her.

* * *

Just a few miles down the two-lane road and Brian saw the buildings and signs that told the grim story of the area. There was a bright billboard announcing Oakwood Condominiums, coming here soon! A stylized couple gazed warmly on beautiful, modern townhouses while other slim, equally beautiful people played tennis or dived into the nearby pool.

Except the sign was all yellow and weathered, with its corners curling in like some magazine left out in the yard for a year or two. Obviously, Oakwood Condos never got off the ground.

Then there were the restaurants—with genuine brickface— new places put up in anticipation of some big tourist boom, visions of thousands of skiers and summer people that just never materialized. Big 'For Sale' signs sat sullenly in front of the closed doors.

And the 'antique shops' looked suspiciously like private homes, with a hand-painted sign outside and probably whatever passed for family heirlooms haphazardly arranged on the lawn.

This, then, was the only business on this desolation trail. Just a slim hope to snag some city visitor who fancied an old chair for his Fifty-seventh Street co-op, or a genuine washboard to prop in the corner—an object d'Americana . . .

So the previous owners could take the eight bucks and buy a six-pack of Genesee beer and two bags of Wise Barbecue-flavored potato chips, wondering just where the hell they went wrong.

Beautiful country didn't always bring a beautiful lifestyle.

Then—an interruption in the desperation parade—he saw a generic green-and-white highway sign. Stoneywood, ten miles.

And another, announcing the Miller Inn.

He thought he should stop and check his directions to the town. Maybe get a brewski. Might help take his backache away.

There was a place just ahead . . . looked like a roadside gin mill.

The neon sign was off, but he could read the tubular letters well enough.

'Bosco's Folly, Eats and Bar' it announced. With 'Folly' taking up most of the sign.

He pulled into the parking area. His car bumped up and down as the holes and ruts gobbled at his tires. He heard the rear bumper smash into the ground.

He stopped.

And checked out Bosco's Folly.

It was a blue and white building. Thirty years ago it probably had looked garishly *moderne*.

Which was probably the last time Bosco's was open.

Brian got out of his car.

Walked up to the splintery blue door.

(There was a faded sign right on the door. He could just barely read it . . . 'Welcome to my Folly.' Then the swirling letters of the proprietor's name . . . 'Bosco.')

Boy, Brian thought, *I'd love to take a look inside and*—

"Bosco's is closed, friend."

"Huh?" Brian said, spinning around. He hadn't heard another car stop . . . or anyone come up behind him.

Yet here was this guy standing there, real close. He was thin, dressed in a T-shirt and jeans. He could have been twenty . . . or sixty. He was the type of guy who'd look the same age for fifty years, and then just up and die.

Brian smiled. "I was looking for some place to grab a cold one. Get some directions . . ."

The man nodded. "Where you headed?"

"Stoneywood."

The man grinned.

Watching stupid city folk probably ranked right up there on the entertainment scale with checking out the bears at the garbage dump.

"Just go straight . . . can't miss it." The man grinned.

"Thanks," Brian said. "I guess I can grab a beer in town."

"I don't know about that, fella. But I do know that you sure as hell can't get one here." The man started laughing, a goofy hiccoughing sound that accompanied Brian back to his car.

The man was still cackling as Brian got behind the wheel.

He started the reluctant K engine.

And he looked at the man in the T-shirt . . . like some roadside mystic, waiting to snare the unwary traveler. He looked at him and wondered . . .

Was that guy Bosco?

* * *

"These are your two uniforms, Miss Mayhew."

Miss Wilcox, dressed in a crisp black dress with a high white collar, slapped down two bundles wrapped in crinkly brown paper. "Cleaning them is your responsibility, and since you have two uniforms, we expect you at all times to be spotless. Shoes and stockings are your responsibility, and Mr. Porter does not look kindly on runs in stockings."

Ann looked around. This was the underbelly of the Inn. To the left, the enormous kitchen was getting ready to serve dinner, while a battery of waitresses and busboys were adjusting their uniforms, lining up their serving trays, and bantering back and forth. Most of the waitresses were much older than Ann. Each one picked up a tray and held it like a knight's shield.

"Miss Mayhew, do you understand?"

"What?" Ann said, suddenly aware that she had been drifting. "Yes . . . my responsibility."

Wilcox didn't look so sure.

"If there is some problem that you can't deal with—on your own—come to me. That," she said, aiming her finger towards a room down the hall, "is my office. You may always come and see me," she said—without much conviction, Ann thought.

"Joanie!" Wilcox said, snapping her fingers.

A younger waitress came over. "Joanie will explain how things are done here . . . and she'll get you through your first day tomorrow."

Ann gave the waitress a quick smile.

"I'll see you tomorrow," Wilcox announced, and then turned sharply away.

"A real sweetheart," Joanie said.

And Ann turned and looked at her assigned guide.

"She seems all—"

"We," Joanie announced with authority, "call her 'The Bitch.'"

Ann nodded.

She looked at Joanie. Pretty light-brown hair, pulled up in a bun. The waitresses wore silly little white caps, right out of *Upstairs-Downstairs*.

"Rule numero uno," Joanie said, popping her gum. "Be nice to the cooks. All of them. They get thirty per cent of your tips, and don't try and screw them." She leaned close to Ann, grinning wickedly. "'Cause they can fuck up your food so bad the guest will have your ass out of here immediately if not sooner. Rule number two, be nice to the old-timers, the bags who have been carrying food around so long they feel naked if they don't have a tray in their paws. They can get you all fucked up almost as quickly as the cooks."

Joanie went over to the pile of trays, great brown oblongs that were heavy even with nothing on them. "You waited on tables before, right?"

"Yes," Ann said. "I—"

"Well, forget what you did there. These fuckers," she said, giving one of the trays a great heft, "hold lots of food and if you don't get it balanced right, you'll lose your orders. Ker-plop. Comes out of your pay, ya know. Start in the center with the heavy plates . . . then work your way out to the side with the other dishes."

"Joanie!" someone called from across the great room, the pace quickening. "Do you have a spare apron?"

"Sure!" she bellowed back. "Hanging in my locker. Take it . . . but bring me a clean one tomorrow!"

She turned her attention back to Ann. "We all help each other. The tips can be great. Be sweet to the old farts and you can pick up some nice change. But don't be surprised—or get pissed—if someone stiffs you. Happens all the time . . . and it balances out."

"Hi, Joanie," said a tall kid in a busboy's outfit, gliding past them. He kept on going, spinning around for a another look. "Who's the new talent?"

"No one you'd like, Billy." She leaned close to Ann. "Another good rule. At least until you get your feet wet. Steer clear of the busboys. They're cute and fun and there are some real hunks. But wait until you can figure which ones can keep their mouth shut and which ones can't."

"Well, I don't think—"

Joanie led her over to the pick-up area, a long line of stainless steel counters. "You pick up here, and—"

Joanie paused, studying Ann carefully.

"Ann Mayhew . . ." she said slowly.

"Yes, Why?"

Joanie smiled. "*You* were in my sister's class. Graduated in eighty-three, right?"

Ann nodded.

"So did she. Patty Cutter? She knew you. . . ."

Ann smiled. So long ago. High school, and its dances and parties. And—

"Where is she now?" Ann asked.

"Married," Joanie said. "Got one kid." Then she snapped her fingers. "Hey, didn't you go with Alan Ward?"

Ann nodded slowly. "Yes . . . before he went into the Navy."

Joanie looked at her. "In fact, didn't you—"

The waitress froze, as if remembering something she shouldn't say.

Ann knew exactly what it was.

"That was a long time ago," Ann said.

"Right," Joanie nodded. "Well, the only reason I mention it . . . but you probably know already, though."

The waitress turned away from her. And took a step.

Ann reached out, put a hand on her shoulder, stopping her.

"Know what?"

Joanie spun around, a victorious smile on her face. And Ann wondered whether she'd known all along who she was.

"Oh, thought you knew. Old flames and all that."

Ann licked her lips.

"What?"

"About Alan." Joanie shrugged. "He's back. Staying in his cottage, up near the gorge . . . Thought you knew."

Joanie turned, and walked towards the locker room.

While Ann stood there.

What's the line . . . ?

No flame burns like an old flame.

She walked into the women's noisy locker room.

The road right in front of their small cottage was deserted. Mary Ward kept leaning forward to see if she could make out the black pickup churning up a trail of dust as it chugged up the hill.

But it was perfectly still outside.

Where in the world *was* he?

Her Alan . . . her baby . . .

He just hadn't seemed the same. That was certainly understandable. She knew he wasn't going to be quite right when she first visited him in Bethesda Hospital. They had prepared her.

It was just the shock of it all, they explained. With time, he'd be fine.

But it was his eyes that worried her . . . sort of all dull and lost.

And they stayed that way.

She didn't ask him what had happened.

The Navy had told her quite enough.

Her poor baby.

But she thought that once they were together, back in Boston, he'd start to come around. Sure he would. He'd go to the movies that he loved so much. Look up some of his old friends.

It didn't happen.

(And she chewed her lip . . . a new habit . . . looking at her son . . . biting at her lip . . . worrying. . . .)

The first week Alan didn't move from the house. He just sat in his room, barely touching the lovely meals she made. And he hardly said a word to her.

"You're going to waste away," she had told him, a smile on her face. "Waste right down to nothing."

But Alan didn't smile back.

Then he said he wanted to go to Stoneywood.

"What on earth for?" she'd asked. "The cottage is so small." It was fun when he was growing up, with the lake and all the other children. But why would he want to go there now?

But Alan insisted.

Until she'd said, "Okay, son. If it will make you happy."

Except . . . he didn't seem any happier.

Mary Ward looked out the window some more.

For a moment she thought she heard a sound, the rumble of the truck, pulling her away from her thoughts. *I get lost in myself so easily these days*, she reflected. *Just can't seem to keep my mind on anything . . . anything at all.*

She turned on the water. It coughed out of the faucet all silty red. She pulled her hand back, waiting for the water to clear.

Mud-red splatters dotted the basin. Then the water started to run clear.

She put her hands under the faucet. Scrubbing them, wishing she had some soap.

The door creaked behind her.

"Alan," she said, starting to turn. "Alan, are you—"

But as she turned she caught sight of something in the

window. The faintest hint of a reflection. Like the twisted image in a fun-house mirror . . . just barely registering.

"Al—"

Then it was right against her. Hard. Pressing close, right up to her body. Something cold, wet—

She smelled something that made her gag, cough, want to throw up.

She tried to turn, but she couldn't; it held her there . . . tight. . . .

"Please," she said.

Then there was this feeling.

Like thousands of tiny needles.

Pressing her flabby midsection right up against the sink. Like tiny little bug bites. Pinpricks. Almost tickling her at first. "What . . ."

She started to talk. But the sensation changed. The pinpricks quickly turned into rough gouges, all along the back of her body, screwing this way and that, digging into her skin.

Her words turned into a horrible gargle. She sputtered, trying to force out some magic word to make it end.

"Oh, God," she moaned, a burbling, liquid sound.

"Oh, please—"

Then she tilted forward, right into the sink, coughing and sputtering, retching violently. She hawked up a reddish glob . . . then another, until she disgorged a whole horrible red torrent.

She watched her insides fill the dingy sink.

The horrible corkscrews crept up her neck, squirreling this way and that, sending brightly colored explosions of pure pain into her head.

She thought . . . *Help!*

Then she merely tried to imagine surviving from one insane moment of the hundred horrible corkscrew turns to another. Just that . . . no more.

Until she prayed, begged, pleaded for death.

As she never before had pleaded for anything.

Seven

"S'ALRIGHT?"

Brian looked around the room. It was small, just a bed, a dwarf's desk, and a chair out of a Turkish interrogation chamber.

"Fine. I'll take it."

The black woman looked confused, as if she'd expected him to turn on his heels and storm out of her boarding house. "Fifteen dollars a day, then. Four days in advance. And I serve dinner, if you want it."

"Not tonight." Brian smiled. "But I'll keep it in mind." He dug out his wallet and handed the landlady sixty dollars. She nodded, then turned and walked briskly toward the door.

"You wouldn't know of a cottage near here . . . a friend of mine owns it. Name of Ward."

"Sure I do. . . . It's a rental, a cottage top of Barrow's Hill," the woman said, barely breaking stride. "Just take Mountain Road."

Nice, close-knit community, Brian guessed. He thanked her as she went downstairs, where he could hear her TV friends screaming out, "Wheel . . . of . . . Fortune!"

He shut his door.

Josh finished yet another grilled cheese sandwich, almost swallowing it whole, washing it down with great spoonfuls of tomato soup.

God, he was hungry. It must be this mountain air.

"Okay?" Grandma asked.

"The best." He popped out of his chair and carried his plates over to the sink. "I'll wash up later, Grandma. Honest. But I want to go sketch Mister while it's still light. That horse of yours sure doesn't move much."

"No," she agreed with a laugh. "His working days are over and I think he's earned the right to just sit in his stall and chow down."

Josh picked up his pad and pencil from the kitchen counter.

"Now, don't go get lost," his grandmother said. "Your mother said she was going to call again."

"I'll just be in the barn," he said, dashing through the kitchen and out the back door.

He saw that the setting sun just touched the tip of Mount Shadow. The last golden rays of the day were in his face. *Great,* he thought. *I can open up the barn and let the light fall on Mister. That old horse stands so stock-still, it's just like painting a bowl of fruit.*

He unlatched the creaky barn doors, kicking them wide open. The two sheep bleated nervously in the murky background. Josh grinned. They always acted like they were expecting bad news. Mister made a hesitant snort.

"Hey, boy, I'm going to make you famous. You're gonna be an early sketch by Joshua Tyler."

The horse, all brown except for a great creamy dollop on his hindquarters, blinked at the boy. It was a grizzly old sway-backed animal. Not good for much of anything.

Josh inhaled deeply; the rich loamy smell of the hay and the animals was wonderful. He heard a small sound in the corner, probably a mouse skittering around. The light behind him turned a bright orange.

He picked up a chunk of cut wood to rest his paper on. Then he snatched a can off a hook on the barn wall and turned it upside down for a makeshift stool.

He sat down. And, for a moment, he did nothing.

You've got to see what you draw. That's what his art teacher, Mr. Leone, preached. *Look before you leap. Find every curve, every line, let your eyes fill it in.*

Leone knew his stuff.

(Of course, that didn't prevent the school board from firing him. Rumor had it that Leone had gotten heavy with the new math teacher, a real fox who had all the boys paying real close attention to her geometry class. One kid said that Leone just quit, left for Europe . . . or California . . . or whatever. His replacement was some baldheaded dork. The class did lots of woodwork and leather projects when he took over.)

Josh looked at Mister. The curve of his head, the way the mane fell so carelessly to the side. The great neck, so powerful, and the legs, looking much too weak to hold up such a big body.

And he thought then, about Clara.

Why the heck is she interested in me? Was she just leading him on, only to spring her bully boys on him?

Ha, ha—what a neat joke that would be.

It made his stomach tighten.

Am I a coward? he wondered.

Did I fight that kid as hard as I could? I tried to hit the jerk. Really tried.

(Sure you did. Then you let him work you over real good.)

Of course, his last experience in a fight had turned out even worse. There was this new kid who entered Wilton in midterm. Fresh out of Hades High . . . Steven Donovan.

(And he'd never forget that name.)

Supposedly you had to be of the least average intelligence to get into Wilton. But this kid was an animal. The teachers didn't have a clue what to do with him.

But nobody laughed at Donovan's stupidity.

No one dared. . . .

Talk was that his father or his grandfather had left the school a bunch of money. The school owed his family a big favor. Like taking in their delinquent child.

It was English class that made Donovan snap. Crazy Mr. Bartley asked the class why in Hemingway's story the old man was all alone when he finally caught his *gigundo* fish.

"Why did Hemingway write it that way?" Bartley had asked, his threadbare black schoolmaster's cloak covered with yellow and white chalk blotches. "The boy *could* have been with the old man . . . so why did Hemingway write the story like that?"

Bartley must have thought that Donovan raised his hand, or an elbow or something. Or maybe Bartley was just tired of the oversized (and probably overaged) eighth-grader sitting on his ass, snickering, and looking out the window.

"Why don't you tell us what *you* think, Mr. Donovan?"

Bartley demanded, plopping down on the edge of his desk, his bald dome reflecting the fluorescent lights . . .

Looking right at Steven Donovan.

The whole class got kind of quiet.

Donovan looked up, the smile slow to melt off his dumb-looking face.

"Well?" Bartley said.

Donovan looked around, his face growing grimmer every second, like he was Mr. Hyde. Then he mumbled something about the boy having to stay with his parents.

"No, Mr. Donovan . . . Ernest Hemingway made up the story." Bartley slipped off his desk. The normally affable English teacher smelled fresh meat. "It's not a *real* story, Mr. Donovan," he said, coming closer to the red-faced Donovan. "He made it up that way," Bartley sang. "And he *could have* made it up differently. . . . The question is why did he write it *that* way?"

Donovan sort of grunted. He may have said something; Josh didn't hear. And Bartley turned around.

And his eyes fell on Josh.

The teacher didn't wait for anyone to volunteer an answer. "Tyler . . . what do you think?"

And now Josh remembered with crystal-clear clarity everything that happened the rest of the afternoon. He remembered shifting in his seat, clearing his throat . . .

All because it led to the Big Event.

"Well . . . I sort of figure the story is about facing challenges alone . . . and finding that the real challenge is inside yourself."

"Oh, really, Tyler? And what do you have to support that?"

Josh cleared his throat again.

"A couple of things. Hemingway's life, for example. He always—"

"Nice try, Tyler," Bartley said, spinning around. "I mean from the novel itself."

"Oh . . . Well, the way the man talks to the fish. It's not like they're enemies. He treats it like a friend, as though the fish helped him do something important. In the end, the old man's sad because the fish has been destroyed by the sharks. The fish had given the man the chance to prove something. But in the end, they both lost."

"Good," Bartley said, nodding. "Not the whole banana,

Tyler, but enough to get us talking about the story at least. Okay, let's look at—"

And the teacher directed everyone to a page of *The Old Man and the Sea*, to a page number that Josh never even heard.

Because his eyes were fixed on Donovan.

Who was sending daggers right at him.

If looks could kill, then Josh was already a dead kid. *Shit. I'm screwed*, he thought. *This monkey is going to murder me. He blames me for what Bartley did.*

The rest of the day passed in a dream. Josh kept expecting Steven Donovan to come leaping out of the rows of lockers, brass knuckles on his hands, wearing his big black ass-kicking boots.

But nothing happened.

Nothing . . .

School ended, and everyone headed home.

And Josh began to breathe easier.

Except Josh had String Orchestra after school, something his mother wouldn't let him quit no matter how many horrible sounds he kept making on his violin. And when rehearsal ended at four, the basement lockers were deserted.

Josh was about to close his locker and hurry up to the Fifth Avenue bus before rush hour, when he appeared.

Almost as Josh had imagined he would.

Sure enough, there was Steven Donovan standing no more than three feet away, looking as ugly as Josh had ever seen a kid look.

"We have something to settle," Donovan grunted.

"What?" Josh asked and, dammit, he thought his voice actually broke.

Donovan smiled. "You know what, asshole. So shut your goddam locker, fucker, and get ready to be punched out."

Josh remembered the way the locker sounded as he clicked it shut. So loud, echoing in the deserted basement.

So final.

Donovan hit him in the stomach. *Boom*, just like that.

"Aww . . ." Josh groaned with the pain, gasping for breath, waiting to see what horrible sensation was going to come next. Then, again.

Josh didn't want to swing back. It would only make the animal get madder. And then what? But after Donovan took a swing at Josh's head and missed by a fraction of an inch, Josh knew he'd have to do something.

He put up his fists—a laughable effort—and started fighting. Donovan kept peppering Josh with shots to the chin and the stomach, chuckling hysterically. And Josh tried to block them, a hopeless effort. He felt his cheeks burning—a ruddy red glow, from Donovan's punches.

"And I've only just started, Tyler . . . just started."

On and on, until Josh felt the tears come, bringing no mercy from Donovan. Josh kept swinging, but only sent his fist slamming into a locker.

Finally Josh couldn't handle it anymore. He screamed—out of control—and jumped towards Donovan.

Yelling.

"You bastard . . . You goddam bastard!"

Donovan laughed as his chunky arms sent fists digging into Josh's body, smashing him down to the floor.

Until suddenly someone was there, pulling a leering Donovan back. Josh got up from the floor.

It was Mr. Moran, the Assistant Head. Or the Ass Head, as they called him.

It was over.

Donovan was out of the school. And everyone kidded Josh. The Basement Brawler, they called him. But during swim class, when his bruises made him look like a banana that's been kicked around, no one said anything.

Josh drew the line of the horse's head. The rolling curve of the nostrils, the flaring bulge near the eyes. The ears.

He sketched quickly now.

The brilliant golden light was gone. The sky was a shadowy bluish color. *No big deal,* he thought. *I can still see the horse.*

Mister snorted. Once, and then again, shaking his head. The horse pulled against the leather strap holding him in his stall.

"Easy boy," Josh said. "Won't be long now . . . not long at all."

He started shading in the back of the horse, holding the pencil at an angle. Maybe later he'd add some color to the sketch. Or maybe he'd just throw it away.

But as he shaded the back he became interested in the pattern his rubbing made on the white vellum. It seemed to pick up the

pattern from the chunk of wood below the paper, giving the
horse's back a certain strange texture, a bumpiness—

He lifted his pencil.

Mister snorted again, and again, louder.

Josh looked at his picture. There were tiny bumps all along
the horse's back. They were all sort of . . . regular. Josh
touched his pencil to one of the marks, extending it just to see
what it would look like. Higher, away from the horse's body.
Then another, until the pointy lines were all streaming off the
horse.

Crazy-looking thing, he thought. *Just ruined my—*

The head! Hey, he hadn't noticed that before. But there were
some marks there too. He started connecting them.

And now he finished the picture, not knowing what in the
world he was drawing, but scribbling fast, letting the bumps
grow, twine around each other, swirling together like vines.
The horse seemed to grow a beard, something nasty, barbed,
pointing down, supporting itself on the ground.

Josh wasn't smiling at his picture anymore.

He worked faster now, barely able to stop, erasing marks for
no reason . . . just with some vague idea that they were
somehow wrong.

"What the—" he said, looking at his handiwork.

The legs became the exposed roots of a hundred-year-old
tree, still trying to clutch at the ground.

No, he thought, adding more details. *Sucking* at it—

He heard Mister.

Josh looked up.

The horse had been snorting and whinnying, but he hadn't
heard it. But now he saw Mister rolling his great head, kicking
wildly at the sides of his stall. Droplets of foamy goo hung
from his mouth.

"Hey," Josh said. "What's wrong, boy, what's—"

Josh looked down at his picture.

Then back at Mister, kicking and snorting. "It's just a—"

The horse pulled back, shaking his head from side to side.
His eyes were wide . . . angry.

The leather strap broke.

And the horse reared back, rising above Josh . . .

The phone rang tentatively. Elizabeth Stoller was used to the
party line.

She had already done the dishes Josh said he would do. She knew better than to depend on a boy's good intentions.

His mother hadn't been much different.

"I was just thinking of you," she said, picking up the receiver and hearing Erica. "Just thinking how much Josh is like you."

But there was a funny silence on the other end.

Erica just wanted to speak with Josh.

"Yes," Mrs. Stoller said, "he's just outside, sketching Mister. I'll go get him." She laid the phone down on the table and walked out the back door, calling Josh's name.

Then, again. "Josh!"

Maybe it was all too much, having the boy here. Erica was so worried. What if something were to happen to him? "Josh!" she yelled, her voice sailing over her still-low cornfield.

She thought she heard something in the barn, a yell maybe . . . someone calling.

And she took a step out towards the barn.

Josh tumbled backwards, falling off his seat onto the hay. Mister's hooves landed, crushing the can. The he kicked it away.

He's going to kill me, Josh thought. *He's crazy, mad—*

"Hey, boy, it's okay," he pleaded. "It's—"

But Mister tossed his head and pulled up again. He was closer now, and Josh would have to crawl right under those stamping hooves to get out.

The horse was breathing hard, spraying Josh with his lather. He pounded the dirt.

Then his grandmother was there. She grabbed what was left of Mister's harness, roughly holding the horse's head down. Mister still jerked left and right, but as the woman spoke to him, the horse slowly calmed down.

Josh saw that the horse's eyes had lost some of the strange glow that they had only a second before. His grandmother whispered in the animal's ears. Soothing him . . .

But she turned to Josh and snapped:

"Get inside, Joshua. Your mother's on the phone."

He stood up slowly.

"Get going *now*!" she yelled.

And Josh ran out.

Leaving his sketch behind.

* * *

Clara stopped walking, just down the block from her house.

And Clara looked down at the darkening street, at the other houses with their flaking paint and crumbling porches, their lawns with great brown patches and odd tufts of tall grass. The rainbow glow of TV's made all the windows sparkle with smeary reds and blues. She heard somebody yelling—a man's voice—then a woman, screaming back at him.

Just like my house, she thought.

She grinned at the funny awfulness of it. *My house, with screaming people.*

But her house was still up the block and even her father's drunken voice wouldn't carry this far. Besides, her mother wasn't home. Who could her father scream at? The TV?

Wouldn't be the first time.

She started walking again, slowly, postponing the moment she'd have to actually go inside.

Things were worse now. A lot worse. Her mother rotated through three shifts at Hudson Valley Community Medical Center. A month doing days, a month on the night shift, and then a month doing what her mother called the graveyard shift. She wasn't a nurse, though her mother liked to pretend she was, saying, "I'm just as good as the nurses. I do all the same things for a fraction, a *fraction,* of the goddam pay."

But Clara doubted it, in a big way. Her mother had trouble whipping together Kraft Macaroni and Cheese, a cigarette dangling from her too-red lips.

No, she knew her mother probably did other stuff at the hospital, stuff like washing people's bottoms and changing bedpans and picking up half-eaten trays of the disgusting hospital food.

(And it *was* disgusting! Clara had spent a week in the hospital after her appendix was taken out, eating the food and watching her mother act so sweet to her. Her sick baby girl. Yuck!)

But when her mother had nights, that was the absolute worst. Clara had to be in the house, with her father . . . by herself.

She looked up. She was at her house, the smallest one on the block.

Too soon, it was there. The lawn dotted with a few broken tiles from the roof, blown off by last week's storm. The grass growing in irregular clumps. The rusty fence, a pint-sized chain-link number, weaved dopily left and right around the small lawn.

It was the worst house on the whole dumb-looking block.

She walked up the steps.

Knowing she'd catch hell from her father.

Where have you been? he'd bellow. *Just what the hell time do you think it is?*

Missy!

And if she was lucky—and if she said absolutely nothing—that might be it. Just that, and waiting in her room for him to fall asleep . . . or stumble upstairs . . . past her door.

She walked inside, letting the puckered screen door slam shut, announcing her arrival. It was no good trying to sneak in. He'd just scream louder when he finally flashed on the fact that she was back.

The living room, his dark den, was right there, just to the left of the front door. He was stretched out in front of the TV, listening to the baseball game. Two beer cans sat on the table, another was in his hand.

"S'at you?" he grunted.

"Yeah, Dad."

She kept walking toward the stairs.

"Wait a minute, *missy*. Just where the hell have you been?"

She stopped.

(*Had* to stop. He'd just follow her. And that could be worse . . . much worse.)

"I was in town, Dad, watching them put up the carnival signs. It's this weekend," she tried to say brightly.

Her father's eyes reflected the luminescent green on the TV screen. His face was sunken, hollow. Like some kind of fish.

He licked his lips.

Took a big slug of his beer.

It's always Miller Time here, she thought.

"Wha . . ." He tried looking at his watch. "What time is it?"

Clara shrugged. "I dunno. Seven. Seven thirty."

He nodded, but then started shaking his head. "No, it isn't," he said. He squinted down at his watch, aiming it upwards to try and catch the light of the TV. "It's . . . damn near eight o'clock. Eight o'clock, missy."

He stood up. Quickly.

She took a step backwards, groaning. Things were getting worse.

But then someone did something in the baseball game, and there was cheering and the announcers got real excited. Her father stopped, caught by the excitement, turning to look at the tube.

But the noise faded and he turned back to Clara.

He came close, his face all dark.

"Now, why don't you tell me just where've you been, girl? Just what the hell have you been up to?"

Clara smiled, trying to calm him down, knowing that it was hopeless.

"I told you, Daddy, I was just in—"

He reached out and grabbed her wrist, squeezing it hard. He yanked her arm roughly, and she stumbled close to him, so terribly close to falling in on him. "Doing what?" he demanded. Another hard yank. Her eyes started watering from the pain.

(She must not cry, she told herself. She must not. It only made him lose it, as if now he had *that* to blame her for. *Look, just look what you went and made me do! You* made *me hurt you. Now I'm really mad.*)

"Please," she begged him, "I'm sorry I was late. I'll be home earlier tomorrow." She forced a smile. "Please, Daddy."

Her father licked his lips. His wet tongue was just about the only thing she could see clearly.

And then he let go of her wrist.

"You damn well better be. Damn well—"

He looked back at the screen, at his untended beer.

Clara stepped back.

"I will," she said brightly.

He shook his head and maneuvered back to his chair, falling into it and, in the same movement, scooping up his beer.

Somebody hit the stupid baseball again and she was free. She hurried to the stairs, taking them two at a time, up to her room.

But she didn't lock the door.

He had warned her about that too.

No locked doors in my house, girl. No, sir!

So she lived with her fear. That he'd come in, all boozed up, unable to stand, over to her bed . . . close to her.

She shut the door. There were no posters on the wall. He had told her that there'd be "none of that shit." The room was bare, *like a cheap hotel room for a kid,* she imagined.

There was a mirror and she saw herself in it.

Still smiling.

Oh, God, she thought. Smiling.

Like some stupid kid-clown.

But as she watched, her face melted, the tears bloomed on her face. Trails ran down her cheek as her hand leaned down onto the cheap bureau.

"Please . . ." she begged to the air.

She blinked. And then she opened the bottom drawer . . .

And felt around in the back, underneath some old sweaters.

She touched it . . . and pulled it out.

A knife.

And she rubbed away her tears, with the short blade held tightly in her right hand.

Eight

Damn, the uniform was uncomfortable! So snug, starched stiff, and the collar was so close and tight around her neck that she just wanted to keep hooking a finger under the collar, yanking at it.

Still, as Ann Mayhew parked her car in the small lot reserved for employees of the Inn, she was excited. This might be another waitressing job, but it was a shot at some good money, maybe getting ahead a bit. . . .

She stepped out of her car and shivered.

It was very early in the morning and cool, the sun only now breaking the horizon. And she hurried to the main building, joining groups of other waitresses and busboys making their sleepy way to the Miller Inn.

The Inn was a fairy-tale castle. There were turrets and gables, and a great flagpole at the very top of the highest roof, flying three flags that flapped noisily. The main building, she read in the official guidebook, was actually the second built. The original Inn, a very Quaker establishment, was the barnlike wooden building that sat perched at the edge of the cliff, overlooking Miller Lake. From there, a great wooden stairway led down to the Inn's tiny private beach and dock.

The cliff was sheer, though, and not too many of the old-timers braved the wooden walkway with its split-rail handholds.

The main building was made out of great chunks of local granite, enormous hand-cut stones that made it look like a fortress. The Grand Dining Room and the Main Ballroom were here, as was the small gallery of shops. Most people, unless they had connections or were patrons of long standing, were assigned to the guest rooms in this buildings.

It was difficult to get a room in the original building, with its master suites, great brick fireplaces in each room, and wrought-iron balconies overlooking the lake.

The third building, sitting right next to the castle, held just a few guest rooms—less desirable and much less expensive— and rooms for the live-in staff (seventy-five or more, according to the guidebook). It also held the storerooms, freezer, and other business areas of the Inn.

Ann entered the service entrance to the main building. The sun popped over the eastern hills, bathing the Inn's orange roofs in a warm glow.

And Ann breathed deep, feeling not unlike a princess.

By 10 A.M., the princess had turned into a toad.

Or so she felt, struggling to get the breakfast orders delivered correctly, navigating the incredibly long trip from the kitchen to the dining room.

Joanie gave her an occasional word of encouragement.

"Lookin' good, kid," she said, floating with ease through the flurry of waitresses and busboys, scooping up hot cereal, griddle cakes, and platters of bacon. "Just don't forget that the old ones like to gab a bit." She breezed past Ann. "And smile, honey!"

Ann nodded, picking up someone else's Cream of Wheat. (And was promptly informed of that fact by some heavy-armed pro who muscled Ann away, shaking her head.)

Ann was left meekly apologizing to thin air.

When an order of Corn Flakes didn't materialize, Ann wasted a good five minutes getting the attention of one of the cooks . . . who rolled his eyes and told her that cold cereal was available from a table in the back.

Duh—the cook gestured, shaking his head.

"Sorry . . ." she groaned.

This was the absolute worst, to be surrounded by all these people who knew exactly what they were doing, and to be so confused.

It was some kind of nightmare Lucy episode.

("Oh, Ricky . . . take me out of here. Waaah!")

A few of the busboys sailed by her, grinning and welcoming

her on board. Joanie appeared and promptly warned her about
one of them.

"That," she said, arching her dark eyebrows towards a
dark-haired kid, "is Tommy Balen. He's going to night
school . . . at least he says he is." Joanie leaned close. "He's
nailed every chippy in the building, kiddo, so if you're not
interested in just being another casualty, better be warned."

Joanie drifted away, leaving Ann to wonder if there wasn't
more than a bit of wounded pride in her advice.

By the time breakfast had ended, she'd had a nice chat with
an old couple at Table Five, the Friedmans, both staying over
for the Mystery Weekend.

"We love murder," the tiny gray-haired woman had said,
grinning.

A lone man at Table Six, gruff and absorbed in his *Wall
Street Journal,* had her take his poached eggs back.

"Too damn hard," he snapped. "I like the yolk runny!"

When she brought them back to the cook, he rolled his eyes
at her.

"Find out how they like 'em," he said, tilting the plate and
sliding the rejected eggs into an overflowing garbage can.

She got through it though, ready, if not eager, for the lunch
sitting . . . starting in a mere two hours. With dinner running
from five to six thirty, it was a long day. And she had only one
day a week off.

But as she strolled back to the kitchen and the locker area,
she found herself thinking, not about the Inn, or the nasty man
at Table Six, or the cute busboys, or even the big tips.

She thought about Alan Ward.

And wondered what she was going to do about him.

After a quick breakfast of whole wheat toast and Raisin Bran,
with a nicely untalkative Mrs. Simpson in her immaculate
dining room—no other guests seemed to be about—Brian
started his exploration of Stoneywood.

The town was slow to awaken. Either that, or there wasn't a
hell of a lot going on in old Stoneywood. The main street was
still deserted by 9 A.M., though there were some cars and vans
gathered near the bank.

(And he could imagine the sob stories the loan department
must hear. Reaganomics surely had done damage here.)

He drove under a gigantic banner announcing a carnival,

starting Friday night. Sponsored by the good ole boys of the Volunteer Fire Department. That might brighten up this trip a bit.

Some hokey games, and kiddie rides. A bit of small-town America. Cotton candy and hot dogs with the works.

Maybe he'd win himself a Kewpie doll.

He went back down Faith Avenue, moving east, away from Mount Shadow. The road split, one spur heading back to the Taconic while the other, according to the sign, led to the town beach and the Miller Inn.

The road weaved past a few small farms, past a few roadside fruit and vegetable stands, all closed tight. The road dipped, and Brian saw that it was actually turning back, circling behind the town. Then, after one long hill leading down, he saw the lake.

It was more like a crater. The beach was just a small sandy strip, probably made by the town fathers of Stoneywood. A lopsided swimming dock was moored out in the circular lake, and he saw a few homes peeking through the thick wall of pine trees that grew right to the lake's edge.

And there, at the other end of the lake, was the Miller Inn.

It sat on a great cliff at the northern border of the lake. Brian pulled off the road and got out of his car. There was a crazy stairway leading down from the Inn complex, crisscrossing the cliff, leading down to a small beach and a dock lined with rowboats.

He looked at the Inn, and grinned. It was unlike anything he had ever seen, something the Seven Dwarfs might have designed, a resort complex for overworked creatures under three feet tall.

Check your pointed cap, sir?

It might be a nice place to have a drink later.

He got back in the car.

The inevitable had been postponed long enough.

And why? *Because I don't know what I'm supposed to be doing here, that's why. I'm a prosecutor, not a goddamn private detective*.

And he drove back, towards Mount Shadow, and Alan Ward's cottage.

The banging on the door startled Josh, making him choke on his Cheerios. His grandmother looked over at him.

"Expecting company?"

He shook his head. When he'd gotten up this morning, his grandmother was still annoyed at him for riling Mister.

He tried to explain . . . the picture . . . the horse's sudden craziness. But she just shook her head.

Then he spoke to his mother, who really pissed him off! He asked her to come up, just to visit for a few days. "There's a carnival," he had told her. "Can't you take a few days off? It will be fun," he said.

For a moment his mother was quiet, like she was thinking about it.

"Please," he said.

But then she was all business: *I've got this to do, and that to do, and that account, and that—*

"Sure," Josh told her. "I understand. Hey, Mom, you've got an important job." Even though he knew it probably had nothing to do with her job.

Another knock, and his grandmother opened the door.

And there was Clara, dressed in jeans faded to a perfect dusky blue and striped T-shirt.

"Hey, Josh," she said, standing at the doorway.

His grandmother stepped aside, and arched her eyebrows.

"An introduction, Josh?"

He pushed back his chair and stood up, dabbing at his milk-moustache with a napkin. "Hi, Clara. This is Clara, Grandma . . . a friend," he said quietly.

His grandmother smiled. "Well, hello, Clara," she said, sticking out her hand. "Come in, it's very nice to meet you."

Josh felt embarrassed, though he wasn't sure why.

"What's up?" he tried to say casually.

Clara looked at him, smiling. Then, quickly, glancing up at his grandmother, she said, "I was wondering whether you wanted to go biking and stuff? Maybe go swimming later?"

Josh nodded. "Sure."

He was relieved to see his grandmother busy herself over at the sink. Josh got up from the table.

"Bring a lunch," Clara suggested, tilting her head.

He turned to his grandmother. "Er, is there anything for—"

"Peanut butter and jelly," she said, turning and smiling at him—at last. "And how does two slices of pie sound?"

* * *

Josh saw her rub her wrist. Quickly, before grabbing the handlebars again. He saw it, and noticed the ugly dark color imprinted on her skin.

They were careering down the hill, bumping on rocks, holding onto their handlebars for dear life.

"What happened?" he yelled over to her.

"What?" she yelled back.

"Your wrist!"

"Nothing!" she called to him, then she pedaled hard, passing him, moving even faster down the hill. Josh worked to catch up with her.

"Where are we going?"

"Just one of the absolute neatest places that I know. And nobody else knows about it. *Nobody*. At least," she said, wrinkling her nose like a rabbit, "I don't think anyone else knows about it. Anyway, just wait till you see it. It's great, really great."

"Okay." He smiled.

The biking was hard, from a country road that seemed to lead nowhere, through grassy fields that grabbed at their spokes, and then up, over bumpy hills, then across meadow, dodging rabbit holes and rocks hidden in the waist-high grass.

Heading towards the mountain.

Looking up at it, Josh didn't see the rut in the road. He hit it with his front tire, and as the bike pitched forward he snapped to attention. He leaned back, trying to get his balance, feeling the bike tilt forward, then sideways.

When he heard a sound. Deep, rumbling. Like storm clouds in the distance. A summer storm, lumbering over the mountain.

Except the sky was clear blue.

The rumbled vanished.

"Josh!" Clara yelled at him. And the bike began sideslipping to the left, taking forever to fall. He stuck his leg out to catch himself but he was going too fast.

He felt himself fly forward, over the bike.

The sandy road and prickers dug into his jeans.

Then Clara was there, astride her bike, looking down at him.

"You okay?" she asked. He nodded. Then he remembered the sound. The rumble. The storm. The thunder—

"Did you hear that sound?" he asked.

"What?" She grinned. "You mean you yelling as you went ass-over-handlebars?"

"No," he said, getting up, picking the tiny thorns off his pants legs, dusting away the grit. "A rumble. A deep sound, near the mountain."

"Nope," she said. "Didn't hear a thing. C'mon, let's get going . . . and puh-leese—watch where you're going."

Josh recovered his bike and hurried to catch up to Clara . . .

Ever since Josh first came to his Grandmother's farm, he didn't notice anything odd about the mountain. It wasn't monstrously big, just tall enough to lord it over the rolling hills that filled the valley.

But there was something about it that made him keep looking at it . . . made him want to explore it.

There were boulders perched precariously along its slope, as though they'd tumbled there and just got snagged. They looked ready to continue careening down the hill.

From the beginning, Josh thought that the mountain looked dangerous.

And the trees! The lower slope of the mountain was dotted with great, lush pines. But they all jutted out at odd angles, leaning off and away from the mountain.

Like they were trying to get away from it.

But something else started to bother him as he looked at the mountain, sketched the mountain . . . something—

Then one day he knew what it was.

The mountain was all rough edges, sharp precipices ending in sheer cliffs and pointy outcrops. There were no soft, gentle rolling slopes covered with bushes and trees. This mountain, small as it was, looked like something from the Rocky Mountains, rough and new.

Fresh out of the ground.

And it looked like it didn't belong here.

"Why the name?" he yelled to Clara, straining to keep up with her."

"What?"

"The mountain—why is it called 'Shadow'?"

"Dunno. Guess cause it throws a big shadow right across the town. Who knows? The shadow reaches the lake. It gets pretty cool there in the late afternoon."

They came to a rough path, all gouged with deep furrows.

"We go up here," she said, taking the uphill path all too easily.

Josh stood up to pedal, his ten-speed not helping him against Clara's beat-up Huffy. His narrow wheels seemed to find every pit and pile of rubble.

His head was down now, concentrating on the path and getting up the goddam hill.

(Having second thoughts about his new friendship with this twelve-year-old Wonder Woman.)

He looked up.

And there, at the crest of the hill, he saw a cottage. It sat off the road, with just enough space to park a car or two.

A dumpy little cottage.

And there, parked beside it, was the black pickup.

Mountain Road? This was more like Mountain Gully, Brian thought as his car labored up the hill.

A couple of times he swore he heard the damn exhaust pipe snap right off. Some ominous sound seemed to vibrate through the cheap car. But then it was gone. A temporary reprieve from whatever threatened the heap.

The dirt road was scarred by years, maybe decades, of run-off. It was knocking his car around like a toy.

He gained a few feet, only to have the rear wheels trapped by some carnivorous gouge that sucked at the tires while they sang out a high-pitched whine of protest.

"Shit . . ."

Having said that—summing up his present circumstances— he looked up the hill.

And he saw what had to be Ward's cottage.

The first thing that struck him was how alone it was. It sat on top of the hill, all by itself, a small, ramshackle joint that had to be a barrel of laughs when Old Man Winter rolled around. The icy wind must sound like it was going to pluck the small house right off the ground.

But even now, with the mid-morning sun bearing down, the house looked isolated and desolate. It was surrounded by tall, wild grass and a scattering of browned-out bushes. The mountain loomed behind it, grim, dark, and closer than it seemed it should be.

And it appeared that Mountain Road ended just few yards ahead.

This was the last stop, end of the road.

And he had to wonder . . . Who the hell would rent this dump? Okay, it had a nice view of the mountain. And, from the crest of the hill you could probably see the lake.

But it was so desolate that it was positively creepy.

A summer place for the Addams Family.

He stopped the car.

(Noticing the thin plume of smoke that sizzled out of the hood. Poor sick engine probably never bargained for a jaunt like this. . . .)

If he drove up closer to the cottage, they'd see him—how could they avoid it? And he wasn't ready for that, not yet.

No. He grinned, killing the engine. *I'm still in the information-gathering stage. That's right, just some court-approved surveillance.*

Only thing is . . . I don't know what the hell I'm looking for. He got out of the car, leaving it right in the middle of the road.

There was nowhere decent to pull off. And, if he didn't spend too much time at Chez Ward, nobody would likely need to get up or down.

And if they did, fuck 'em.

At first he thought he'd just walk straight up the hill, right to the house.

(Like a door-to-door salesman. "Excuse me, folks, I'm your Local Electrolux representative and . . . Say, I see you have a dirt floor here. Now, we've got—")

But he walked off the road, into the tall grass.

Let's pretend we're trying to do this quietly.

Don't want to get anyone riled up.

Now, do we?

No. Brian knew how that could turn out . . . knew from personal experience.

Yeah, and it probably explained how his meteoric rise in the Navy Judicial system had come to an abrupt halt. When you screw up, no matter whose fault it is, the government has a nice way of remembering.

(His foot got caught in a hole—a gopher hole, he guessed—and he tripped and tumbled to the ground.)

And he thought about his fuck-up.

It was a drug case, always an embarrassment for the armed forces. Some lieutenant, j.g., working in the goddamn Pentagon, if you could believe that, and supplying a dozen bases on the East Coast with coke. Magic nose powder.

But he was a smart little dealer. There were no smoking guns, no tapes of telephone calls, nothing that could be used to pin his ears to his ass. He had a pretty Navy wife and two cute kids.

Sweet guy.

Enter the rising star of the Prosecutor's office, everyone's fair-haired boy, Brian McShane. Brian remembered trying to pass on handling the actual investigation. There was, after all, a whole department in the Shore Patrol unit devoted to drugs. "Why me?" he argued. But this was sensitive, they explained. It might have ramifications.

Brian remembered grinning as they handed him the sticky lollipop.

The first week was pretty quiet—getting photos, license plates of who came and went, following cars, getting search warrants ready for the big raid.

But what they didn't know was that the lieutenant had been warned by somebody. He was getting ready to go AWOL. Take his profits and split.

Hello, Rio . . .

But Brian felt it in his bones and, even though he didn't have everything locked up the way he would have liked, he gave the order for the raid.

There was only one problem.

All the pressure on the lieutenant made him dip into his own product more and more.

Until, on the night of the raid, he was absolutely bonkers.

Brian's team, not especially experienced in such things—this wasn't, after all, 138th Street and Amsterdam Avenue—tried to make an orderly entrance.

The lieutenant's snub-nosed Uzi ripped a foot-wide hole through his apartment door, taking out two of Brian's men. Scratch two Navy pensions. And the glassy-eyed dealer kept coming, dragging his wife along, using her as a shield, taunting Brian's men to try and stop him.

(And just thinking about it made Brian lick his lips. It was so dry out here. Or maybe it was just the memory of how out of control the whole situation had been. *What the fuck do I do now*? he had wondered, clinging to the apartment wall, so scared his balls almost rattled. *Oh, Jesus . . . what do I do?*

Then the kids came out, crying, screaming for their mother, and Brian knew he'd just taken an express elevator to hell.

Your floor, sir, bedlam.

Some of the Shore Patrol he had in tow were a bit more experienced in dealing with armed crazy people.

They fired back.

Even though the guy's wife was being dragged alongside. Even though the two kids were staggering out behind Daddy.

While the dealer's Uzi peppered the wall with pizza-sized craters, they fired back. Ignoring Brian's scream, "No!"

(Or did he only imagine that he screamed out something? Maybe he was just cowering there, scared shitless, unable to do squat.)

They cut down the lieutenant . . .

Missing his wife.

But one bullet—

And everyone *said* it came from the dealer's gun, insisted that it *had* to have come from the dealer's gun—took the little boy and sent him flying back into the apartment.

And when the roar of the bullets stopped—and the bluish smoke hung in the hallway, and drifted into the apartment—the mother went around, pounding on everyone with her fists, screaming at them. . . .

"You killed my *baby* . . . *my baby!*"

The official report disagreed.

But Brian's career advancement came to an abrupt, and permanent, halt.

Rightly so, he admitted every time he replayed the worst five minutes of his life.

He neared the top of the hill. Some huckleberry bushes clung to the side of the hill. Their tough, waxy-green leaves should give him some cover, he figured. And he took out a small pair of Zeiss binoculars—good old German optics—and hunkered down, close to the bushes, looking forward to his first glimpse of Alan Ward in the flesh. . . .

Nine

"WE'VE GOTTA LEAVE the bikes here," Clara announced.

Josh looked over his shoulder at the cottage up on the hill. He didn't like the idea of it being so close.

(*Oh, stop being a wussy,* he told himself. *Some country bumpkin in a pickup gets a little too close on the highway and I'm ready to call the police. Jeeez!*)

"We have to make our way through the gorge . . . there's a neat climb . . . and then we come to these caves."

Josh had to voice his suspicion. "And your friends?"

Clara grimaced, disappointed.

"Hey, I told you they only come here to have some beers. And they *always* invite me."

"Uh-huh," Josh said uncertainly.

"What . . . you don't trust me?"

"It's not that, it's just—"

Above him, a bird called. He looked up and saw the dark, soaring shadow, circling over them.

He thought of the dead deer.

"No, I just—"

"If you don't want to go see the cave"—Clara shrugged—"that's okay. We can go back." She started back over to her bike.

"No," Josh said. "Come on! Let's go."

Clara's grin filled her pie-shaped face. "Great! Follow me!"

She led him through the gorge, jumping on top of rocks, skipping from one safe perch to another. A few times Josh slipped and lost his footing.

I'm looking for the deer, he thought.

But it wasn't there.

What happened to it? he wondered. He thought of asking Clara.

But he didn't.

The bird called again, its screeching call growing fainter as they moved into the narrow cleft of the gorge.

"There are pools ahead," she called back to him. "Deep places where we can swim. I mean, not today, without suits and all. Ice cold. You'd freeze your nuts off." She laughed.

(And he felt himself redden.)

She looked back at him. "If you know what I mean . . ."

Clara was skipping ahead when Josh saw something stuck in the wall of the gorge.

"Wait!" he said. He bent close to the rock.

It was a fossil, just sort of stuck on the wall, ready to fall out. He tried to work his fingers under the stone, to pry it loose.

Clara walked back to him.

"What is it?"

"Some kind of fossil. See, it's all bumpy here. But it won't come—"

"Here," she said, picking up a piece of rock from the stream and handing it to him. Josh saw that it was a sharp chunk of slate.

"Good," he said, working the sharp edge of the slate under the fossil. It didn't look like it was going to budge. He was chewing all around it but the fossil simply didn't move.

(As if the rock wall didn't want to release it.)

Then it popped out, leaping off the wall, flying through the air.

Clara caught it.

"Good catch." He smiled.

Clara turned the bumpy chunk around in her hand. "What is it?"

Josh took it from her.

Good question. What was it? It looked like it was part of something larger, all bumpy, then tapering near the end. Or maybe it was just some kind of weird prehistoric plant.

"I don't know. . . ."

He popped it into his back pocket. "I can check it later. You've got a library in town, don't you?"

"Sure we do!" Clara said. "Let's get going. . . ." Then she turned and started climbing up the side of the gorge, leaving the stream bed behind.

She moves so easily, he marveled. *What is she? Part mountain goat?*

And he caught himself looking at her . . . in a different way. . . .

The line of her leg when she stretched up, grabbing a handhold. Her T-shirt tight against her back.

And his foot slipped.

The rock gave way, and he found himself slipping down a few feet before his hands were able to claw into some crack in the granite.

"Okay?" Clara called down to him.

He smiled at her. "Sure. Just wasn't paying attention."

She smiled at him—

(There was something about that smile that worried him, scared him. It was too easy, too warm. She seemed to know what she was doing, so damn confident all the time. But something about that smile made him worry about her.)

Josh paid more attention to the climb now, checking each new perch before letting it carry his weight.

And when he glanced up, he saw that Clara was already standing on top of a ledge.

"There," she said, as he crawled over the lip. "That wasn't so bad, now was it?"

He stood up.

"We're on the mountain," he said, looking around. He could just make out the tops of some of the buildings in Stoneywood, and then, to the north, the lake, glistening and brilliant in the sun.

He looked down.

The gorge swung around to the left, probably leading to those pools Clara was talking about. He couldn't see his house—they'd need to get still higher.

But he saw the small cottage.

And he saw someone outside.

"The caves are this way," Clara said.

Josh nodded.

But he watched the cottage, and the man walking around outside. . . .

* * *

Ward came out of the cottage quickly, almost rushing.

Brian crouched down, noisily snapping a branch of the huckleberry bush.

Shit, Brian thought, looking up to see if Ward heard anything. But Ward kept on moving, oblivious to the fact that he was being watched.

He went over to his pickup, and let the tailgate creak down. Then he pushed some stuff to the back and hurried into the house.

Looks normal enough, Brian thought, bringing his binoculars up in case Ward reappeared.

Which he did almost immediately.

Ward carried a large, black plastic bag. And from the way he held it, it looked heavy.

Then someone else came out—a woman, struggling with every step.

Mama, Brian thought.

Ward tossed the bag into the back of the truck.

Then Ward slammed the tailgate back into position.

And he walked back into the cottage with his mother.

Now, what the hell do you suppose that is? Brian thought. Garbage?

Sure. There were no big trucks that came by twice a week to snatch everyone's trash from their doorstep. This was the country. You took your garbage to the dump—located, to be sure—in some less desirable area.

People here had a more direct relationship with their environment. They made their trash and they got to see it build up, year after year, until it became a mountain of plastic bottles and cans and six-pack holders, a wonderland for the crows and bears to sample Cheetos and Coors Light.

Everything looked pretty normal.

Ward . . . his mother . . . taking it easy on Barrow's Hill.

American Gothic.

More gothic, he thought, than American . . .

"Go ahead in! There's nothing to be afraid of. . . ."

Josh wasn't too sure of that. The cave entrance was black and cool, with a strange odor.

He stepped closer and peered into the cave.

"Okay," Clara said, not unkindly. "I'll go in first. I've gone in hundreds of times."

He watched her walk into the darkness and disappear.

"Clara," he called.

Then, again, "Clara . . ."

"Well," she yelled out, her voice echoing, "are you coming in or not?"

"Sure," he said.

Not at all sure.

Then he heard a click, and Clara's face was bathed in the pale yellow light of a small flashlight.

"Hi ya!" Clara grinned ghoulishly at him.

The light was a small, puny thing in so much darkness.

"Didn't think I'd come in here with no light, did you?" She aimed the light right and left, outlining the nearby walls of the cave, the floor. "So, are you coming in or do I have to drag you in?" She laughed.

He walked in.

So cool!

The air was damp, and he wished he had a sweatshirt. It was actually *cold*. Clara came close to him, the small flashlight pointed up at their two faces.

"Ain't it great?" she said, looking up at him.

(And he realized that this girl—as exciting as she was—probably had a whole bunch of experiences that he had only daydreamed about.)

Until now.

But then, as if sensing his discomfort, she turned around and pointed the light farther into the cave, down an incline.

"That's where we go," she said.

"Why?"

"Just wait . . ." And she walked away, with the light.

He hurried to follow her.

The roof started to slope down, getting closer and closer.

"There are bats if you go the other way, thousands and thousands of them, nasty suckers, all stuck on the top of the cave like vampires. That's pretty neat to see too," she said. They both had to crouch down now. Drops of icy water plopped onto Josh's head.

Then the cave seemed to end.

Clara knelt down.

"Come on," she said. "Crouch down here."

He knelt down, next to her.

It was a hole, going right into the mountain.

"No way," he said, backing away from it. "No thank you, but I don't need to crawl in there and prove anything."

But Clara shook her head, and aimed her light into the hole.

"Hey, Josh, I go in there all the time. It's great. Look, you can see light . . . see?" she said, pulling him close to the hole. "There's *light* on the other side. It leads to an opening at the other end of the gorge, right by the falls."

"Falls?"

"Well, they're dry now, but in the spring there's these great falls. We can crawl through . . . and come out the other end."

Josh shook his head.

"Thanks, but no thanks. Maybe some other day."

"Oh, that's too bad," Clara said, ". . . 'cause that's the way I'm going."

And then she squirmed her way into the hole, wriggling on the damp ground. He watched her scissoring legs disappear into the hole, swallowed up.

And with her went the light.

Then he looked around. The cave entrance was . . . somewhere back there.

He saw a faint glow of light.

But not much.

The real light—Clara's sickly flashlight—was quickly disappearing into the hole.

"Dammit, Clara, I knew I shouldn't have trusted you, you and your dumb-ass cave—"

"Quit your complaining," she called back, her voice all muffled and weird. "Come on"—she laughed, trying to sound like Dracula—"bee-fore the bats get hun-greee!"

On cue, Josh heard some high-pitched sounds from behind him.

He stuck his head into the hole.

Like he was following Alice in Wonderland.

He started crawling. . . .

So that's what Alan Ward looks like.

Brian walked down the hill, staying on the road now that he was out of sight of the cottage.

Ward didn't look too much different from his official Navy

Before the tunnel began to close. The stone walls seemed to fight against the terrible shaking. But then they gave up . . . and started moving—

A stony mouth chewing down.

The tunnel squeezed . . .

Pressing his head down . . . his chin. The rocks, rubbing and scraping, screeching out a high-pitched whine of protest.

He was flush with the floor. Unable to move.

His arms were pinned under him.

Something dug into his ass. Something hard, pushing into him.

He felt the fossil in his back pocket grind into him. Printing itself into his buttocks. The pain made his eyes water.

"Oh, God," he cried.

His head was turned sideways, in a stone hammerlock.

"Josh! Josh!" Clara screamed.

The rumble stopped.

And Josh was stuck.

Clara was crying.

The first rumble had just startled her, sounding far away, on the other side of the mountain. But then she had to grab the side of the rocky wall to steady herself. It felt as if the rumble had traveled here, rippling through the stone like a wave.

She had felt earthquakes before. Small ones happened all the time here. But this was different. It came suddenly, then grew. As if it were attacking the mountain.

Maybe, she thought, it wasn't an earthquake.

And when it stopped, she could see that the tunnel was smaller.

Not a lot. She wiped her eyes.

But smaller. Small enough to hold Josh fast.

"Josh!" she screamed.

"Yeah . . ." he answered, almost too calmly.

She leaned into the hole, aiming her small flashlight into it. "Are you all right?"

"I guess so. Something is jabbing into my side. I don't know what it—"

"Josh . . ." Clara said, chewing at her lower lip, "can you move . . . Can you—"

"No. I'm stuck, Clara. I can't do anything." He waited a minute. "Clara—"

"Yes?" she called into the hole.

"You better get some help."

"Okay," she said, pulling back from the opening.

"Clara!" he yelled. "Leave the light, will you?"

Josh sounded like he was going to cry—or scream.

"Oh, sorry."

She found a small rock and propped the flashlight on it. Most of its yellow light was aimed at the ceiling, but enough made its way down to Josh.

"I'll get help," she said, taking a step backwards. "Don't worry, Josh."

And she turned away from the hole, climbing down to the gorge, to the rocky path that led along the stream, that meandered back to the wall they climbed and, further, the entrance to the gorge.

She climbed quickly, jumping down two and three feet at a time, before she reached the rocky ledge that went alongside the stream.

I've got to hurry, she kept telling herself. *Got to hurry.*

'Cause what if it moves again . . . ?

What if it moves again and Josh is there, stuck there, when the tunnel closes some more?

Her sneakered feet slipped on a wet rock and she went tumbling into the shallow stream. She caught herself and popped up, still running.

There was a cottage, she knew. Just on the hill, right near the mountain.

A cottage and a truck and, *God, there just had to be people there*. They could help . . . do something.

And with every step she took, she tried to listen, listen to the mountain.

Hoping it was quiet now.

Every sound that Josh heard he had to identify.

Had to!

That's a bird outside, he thought, hearing a crow's screech. *And there, from behind, that's some loose rock. And that's a . . . a—*

Oh, God, hurry, Clara. Please.

The light, aimed at the ceiling of the tunnel, was now so faint he could barely make out the pattern of the rock, the black swirl running through the gray stone. And then he saw the light begin to fade some more. First it seemed just a bit dimmer, and then it was just a sickly yellowish glow.

The batteries were nearly dead.

And in a few minutes he'd be trapped in the dark.

(He heard a sound from behind him. Something moving back in the cave. It sounded like feet.)

He grunted and pushed against the rock, as if one incredible effort would magically free him. But his body wouldn't budge.

Not an inch.

And he watched the light melt away into total blackness.

She was panting when she reached the top of the hill, breathing hard, her lungs in pain.

There was the cottage!

Just ahead of her.

She risked a look back at the mountain.

It was as if nothing had happened at all, as if she had gone to the mountain for a hike, all by herself. As if she had just imagined the whole thing. Just another silly pretend game, like she played so often when she went there alone. The wind blew the tall grass, and some crows soared overhead.

Yeah . . .

As if Josh wasn't there at all.

She let her lungs ease up just a bit. A moment's rest, to make the burning feeling stop.

Then she bolted towards the cottage, not stopping now, climbing the last twenty feet of the hill. Her eyes locked on the small gray clapboard cottage, sitting so alone on the hill.

It wasn't a nice place to look at.

Something about it was ugly.

She reached the top of the hill, reached the beginning of the road. And she ran up the path, past the truck, to the front door of the cottage. . . .

Ten

IT WAS DURING his break that Jeffy Post decided to hoof it over to the Mohawk and see just what the hell was going on.

Every day, like clockwork, he watched that little cunt Ann Mayhew drive in and walk her pretty little butt into the diner.

Hell, it was something to look forward to! And then, during his break, he always liked to go over for a burger or something and watch her move around the place. Somehow, it made working for that old cracker, Bob O, big Bob O'Connor with his white Lincoln Town Car and fat-ass wife, something he could almost stomach.

I'll get a crack at her, Jeffy told himself. Even though the waitress had brushed off all his attempts to get friendly. One day, his grin would break through that tight-ass composure of hers, yeah, and then she'd go out with him.

And he knew that as soon as she sampled some of his long john, it would be all over.

Sure. He could tell, just by looking at someone if they liked to fuck. He could *see* it.

And there was no doubt about that waitress. . . .

"Besides," he kept kidding her as he held his hot coffee close in the icy diner—'always Kool' the sign said. Always fuckin' frigid was more like it—"besides, what other prospects you got, babe? Who else is knockin' on your door 'cept some lard-butt truckers who just can't face the idea of dragging their rigs and their beer bellies home to the little wifey and their wacked-out kids.

"We'll have some fun." He grinned, winking at her.

She always said *no*. Always.

But not, he noted, thinking about it—playing it over in his head—not in any kind of pissed-off way.

That door will open, he always told himself. *Just gotta be patient and find the right key.*

But now, walking into the ice-cold greasy spoon, he didn't get that same charge he usually got. The rest of the waitresses were dogs, just a bunch of middle-aged broads with bowling-pin arms and dyed hair.

Jeffy squatted on one of the stools. He ordered a piece of blueberry pie and some coffee from someone named Tammy.

"Hey," he grunted, digging out a Marlboro and lighting it, as if he didn't give two shits about his question. "Where's that other waitress? You know . . . the young one?" He grinned.

Tammy didn't stop moving, setting up other places along the counter with a napkin, fork and knife.

"You mean the one you're always hitting on, Jeffy?"

"Hey, I just like her. At least," he said, blowing the smoke towards Tammy, "she wasn't all gone to blubber." He nodded to himself. "She's a cute little number."

Tammy was filling one of the glass sugar cylinders. Jeffy marveled that none of the sugar spilled onto the counter.

I could use one of them things in my apartment. Fuckin' sugar bowl was always empty. And he usually tried to fill it when he'd had too many beers. Fuckin' ants always had a field day.

"So where is she?"

Now Tammy screwed up her face at him. Like get off it, creep. Leave it the fuck alone.

"She's quit. Got herself a job at the Inn. She's gonna make some decent money. . . ." She smiled at Jeffy. "Nicer clientele."

"No shit," Jeffy said.

And Tammy was gone.

Now, ain't that a kick in the head? he thought. He sucked on his butt, enjoying the smoke, the way it seared his lungs, the rheumy cough it created, the sting of the smoke in his eyes.

Now, what the hell do I have to look forward to?

He looked through the window at Bob O—at the big cheese himself, outside, pumping gas with a disgusted mug. *Pumps all of twenty-five minutes a day and hates it.*

The answer to his question was clear.

Even for Jeffy Post.

Nothing.

There was nothing now to make each horrible little goddam day even the slightest bit decent.

Absolutely nothing.

Jeffy squashed out his cigarette in his half-eaten blueberry pie. One way or another, he'd just have to do something about that. . . .

Clara took three steps to the door . . .

When a bit of movement down the hill caught her eye.

It was someone—a man—walking down the hill.

She saw his car. Clara looked back at the cottage. The windows were closed, and tattered curtains made it impossible to see anything inside.

The man opened his car door, getting ready to leave.

And something made her call out to him.

"Hey!" she yelled, running down the hill. "Mister! Hey, wait."

The man got into his car. His hand reached out to shut the door. Clara ran full out, yelling at him. "Please!" she screamed. "Wait."

The door shut.

Then it opened again.

And the man came out of the car, a very confused look on his face.

Brian took a breath, looking around at the narrow tunnel.

"You okay, son?"

"Yeah," Josh said. "Just a bit crampy."

Brian nodded, smiling. "Well, don't worry. We're going to get you out of here in a jiffy."

And how am I going to do that? Brian wondered, still puffing from the run. The girl had set a wicked pace, begging him to hurry.

But now that they were here, in this strange, twisted grotto, he wasn't sure there was anything he could do for the kid.

The boy's head was beyond the reach of Brian's arms, and the boy—Josh, the girl called him—couldn't even turn around to look at Brian. There was a bit of room on either side of his head, but not a lot.

Brian's first thought was that he should hustle back to town and get the police or firemen to come and take a look.

And he told that to the girl, a lanky, tomboyish kid whose face and eyes held a deep, dark beauty.

"You can't do that," she said flatly.

"Why not?"

"It might move again. That would take too long," she whispered. "There could be another earthquake and—"

"Earthquake? What do you mean?"

"It moved. It sort of closed on him. . . ."

Brian hadn't felt anything when he was standing out there on the hill. What in the world was she talking about?

"It moved? You mean, he didn't just crawl in and get stuck?"

The girl nibbled at her lip, looking almost guilty.

"No, it started vibrating, sort of, like an earthquake. Then it closed on him."

Brian took another look inside the tunnel. He couldn't imagine any earthquake so localized that he wouldn't have felt it at all, just down the hill.

The narrowest part of the tunnel was just where the boy was stuck. If Josh could just get past that point, he might be able to get out. But for that to happen, he'd have to get his arms free.

Brian licked his lips. It was cool here, shaded by the mountain, and an even cooler breeze wafted out of the tunnel.

"Okay, Josh," Brian said, trying to make his voice sound as jaunty as possible. "Here's what we're going to do. We need to get your hands past your head. So, one at a time, start working them up your body. Force them if you have to, but get them up."

There was some grunting—Brian couldn't see much in the faint light. Then . . .

"I can't. All I can do is just get my hand up near my armpit. But then I can't move it anymore." There was panic in the boy's voice. Brian spoke to him calmly.

"Right. Okay, Josh. Try this. Push your body away from one wall—all the way, as close as you can get it to the other wall. Got it?"

There was silence. Then some more grunts.

"I'm over."

"Good work. Now try the hand."

Brian watched the boy's upper body squirming in the hole.

Then, like worms, his fingers crept past his arm. Josh grunted. And then his arm was out, looking like some odd appendage not really attached to his body.

Brian leaned into the hole and reached out. His fingers touched Josh's hand.

"Way to go, Josh. Now let's get the other arm."

And Brian thought he heard something then. Maybe from inside the tunnel. He looked up . . .

Bumping into Clara, who hung at his shoulder, her face a mask of concern and fear.

"I . . . I got my arm out!" Josh called out, and his two arms dangled weirdly ahead of him.

"Okay, Josh, I'm going to reach in and try to pull you out."

Brian actually had to crawl into the hole, filling it like a human cork. But his fingers found Josh's hands in the darkness.

It was hard to pull back. But Brian brought his knees against the stone wall, just outside the tunnel, and started pulling on Josh.

The boy groaned.

He wasn't moving.

Damn, Bright thought, careful not to say anything to scare the boy.

"I'm not moving!" Josh said.

The boy's fingers twisted in Brian's hand, eager for freedom.

Brian tightened his grip.

"Hold onto me!" he yelled back to Clara. He felt the girl grab around his midsection, her grip surprisingly strong.

"We're going to try it one more time, Josh," he said.

Because if it doesn't work, then you're going to be stuck here until we can get some real help.

Some competent help.

Oil, he thought. *I should have stopped a moment and brought some goddam oil from the car. Or maybe I could have gone to Ward's cottage and asked for some cooking oil . . . anything to make the boy's body slippery.*

Hindsight always was my forte.

"Here we go, Josh. Help me if you can. . . . Squirm your way through. Ready?"

The boy hesitated, not at all sure.

"Ready . . ."

Brian started pulling.

At first, nothing happened. Brian could imagine the stone digging into the boy's jeans, scraping at his skin through the thin material of his T-shirt.

The boy grunted, then something hurt him and he howled like a trapped animal.

Clara's hands dug into Brian even harder.

"Keep at it, Josh," Brian panted. "You're almost—"

—There. Josh felt his body, suddenly such a twisted, oversized thing, move. Just a bit. His cheek rubbed roughly against the rock. He tasted something then, some salty liquid on the rock.

The man kept pulling him.

He's just getting me stuck all the worse. He isn't helping me at all . . . not at all!

Josh thought of all his childhood playgrounds, and all the climbing toys and tubes, things to crawl through and under.

He used to love them, turning them into spaceships or pirate coves.

But this—*this* was just a trap.

It was a horrible, dead feeling.

As if the mountain were saying, "You're not going anywhere, kid."

His ass cheeks were pressed flat. No give left. That seemed to be the problem. Then he thought he felt something moving again.

Oh, Jesus, he thought. *The rumble! It's starting again. It's going to finish me. It's—*

Brian heard the rumble. Low, and in the distance.

He looked up, knowing what it was. Clara stared at him.

It was dynamite. Someone was blasting, somewhere on the other side of the mountain. Someone trying to blast great chunks of the mountain. Do it in the right place, and the vibrations could travel right through the mountain.

Right to Josh.

Brian tugged even harder, not caring whether he hurt the boy, knowing he'd better get him the hell out of there.

The fossil. It dig into Josh, imprinting itself on him. Then he felt something give, and somehow his twisting feet were able to kick him up. The man's hands felt surprised by Josh's sudden release.

But they recovered quickly and pulled him out.

Into the daylight.

Josh stood, his legs suddenly useful.

And he looked at Clara.

Wondering whether he was going to be angry at her, ripping mad that she had led him into the hole.

He heard the water rippling below him.

But that was all.

He looked at Clara, and smiled.

"You okay?" she asked, her voice unsure. Just looking at her face he knew he didn't look good. He licked his lips, tasting blood. His face was probably a mess.

"Sure." He grinned back, forgiving her.

(Knowing that she hadn't anything to do with this. This was . . . something else.)

He looked at the man. "Thank you."

"I'll take you home, Josh," the man said.

Josh nodded.

Then he reached to the back of his pants, back to where all that pressure had been.

The pocket of his jeans had been ripped open; it dangled like a loose flap of skin from his fanny. And the fossil, crumbled by the tunnel, was gone, scattered in pieces behind him.

The man put an arm on his shoulder, leading him down to the stream.

That's what let me get out, Josh thought.

He touched the flap of denim, fingering it.

Then he reached up and felt the impression of the strange fossil on his body.

Everyone was real quiet on the way back.

But then the man asked how he ended up in the tunnel.

And, like a light bulb coming on, Clara started telling, in lively detail, the whole story. . . .

Brian stood by the kitchen door and watched the old woman tend to the boy's wounds. She kept up a steady stream of tsk-tsking, shaking her head. Pinching Josh's chin between her thumb and forefinger, tilting the boy's head this way and that as she dabbed at his messy-looking face with a washcloth.

She demanded, and got, Josh's explanation of what had happened.

"The mountain moved?" she said, her voice dripping with disbelief. She looked over at Brian. "Funny we didn't feel anything here, Joshua."

"Ouch," the boy yelped as she took a swipe at another scrape.

"Is anyone doing any blasting near here, Mrs. Stoller?" Brian asked. "I heard something that sounded like dynamite."

Josh's grandmother shook her head. "No," she said. "Not that I know of . . ."

Josh's cuts and scraps only looked nasty. There was nothing on the boy's body that would leave anything like a scar.

The girl, Clara, lurked behind Brian, almost edging to the door, ready to bolt should this fierce grandmother turn her attention on her.

When Josh's wounds were finally cleaned up and dabbed with brilliant red streaks of mercurochrome, the woman finally came over to Brian.

"Thank you, Mr. McShane. My grandson seems to be spending his summer getting in trouble."

"I think that's what thirteen-year-old boys are supposed to do with their summer," Brian said, smiling over at a glum Josh.

Then the woman looked down at Clara, but not, Brian noticed, with any warmth. She obviously placed a good deal of the blame for her grandson's misadventure at the girl's doorstep.

If Josh got hurt, it was clear from her no-nonsense tone of voice, it was due to the boy's own foolishness . . . and getting mixed up with Clara.

"Well, I'm going to have to do . . . something," she said again, turning back to Josh.

"Right," Brian said. Then he looked at Clara. "I'd best take this young lady home. They've had a bit of a scare."

The old woman looked at Clara and then shook her head at Josh. The girl, it would seem, came from the wrong side of the tracks.

Wherever the tracks were in this burg.

Brian opened the kitchen door.

"Feel better, Josh," he said.

"See you, Josh," Clara said quietly, apologetically.

The boy looked right at him. He wasn't himself yet—still a bit fuzzy.

"Thank you," Josh said. "Thanks a lot."

"Any time."

Josh smiled.

Then Brian walked out.

Once outside, Brian brusquely overrode Clara's objections when she said that she'd just as soon bike back home. "It isn't far," she claimed. "I don't need you to do this, *really*."

"I know, *really*." Brian grinned. "It's just that when I save people I like to see them safe at home. Part of the job."

But there was no light in her face now. It was all doom and gloom as she sat there, sullen, gnawing at her lip.

Driving her back home, it didn't take him long to see why.

She lived down a small dead-end side street.

And if Stoneywood had a slum, this was it. Ten, maybe even five years ago, the block probably didn't look all that much different from the other blocks. But times were different . . . and too many families with out-of-work bread-winners led to roofs past repair and flaking paint jobs.

Then it just becomes a matter of drowning your troubles with a few brewskis and letting the lawn go to hell.

Just hang in there and wait till midsummer.

Wait till all the grass browns out, burned by the summer sun.

"This will be fine," Clara said quickly.

And Brian knew that they were still probably a good distance away from her house.

"Here?" he asked, cruising slowly up to the nearest house.

Clara shook her head, all perturbed. "This is *fine*, Mr. McShane. It's close enough." She popped open the door.

"Can I at least pull the car over to the curb?"

She pulled her door shut while Brian parked.

Then she turned and looked at him. "Thanks . . . for everything. You probably saved Josh's life."

"More likely, I just spared him a few hours stuck in that hole."

Clara got out. "Well, thanks anyway."

"Sure."

And she stood on the sidewalk.

And waited for Brian to pull away.

Okay, he thought. *I don't really need to see which one of these ramshackle joints is yours.*

But as he pulled away, he had the odd feeling that he'd just left behind someone who was really in trouble. . . .

Ann finished touching up her makeup.

She would have liked a shower after finishing her first day, just the thing to really freshen up.

Now that she knew what she wanted to do.

She had thought about it all through dinner. As she started to feel at home at the Inn. *They're all so decent*, she thought. Everyone. Even the cooks—hard to believe—treated her like a person. She was so used to feeling battered after a day at the Mohawk. Well, this was quite a change.

"Heavy date?" Joanie grinned, walking by her.

Ann turned and smiled at her. Joanie had been friendly and helpful all day. She could do worse for a new friend.

"Sort of." Ann grinned back.

Joanie kept on walking out.

"You did good today, kid." she called back. Then, looking over her shoulder, making a witchy motion with her hands she added, "Just watch out for them busboys, sweetie."

Ann took one last look in the mirror, wet her lips with her tongue.

There, she thought. *Not bad. A bit like Debra Winger.*

Sure.

She went over to her locker and shut it.

And she thought about what it was going to be like to see Alan Ward after all these years. . . .

"DOWN IN KOKO-MO!"

Jeffy opened the door to Peek's Lounge, and the blasting jukebox greeted his arrival.

He looked into the darkness.

Good, he thought. *I know that dancer on the small stage behind the bar. Jill . . . Jane . . . something like that. Something with a* J.

A real fuckin' tease.

Yeah, she had sucked a few drinks out of him one night before disappearing into the back room. And when she came out she made tracks for someone else, some nervous-looking schmuck wearing a jacket and a tie, for Chrissake. Jeffy wanted to go over and tell the wimp that he had the wrong place.

*No, Mac, the Starlite Room of the Holiday Inn is down the
road. This is a—*

Burp!

*—Topless joint. T&A, man. See, naked wimmen, jiggling
titties. For real men.*

Now, Jeffy saw a free stool right in front. He plopped down,
and Jill—or Jane, or whatever—looked at him.

Her eyes were locked on his, sucking the blood right into his
pecker.

And, big show now, Jeffy dug out his wallet and put down
a twenty on the bar. To say, *I've got a full tank, baby, and I'm
ready to go.*

The bartender, a meaty old bag who didn't look at anyone,
knew what he wanted. She opened a Genesee and exchanged it
for his bill.

Jeffy kept his eye on the dancer.

"Down in Koko-Mo . . ."

She had her little ass moving in time to the Beach Boys,
dipping up and down, no fat on her stomach. She still had a
little bra-thing on, but Jeffy knew that would come popping off
soon.

Jeffy sucked at his beer and then picked up a dollar, folding
it into a crisp V. He reached out over the bar, watching the
dancer smile. She leaned out to his hand, caressing it, tilting
her tits toward him, grinning and licking her lips.

Then she took his buck and stuck in her G-string.

"Aruba, Jamaica . . . Montego . . . Down in—"

Before he knew it the song was over and his beer was
finished.

And another, magically, had taken its place.

Some shitty song by some high-pitched black singer started
up.

*Man, if there was one thing he had problems with, especially
after Attica, it was any damn black music. That's all there was
in Attica. Twenty-four hours nonstop, every fuckin' day, all the
time, thumping, jabbering soul music.*

Jill popped off her bra—let it hang there a moment—and she
watched him grinning at her before letting it slide off her nice
pointy titties.

And Jeffy picked up another dollar and folded it in
half. . . .

Eleven

ANN WENT DOWN Faith Avenue, past the large banner announcing the carnival, before turning right, up towards Barrow's Hill . . . to Mountain Road.

She thought about not going at all.

After all, it had been years since she had seen Alan.

Their relationship had been in another time, in some other life. They were both different people now.

Things change.

And she didn't blame him for what happened. Not for joining the Navy. For leaving . . .

After it was all over.

He had always told her, "No commitments, Annie. I don't know where I'll be or what I'll be doing, so let's just take things one day at a time. Just like the bumper sticker says."

And he grinned, a great blooming thing that she loved more than anything else. And they'd end up screwing. In his car. In her car. Or, when no one else was around, in his mother's cottage.

She knew that small cottage as well as her own home. It was fun to fuck and then pad around the place naked, making coffee, fixing eggs, just like they were an old married couple.

No, she didn't blame him for what happened.

Not really.

In fact, she thought—

(Pulling up Mountain Road, her heart beating fast, her fingers all tingly with excitement.)

—It was really her fault.

"Oops," she had said, laughing when she told him. "I guess I screwed up and forgot to take the pill. I'm pregnant."

A two-word sentence that had to be the oldest bad-news message in history.

And he had hugged her and said, "Hey, it's okay. I'm with you and everything's going to be fine."

(And for a while she thought that was true, maybe . . . yeah, maybe they could get married, even before he went away. Sure, and she could have the baby. Right here, in Stoneywood.)

I'm married to a Navy lieutenant, she imagined herself saying. *He's stationed in Antarctica. . . .*

And when he gets home I'm going to warm him up the way a good wife can.

That was the fantasy.

It lasted all of twenty seconds, before his grin went all sort of rigid.

"Yeah," he said, "I'm with you. I'll help pay for the abortion. Don't worry," he said, squeezing her shoulder. "Everything's going to be *fine*."

And he was there. Even when things went wrong with the operation. Some hick doctor just didn't have steady enough hands.

He was there, when the doctor told her, gently, that, sorry, she wouldn't be able to have any more babies.

"Any more?" she repeated.

Any more?

"You mean," she asked, her voice slowly sliding out of control, turning into a terrible wail, "that the only baby I'll ever have is dead? *That I just killed my only baby!*"

He was there.

Then.

But when she finally got out of the hospital, he was gone. The Navy called him earlier, he explained by phone.

She forgave him that, too.

After all, it hadn't been his fault.

She wrote to him. Lots. He sent a few letters back. Short, breezy.

Then one day she got up, looked at herself in the mirror—

And when she had finished crying—silly, silly thing, it had been so many months ago—she never wrote again.

(Her car tumbled into a rut as if jostling her memory, trying to shake the past away.)

But now . . . Well, Alan was back.

She wanted to see him. Wanted to see if maybe somehow, she still didn't love him . . .

Hoping to God that she felt absolutely nothing.

"It's Jill," the dancer said slipping onto the stool beside Jeffy, answering his question. "What's your name?"

"What'll it be?" the bartender asked the dancer.

Jeffy knew what she'd say. They always ordered the same thing, no matter what.

Can't fool me.

Champagne cocktail. A no-booze concoction for five bucks.

There used to be a place right near Stoneywood, not out in the middle of the woods like Peek's Lounge. And there you could buy the girls real drinks, with alcohol, for Crissakes. And they'd drink them. One of the night gas jocks—some kid who went off to college—said he conned one of the bimbos into a hand job.

But none of that shit went on at Peek's place.

At least, he thought, *not for me.*

If he got lucky he might be able to reach down and feel her leg. Not too high, though. Anywhere near home plate and her hand would fly out like a fuckin' bat.

No, no, she'd shake her head, like he was some naughty schoolboy.

And he'd think, his mind running away with crazy ideas of what he'd really like to do, *I ain't no school boy.*

He finished another Genesee . . . his third . . . maybe his fourth. He didn't bother keeping track.

Jill had on an tissue-thin robe that let him see her body, so damn close now.

"You know," he said, leaning close to her, smelling the incredible aroma of her perfume, "we could have a good time if we got out o'here."

He watched her shift uneasily in her seat.

"I bet we could, Jeffy. But," she said, looking around at the rest of the crowd at the bar, "I'm working till real late." She leaned forward and sipped on her drink.

Then, before Jeffy knew what was happening, she slid off the stool.

"Hey," he said, "Where are you goin', babe? I—"

She shrugged her shoulders. "I've got to freshen up."

And she turned and walked to the Employees Only back room.

He saw every other guy in the bar following her with their eyes as she walked away.

Jeffy chugged his beer.

Goddam waste of time, Jeffy thought. The only person who got a taste of that stuff might be Peek himself . . . a slick-haired dago bastard who dropped by in the evenings, leaving his red Jap sports car parked right by the door.

Jeffy looked around the bar.

The rest of us are suckers.

Stupid-ass suckers.

He looked at a guy in a shirt with an alligator on the pocket. Jeezus! Whadda they call them? Yuppies. Yeah, that's a yuppie. Melting into his fuckin' seat.

Like to punch your big owl eyes out, Jeffy thought, looking at him. *Punch your glasses right into your stupid little head.*

But the yuppie didn't look up, just sat there, his two hands wrapped around his bottle of beer, eyes locked on the back door, waiting for the dancer.

Jeffy stood up.

Not too bad, he thought, checking his balance. He grinned. *Pretty fuckin' steady.*

He had some blow outside, in the glove compartment of his beat-up Imperial.

Just the thing to perk him up.

Yeah. And then he could see what else he'd like to do tonight.

Something good, he thought, as he chugged his way to the door.

Something fun . . .

She saw the cottage.

There were no lights on.

Ann licked her lips.

Well, that didn't mean anything. The sun was still up, even if it was kinda dark here, with the mountain shading everything.

And besides, their car was there. The same junky pickup they had bounced around in years ago.

She and Alan used to laugh . . . maybe his mother could smell it.

"Can you smell sex?" she asked laughing.

And he'd grin—

"I don't think so."

Still, she thought, maybe nobody was at home.

Mountain Road made one last attempt to snag her car—the road was worse than she remembered it, more years of eroding away.

Then she stopped. Just outside the house.

She waited there a moment, fighting the urge to start the car again and pull away. Maybe ghosts from the past should be left alone.

She opened the car door and it made a groaning sound.

(And the sky darkened. The sun, invisible—hidden by the mountains—had finally set.)

She took a deep breath. And got out of the car.

Josh lay in his bed, his pad on his lap.

His grandmother had mellowed a bit since he came home. But she was still mighty angry at him, and she wasn't afraid to let him know it.

"You have no right to make me worry about you, Josh. *No right!* You're big enough to be careful about what you do."

And all his apologies did nothing to take the edge off her anger.

Then she even went to bed early, complaining of her arthritis . . .

While he was left to deal with his guilt.

And just what *is my problem?* he wondered.

All of a sudden I'm getting into trouble. Strange kind of trouble.

(And by now he wasn't sure the mountain had moved at all. Maybe he just went and got himself stuck. Maybe it was just some weird thing, some mental thing that he and Clara imagined. . . .)

Was Clara to blame for everything, getting him to go there in the first place?

But no. If anything, Clara seemed to really like him. She seemed to find something exciting and adventurous in him. Josh liked the feeling that gave him.

He felt his cheek.

He looked in the mirror. It looked like he'd been in a wicked car wreck. His cheek carried a burning-red swatch of open skin. It would heal quickly, his grandmother said.

Josh started drawing. Knowing that he wanted to remember what the fossil looked like. It had been special, unlike anything he had ever seen in the Museum of Natural History.

He started sketching it from memory, making careful, very light pencil strokes—just faint lines to capture the outline of the fossil. Then, darker lines when he felt he was starting to get the shape.

He added details. The funny hexagonal bumps on the fossil's surface, like the mosaic pattern blocks in Math Lab. And at the center, something raised, like a tiny needle.

(Reminding him of . . . something. But what? Where had he seen it before?)

Then, more lines, and finally he held the sketch up to see what he had.

Not bad, he thought. *Not bad at all*. It would have been a whole lot better if he'd had the fossil to work from, but the sketch was pretty good. It would certainly help him look it up.

He put down the pad.

And picked up the dog-eared paperback by his bed—his mom's old bed. From when she was a kid, if he could believe any such time actually existed.

Vampires Incorporated. He read the book title aloud.

Highly recommended by his best friend, the ever-weird Gary Friedrich—who was, at this very moment, flying to Portugal with his parents.

Lucky dude.

Josh opened the book and started reading Chapter One.

"Neck & Neck . . ."

She knocked on the door.

And waited.

(The wind rustled her hair.)

Ann looked at the cottage door. It was the same . . . but it was different. *There used to be a screen here*, she remembered. And the brown paint used to be new and glossy.

Now the house seemed tired and neglected.

She knocked again.

(Thinking that maybe Joanie had been wrong; maybe Alan Ward hadn't come back. And maybe that was just as well.)

She heard a sound. Something from inside. A shuffling. Alan's mother?

Or a mouse getting all stirred up?

She thought then she'd just turn around and leave. It was dark now, the rich purple velvet of the sky, so clear, almost electric, had changed. The moon wasn't up yet and the only light came from the stars.

Yes. That's what she was going to do.

Except she thought she'd try the doorknob first.

Probably locked, she figured.

She reached out and turned the door handle, expecting it to catch.

Instead, it turned completely around and the door slid open a few inches.

(*If it's open, then they're here*, she thought. *At least, somebody's here. . . .*)

Ann called into the murky darkness of the cottage.

"Alan . . ." she said gently. Then, louder, "Alan . . . Mrs. Ward . . . ?"

(*She never liked me, not his mother. I was beneath him, that's what she thought. She never had a smile for me. Never. And she gave me that look . . . like, "I know you're fucking my son. But you'll never keep him. Never . . ."*)

"Alan!" she said louder.

Her hand was still on the door. She pushed it open a few more inches.

She took a step.

And she smelled something.

Her nose actually twitched from the strange, pungent odor, like some meal gone terribly wrong. Burnt onions . . . old cauliflower . . . or some moldy dish, something covered with so much black mold that you just have to sniff it, just to guess what in the world it once was.

Were you a hamburger? Or sour cream? Or some tomato slices?

The stench was like that, but stronger. Fresher.

Mom's home cooking, I bet. And she grinned at the thought. *That old bitch . . .*

Ann opened the door.

So damned dark inside the cottage. She glanced back over her shoulder. There was her car, just a few steps away. Now she heard no noise from inside.

There was just the terrible stench.

And all the window shades pulled down tight.

She felt on the wall for a light switch, her hand flapping against the wall like a flounder.

But there was nothing.

Her eyes started to adjust to the gloom.

She took another step.

"Alan?"

Could be he's sleeping . . . in the bedroom.

She saw the outline of the couch—sticky knotty pine and some under-stuffed plastic covered cushions. And a cheap coffee table. And, in the corner, an easy chair. With some clothes piles on it, or some bags, or—

Someone sitting.

(Her heart skipped a beat. And her lungs went funny as she gulped at the air.)

She cleared her throat.

"Mrs. Ward?"

(No, she thought. *It's nobody. Just some clothes on something.*)

Another step.

"Hello—"

Ann moved a bit to the side, and there was the smallest bit of reflected light—not a twinkle but just a pinpoint of light. Coming from the corner chair. Just about where a head should be.

She froze there.

For what seemed like hours.

(A small voice quietly but urgently said something to her.)

Get the fuck out of here.

The smell seemed stronger.

Ann stepped back.

Then again, another step . . .

Not wanting to turn her back to the thing in the chair. Looking forward to that moment when she could laugh at her silly fears, outside. *Ha, ha, just like a kid, scared of something in the closet.*

She kept her eyes fixed on the corner . . .

Because if that thing or person or whatever moves, I'm running the hell out of here.

Another step back.

"Alan . . . ?"

The door had to be right there.

The thing in the chair didn't move.

She reached behind to grab at the door, not wanting to be clumsy and smash right into it.

Ann reached back. Ready to grab the open door, turn and bolt.

She touched something.

At first she thought it was the couch. Her movement backwards must have been way off course, with all her stupid stumbling in the darkness.

But she looked to the side.

The couch was right there, to her left. Right where it should be.

She started to turn.

(*What am I touching?*)

There was a sound from the corner. Her head snapped back.

The thing on the couch stood up. The pile of clothes . . . the bags . . . the big pillows.

Stood up, and walked towards her.

"Who are you . . . ?" Ann asked quietly.

She backed up.

(Forgetting that something was there, just behind her.)

How silly of me . . .

Two hands grabbed her tightly.

(It was a woman . . . shuffling towards her. An old, twisted woman. Mrs. Ward!)

And she twisted her head away, turning around.

Then, that had to be Alan right behind her. Alan. Playing some kind of dumb joke, some trick, just to frighten her.

She smiled.

And called his name.

"Alan!"

But it wasn't Alan. It wasn't any—

(The pain started traveling through her arms, digging into her skin. A thousand dentist's drills, whirring, chewing into her flesh. Someone was screaming, yelling, cursing—"Oh, Christ . . . Oh, God . . . no. Please . . . No!")

The screaming filled the cottage.

(*It's me*, she thought with sudden clarity. *I'm the one screaming.*)

This is happening to me. . . .

And that one word exploded in her brain, like fireworks flashing over and over.

Her last thought. Unshakable. Final.

Meaningless.

Me.

The fuckin' car climbed onto the curb and Jeffy inched ahead to get the damn front tire back down onto the street again.

Piece of shit.

He shut off the ignition. Popped open a beer. Lit up a Marlboro.

Ann's apartment was just to his right.

He knew where it was. He had followed her home once. And she hadn't even known it.

He'd just been curious.

Just wanted to know where she parked her ass at night.

It was always good to have information.

He grinned. Yeah, you never can tell when it will come in handy.

He looked in the driveway. Her car was gone. And there was no light on in her apartment, some el cheapo studio above Gelson's Hardware.

No problem, Jeffy thought.

He opened up the glove compartment. His small vial of coke was just about gone. Enough for one more tiny little toot. Just enough to light a little fire in the old brain.

With the help of half a six-pack sitting in the back seat.

He sucked on the cigarette.

Yeah, I can just wait here until she gets home—

(He grinned in the darkness.)

—And pay her a little surprise visit. . . .

Twelve

HE WAS WITH Clara, knowing it was a dream, from the golden warmth of a too-bright sun to the brilliant green grass that covered the hill. He was with Clara, and they were running on the hill.

Playing tag. Chasing each other.

She was fast, too fast to be caught.

Unless she wanted to be.

She came rushing past him, her laughter, so clear and wonderful, the only sound on the hill. But every time he reached out to grab her, to snatch her arm or her leg, she easily jerked away, leaving Josh to tumble down onto the grass, rolling around on the wonderfully soft grass, letting the sun warm him all over.

Then she stood in front of him, blocking out the sun.

An eclipse.

And Josh tensed, ready to spring at her.

(He rolled around on the old bed in his grandmother's house, making the ancient springs creak.)

She said something to him, daring him to try yet again.

And now he sprang up, flying at her. Clara squealed. She backed away.

But this time he found his mark.

His hands grabbed her waist.

Falling there almost naturally. He held her tight.

She was off balance and instead of falling backwards, she started falling forward, pushing Josh back onto the bed of grass, landing on him.

But so gently! Like a feather, falling on him in slow motion.

Until she was there, right on top of him, laughing in his face.
So close to his face, laughing, giggling.

He felt the funny way her body rippled with each laugh.

Then they both became silent, slowly, the laughs dribbling away . . .

As they felt something else.

Something dark and mysterious.

She moved a bit against him.

He gulped.

His hands didn't move from her waist. Instead he brought them around her . . . and, after a moment's hesitation, he embraced her.

(He turned again in his bed, sending an arm flying out to the side, dangling off the bed.)

Clara pushed away, getting ready to stand up . . .

When they both heard something.

And the sun went behind a cloud. And the grass turned a darker green, almost blue. The sky was filled with birds.

She pulled away from him, her face suddenly small and worried.

Josh sat up, and looked around.

They were right near the gorge . . . right near it.

Why hadn't he seen that before? It was so close. The gorge . . .

The sound was loud, a deep, gurgling sound. Then the sound of popping bubbles, right in their ears.

And voices . . . Thousands and thousands of voices . . . coming out of the gorge . . .

Josh woke up.

And heard one voice.

His grandmother, calling from the room down the hall.

He untangled himself from the web of bedsheets and stood up.

All the feelings from his dream started to fade. The warmth. Clara rolling on top of him. Those weird popping noises.

Every step he took into his grandmother's room made the dream melt away, like butter on a griddle.

"Grandma?" he called, stopping at her door.

He heard her groan. A quiet sound. He called to her again.

"Grandma . . . are you okay?"

He looked into her gloomy bedroom and saw her turn towards him.

"Oh, Josh," she said. "I'm having some—"

She grunted a bit.

"—Pain, honey . . . Could you go to the medicine cabinet? There's some pills . . . in a brown container."

Josh hurried to the bathroom and returned with her pills. He handed them to the old woman, now sitting up in the dark.

He could just make her out, working the cap, popping it off, and then shaking out the pills.

"Can I get you some juice . . . maybe some water?"

"Yes," she nodded. "That would be nice."

He bounded down the stairs to the kitchen.

The moon, full, bright, but a painted yellow, sat just over the hills in the east. It filled the kitchen with a weird light.

The only sound was the noisy hum of the refrigerator. Josh poured a glass of orange juice and hurried back to his grandmother's room.

She had the light on.

"Thank you, sweetheart," she said, taking the glass from him. "I've been having these attacks"—she smiled at him—"always in the night." She reached up and ran a wrinkled hand through his hair. "Usually I have to get up myself and get the medicine. . . . Thank you."

She put down the glass. "Now we both better get back to sleep. Okay?"

Josh nodded.

And he went back to his room.

The Stoneywood Police Department shared space with the Stoneywood Town Hall and the Stoneywood Water Department.

There was enough room for each official department to have one crowded office and a shared secretary. In the basement were two cells, rarely occupied at the same time.

This morning, like most mornings, the cells were empty and Captain Torey Watson, Chief of Police, was alone in the building fixing the first pot of Mr. Coffee.

For anything major, like the time some wild-eyed bikers started raising hell all along Route 122, the State Trooper barracks was only eight miles away, just north of Stoneywood.

The troopers were real police.

His job, at least the way he saw it, was simply to be there, so the good—and bad—people of Stoneywood could see a figure of authority.

Law and order, and all that crap.

But there was rarely any need for him to actually *do* anything.

Sure, once in a while there was a family squabble that got out of hand. And he'd have to go plant his gut between two people. But that was mostly words. Violence, real violence, just didn't happen here.

And his deputies liked that well enough. They were two young cops, both married, both glad they didn't have to walk the hairy streets of the Big Apple.

Fun City.

If New York was a war zone, this was a country club.

But still, there were things that even Watson in his quiet way, felt had to be checked up on.

Like the new fellow at Agnes Simpson's boarding house.

Yes, Watson thought, sipping on the black coffee—always cold by the time he got to the bottom of his cup—that guy might bear watching.

Especially with the carnival coming to town tomorrow. He always deputized a few of the volunteer firemen at carnival time. To watch the crowd and the games. No big deal. People came from thirty, even forty miles around. Watson didn't want anything bad happening to them while they were in town.

He took another sip. The secretary would show up soon. She was always good for some doughnuts or sticky rolls.

"Here you go, Chief," she'd say with a grin, flirting like crazy. Even though her best days were a decade behind her. "Something to help keep up that old waistline."

And as much as Torey promised himself to stay away from all that good fattening stuff, he'd end up walking into the outer office for more coffee and a cruller.

We all got our vices.

Yeah, he thought. Best to check out this fellow before Friday. Simpson usually took in traveling salesmen and other businessmen, down on their luck types who couldn't afford the price at the Holiday Inn and dinner at Risoti's.

It wouldn't hurt to see who this guy was and why he was in town.

Captain Torey Watson smiled.

Why, it would almost be like real police work. . . .

Josh heard voices downstairs. He blinked awake, staring at the small battery-operated clock sitting on the desk.

Ten o'clock.

Boy, it was late and he was starved.

He snatched a fresh pair of jeans out of a drawer, his black Forbidden Planet T-shirt, and, still slipping into them, he opened his door, hoping that he could talk his grandmother into some scrambled eggs, maybe some french toast. . . .

Josh went down to the kitchen.

And he saw his mother, sitting there.

"Hi, Josh," she said.

Erica had wanted her mother to say it was okay, that she didn't have to worry, that she didn't have to come here. She had a hard time believing that it was her son that her mother was talking about.

"Josh?" She laughed on the phone. "Getting into trouble?"

"Yes," her mother said very seriously, "and he doesn't seem himself, either. He's made friends with this girl—"

"Girl?" More amazing news . . .

"Yes. A tough-looking townie named Clara. She lives on Charity Street."

"Uh-huh . . ." Erica knew what that meant. The once-respectable block of houses was now more than aptly named.

"His face is a mess, Erica. Nothing permanent, but it looks just terrible." There was a pause, and Erica knew her mother was waiting for her to say something.

But then mother, never one to pussyfoot about such things, made the point clear. "If he wants you to come—to spend a few days with him—then, by God, you should do that, Erica. No matter what 'important' work you're doing."

And Erica surprised herself by saying, "Sure, Mom . . . sure." There was nothing really pressing in the office. And she'd had enough of her mother's guilt-provoking talk, at least for tonight.

Besides, she thought, it might be fun. Carnival time in Stoneywood. Hokey, sleazy fun. Where everyone who survived the winter got a chance to come out under the stars and compare notes.

Complain about the heat if it was too hot.

Or complain if it was too cold.

What's wrong with the summer? There was always something wrong with it. It was never just right.

It might be fun.

Might be . . . if she could deal with all the memories . . . that tremendous wave of feelings she'd just as soon miss . . .

Erica looked up at a very surprised Josh.

"Mom? What are you doing here?"

She stood up to inspect Josh's face. There was already a thin, fresh scab stretching clear across one cheek.

"Well, you wanted me to come up for the carnival, didn't you?" She came closer to him, raising a hand to his cheek . . .

(And seeing his father, like she always did. Remembering that last morning. Just a quick peck goodbye. *Goodbye, honey*. Not knowing it was forever.)

"Your grandmother tells me that you've had a few adventures since you've been here."

She saw him shoot a look at his grandmother, surprised at her betrayal. But his grandmother busied herself clearing the table.

"Well, yeah . . . I mean, yesterday I got stuck in this—"

"I told him not to go to the gorge. *Twice*."

"It's dangerous, Josh," Erica said.

(Remembering how many times she went there, her mother never guessing.)

Josh squinted, outnumbered two-to-one.

"But it's a neat place, Mom. There's some great fossils there."

She touched his cheek again. "Maybe we can hike there together, Josh." She smiled at him. And took a breath.

"Now, tell me . . . *who* is this Clara?"

Mrs. Simpson showed Brian where the pay phone was, and then disappeared into the kitchen.

Brian waited until she was gone and then picked up the receiver. He punched in the three sets of numbers for his MCI Expressphone Calling Card and waited for the fabled fiber-optic connection to kick in.

"Commander Alexander's office," he told the secretary.

He was on hold, then his superior officer got on the line.

"Well, Mac, how are you doing?"

Brian cleared his throat.

"Okay, Commander. I mean, I guess I'm doing okay. I found Ward. He's with his mother, at their cottage."

"He didn't stay in Boston?"

"No. He left pretty quickly."

The Commander was quiet for a moment, as if chewing over something.

"What else?" he finally asked.

"Well, I saw him, and his mother, outside their cottage. I guess he's been into town. But I have to say that, from just looking at him, everything seems pretty normal for someone recuperating from, er, a—"

"Right. Well, that's what you're there for."

Okay, Brian thought. *Now tell me that we're all done here and I can go back to Washington.*

As if reading his mind, Alexander spoke:

"We want you to stay there, Brian. For a while, at least. Keep a low profile and watch Ward. If he seems to do anything . . . unusual, let me know."

"Unusual? What do you mean 'unusual'?"

Alexander didn't answer.

"Just watch him."

An order plain and simple.

"And call me in a couple of days."

"Right, Commander."

Then Alexander said goodbye, and Brian was left hanging up the phone, wondering—

What the hell is going on here?

Because now, for the first time, he had a gut feeling that Alexander hadn't told him everything. That there was another story he was keeping from him.

And if that was true—if there was something they weren't telling him—could he figure it out?

The kitchen door swung open.

Mrs. Simpson passed by the phone, on her way upstairs.

"Everything all right?" she asked, seeing his concerned face.

"Yes . . . everything's"—he looked at her, smiling now— "Fine."

* * *

Erica watched the breeze catch the fine strands of Josh's hair. His hammering was barely audible.

"I'm sorry he's been trouble, Mom. I just didn't imagine—"

Her mother was close to her, leaning on the fence. Josh braced one of the wooden rails with his knee while he hammered two-inch nails through the splintery wood.

"He's being pretty helpful right now, Erica." Then, a pause. "I'm not upset. I'm just a bit concerned."

Erica nodded.

The memories, the mix of feelings that just being here brought to her! It was all too much. How did this fit in with her life? Her *real* life of New York cabs, and restaurants where dinner for two cost what some Stoneywood people earned in a week of work.

Her world was built on quick success and stress, where there just wasn't too much time to think about things. Here, it was all different. Here you had to think, and had to remember.

She felt a hand on her hair.

"It's a shade darker, isn't it, sweetheart?"

Erica nodded.

"You always had the most beautiful hair . . . beautiful. It would be beautiful even if you let the gray show through."

Josh stopped hammering and waved at them. Then he raised another one of the split rails back into position. And her son stood there, lanky, his string-bean body catching every ray of the morning sun. Then he walked over to the other fallen rail.

She used to help like that, she remembered. She helped plant the corn and, before her father died—so gently, carried away in his sleep—she'd helped harvest the sweet corn and the small pumpkin patch, enjoying the apple-crispness of October, with its icy blue-sky mornings. She loved the farm then, the smells, the quiet, the feeling that this was the world, everything. There was nothing worthwhile beyond the horizon.

But in high school something started pulling her away. Maybe it was the death of her father, or watching her mother get older and grayer, not wanting that to happen to her.

That's when she started dreaming of leaving.

And once she went away to college, all her thoughts of her childhood, and October, and biting into just-picked corn, vanished.

Josh hammered away, a human woodpecker.

"I can take him back with me. . . ." Erica said quietly. "There are camps. He won't want to go, but—"

"Nonsense. If the boy wants to stay here, he can stay here. He wouldn't be normal if he didn't get into some trouble. I don't mind that. Not at all. Your father always wanted a boy. Just never happened. He would have loved Josh."

Erica felt her mother's hand take her chin—a hand so steady, so sure of itself! She turned Erica's head towards her.

"That's not why I asked you to come home, Erica. The boy is still hurt, still confused. Maybe you can put it behind you. We adults are supposed to be good at that. But he's still very much in pain. He needs to know you understand that."

Erica nodded, feeling a funny stinging in her eye. As if the wind had just whipped up a bit stronger and sent a stray piece of dust flying into her eye. She rubbed at the watery eye.

"I understand, Mom."

And her words, even her voice, sounded suddenly like the voice of a child.

We're always children to our parents. No matter who or what we become. Murderer or President. It makes no difference.

Josh stopped hammering, picked up his grandfather's tool kit, and started walking towards them.

He walked around the side of the small cornfield, by the small road . . . past the violets that grew chaotically from the fence right down to the edge of the dirt path. It was a sea of purple, stretching from the farmhouse all the way to the start of Barrow's Hill. Tiny dots flitted from flower to flower, hundreds of bees tending to their chores.

Erica watched him. She remembered picking up armfuls of the flowers until they went right up to her nose, the smell dizzying, watching an occasional bee dart away.

And sometimes, in her bare feet, she stepped on a bee.

She put her hand on top of her mother's.

"It's good to be here," she said quietly.

Josh swaggered up, letting the tool chest fall to the ground with a noisy, no-nonsense rattle.

"There, that should hold the fence for a while, Grandma."

"Thank you, Josh."

Erica felt Josh turn and look at her, studying her distant expression.

"Mom . . . is everything okay?"

And Erica nodded, no longer a young girl.

"I was just thinking, Josh, how I could use a few days' vacation."

A smile bloomed on the boy's face. "You mean you'll stay?"

She nodded. "At least till Sunday."

Her mother turned and started back to the small house. "Couldn't have picked a better night," she said. "It's the Firemen's Pancake Supper and Silent Auction. Remember how you used to stuff yourself, Erica?"

"And tomorrow night is the carnival," Josh added.

The carnival. More memories. But this time there was a quick glimpse of a memory she'd rather forget.

She gave her shoulders a little shake, throwing off the unwanted thought. Then she took Josh's hand. "C'mon. Your mom needs another cup of coffee . . . prontissimo!"

And she walked with her son, back to the house.

Thirteen

BRIAN CROUCHED BEHIND the huckleberry bushes. The wind was strong this morning, rustling the waxy green leaves noisily.

But there didn't seem to be much happening at Maison Ward.

His car was parked at the bottom of Mountain Road, pulled off to the side. That way he could watch Ward's comings and goings. But outside of catching Ward's mother shuffling past a window, things had been mighty quiet.

It *is* quiet today.

Maybe he'd put in just one more day watching the house, he thought. Then, if he got lucky, old Alan might show up at the carnival. And wouldn't that be fun, watching him up close . . . and seeing just how tightly his springs were wound.

(Waiting for what? For Alan Ward to snap? And if he did, what the hell was Brian going to do about it?)

Who the hell knew. Not the goddam Navy, that was for sure.

Brian lowered the binoculars, and tried to dig out a piece of gum. But his revolver was in the way. He took the gun out of its small holster. He put it on the ground.

(Thinking, *Jeezus! When's the last time I even fired it?*)

He fished out a piece of sugarless gum. The Navy paid for all dental work, but going to the dentist still wasn't one of his favorite activities.

He unwrapped the gum and stuck it in his mouth. It tasted too sweet, with its goddam chemical crap that made those first chews unbearably cloying.

He picked up the binoculars and was checking the cottage . . .

When he felt a hand touch his shoulder.

Bob O, as announced by his license plate, pulled into his service station, bringing his white Lincoln Town Car around to the side of the station. The rubber snake gave out two rings as he drove over it, passing the pumps.

He caught Jeffy coming out of the office, lumbering, lurching in his usual way towards a nonexistent customer.

I'm such a sucker, he thought. *Giving a job to an ex-con. A real sucker. The guy is probably ripping me off somehow. Probably doing something to screw me.*

Bob O cut the car's ignition, and Elvis—Live from Hawaii—died. The car's sound system, a custom-designed powerhouse that had set him back a grand, regurgitated the Elvis tape. Bob O took it out and tossed it in the glove compartment, with a dozen other Elvis tapes.

As he liked to tell people, he saw Elvis in Vegas.

Five times.

And Elvis *was* the king.

"Hey, Jeffy . . . relax," Bob O said, taking care not to step onto any oil or gas smears in his white shoes. "It's just the boss." He grinned.

Jeffy nodded.

"Good morning, Mr. O'Conner."

So damned polite, Bob O thought. You hire an ex-con, someone who couldn't get a job scraping dog poop off the sidewalk, and they're so damned grateful. They'd do anything for you.

Anything.

It was a debt that Bob O thought he might have to call in some day.

"Take your break, Jeffy. I've got about ten minutes before my meeting."

And wasn't that going to be a pisser, he thought.

Everything comes on home today. Oh, yeah. By this afternoon, Stoneywood becomes my personal golden goose.

"Come on, boy. I don't have all A.M. Go over and get your coffee and cruller, for Pete's sake."

But Jeffy stood there, and it was then that Bob O noticed that Jeffy didn't look too well. He always had a sort of sad-sack, hangdog expression. A droopy character, to be sure. But today, Jeffy seemed a little spaced-out, even for him. Standing so still, blinking his eyes.

You better not be using drugs again, you fucker. No sirree, Bob O thought. *I'll have your ass out of here and back in jail before you can say "nose candy."*

Then Jeffy looked up, his grin suddenly warm.

"That's okay, Mr. O'Conner. I had a big breakfast before I opened up. I don't really feel like anything now."

Jeffy took a few steps towards O'Connor.

"I don't need no break—you can go, Mr. O'Connor," Jeffy said quietly.

And damned, if O'Connor didn't feel something then. Not a threat exactly, but, damn, something. *Who's he to tell me to go? It's my goddam station and—*

But Jeffy smiled and Bob O saw it for no more than it was. *The stupid-ass kid doesn't want his break. So what's the big deal?*

I'll go on over to the site early.

Yeah. Savor the moment of the coming victory.

"Okay, Jeffy. Sam will be in at five . . . as usual."

Sam Kashir was a Pakistani. He said nothing, pumped the gas, and grinned a lot. The country was being inundated with Sam Kashirs.

Jeffy nodded. And O'Conner turned away from him, feeling Jeffy watch him walk over to his snow-white Lincoln.

And he pulled away, quickly, before rooting around in the compartment for another Elvis tape—the Sun sessions. The early stuff.

Elvis before Hollywood, and Priscilla, and drugs . . .

And success.

Just like me, thought Bob O.

Just like me.

Guests started drifting into the massive dining room for lunch.

Wallace Porter liked to stroll past the room to make sure that nobody was flouting the house dress code.

He didn't want any clattering sandals or flip flops making the Inn sound like some summery chowder house. And no obnoxious T-shirts, Good Lord no.

Every guest knew the rules. Real shirts, with buttons, slacks for the men, dresses or skirts for the ladies. No shorts.

The air conditioning kept the room a tad chilly, just to make sure that no one forgot the regulations. So damn cool, the old ladies brought sweaters to lunch.

The older guests appreciated such niceties.

And for the younger ones, it was a novelty. Dress code? How quaint . . .

Just like the rickety stairs leading down to the lake.

The Inn oozed old world charm—a timelessness.

Which made Porter even more unhappy about the meeting he was off to.

He passed the dining hall, greeting some of the guests by name, nodding to others. And he saw the new waitress, Ann Mayhew.

He watched her for a minute . . . She moved slowly, as if she was distracted.

Hoping no one saw his lingering glance.

She was attractive, that was for sure. In a kind of cheap way. More of a tart than most of the girls he hired. Full lips, dark, lustrous brown hair, all done up in a bun. The Inn's outfit was if anything demure, but Wallace could imagine what she looked like without it.

Then she turned and looked at him. Her eyes were dull, blank as if she was sick. Then . . .

She smiled.

He smiled back.

(Hoping that she didn't see him redden.)

He walked over to her.

"Everything coming along well, I trust?"

Ann smiled at him.

(So very pretty, he thought.)

"Yes. Everyone has been very helpful."

She seemed to hold his gaze as he nodded.

"Good . . . I was just wondering how you—"

God, the way she looked at him. As if she knew. Was he so transparent?

"Yes, well, carry on," he said smiling, gesturing at the great dining room and the sea of tables.

"Thank you," Ann said, still looking right at him.

Porter turned and walked away, out to the great stone staircase leading to the main entrance and his car.

While he felt—all the time—that Ann was watching him . . .

Knowing his dirty little thoughts.

"Now just bring both of your hands up in the air, nice and slowly, friend. We don't want any nasty accidents just 'cause I'm getting a tad nervous in my old age. There you go—nice and slowly."

Brian felt the gun touching him just at the midway point of his spine.

Not a bad location for a single shot that could cripple him for life.

And his first thought was that Alan Ward had somehow circled around the cottage and come up behind him.

But this guy's voice belonged to an older man.

Brian had a funny tingling in his bowels.

(*And yes, I know that feeling*, he thought. *That's fear! Sure it is! And it can get worse, pal. A lot worse.*)

Brian raised his hands awkwardly in the air.

"Good. Now if you'll just stand up slowly. . . . That's it," the man said as Brian dug his feet into the ground and pushed himself up with difficulty.

And the Navy prosecutor turned around, and found himself staring into the face of a local gendarme.

Brian smiled and started to lower his hands. "Oh, good. Boy I thought some maniac—"

"Keep them up, please."

Brian shook his head. He read the name above the cop's pocket.

"Captain, er, Watson, I know this looks bad. But I can explain everything. If you'll just—"

"Fine," the Captain said. "I'd like that." Then he reached over and removed Brian's gun. "You seemed so interested in Alan Ward, let's mosey on up there, and let Alan hear what you have to say."

Brian shook his head.

This was not good. Not good at all. If Ward knew he was being watched, he'd vanish, just the way he disappeared in Boston. "I don't think you understand," Brian said. "I can't let—"

"C'mon, pal. Start moving."

Watson jabbed the gun into Brian's back.

He trudged up the slope.

Shit, I can't go in there. Can't let Ward see me.

"Captain—" Brian said, still walking. "I'm an Assistant Prosecutor in the United States Navy. . . ."

"Yes, and I'm the Good Witch of the North."

They were almost at the side yard, only a few steps away from the path leading to the front door of the cottage.

"Alan Ward is under surveillance. He was in Antarctica, Captain. Eight men were brutally killed. Ward came back alone. If he sees me, he'll be gone by lunchtime."

More steps, and if anyone was at the cottage window looking out, they could see the pair of them.

"You can call Washington. Use your police radio. Commander Alexander. The Pentagon."

A few more steps.

"Because if Alan Ward splits, Captain," Brian hissed, whispering, "it will be your fucking fault."

The gun left Brian's back.

"Okay. Turning around, friend. And you sure as hell better not be shitting me."

Brian looked over his shoulder, and sighed. "Thank you."

And now he hurried back down the hill, the gun still at his back . . .

Hoping that no one was watching the scene from the cottage.

Bob O clapped his hand on Wallace Porter's broad shoulder.

"Now, listen big fella. Just listen."

There was nothing for a moment, then Porter heard the deep, rumbling sound. A low, gentle roar in the distance. He felt the rock underneath his feet tingle, vibrate.

Bob O was all smiles. "There, what the hell did I tell you? It's like a baby's whisper. Hardly audible, now was it?"

They were standing on a giant outcrop of rock that ran from the Inn all the way to the base of the mountain. All this rock, this tremendous chunk of granite, belonged to the Miller Inn.

Porter shook his head.

The rumble, the distant roar, was the dynamite exploding at the quarry at the other side of the mountain.

"Not bad at all, eh? Now, let's go back to your office and talk turkey."

"I want to see it," Porter said softly, uncomfortable out here in the midday heat. He was used to the Inn, and his car, where everything was cool, controlled.

"See it?" O'Connor asked. "See what?"

"The quarry. I want to see what it looks like . . . what this would look like if you started digging here."

O'Connor shrugged as if to say it was a pretty stupid request. "Okay. If that's what you want." He led Porter to his car, and drove him around, off the outcrop of granite, down to the woods and the road that ran from the lake to the northern face of the mountain.

They came to the quarry.

O'Connor hopped out of his car. Porter watched men in hard hats wave at O'Connor. Heavy-duty bulldozers were moving great chunks of just-exposed stone over to rock-crushing machines—great pneumatic jackhammers that filled the air with a terrible concussive pounding.

It was a horrible place. Something out of Brueghel.

A kind of hell.

A red and white sign announced that the work was being done by 'Big Ten Construction Company. R. O'Connor, Pres.'

"You see!" O'Connor yelled at Porter as he slid uncomfortably out of the Lincoln, "the rock here is down to conglomerates and shit. Lots of quartz, feldspar. It's only good enough for gravel. But the other rock—your rock!" he said, clapping Porter on the shoulder, "is grade A stone, big guy. The type of granite you just can't get anymore. Buildings and restorations are begging for the shit, paying through the nose. Together, we'd make a killing."

Porter nodded.

But his eyes were fixed on the quarry.

The first disturbing thought was that this place, where they were standing, used to be inside the mountain. Porter could look left and right, and see the natural slope of the mountain. But here a bowl had been carved out of the mountain, a great chunk of stone just blasted away. Everywhere there were gouges and ragged edges of the digging and explosions. The quarry had produced an abrupt, jagged cliff leading up Mount Shadow, filled with loose boulders lodged precariously, ready to tumble down.

The bottom of the bowl, this basin they were standing on, was dotted with scrawny pines and sick-looking trees entwined with thin, thorny vines.

Porter looked at the ground. Not much soil here. Just a foot or so scattered by the excavation.

Environmental restoration, it was called.

It was another planet.

Alien.

Sinister.

"I don't like it," Porter said.

But O'Connor signaled that he hadn't caught any of what Porter said.

"I don't like it!" Porter yelled, now just barely audible over the rumble of the heavy trucks.

He looked at O'Connor.

"But you will, Wallace me-boy."

O'Connor smirked, hugging Porter close to him.

"Yes, you will!"

Torey Watson hung up the phone.

His face was tight and drawn. He wasn't used to big problems in his quiet little town, Brian suspected.

"Sorry," Watson said quietly. "I just wish you had checked in with me before—"

"Alexander didn't want it done that way," Brian said. "For all we know, there might be nothing going on here . . . nothing more than what Alan Ward told us."

The Captain arched his eyebrows.

"Which is?"

Someone knocked at Watson's office door.

"Come in," Watson said.

A young cop opened the door a crack. "Mrs. Watson on line two, Captain. Something about the Pancake Supper."

Watson nodded. "Tell her I'll pick her up, Tom. Around six."

The cop shut the door.

"One of my two detectives." Watson smiled. "You were going to tell me—"

Brian shifted in the uncomfortable wooden chair. The office was small, just enough room for a beat-up desk and a pair of straight-back chairs.

No computer terminals here. This was policework done the old-fashioned way.

"I can tell you what I've been told, Captain. What the official records show."

(*But not*, Brian thought, *my suspicion that I haven't been told everything, not by a long shot.*)

"Go ahead . . ." Watson said.

"The facts are these. Alan Ward was on duty at Naval Research Station Five. It was called Ice Box. From there, a team of scientists, headed by Dr. Clement Wynan, were studying an area called Emperor Two, about one hundred miles from the magnetic South Pole."

"Colorful names," Watson said. "Care for some coffee?"

Brian started to shake his head *no*, but he stopped. This might take longer than he thought.

Watson spoke to his deputy using an antiquated intercom, full of hiss and static. This was a sheriff's office right out of Mayberry.

"I'm not privy to whatever information triggered the original investigation of the region. That's still classified. I assume that even Ward doesn't know why the research party was there. It may not be important, because that's not where it happened. At least, according to Ward."

"Where what happened?"

"The scientists worked in teams of two, each time out taking two Navy people with them, using high-powered, precision snowmobiles. Not toys, these were machines designed with the same ruggedness as lunar rover vehicles. They could easily operate at well below forty degrees below zero.

"Ward was at Ice Box, monitoring the weather—his specialty—while the other crew slept. He picked up a storm, told Wynan to get the hell out of there. Then he lost contact."

The young cop opened the door, two cups in his hand.

"Oh," Watson said. "Thanks, Tom. Brian . . . would you like some food?"

"No, thanks."

The cop left.

Brian reached out and took the steaming hot cup.

And he saw Watson reach behind him and turn down the air conditioning.

Mind over matter, Brian thought. It *was* feeling chilly in here.

"He lost contact with the party. But then Ward heard a snowcat outside—only one, when three had left. And Dr. Wynan came back into the hut . . . a bloody axe in his hand."

"Jesus!"

Brian took another sip of the black coffee.

"What happened?" Watson asked.

"Here's where things get a bit screwy, Captain. According to Ward, Wynan proceeded to start chopping up the other men while they slept, cutting off their heads, hacking away at them like a mad butcher."

Watson sat perched on the edge of his seat.

"Working his way to Ward. But Ward broke open the weapons locker and—just before the scientist got to him—he blew the madman to bits."

"God. What a story. And poor Alan."

Brian nodded.

"Yeah. Poor Alan. It must have been terrible. A nightmare. Except for one thing."

"Eh, what's that?"

"The Navy doesn't believe him, Captain. Sure, they found the bodies scattered around. But by the time they got the place checked out, it was nearing Antarctic winter. So Emperor Two was left for spring. But when they got Ward back here, there were things about his story that bothered his doctors. And then the Research Station officials noticed something odd about his story."

"Like what?"

"It was the same. Every damn time he told it. Absolutely the same. As if it had been rehearsed or something."

"Maybe it was just the truth."

Brian shook his head. "It was all too pat. And too unbelievable."

"How's that?"

"Here was a scientist, no young fellow, who kills eight other people, including trained Navy officers. Eight . . . And then Ward takes him out? Just like that?"

"What else have your people found out?"

"Not much. Ward's emotional state seemed peculiar, to say the least. He had no trouble talking about what happened. As if it all happened to someone else. And there were these blackout periods—temporary aphasia, they called it. Ward just seemed to tune out. And just as suddenly he'd snap back."

They were both quiet then. Brian finished his coffee, now cold with an oily film on the top.

He'd drunk worse, he knew.

"Mind, you, Captain, I've never seen any of it. I was just rought in a couple of weeks ago . . . to keep an eye on old lan."

Watson nodded. "What can I do, Brian? We're not a ig-league police department, but I'll be glad to do what I an."

"Thank you, Captain. I guess the only thing I might like ould be a little help watching the cottage . . . keeping track f Ward."

"No problem. I'll have Tom Smith spend some time there onight. We always take a run through those back roads nyway. Tonight, he'll just stick around up on Mountain Road. t least until Ward and his mother are asleep."

Brian stood up. "Thanks. That will make things a lot asier." He took a step to the door. "Hey, did I hear mention f a pancake supper tonight?"

"Oh, yeah. Big event in our little town. It's always the night efore the Carnival Weekend, at the firehouse. Lots of fun. he whole town shows up."

"Maybe Alan Ward will show up. . . ."

Watson came close to Brian. He cleared his throat.

(And Brian thought, *I know what he's going to ask, don't I? Because it's the same question I ask myself.*)

"Brian, what do, er, you think really happened? In Antarctica—"

Brian smiled. "I don't know, Captain . . . I haven't the foggiest idea. . . ."

Fourteen

LOOK AT HIM wiggle in his chair! His big ass squirming all around.

O'Connor grinned at Porter.

"I *love* this office, Wallace. Love it! I really do."

And I'd like to send a pair of bulldozers crashing into the Inn and push this wooden shithouse right into the lake, with your fat ass inside it.

Make room for the Hudson Mall.

A Big Ten Development, baby.

Porter grinned back, visibly uncomfortable.

Good . . .

O'Connor saw him lick his lips.

"Thirsty?" he asked the manager. "Got a nip squirreled away some place here?"

He caught Porter's eyes darting to a wooden cabinet to the left.

"I'd like one too, if you don't mind," O'Connor said.

"Sure, Bob."

He watched Porter slide off his leather chair, the loose seat cover sticking gummily to his sweaty behind. No sir, this fatso was *not* going to stand in his way.

Porter opened the cabinet, leaned over it, and looked back at O'Connor.

"What would you like, Bob. I've got—"

"Some Scotch will do fine. Neat, if you don't mind."

He waited, watching Porter fiddle nervously with the bottle

top and then pour two generous drinks. Then the manager waddled over and handed him his drink.

"Much obliged, Wallace. Now have a seat and let's talk. . . ."

O'Connor brought his chair closer, right up to Porter's desk. The manager was framed by the picture-window view of the lake, just behind him. Another window, to the left, showed Mount Shadow.

It was one damn good-looking office.

"Now, Wallace, you know your board wants to give my company permission to extend the quarry just south of the Inn." O'Connor squinted. "You *know* they do. The Inn, beautiful as it is, just can't seem to turn a profit, now can it? Times have changed. It's just not an efficient place, now is it, Wallace?"

"Well, we have turned things around a bit and—"

Bob O raised a hand. "Hey, I know the job that you've done here. You've done great . . . just great." O'Connor took a hit of his drink. "But the cash flow just ain't there, Wallace. Just ain't there."

"But the board told me that they would wait, at least—"

"Yes, they'd wait *if* you weren't happy with my proposal. But hey, you heard the blasting. A baby could sleep through that, right? And it won't affect the Inn at all, now will it?"

"People like to climb that way . . . to Mount Shadow."

"Then they'll have to do something else, now won't they?"

Porter looked out the window, the one to the left, at the brooding mountain, its jagged edges cutting into the blue sky.

Don't fuck with me, O'Connor wanted to say.

Do—not—fuck—with—

Me.

He smiled.

"I understand what you're saying. I do. But financial reality is financial reality. Wallace, if this deal goes through, everyone makes out like a bandit. Including—"

O'Connor dug into his jacket pocket.

"You."

He pulled out an envelope.

"So this is a little something for you. A little recognition. And there will be two more, when the contract is signed . . . and when we start blasting." He put the envelope on the table and slid it towards Porter.

A little something for lard-ass. Hell, there was ten grand in there.

Porter looked at it like it was some kind of reptile slithering across his desk.

"Take it, Wallace. And then tell the board that everything looks fine."

Porter kept his fish eyes on the envelope.

Reach out and take it. Grab the fucking envelope in your pudgy little fingers.

"I . . . I don't—"

Bob O smiled. "Okay. Take your time, Wallace. Let it sit there. Overnight. You think about it." O'Connor stood up. Best not to push too much. "And think about the other two envelopes. And I'll call you tomorrow."

He walked to the door . . .

And then stopped and looked up at the great wooden cross beams that stretched across the office ceiling. "You know, this place is getting old." He looked back at Porter. "It would be a shame if anything happened to it. . . ."

And he grabbed the brass doorknob and let himself out.

Clara heard her mother downstairs.

She looked at the clock. It was only 3:30 P.M. She couldn't be leaving this early. Not yet.

She ran downstairs, swinging around the banister.

"Mom? Mom!"

"In here," her mother called from the kitchen.

Clara hurried in. And there was her mother, dressed in a pale blue dress and white rubber-soled shoes.

"Why are you going to work? It's not time yet."

Her mother took a gulp of coffee, and Clara wondered whether there was anything else in the cup. She was wise to her mother's coffee.

"I know, honey, but Janice asked me to spell her early. She's got a doctor's appointment or something." Another sip. "It's a favor."

Clara came close to her mother. "I wish you didn't have to go."

Her mother nodded.

"There's macaroni for dinner," she said, gesturing at the cupboard.

Macaroni and cheese. How many times a week did she end up fixing that? Clara wondered. Stirring the shrimpy noodles, adding the radioactive cheese powder and great gobs of margarine. God, it was disgusting!

"I don't like being here alone."

Her mother looked up at her. "I know, Clara, sweetheart. I *know* you don't. But your father will be home soon." She laughed to herself. "If he doesn't get waylaid." Her mother looked at her watch. "Oh, damn, gotta go, sweetie."

Clara watched her stand up and wipe her lips on a dish towel.

"Now, don't you go get your father all upset, honey. You just fix the macaroni and I'll see you tomorrow."

Clara grabbed her hand. "Can I go to work with you?"

Her mother smiled. *"No,* honey. They wouldn't like that at all. Now, goodbye . . ."

Her mother left, and Clara saw the open cabinet. The bottle of vodka, looking just like water. She heard her mother's car start, the muffler growling.

She looked at the clock.

Her father would be home in an hour.

Maybe less.

But Clara wouldn't be there.

No way . . .

"Excuse me, but do you have a map of Upstate New York, the Saratoga region and north?" Ed Stein, his seersucker suit hot and sticky, stood by the gas station attendant, this Jeffy character, watching his dull face light up with something that began to approach an answer. "Look, pal—a simple question. Do you got any maps?"

God, these hill people. Ed Stein hated doing the advance work for the carnival, checking out each town, making sure that there were no problems. No problems, that's what the Pardones liked. No fuck-ups. Make sure the site is okay, that there wouldn't be no hassle with the porto-johns, or the noise from the generators. No problems, that was his job.

And it meant that Stein had to wander the back roads of New York, all by his lonesome, talking to Town Councils, or Town

Boards, or whatever the hell they called the shmucks who ran
the towns.

The Pardones kept promising that they'd get someone else to
take over the advance-man job, let Stein come back and
manage the concessions, or the games. Some easy job.

But Ed Stein thought that if they ever took him off the road,
they'd can his ass.

A carnival wasn't a good place to get old.

So he didn't bitch about the traveling, about dealing with the
rubes, so concerned about their clean town squares and spotless
Main Streets. A little trashy fun, that's what the carnival
brought. And the towns were just as happy to see it leave
again.

Jeffy finally answered Ed's question.

"Sure. Got a bunch inside. Come take a look. There's a
bunch of them." Ed smiled. Somewhere between here and the
last bar he'd stopped at, his old map had disappeared. He
watched Jeffy pull the gas nozzle out of the car and hang it back
on the pump.

Good aim, kid. You've found your notch.

"Great. I'd hate to head back north and get lost in the
Adirondacks. It's bear country, you know." Ed laughed. Jeffy
kept walking.

*You'd think the guy would like some conversation. Standing
out here or sitting inside all day. A little conversation, you
know what I mean?*

Yeah, this Jeffy character was one of those new species of
human.

Homo Sub-intelligensia. The post-nuclear man, ready for
anything 'cause, *hey, what the fuck does he have to lose?*

He followed Jeffy into the office.

And expected to smell gas and oil and the odor of new
rubber tires.

But he smelled something else. Something repugnant.

Like barf.

(Yeah, that smell that filled the halls of St. Vinnie's when the
first graders tossed their cookies before facing Sister Herman
Goering. That's all he remembered about grade school . . .
piles of upchuck, covered with some green absorbent crud.)

But this was worse than that. This was foul . . .
nasty. . . .

"You keeping animals here, pal?" Another joke that missed

its mark. The gas jockey only pointed at a rack filled with Hagstrom's maps.

Always impossible to refold.

Ed Stein walked over to it, looking at the two dozen different maps. "Didn't think that the state was that damn big. They've got it broken down into sections I ain't even heard of. Guess I'll have to just look—"

He fingered his way through the maps, realizing that he'd have to buy a few just to make sure he got the right area he needed.

"All I really need is a good atlas. Shit . . ."

He felt Jeffy watching him.

And a cold prickle ran up his back.

He felt those dead eyes. Stupid eyes.

Ed's knees went funny. He cleared his throat.

Started to turn around—

"I guess these will be okay. Don't know if—"

Ed tried not to turn too fast. Didn't want to panic. Nothing to be worried about.

He smiled at Jeffy, handing him the maps he wanted to buy.

The window of the station was behind Jeffy. Outlining him.

Then Jeffy took a step closer. Ignoring the maps. He reached out and grabbed Ed's wrists.

"Hey, what the hell you—"

The smell was stronger.

And now Ed knew where it was coming from.

It came from Jeffy.

From his skin. From his clothes.

But especially from his breath.

Ed pulled back, stumbling into the map rack. And New York, and New Jersey, and Connecticut and Massachusetts all went tumbling to the floor while the rack clattered into a dozen unrecognizable pieces.

Ed kept jerking back, trying to pull away from Jeffy's grip.

Like a fish caught on a hook.

Then he tried to skip backwards, back over to the desk.

(To the *door*.)

And Jeffy swung around.

And the light was on him.

Jeffy smiled.

(No. He just opened his mouth. That was all. Opened his mouth.)

For the tendrils to come out.

"What the fu—!"

Ed screamed.

(And he looked out the smeary window, praying that someone would drive up, ring the bells. Honk their horn. And Jeffy would just let go.)

Go pump gas.

Tendrils. Little vine things. A few, at first. But Jeffy opened his mouth wider, and wider still—the lips rolling away from his open mouth—until a whole forest of them wormed their way out of his gullet. Thin, white, maggoty things, waving their way towards Ed.

Now Ed jerked and went into a spasm like a madman, yelling, then gibbering, the drool pouring out of his mouth.

(He knew that. He really did. Because he saw his reflection in the plate glass. Wondering . . .)

Who's that?

And the sound they made as they slithered out of Jeffy! The same tearing sound made by pulling the skin off a chicken. The sound he once heard when he stepped on a dead flounder and made its eyes pop out like marbles.

They touched his face.

"No . . . God . . . please . . ."

The tiny worm things landed stickily on his face, and for a moment Ed thought that was all that was going to happen.

He had a sick grin on his face.

(*I'm okay . . . I'm okay . . . I'm—*)

Then they started boring under his skin, into the cheek, right through his lip. Until they were in his mouth and he was gagging on them, tasting his own blood, coughing.

He fell to his knees.

And Jeffy didn't have to hold him anymore.

Eduardo opened the backdoor of the Mohawk's kitchen. Too damn hot in there. *The air conditioning didn't do shit, man.*

Nada.

He chewed his toothpick.

And heard a car start.

It came from across the road, over at Bob O's. He saw Jeffy behind the wheel of a big black car. He pulled it around the side, got out, and looked up.

He saw Eduardo.

Eduardo waved.

Thinking . . .

I wouldn't let that monkey work on my car. . . .

Pancakes!

Erica sniffed deeply.

It was amazing, she thought. A couple of hours away from New York, where the most esoteric cuisine from every part of the world can be found, even at 3 A.M., yet the smell of pancakes could seem like the best thing the planet had to offer.

Add the spattering and crackling of bacon and links of sausage (with what had to be real maple syrup) and you're in heaven.

She brushed Josh's hair off his forehead. Thinking . . . *the boy needs a cut*.

She felt him pull away.

"Mom," he wailed, in an exasperated tone that said, *I'm not a kid and I hate it when you treat me like one*.

They were elbow to elbow with the good folks of Stoney-wood.

Some older people, cut from a generic cookie mold, with their ruddy cheeks and gray hair, bustled about making sure that each of the tables, stretched out on the lawn behind the firehouse, was set with stiff plastic plates, white plastic utensils and, incongruously, great glass syrup pitchers.

Erica felt cool. A break from the sweltering city. The town, as usual, was already swallowed by the shade of Stoneywood's pride and joy, Mount Shadow.

Should have brought a sweater.

"Why don't you get us a table, Mom?" Erica said to her mother. "Josh and I will bring the flapjacks over."

Her mother nodded and walked away, greeting a half-dozen people, clasping hands, touching women that she had spent her whole life with.

Most of them, like Erica's mother, living alone now.

Like me, Erica thought, surprised to see that she had somehow let herself slip into that group.

Ooops . . .

I seem to have lost my husband.

She stayed on line with Josh. He was ready to leap ahead, his nostrils filled with the wonderful smells. The volunteer firemen manning the stoves made a big show of flipping the pancakes in the air, laughing and talking to each person before they walked away rewarded with a steaming stack.

Erica glanced back at her mother.

She didn't look right. Her mother was strong, one of those people always doing things for others, making a stew for a family after a baby was born, cleaning house for the older ones who couldn't even get out of bed. But now, looking at her, studying that great wrinkled face, the way her hands moved, Erica was worried.

Her mother looked pale and tired.

"Josh," Erica said softly, "has Grandma been okay? I mean, how—"

Josh looked at her. "Grandma? She seems fine. Oh, she did complain about some pain last night. I think it was her arthritis. But she's been okay. Why?"

"Nothing. I just thought—"

"*Erica*?"

The voice boomed from across the great lawn that led to the picture-postcard town square. "Erica Stoller?"

She turned . . .

Recognizing the voice.

Knowing that old flames never die.

They just marry someone else.

Bob, she said to herself.

(Of all the damn luck!)

She saw, gratefully, that he had a woman and a pair of kids in tow. They were young kids, one five or so, the other about eight. The woman looked disinterested in the universe.

And large.

Someone who didn't need a pancake supper.

Erica shifted uneasily on her feet.

Damn, she knew that she'd run into people, people she knew. There was no way to avoid it.

But did it have to be Bob O'Connor?

"Er-i-ca!" he said, stressing every syllable, arriving, at last, next to her. It didn't bother him that everyone watched his big greeting.

He stepped back.

"You look marvelous." Then he aped Billy Crystal doing Fernando Lamas . . . "Absolutely *mah*velous."

Erica smiled.

"Hello, Bob," she said.

"And this big fellow must be your son." She saw O'Connor look at Josh, winking at him.

Christ, she thought. *Is there no way to end this?*

"Your dad must be some big guy, eh, son?"

"His father's dead, Bob," Erica said quickly, quietly.

But Bob looked confused, like he hadn't heard her.

And now she'd have to repeat it. Nice and loud.

So every damn person there could hear it.

But O'Connor's face went wide with exaggerated concern. Mouth open.

Like a surprised fish.

Back when they had dated, she was a dewy-eyed sophomore and O'Connor was the brash star of the football team.

He had great hands.

But he also had the soul of a lizard.

For a couple of weeks he had been fucking her best friend only minutes after dropping Erica off at home. And then, when she confronted him, he tried to weasel out of it with some bullshit about 'male needs.'

She dumped him.

And spent the good part of a year regretting it.

God, the dumb things we do before adulthood rescues us.

But it was good to see him now, living the middle-aged nightmare, his wife transformed into this oversized creature.

The local sweetheart gone to pot. In a big way.

"Very sorry to hear that," O'Connor said. He took her hands in his. "We'll have to catch up . . . perhaps later."

She smiled. "Yes, that would be nice."

And Erica knew she'd have to make sure that Bob O'Connor didn't succeed in cornering her later.

But as she watched him plow through the crowd of pancake fans, she could see that Bob O'Connor had become a big fish.

In a small pond.

Good for him.

"Hey," Josh said, grabbing his mother's arm. "There's Clara . . . and Brian!"

Erica knew who Clara was, and she looked forward to meeting this femme fatale who was luring her son into danger. But she was disappointed to look over and see a decidedly tomboyish girl, all of twelve, grinning at Josh, walking towards them . . .

With a man.

"And who is Brian?" she asked, scrutinizing the man next to Clara.

She saw him smile at Josh, but then, too quickly, turn his attention to her.

"Who is he?" she whispered again, before they got there.

"He's the guy . . . the one who pulled me out of the tunnel."

She nodded. "Yes, but who is—"

But Clara jogged too quickly up to Josh.

And then Brian was there.

"Hi, Josh," he said, "I saw this little lady walking around as if she had nowhere to go. So I told her I'd spring for dinner."

"Hi," Josh said. "Brian, this is my mom."

Erica offered a hand. "Erica Tyler, Mr.—?"

"Brian McShane."

"I want to thank you for helping my son. He hasn't been himself lately . . . since coming here . . . since . . ." She rolled her eyes in the direction of Clara.

Brian smiled, warm and confident. And though there was something about him that didn't seem right, like he didn't belong here, he was easy on the eyes.

"I guess it's just a case of the city boy in the country, Erica. I wouldn't worry about Josh. He seems pretty levelheaded to me."

The pancake line moved up a bit, closer to the flotilla of portable stoves. The smoky smell of the batter billowed around them.

And, she noticed, Brian joined their line.

She turned towards him and lowered her voice. "He may be levelheaded, but I'm not so sure about this Clara. What's her story?"

He grinned, amused. It made him feel protective. "Well, maybe it's just puppy love. Or it might be friendship." He looked up at her. "Kindred souls whom fate has thrown together." He laughed, and looked over at Josh and Clara, talking animatedly. "I wouldn't worry about them. . . ."

He paused, as if just noticing that he had moved onto line with Erica.

"Er, mind if I join you for dinner?"

You already have, Erica thought.

(And what is *your* story?)

"No . . . be my guest. . . ."

* * *

Clara grabbed Josh's arm and squeezed it. Her mouth was full of half-chewed pancake, but that didn't prevent her from talking.

"Josh," she whispered—bits of pancake threatening to tumble from her overstuffed mouth—"we gotta talk."

Josh looked at his mother and grandmother, talking to Brian. No one was listening to him and Clara.

"Okay, talk."

He saw her look right and left. Then she held her head still, looking to the side. Josh turned.

And he saw the kids from the gorge. The infamous Tamm brothers looking like a pair of teen-age hit men from Murder Inc.

"Oh, brother," he groaned.

"Don't sweat it," she mumbled, turning back to him. "They're here for pancakes, not to make grief for you."

But Josh wasn't too thrilled about the way the oldest Tamm kid was looking at him.

I guess he hasn't beat up anyone today, Josh thought, worried about the kid's quota.

He's getting itchy.

Then Bobby Tamm shook his head disgustedly and turned back to the pancake line.

"So talk," Josh said.

Clara looked at him, and Josh saw her face go sort of funny. Dark, serious, not the Clara that he was starting to know . . . and be wary of.

"Not here. You done eating? Then let's go over to the gazebo."

"Huh?"

"Over there." She pointed to a little open-sided hut at the center of the town park.

"Oh, that."

And he turned and told his mother he was going to walk around a bit.

He sat next to Clara on the top step of the gazebo.

The pancake supper was still going on strong, but people were circling the silent auction tables, writing bids on everything from apple pies to tractor tires.

Sitting there, it was like watching a movie.

"Okay, what's the big secret?"

She leaned closer to him.

Though there was no one else around for yards and yards. A breeze rustled a willow standing to the side.

"Do you know what tonight is?"

"Sure." He grinned. "Thursday night."

She shook her head.

So serious. It was a side of Clara that he hadn't seen before. And he wasn't sure he wanted to see.

"It's Midsummer! Tonight, and there's a full moon."

"Midsummer?"

Now she smiled. "Yeah, the middle of the whole summer. It's like a special night. . . . And this year there's a great full moon."

Josh nodded. Not sure that he liked the direction this was going in.

"So . . ."

"The moon rises near eleven, and we gotta, just gotta go out and see it."

Josh laughed and stood up.

"No, Clara. Maybe you have to, but I can spend the night sleeping, thanks." He started off the steps.

"Josh!" she called loudly. He turned around.

She was angry, he thought, her face flushed.

But no. It wasn't anger. She was—

Scared.

(*Maybe she's crazy*, he thought. *I don't know her* that *well*.)

"Josh, come on. It's only one night . . . in the middle of summer. Then fall's here before you know it. Fall! And school, and snow—"

And what else? he wondered. What had her so crazy . . . like she was ready to cry or something?

He thought he should touch her. Pat her hand, her head . . . something.

(He felt people watching them from across the great lawn. You always knew when people were watching you.)

The Brothers Tamm.

Perhaps there was more going on here than just bored town bullies terrorizing the newcomer.

Something with Clara and Bobby Tamm.

Something that he broke up.

The realization made him flush.

"I'm sorry, Clara. But this is an adventure you'll have to go on without me. I'm in enough stupid trouble. My mom's this close to packing me off to camp for the rest of the summer."

Clara looked up at him.

"Josh. C'mon—"

Begging. "*Please*."

He thought of her arm then. The purple-black bruise that just didn't fit with her smiling and pumping away on her bike.

"I'll go out alone," she said flatly.

Josh nodded. She stood up and grabbed his arm, squeezing it.

"It only happens once every thirty years, Josh. *Once!* You'll be an old man the next time. . . ."

Josh shook his head. He looked up at the sky, a clear blue with just thin patches of white off to the north, streaking away from the mountain.

Clara held onto his arm.

"Please?"

He looked at her.

Smiled.

And said—

(*I'm going to regret this, I know it . . . I know it!*)—

"Okay . . ."

McMurdo

"Jee-sus! Will you shut that fucking hatch?" Wilson screamed.

Aguerra, whose Latin blood seemed totally unaffected by the sub-zero temperatures and mad-dog winds, looked up and grinned.

"I don't got all my shit on, Wilson. And we ain't leaving until I got it all loaded." Aguerra paused, still grinning, the glow of the helicopter's thousand idiot lights giving his dark face a ghoulish glow.

"Great. You just take your goddam time and I'll sit here and freeze my nuts off."

"What else are they good for down here?" Aguerra laughed.

Then Wilson watched the pilots come out of the McMurdo station. Their briefing took longer probably because of the weather.

And what weather!

No snow falling now. That was never the problem down here, even at McMurdo Base, sitting right by the ice pack.

Antarctica, as the Navy's manual explained, is a desert.

It's covered by mile-high glaciers, but still a desert.

But it might as well have been snowing. The winds grabbed granules of snow, swirling them into nasty tornadoes, walls of sharp, frozen ice that could lacerate your skin like a rusty razor.

The dogs hated the shit.

The men in the base usually didn't even leave the station.

Not during an Antarctic winter.

So how the hell did this junket get approved?

What could be of such phenomenally great fucking priority that an expedition was flying in this goddam mess? With six men, climbing gear, a pair of snowcats, field radio, and who-knew-what-else in the back of the Sikorsky?

At least they had the best chopper available. It wasn't even a real helicopter. No, the Sikorsky SK-19 had a tail rotor and a main prop, but that's where comparisons with an ordinary helicopter ended.

Its rotor was made of a lightweight tungsten, coated with the same shit they use on the shuttle. Totally resistant to heat or cold. And there were twice the number of blades. The tail rotor was the size of an old Pan-Am propeller.

The Sikorsky even had wings, stubby things that could keep it aloft. Yeah, as long as the two jet turbines were working. And the turbines were identical to those on the F-14.

There were no weapons on this baby. None needed here, unless you wanted to go shake up the penguin population. But the thing could be outfitted with everything from front- and rear-mounted machine guns to heat-seeking missiles.

A nice little machine.

Now if Aguerra would just finish getting his climbing gear in and shut the fucking door.

The pilots climbed up and went to their cabin, quickly followed by Captain Finch.

So what the hell is going on?

There were the rumors.

Stupid stories.

Something to do with the Emperor Two party.

Weird stuff. The radio man had told him something just last night, while they sipped a beer in the common room.

"You're going with body bags," he said. "A whole bunch of them." Then he grinned and took a slug of his beer.

"No shit," Wilson had said.

Fuckin' body bags.

Captain Finch walked to the back to the copter, stepping around the two snow cats.

"Everybody all set here?" he asked.

Wilson answered.

"Yes, sir."

The captain turned to Aguerra. "Everything stowed, Lieutenant?"

"Tied down tight, sir," Aguerra answered.

Wish I could tie your mouth down tight, Wilson thought.

The turbines started. The roar was tremendous. Banshees from hell. The engines were perched just outside the walls of the copter. The Sikorsky was not designed as a passenger vehicle and no expense was wasted on soundproofing.

Finch went back up front, to the pilot's cabin. He shut the door behind him.

The whine of the turbines rose in pitch, higher and higher, a crazy, mad sound. Like the wind whistling through the goddam barracks.

Then the rotors started turning, the tail rotor keeping the chopper from spinning around while the main rotor struggled to get all the dead weight up into the air.

Wilson felt the vibrations of the shaft as it whipped around, picking up speed. Another crazy sound.

The chopper rocked.

More screeching. And he saw Aguerra's face vibrate, grinning at him.

Fucking winter, and they were heading south!

Where it was colder.

Jeezus!

The Sikorsky rocked some more, freeing itself from the ice. Then the runners popped up and they were in the air.

Straight up . . . getting enough altitude to cruise right over the ice barrier . . . up to the Great Antarctic Plateau.

Wilson took a deep breath.

And he saw Aguerra looking right at him, a great big shit-eating grin on his face.

"Hey, Wilson," he yelled over the crazy sounds.

"What, Aguerra?" Wilson yelled back. "What the hell do you want?"

Aguerra's smile filled his dark face. "Nothing, man. Just . . . hey, man, you don't look like you're enjoying the ride."

And Aguerra's laugh, high, squealing, joined all the other sounds.

As the Sikorsky tipped and roared through the Antarctic sky.

II

Midsummer's Night

Fifteen

WHAT A LOAD of crap!

Walt Johnson, balding and feeling too old for this garbage, snorted. Not to express his opinion of the Brothers Pardone, the Mutt and Jeff of two-bit carnivals. But damn! The air inside the Pardones' trailer was thick with smoke of every kind— butts, cigars, and weed—and the rank smell of sweat.

What was the matter with this bunch of animals? Never heard of a bath before? Allergic to water?

No fleas traveling with this carnival.

They all died from the stench.

And Jesus, did Little Lou Pardone really think anyone was listening to his rap? It had to be the hundredth time he was laying down the same load of bull that his father used to sell:

Don't fuck with the rubes . . . Don't do any drugs . . . Make nice with the locals . . . No private back-door games of chance . . . Keep your dicks in your jeans.

And no spare-time hooking by the members of the fairer sex.

Though a rube would have to be absolutely careless about his state of health to troll *those* waters.

While Lou Pardone went on with his sermon, Johnson squirmed in the corner of the big trailer, right by the mini-fridge and a fold-down Formica kitchen table right out of *Father Knows Best*. The two brothers, Henry and Lou slept here, counted the money here, and held these little fireside chats before the worn-out carny hit another town.

Just like their old man used to.

But their old man was a different kettle of fish. Big Lou *was* big. Even when he was well past sixty his meaty hand could knock around any wiseguy asshole who thought he'd give the boss-man some lip. Lou prowled the carny like a bad-tempered lion.

Right up until the day he died.

And then his two idiot sons took over. Both of them were half the size of their father. And the show slowly started going to hell. The rides only passed inspection because of the payoffs laid on the inspectors. Some bad-ass disaster just had to be only months away.

(And which ride would give out first? The Round-Up— Wouldn't that be a sight? With its barrel full of people, spinning around, held in place by the wonder of centrifugal force. Or maybe the rusty ferris wheel might decide to start rolling through the midway on its own, filled with screaming kids and grandmas, over and over, plowing through the rubes playing the sucker games. Or maybe the Devil Coaster might fly off its track and take some unsuspecting folks on a direct run to the Prince of Darkness.

Something bad had to happen soon.

Little Lou finished talking. The runt looked upset that nobody was paying attention: Not the ride monkeys, the greasy, acne-scarred potheads who operated the death machines. Not the food people, who knew better than to eat the weiners they served. And not the barkers.

Yeah, Johnson thought, *'cause I'm a barker and I sure as hell ain't listening.* There was only one guy who seemed to be giving Lou and Henry any attention at all.

The Bozo.

Jim.

That's all the name he had.

Old Jimbo.

The Pardones said, "Jim do this, and Jim do that," like he was their personal servant or something. And the six-foot five-inch lug nodded, grinned a toothy smile, pointed his hand like a gun, and bang! The job was done.

Everyone figured that the Pardones had some kind of hold on Jim, something that kept the wild-eyed mother in check.

But nobody asked Jim. No, he was given a wide berth, lots of breathing space. There were rumors—rumors that Johnson didn't doubt. Bad rumors. About Jim's past.

Some townie girl. A broken neck. In the heat of passion and all that.

Like Lennie in *Of Mice and Men*.

(Hey, George, I'm sorry! I didn't know her neck would snap.)

That was before he became the Bozo.

But hey, that's what the carnival is all about. People without a past. Fringe people who have taken a nosedive in society, going undercover, swimming with the nameless, the faceless, the lifeless.

Johnson moved around a bit, trying to stretch his aching legs. After breaking down his booth and helping the ride honchos fold up their rusty contraptions, they still had a two-hour drive ahead of them, only to set the mess up again.

It would be goddamn dawn before the Pardones would finally look everything over, standing together like Tweedledee and Tweedledum, and tell everyone to go to sleep.

A new girl, Pat—blond, blue-eyed, and hard as a ten-penny nail—kept looking over at him.

Big hooters. Big smile. But probably a big pain in the ass. *I've been in the carny too long*, he thought. *Losing my taste . . . for everything*.

But he smiled back anyway, before looking away.

Then, Johnson heard a car pull up, beside the trailer. He pushed the blinds apart to see who it was.

And he saw Ed Stein, balding, pudgy, and looking like one tired hombre, slide out of his car.

Funny thing . . . instead of coming into the trailer, grabbing a brew, saying Hi to everyone, old Ed, the carny's honcho for dealing with the local yokels, lumbered away.

The meeting here was over anyway, Johnson knew.

And the collected personnel of the Pardone Brothers Combined Shows slowly stumbled to life.

The real living dead.

Staggering out the cheap-jack trailer door.

Ready to haul ass to Stoneywood!

Wow! thought Joanie. What a difference a day makes!

She had showed up late for breakfast service and had to hustle to get ready. And she said a quick hello to Ann Mayhew, the new girl who had seemed so scared yesterday.

I showed her the ropes, *everything* I know to make this job possible. She had seemed so sweet . . . yesterday.

But now today she doesn't say a word. When I said hello it was like the girl was getting a message from beyond. She was acting like little Miss Stuck-up, not even smiling.

And she had been so grateful last night.

What the hell did I do?

But Joanie was never one to let such things lie.

If there was a bull with horns, she grabbed at it. "You're just too direct," her dead mother used to say. And that was only too true. Better that than wondering all the time what the hell was going on, what people were thinking about you, or saying.

So she decided to, yes, confront Ann after dinner clean-up, when everyone was leaving. *Who knows?* she thought. *Maybe I did do something. But she damn well better tell me what it is. . . .*

The waitresses and busboys cleared out of the Inn with amazing speed. Their hustle was at maximum after dinner, when they got their tables all set up for breakfast and the pick-up area cleaned up. Nobody wanted to hang around any longer than necessary at Ye Olde Inn.

Tonight, Joanie couldn't enjoy any of their chatter. Her eye was fixed on Ann, waiting for a good time to talk to her.

What gives, babe? Whose stink are you smelling?

The locker room started to clear out.

But then Ann walked away.

Towards the back door.

Huh? Joanie thought. *Now where is she going?* That door only led to the back of the kitchen and then the woods.

There was nothing out there, nothing at all.

Did this girl have a screw loose?

But this might be a good time to talk with her. Get her alone. Pin her down.

Joanie slammed her locker shut. It echoed in the now deserted rows of lockers. She heard the kitchen crew working, lucky folks from south of de border who got to scrape and clean the enormous griddles and run the monster dishwashers.

(And that was fun work, heating up the table-sized griddle, pouring oil on it and then rubbing it with a whetstone over and over. Great on a hot summer's night.)

She hurried, thinking . . . *I don't want to lose Ann out-*

side. It was getting dark, and the pine trees were thick. And why the hell was she going that way?

Joanie went through the kitchen, too bright from all the brilliant fluorescent light. And she followed Ann to the back door.

"Oh, I don't know. He seemed like a nice man."

Erica sipped the herbal tea, inhaling its cherry-cinnamon scent. She smiled at her mother's evaluation of Brian. "The days of *nice* men helping kids in trouble are over," she argued. "Josh may be nearly thirteen, but it wouldn't take much for some sicko to pick him up and take him away. Now, sit down and have some tea with me."

"Well," her mother said, turning away from the sink.

(*And how many conversations have I had with my mother's back?* Erica thought. *Looking at the back of her head nod at what I said, watching her turn around and deliver the official pronouncement on whatever lofty issue was being discussed— dating, makeup, school.*)

"That kind of thing doesn't happen here, Erica. This isn't your New York. I still think he seemed nice." Her mother turned back to the sink. "And he seemed interested in you."

Erica smiled. *I might as well be a ten-year-old again. Life advice freely dispensed.*

She took another sip of tea.

"Well, it wouldn't hurt you to invite him over for dinner . . . to thank him."

Erica downed the tea.

"And maybe," Erica answered, standing up, "I should just go to bed."

There was no cable TV here. Stoneywood had it, but the line stopped at the bottom of the hill, well away from his grandmother's house. And Josh knew it would never be coming up. There was a small color TV in the sun room which picked up exactly two channels, and neither of them too well. There was WTEN from Albany and WSCY from Schenectady. And that was all he'd have for the summer.

Pretty grim.

Josh turned it on, hoping that his mother and grandma would go to sleep, leaving him up.

I've gotta be crazy to go with Clara, he thought.

He flicked back and forth between the two channels, guessing he'd be stuck with *Mash* re-runs and the even more horrible new *Family Feud*.

But WTEN had a movie.

And not just *any* movie.

One that Josh had seen before.

With his father.

It had been a rainy Saturday, about a year ago. Josh had been scanning the dial and gone flying right past the black-and-white movie. Couldn't stand black and white. But, hearing the high-pitched screeching of the opening, his father put down his book. "Hold it right there, Josh," he said. When the title came on—all wavy lines, corny, but eerie—his father grinned. "You're gonna love this, Josh. It's a classic."

Josh remembered rolling his eyes.

Some of Dad's *classics* were hard to take.

But that one, yeah, that one was great.

He was hearing that strange music again.

The title wiggled onto the screen . . .

The Thing From Another World. He grabbed his pad off the small coffee table. Though he had seen the film a few times, he had never gotten a really good look at the alien. Just a flying arm here, a big head, some thorny bumps on his fingers.

So, he thought, *maybe I can do a quick sketch. Sort of catch it in bits and pieces*. He grabbed a pencil that had a bluntish point and nearly no eraser.

It didn't matter. It was just for fun.

And he tucked his feet up on the ratty couch as the black-and-white movie started.

And he thought . . . *Who needs color?*

Tom Smith brought the patrol car to a sudden stop right beside the Ward cottage.

The lights were on. Watson had told him that if the lights were on, he should just make his normal, slow loop, patrolling the back roads of Stoneywood before coming back later to watch the house.

So he backed the car to the left, spinning the wheels in the gravelly dirt. The house was in his rearview mirror. The windows were lit, the curtains drawn.

And he thought he saw some movement by one of the windows.

They're just checking who's outside.

That's all.

Then Tom Smith—married a mere two months ago and wishing he was home right now with his Poopsie, squeezing her sexy little buns—drove back down the road.

Thinking: *I'll come back and check later.*

Nancy Skye hung back, watching the emergency room doctor and a pair of snooty nurses roll the young man into an empty room. The IV bottle and tube swung in the air.

Then she followed, just curious.

There wasn't much to do, with the patients' dinner done and all. She thought of calling Clara, to make sure that she had some dinner, that everything was—

Okay.

But she put that thought away. She didn't want to call home. She wanted to forget that house . . . her daughter . . . her husband.

She stood by the bathroom door.

"Give us a hand," one of the nurses ordered. And Nancy Skye went to her side. Who the hell did these nurses think they were?

The man was out cold. An accident, she guessed.

Good-looking fellow, though. Nice face. Thin lips.

"Get under his legs," the doctor told her.

Nan nodded, and grabbed the man's upper thigh and leg.

"Okay," the doctor said. "On three . . . one . . . two . . . "

They moved him smoothly onto the bed.

And Nancy stayed there a minute, watching the doctor lift up the patient's eyelids and flash a small beam of light into the pupils. One of the nurses checked that the IV solution was still flowing into him.

"What happened?" Nancy asked, directing her question to the nearest nurse.

"Smashed up his car," the nurse answered, taking the man's pulse. "Not a scratch on him, though, but he's got a bad concussion."

The doctor looked up sharply.

"Could you get that out of here?" he said, gesturing to the now-empty emergency room bed. Nancy went over and

wheeled it out of the room, backwards, watching them finish
their work with their man.

Nice-looking man.

She'd have to come back later.

When the nurses were gone.

Before her shift ended . . .

Everyone became just a tad quieter when they saw who opened
the door to Sheehan's.

The regulars, the guys who came every night and bullshitted
their lives away, looked at their beers or their watches. Two
younger guys looked over at the door and then gave each other
a "look what garbage the wind just blew in" look.

No, Max Sheehan thought, having Jeffy Post stroll in was
not the best thing for business.

Jeffy took a corner stool, down where the TV was, his back
to the baseball game. *Shit, if anyone wanted to watch the game
now, they'd have to look at Jeffy too. Damn nuisance!*

Sheehan took his time walking down to him.

Maybe he'll go if I give him the idea that he's not welcome.

"What'll be, Jeff?"

And Jeffy opened his mouth and smiled.

One of the midget Ecuadorians slaving at the grill looked up at
Joanie.

But she kept walking to the door, expecting to see Ann
standing right there, having a smoke or something.

What's your problem, girl? That's what I'll say.

'Cause whatever it is, I want to settle it right now.

But when Joanie opened the door—

(Smelling the pine trees that grew right up to the door)

She saw nobody.

It was quiet and still, much darker here than on the other side
of the Inn, overlooking the lake.

She thought then about a movie she caught the tail end of a
few nights ago . . . on *Chiller Theater*. Bunch of girls at
camp or something, all of them running around in bras and
panties while some fruitcake cut them down one . . .
by . . . one.

The only thing she thought at the time was, *Damn, wish I
had a body like that. My stomach wasn't that flat when I was
ten, let alone thirty-five.*

"Ann!" she called.

Hell, it was like she had just disappeared into the woods.

Which was a possibility.

Maybe Ann was taking a walk, working around to the employees' parking lot. Of course, to do that you had to climb over some rocks as tall as the Inn.

"Ann?" she called again.

Then her eyes, adjusting to the darkness, picked out a trail . . . of sorts. Probably used by Tommy Balen when collecting notches for his pee-shooter.

(*And I'm a notch, aren't I? Enjoyed it too.*)

Damn it, she said to herself. *I should probably just forget it. It can wait till the morning. Have it out with her then . . . right before work.*

She turned to go . . .

When she heard a sound.

Not too far away. Someone was walking around.

Or something . . .

She followed the noise.

Bill Hammer, good for three mugs of Genny on tap, got up from his seat. Hammer had a new baby girl at home, though he didn't usually seem to be in any hurry to get there.

But tonight was different. "Can't sit here and watch that mug," he muttered to Sheehan, none too quietly.

The Mets were down by three runs—a good game was in store. Sheehan made a face, and then scooped up the empty mug and four bills scattered on the bar.

He looked up to see Jeffy nursing a beer and watching them.

Damn if the punk doesn't look like he's enjoying what he's doing, for chrissakes. Spooking all my customers.

Goddam ex-con.

And goddamn O'Connor for giving him a job.

Sheehan watched Hammer walk to the door.

Faith Avenue was as quiet as a graveyard. The carnival was due in this evening. Maybe that's what had lured Jeffy out.

Hammer stopped at the door and looked right over at Jeffy.

Bob Hammer was a strong bastard.

Sheehan and the rest of his customers watched the action.

Hammer gave Jeffy Post his best disgusted look, standing there at the door.

Just hoping, Sheehan knew, that Jeffy would say or do something.

But Jeffy just looked straight ahead.

And Hammer went out the door.

While Darryl Strawberry came to the plate and a crackling cheer erupted from the TV.

"Come on, Darryl . . . *do something!*" one of Sheehan's customers called.

"Fuckin' guy is cruisin'," Sheehan added, glad to have the game to distract him. "Taking it easy, for Chrissake." He saw Jeffy move.

Jeffy slid off his stool real creepy-like.

(*Try and rob this place, slime ball, and I'll put a hole in you a Coke bottle could fit through.*)

The ex-con dropped a few crumpled dollars on the bar and quickly left.

Strawberry struck out.

"Shit!" someone said.

But Sheehan was watching Jeffy through the window.

He turned left.

Like he was following Bob Hammer.

But then Sheehan grinned. Shit, no, even Jeffy wasn't *that* stupid. He'd have to be crazy to mess with Hammer. And Sheehan reached up and raised the volume just as the Mets took the field and sports fans were treated to some fast-ridin' and good-ropin' beer-guzzling cowboys heading for the mountains of Busch . . .

Beer . . .

The crazy, thumping music from the Spanish station blared away in the kitchen. But as she walked the music faded.

And the trail that Joanie thought she was following soon turned into a maze of a hundred possible pathways, all lined with pine needles, all identical.

She couldn't hear anything in the woods now.

"Ann?" she called.

And Joanie waited, losing her appetite for this little confrontation.

She looked back to the kitchen.

The bright kitchen lights looked small, sliced by the great fat pines. A few more steps, and they'd disappear completely. *I should strip down to my bra and panties*, she thought.

"Oh, forget it," she said, waving her hand at the air and turning back to the Inn.

But then, like it was teasing her, tempting her, she heard a sound. Someone stepping on leaves . . . or pine needles.

"Ann? Is that you? Are you there?"

Joanie took another step.

"Christ, what the hell—"

Then she took a few more steps along the nonexistent trail. She saw a shadow that was not a tree.

A person. Standing quite close.

"Oh, there you are," she said, relieved to see Ann. "I hope you don't mind my following you." Ann had her back to her, but Joanie recognized her hair, and the jeans and light-colored blouse.

"Ann . . . I've got a bone to pick with you. I mean, I've been nothing but helpful to you, and all day I've been getting this cold shoulder from you, like—"

Ann turned to face her.

It was so quiet here.

Almost no sound.

The radio had been shut off. The kitchen crew were heading to their Catskill haciendas.

But there was a noise. Coming from Ann's face.

"I—I like things out on the table," Joanie went on. "If you don't want to—"

A small mewling sound.

Ann turned around.

At first Joanie thought she'd have to laugh. It was funny, but Ann was *eating* something out here, some leftover cake, a turkey wing, something—

Except whatever it was that Ann had up near her mouth was moving.

(Moving.)

Squirming around in her hands.

Making tiny terrified noises.

A small animal. Ears. A tail.

A squirrel. Twisting this way and that, crazed.

Joanie's mouth fell open.

She backed up, right into a tree stump. One hand felt the stump, felt a sticky glob of sap stuck on the tree.

She thought it was sap.

"Wha . . . what . . ."

She started to ask something.

But Ann turned her head just a bit, enough to catch a tiny glimmer of light on her face.

Joanie screamed.

(Would the Inn's guests hear? she wondered. Sitting on the great stone porch overlooking the lake, sipping a sherry.)

Joanie tried to say something.

The squirrel was up near Ann's mouth, writhing around, its BB eyes tiny slimy dots in the darkness. But then Ann brought her hands down.

(No.)

And the squirrel didn't fall. No. It—ha, ha—held up just fine. Sure, it was okay. There were all these things holding it just fine. White things. Hundreds of them . . .

Coming from Ann's mouth.

And Ann took a step toward Joanie, her hands free now, perfectly free, reaching out for her. Joanie slid to the side of the tree, and then looked at the kitchen. Someone had shut the lights off.

But Joanie knew the kitchen was there, just there. Only a few yards away. And a door to the inside.

I can run away.

(She thought of saying something then. Something crazy. Something like . . . *I don't want any of your squirrel. It's all yours. Fair and square. You found it.*)

But that wouldn't work. No sirree!

Ann wasn't eating it. She was doing something else.

The squirrel was still alive.

Still making its terrible squealing scream.

Joanie turned and ran.

(She felt Ann's hands grab her; then there were other things, digging into her. Her stomach heaved, twitching violently. She vomited on the ground.)

And all the time Joanie could smell the crazed squirrel. Its breath. Its wet fur dotted with saliva.

And its blood mixing with her own.

Sixteen

BRIAN PUSHED ASIDE his yellow pad, with its pages and pages of scrawled notes and questions about the Navy's Antarctic stations.

Don't want to spill any vino on my careful research.

Then he held the bottle tightly and pulled up on the corkscrew. It popped out cleanly, with a smooth and satisfying pop.

Success! He picked up the chilled bottle—still amazed that the local package store stocked a cold bottle of Pinot Grigio.

I shouldn't be drinking this, he thought. It was the latest yuppie wine, and *Italian* white wine, no less, pushing the Pouilly Fumé and Pouilly Fuisse right out of all those George-town wine cellars.

It was the preferred drink of the Dinks.

The Dinks . . . the double-income, no-kids set.

Or, as Brian liked to call them, the pod people. They were the new breed, a genetic strain of human being that was clearly and cleanly focused on just one thing. Self. Everything revolved around that simple concept. Career, relationships, diet, even the décor of their apartments. And fuck everyone and everything else.

He looked at the label. Pinot Grigio . . .

And poured some of the wonderful amber liquid into a tacky plastic cup.

So why the hell am I drinking it?

"Because," Brian said aloud, needing to hear another voice,

"it tastes *so* damn good." It may have cost him twenty bucks, but he was going to enjoy every drop.

And with that first luxurious sip, so right on the money—just what the taste buds were clamoring for—he thought of Josh's mother.

Erica Tyler. Now, there was a woman he wouldn't mind sharing a glass with. Beautiful dark hair, and great dark eyes, and those lips . . .

But, damn, what a cold fish. Here he saves her son, hauls his butt out of a cave, and she treats him like the overcoat man from P.S. 212. (*Here, sonny, want to see my meat puppet?*) Brother, if she wasn't filled with New York paranoia he didn't know *who* was. And it was too bad. As long as he had to stay here, babysitting Alan Ward, it would be nice to have someone to treat to a McDLT—

Or a glass of Pinot Grigio.

Oh, well, there was still tomorrow night.

Perhaps at the carnival.

"*Sí*," he said, raising his glass, letting the wondrous wine catch the dim yellow light. Then, a toast.

"*Amore* . . ." he said, taking a sip.

He had been doodling, making small swirls and lines, a hint of the alien's hand here, there a little alien garden feeding off human blood. A commercial break came on, and some leisure-suited monstrosity was chomping on crab legs at the Cohoes Lobster House. Josh put the pad down and went to the stairs.

He stopped on the bottom step and listened. It sure sounded quiet up there, he thought.

There was a rumbling snore. That was Grandma. But what about his mother? Was she asleep, awake, or what?

He started tiptoeing up the stairs. If he was going to sneak out with Clara, he had to be sure that his mother was asleep.

And why am I doing this? he wondered. Hadn't Mom had enough grief . . . enough problems . . . without worrying about him? But this wasn't any big deal. No way. What was he doing, after all? Just sneaking out to catch a midsummer's full moon. With a girl, no less.

He was halfway up the stairs when he heard his mother.

"Josh? Is that you, honey?" She came to the top of the stairs, just in time to catch him turning around, sneaking back down.

"Josh, honey, *what* are you doing?"

He stopped—trapped by the Gestapo—and turned around.

His mind searched for a semi-reasonable explanation. And one appeared, though he wouldn't know how reasonable until he finished saying it. There just wasn't any time to think about it first.

"I . . . I wanted to get my book. The vampire novel I'm reading." Then another useful detail fell into place, embellishing his tale. "To read during the commercials. I didn't want to wake you . . . or Grandma."

His mother cocked an eyebrow at him in that way she had. He never could put anything over on her. "Well," she said matter-of-factly, "I'm up and your grandmother is sawing wood like a buzz saw." She turned, heading back to her room. "No need to creep around like that . . . it's spooky."

Josh bounded up the stairs, putting on his most innocent smile, and went into his room. He snatched the unwanted paperback off the end table and went downstairs.

He caught a glimpse of his mother lying in bed, reading. *Come on*, he thought. *Go to bed. Before Clara gets here. Please!*

And he went back down to the TV. *Chiller Theater* was back on. He threw himself onto the couch, in an eerie iridescence from the flickering glare of the TV. He put his feet up on the coffee table.

Right on his pad.

Oh, yeah, he thought, remembering his plan to sketch the elusive Thing. He reached over and picked up the pad.

He glanced at it.

Doodles. A few odd sketches. And then he saw something.

All the pictures were connected. A twirling coil worked its way to each of his pictures, connecting them, as if it were all one sketch, one thing.

A blast of arctic air blew out of the TV speaker. Someone opened a door to the outside. Kenneth Tobey listened to the huskies howling . . . at something.

Josh looked at his sketch.

I don't remember doing that, he thought. Then, aloud:

"Did I do that?" he whispered. "And if I did, why can't I remember it?"

And why, he wondered, did it bother him so much to look at it?

He looked at the movie, then back at the sketch.

Then he ripped the sheet from the pad, tossing it away to a dark corner of the room.

As he tried to scrunch back and enjoy the rest of *The Thing*.

Clara looked at her father, slumped over in his chair. She chewed at her lip. Not from any fear that she'd be caught. No, he was too far gone for that.

Too far gone . . . that's what her mother always said. *Oh, your father's too far gone . . . to remember that he slapped you. Don't hold it against him, honey. He works hard at the quarry and tries to relax. He's got a temper. Always did . . .*

Too far gone.

The can of beer drooped from his hand, its open spout pointed at the floor.

Empty. She grinned.

Leave it to him to fall asleep only when the beer was all gone.

Her mom wouldn't be back from the hospital until one or one thirty in the morning. *By then*, Clara thought, *I'll be home*. Mom would wake up dear old Dad and he'd stagger up to his room, or maybe start drinking some more.

(And sometimes, in the middle of the night, Clara was awakened by the drunken sounds they made, the wild laughing and shrieking noises. Cackling. Yeah, that was the word. They cackled, like the witch in a comic book she'd read. And Clara didn't sleep then; she would just lie there, waiting for them to stop, watching the black outline of the door . . . wondering if they might stumble into her room.)

Let's go play with Clara.

Clara walked past the living room, the sound of the TV and the flickering light of the picture tube helping her escape. *I'd love to just keep going*, she thought. To leave, walk out and never, ever come back.

I'd give anything for that.

Anything.

She opened the door. And left her house.

Nancy Skye ducked into the man's room. It was dark and cool. The other bed was empty. She walked close to his bed.

She heard something in the hall. A voice, some steps.

Damn, she shouldn't be here. They'd wonder what she was doing, what she wanted.

She froze.

The voice got louder, and then faded.

She waited. Until she was sure that whoever it was had gone away. The night nurses liked to sit on their butts, eating and smoking and reading their dumb romance novels.

She waited. Then she looked at the man.

So handsome, and young too. His eyes were closed, but she could imagine what they were like, a deep blue. And what a smile he'd have. Warm, and open.

She took a step closer to his bed.

Rested her hand on the rail of the bed guard.

Another voice echoed down the hallway.

Nancy quickly cleared her throat. "W-would you like something . . . ?" she said, almost whispering. "Some juice, or—"

But her ears were cocked for the sound in the hall, not some answer from the sedated patient. She heard a big laugh, and then it was quiet.

The man in front of her wasn't waking up to ask for anything.

I should go, she thought. *Go do . . . something else.*

Instead, she leaned against the guard rail.

Pressing her body tight against it. Almost unawares, she let her arm snake down to the crisp white sheets. Then she let it lie there gently. She felt the slow rhythmic rise and fall of his chest. Now, made bold by the silence, the absolute stillness, she traced a line up to the man's chin. Her fingers touched the smooth skin of his cheek. *Such a good-looking young man.*

She extended one finger and touched his lower lip.

Opening it just the tiniest bit.

She made a small moan.

Pressing harder against the rail.

His lip slid from her finger, making a small pop as it flapped closed.

Her hand pulled away from his face, down, crawling under the sheet, while she listened, all the time listening, for any sound in the hallway.

Just fixing his sheets, she'd explain. Tucking him in . . . seeing if he was awake . . . if he wanted—

Anything.

Down, lower, feeling his skin, warm, barely protected by the thin hospital gown. Lower, until she felt his skin, and the bed was becoming seriously disarrayed.

She touched him.

In the cool darkness . . .

Played with him while she ground her body against the bed . . .

So what do we have here?

Brian looked at his pad. Line after line of questions, all of them ending in big question marks, circled, underlined.

Question numero uno.

How did Ward kill Dr. Wynan? Wynan had, by all accounts, cut up a party consisting of experienced Navy personnel and other scientists, with no difficulty. So how did Ward stop him? And how come Ward couldn't save anyone else at the station. Everyone else was cut to pieces, hacked up like so much ground beef.

Everyone except Stoneywood's own, ladies and gentlemen, Alan Ward.

Brian took a gulp of the wine.

I should be sipping this shit. And here I'm drinking it like it's Riunite.

No class, no class at all. He refilled the plastic cup, noticing that he had passed the point of no return with the bottle.

Next question, if you please.

How come every transcript of Alan Ward's, from the moment the Navy choppers pulled him out of Ice Box to just two weeks ago reads exactly the same? Exactly. *If there's one thing you can say for him, he's consistent. His story is more than pat.*

The same words. The same events in exactly the same order.

Like it was a goddam script . . . a program.

Even the truth grows fuzzy with time. But Alan Ward's testimony was carved in stone.

Then Brian came to a scratchy pair of double lines.

These were newer questions, hot off the press, and one of them made him feel a little strange. Like someone was playing a practical joke on him.

What is the hell is the Navy up to?

Alexander never told him the purpose of the Emperor Two expedition. What were they doing? Why was it classified? But there was no more information. Nada. It didn't impact on the case, Alexander assured him.

Bullshit, Brian thought. *If I'm hanging my ass out here with Ward, I should know everything. Alexander said he'd see what he could do.*

Which meant, Brian knew, that his request for more information was crawling like a slug through the labyrinthine sewers of Navy bureaucracy. If an answer took forever that would be considered speedy.

And then, there was this last question.

(And shit, this one worried him.)

He heard a noise from outside. A heavy truck. Then another truck. And some cars. He grabbed his cup and went to the window.

The streets of Stoneywood were dark, quiet. The one stoplight in the center of Faith Street, right across from the bank, blinked its pointless warning to empty streets. But up by the town park, near the fire station, there was a circle of trucks and vans. Flatbed sixteen-wheelers cradled strange machines folded in on themselves.

He didn't have a clue as to what they could be.

Backhoes from Mars?

There was no light, no heavy-duty crimebuster tungsten lamps to let him read what was written on the trucks. But then one of the flatbeds backed up and Brian saw just what its strange lifeless cargo was.

"A ferris wheel," he said, taking another gulp of the wine.

It actually looked more like the carcass of a ferris wheel, a dead one, killed by one too many turns.

This should be interesting, he thought. *I never saw a carnival set up*. They always just seemed to *be* there . . . and then, a few days later, poof! they were gone. Summoned by some sleazy genie who helped the Catholic schools and the Volunteer Firemen with their budget problems.

He heard voices, and he opened the window wider. The air felt good. Summer in the mountains. It was cool, almost cold. But the crisp air felt nice, refreshing. He watched men hurry to the trucks, whistling at the drivers, helping them back into position.

Then he thought of his last question.

The one that really bothered him.

Why did the Navy want him here? What was the point? he'd

asked himself a dozen times a day. It couldn't be just to watch
Ward. What the hell for? There had to be something else going
on here.

But damned if I know what it is, he thought. *Damned if I
know.*

Except—

(He saw the crumpled ferris wheel slide off one of the trucks,
clanking its metal girders and pulleys and chains, rattling them
like some ancient torture device.)

He was starting to feel very bad about this whole thing.

The men pulled at the dead ferris wheel, yanking at wires
and rope, and it opened up, its two halves suddenly standing
erect. *You won't catch me riding on that thing*, Brian thought.
No way.

Too fucking dangerous.

He went back to finish the wine.

It didn't make sense.

I mean, Josh thought, *here's this alien, a guy who piloted a
spaceship through space, a spaceship his people obviously
built. And he lets himself get fried?*

Duh . . .

The Thing, vegetable or not, couldn't be *that* stupid.
Grunting and stomping its way down the dark corridor. Acting
more like Frankenstein's monster than a fairly intelligent
invader.

Then Josh's favorite part came. The scientist, the weasely
one with the beard, shuts the power down—at the last minute!
And then he tries to reason with the creature.

*What a dork! You don't talk with the enemy, man, you waste
it.*

Before it wastes you.

The ending was always a drag. It came too quickly, too
much like the witch melting in *The Wizard of Oz*. Then there
was that cornball wrap-up from Scotty, the wisecracking
reporter, broadcasting a warning to the people of Earth.

"Watch the skies!"

For what, meathead?

The WTEN news team came on. They sounded like *they*
should be working in the Arctic.

He looked at the clock.

Clara had said to get out by 11:10 . . . like they were

planning some mission behind enemy lines. *Synchronize watches, gang.* It was 11:05. In five more minutes she'd be standing outside, waiting for him.

It made his skin feel cold and tingly.

And he was anything but tired.

Still, there was Mom to worry about. He didn't want to be caught on the steps again, prowling around like a cat burglar. He went back upstairs.

This time he made it all the way to the top.

And his mother's door was shut. Josh stopped by his room to quickly arrange the pillows on his bed. If she happened to check later, it would look like he was all twisted up in his blanket and sheets.

Then he shut his door.

And went out to meet Clara.

Tom Smith left the Mohawk Diner. Always a big welcome for him there. They liked him stopping by, yeah, sitting at the counter with his gun jutting out. Probably gave them a nice feeling of security.

While all it cost them was a nice slice of blueberry pie and black coffee.

Not that anything much ever happened at the Mohawk or anywhere else in Stoneywood.

He got into his patrol car and checked his watch. It was time he headed back to Mountain Road, to spend the rest of the night keeping an eye on the Ward house, like Watson wanted.

Though who knew what the hell for?

He pulled out of the Mohawk parking lot, noisily, as if he were roaring off to some emergency. And, as he headed north on 133, he saw the full moon, big and yellow, peeking above Mount Shadow.

Damn, it was going to be one beautiful night.

Nancy Skye opened the heavy door to the fire exit. She let the door shut behind her with a heavy thud, and then dug her cigarettes out of her pocket.

She didn't regret what she had done.

In fact, as she started shaking the pack to get a cigarette out, she thought it was perfectly fine. Just a bit of fun, that's all. If the man had been awake, he might have even liked it.

That's what she told herself.

She was still shaking the pack, but nothing was coming out.
No cigarettes.

Shit, she thought. And the fucking hospital refused to allow
a vending machine in the building.

She looked at her watch.

She had another hour left. She sure as hell didn't want to go
without a butt for that long. An idea came to her.

She could go on down the stairs, out the back door.

Sure. No one would see her. And she could drive over to
Bob O's gas station and get some cigarettes.

She licked her lips, tasting—in her imagination—the wonderful burn of the cigarette smoke.

And she hurried down the stairs.

The gas station looked open. But not one of Bob O's
crackerjack employees was in sight. She got out of the car and
went into the small office.

The floor was filled with maps.

"What the hell?" she said, looking around.

She heard a sound coming from the garage. The clang of a
wrench. Someone doing repairs.

Then steps, coming towards the office. *Good*, she thought.
I need change for the damn machine. Nancy Skye looked at her
watch. She didn't want to be away too long, catch hell for not
being on the floor.

"Hello," she called. "Hey, I need some change . . ."

Then the attendant was there . . . someone named Jeffy.

"Glad you're open," she said. "I thought I'd have to—"

He didn't say anything. He looked bleary-eyed, doped up.
His hands hung by his side, like they were useless.

"Some change?" she said, pointing at the cigarette machine.

Jeffy nodded. He blinked.

He opened his mouth.

(It reminded her of something, a story, a fairy
tale . . . something every kid knows. Every kid. *But what
the hell was it?*)

Yes.

She remembered.

Red Riding Hood.

He opened his mouth.

So very big . . . bigger.

The better to—

What?

(She thought of the hospital then, where she should be. How horrible it could be there sometimes, with the sound of the patients, screaming in pain, begging for their medicine five minutes ahead of schedule, *just five little fucking minutes, please nurse, for Christ's sake.*

Please.

Nancy Skye backed up—thinking, for just a minute—of her shitty house, and her daughter Clara.

(Wider . . . wider . . . his mouth was a bottomless pit. Now with something shooting out.)

The door was just behind her.

But her hand didn't even come close. . . .

Josh shut the door gently behind him, fearing that even its tiny click would be too much noise. Then he looked around.

Wow, it was dark out here.

Bartley had once read the class a story that felt just like this. And he read it like a wild man, he did.

The Tell-Tale Heart.

About an old geezer who heard everything, every creak, every tiny movement of a door as it swung open just a tiny bit. The old guy had real good ears.

Now, Josh waited on the other side of the door. Waiting for his mother to come flying down at him.

And where do you think you're going, buster? he could hear her say. *Just what is going on here?*

Getting some air, Mom . . .

He waited.

"Yo, Josh," Clara hissed, making him jump into the air.

"Jeeezuz, Clara," he hissed back, seeing her face at the edge of the pool of light made by the living room window. "You scared the hell out of me."

"Sorry. Hey, look," she said, pointing over her shoulder. "The moon's just coming up over the mountain. What did I tell you?"

But Josh shivered. He heard all the bugs making hungry noises in the dense fields. But it didn't feel like summer. It was too darn cold.

"I think I need a jacket. . . ."

"Nah . . . once we start moving we'll be plenty warm."

"Shhh . . ." Josh said. Clara had started talking in her normal voice.

"Come on," she said, hissing again. "This way."

She led him out to the road, where the bug sounds were even more deafening, filling the tall grassy fields. "What's that noise?" he asked.

"Cicadas," Clara said. "Big, gnarly-looking things. About the size of your thumb. They rub their legs together, I think. My teacher once brought in a body or skin of one. It was really big."

Josh nodded. Of all the things that made him uncomfortable in the woods, insects were at the very top of the list. They were everywhere, biting, crawling, spinning. Everywhere. It was their turf. He looked up, away from the ground. The sky was still a deep blue-black, but the great yellow ball of a moon was starting to wash away the stars.

"Ain't it great?" Clara said.

Josh nodded, none too sure.

"So what now?"

"To the top of Barrow's Hill. We'll see everything—the mountain, the lake, the town. It will be super!"

"Okay." She marched briskly up the road, moving away from the pale glow of the windows. "Any trouble getting out?" he asked her, hurrying to catch up.

"From my house?" she said. "You've got to be kidding me. When my old man passes out, he stays passed out."

Funny, he thought. *The way she talks about her father. So different from the way I feel . . . used to feel. And who decides who gets to keep their father and who loses him?*

"Is it always cold here?" he asked.

He saw that Clara had on a sweater, buttons open.

"Depends," she shrugged, walking close to him. "Some days—some really hot days—it can get absolutely ugly hot inside. That's when I go sleep in the backyard."

The more they climbed, the more the moon rose to light the valley and the hill for them. The ground was no longer black, but a milky white. He saw a toad hop away, startled by their steps.

"Clara," he said, "maybe this is far enough. I mean, we can see everything pretty well from—"

"Look, Josh. The top of the hill is only up there."

He looked where she pointed, and it wasn't far. But all Josh could think about was his mother waking up. Finding him gone. Banishing him to camp.

Imagine. Eating your meals with 150 other kids.

Groan.

But Clara fixed him with her bright eyes. "Okay?" she asked. He nodded his reluctant agreement.

His back was to the farmhouse.

And he didn't notice the light flick on upstairs.

Smith killed the patrol car's engine.

The Ward house was quiet. No lights on. There was just the beautiful moon sitting almost on the roof.

He stretched in his seat, pushing back against the upholstery, and yawned loudly. Then he searched the floor for his thermos, hoping that the coffee his little Poopsie made was still a little bit hot.

He looked down and picked up the silvery thermos. He unscrewed the top and smelled the strong coffee . . . noticing that there wasn't a hell of a lot of steam.

Lukewarm at best.

He filled the metal thermos cup.

Looking down as he poured.

Not watching the cottage.

He whistled something. Not knowing what it was. Then he wondered . . . *What the hell tune is that?*

The cup was filled.

Oh, yeah, I know now.

It's the theme from The Cosby Show.

Nice tune.

He looked up. . . . .

Seventeen

"THERE WAS THIS kid in sixth grade—Richard Barr—who was really out of control. I mean, he would do *anything*. He was transferred from some place upstate, and he must have wanted to make an impression on everyone."

Clara turned and looked at Josh. "You know what it's like when you're new to a place and all. He was a big kid too, looked like he should have been in high school."

"Probably been retained," Josh said.

"You mean left back? Yeah, that's for sure. Four or five times at least. Anyway, nobody wanted to mess with Barr. Except the teachers, though. They weren't scared at all."

Josh moved his butt around on the ground, the small pebbles beginning to bother him. He made an O with his mouth and blew out, half-expecting to see a frosty cloud.

It wasn't that cold. But it sure didn't feel like summer.

The moon was blinding, it was so brilliant. The light made everything stand out, the slope of the hill, the gorge, and especially the craggy cliffs of the mountain. But it was all a ghostly, milky white. No color. No life.

Like the moon itself.

This, he thought, *is fun.*

Sitting on top of the hill, looking at the moon climb, talking about stuff.

It was really neat.

"Anyway," Clara continued, needing little encouragement, "this kid Barr did zippo homework, None. Nada. Like he was daring the teachers to do something. Any notes they sent home disappeared—I think he was living with some old aunt, and we loved watching all the teachers go bonkers trying to get this big gorilla to do something."

Josh grinned. Clara sure could tell a story.

She grabbed his arm, turning away from the moon, locking her eyes on him. "So get this. His math teacher keeps him in during lunch. He tells Barr that if he doesn't want to do any work, fine, he can just sit there. Of course, Barr stayed in, but, wow, the look in his eyes . . .

"The next day the math teacher breezed into class, asked for homework and Barr *still* had nothing. The class freaked out! It was a regular revolution."

She stopped, relishing the moment.

"Okay," Josh finally said, "what happened?"

"So the teacher makes Barr get up in front of the class and do the homework right there! On the board! In front of *everybody*. Of course it was all wrong, and we were laughing and the teacher made him stand there, until Barr finally ran out of the room, slamming the door behind him."

"Hello reform school?"

"Not yet. Though none of us expected him to, Barr showed up the next day, wearing the biggest, goofiest grin I ever saw."

"Uh-huh . . . go on," Josh said, shaking his head, eager to hear the end of the story.

But then—

(He heard something. At least he thought he heard something. From far away. A car door slamming. Or something like that. But Clara's story pulled him back to attention.)

"The teacher comes in . . . good morning class, and all that, and opens up his desk—"

Clara let out a great whoop and rolled backwards, kicking her legs in the air, laughing crazily at her own story.

"Come on, Clara, what happened?"

"The teacher went to his desk. I don't know, to get a piece of chalk or something. And Richard Barr is sitting there good as gold. The teacher opens the top drawer . . . and his desk explodes! Boom!" Clara shrieked and rocked back and forth on the ground.

Josh laughed. "What? An explosion?"

"Yeah, not so big that it could kill anyone—Barr obviously knew what he was doing. He was experienced. But it filled the room with smoke. The teacher looked like one of those cartoon guys. You know, like Elmer Fudd looking down the barrel of Bugs Bunny's gun just as he's about to pull the trigger. Pow! The teacher was covered with black soot, blubbering at the whole screaming class. Barr just sat there, grinning, loving every minute of it and—"

(Another sound. He definitely heard it that time, from right behind them. He stood up.)

"Hey, what's wrong, what's—"

Josh turned around, looking at the downslope of the hill, all white and icy.

"I heard something. . . ." he said slowly.

"Probably just a gopher or a screech owl. Probably—"

He shook his head.

"It sounded like a scream."

The sound jolted Erica awake. She was so used to sleeping alone, to the quiet, just the hum of the air conditioner and the muffled roar of New York traffic.

It was her mother. Moaning.

She got up, turning on her light, running down the once familiar but now strange and distant hall. A hall she grew up in—getting up to take a pee in the middle of the night, getting a drink of water, coming into her parents' room when she was scared. Now here she was, hurrying to see what was wrong with her mother.

The moan was a low, lost sound.

She reached her mother's door and hurried to her bed.

"Mom . . . Mom, what's wrong? What is it?"

Her mother coughed. Gobs of spittle flew out uncontrollably. Erica put a hand behind her mother's head. "Mom, can I get you something?"

More spasms, more coughs, terrible barking things that threatened to shake the old woman to pieces. Finally her mother opened her eyes, returning from some grim trip.

Her eyes opened on Erica. Old eyes. Eyes that have seen their world together grow, change . . .

"My medicine," she said hoarsely, tilting her head slightly to the left. And Erica quickly found the prescription container. It took forever to open. The damn lock-caps. Then it popped off. Her mother's hand was out, eagerly awaiting the pills.

She took two, still heaving and choking in the bed. Erica held her close.

"I had no idea you were this sick, Mom. I thought everything was fine."

A few more spasms and then, a storm passing, they stopped. Her mother looked up. "Oh, I'm okay, Erica. I just have these attacks. At night. Something to do with my lungs filling . . ."

Erica knew she wasn't being told the whole truth.

She thought: *I'll call the doctor myself tomorrow.*

"It's just very painful, sweetheart. That's all. Nothing to worry about."

She nodded, letting her mother's head fall back onto the pillow. Why did people always lie about their health? *I'm fine . . . got only a week to live, but otherwise everything's just hunky-dory. . . .*

"Get some rest, Mom. We'll talk tomorrow."

Erica backed out of the room. *Why this?* she wondered. *And why now?*

It's fate, girl, she told herself. *Redirecting my energies. Whether I want them redirected or not.*

She half-shut her mother's door and headed back to her room.

And stopped.

Perhaps she'd look in on Josh.

Such a quaint and motherly thing to do.

(Knowing she wouldn't dream of doing it in New York. He was independent. Her young man. That umbilical cord had long been cut.)

But why not?

She turned back for the room at the end of the hall.

It used to be her room, and it still bore the battle scars of her youth. Boys' names written on the pink-flowered wallpaper. Some dolls wrapped in plastic, tucked away up in the closet.

It was weird to come back to a place years later, someplace that had been important to you. It should all be the same, frozen in time. Waiting for that part of your life to just start again.

She came to the door.

It was shut.

She opened it, ever so gently.

Don't want him waking up. Wouldn't do for him to catch his mom checking up on him.

About an inch into the opening, the door creaked.

And she felt creepy, standing there in the darkness. Then she just pushed it open the rest of the way.

She saw Josh, the sheets and blanket wrapped around him mummy-style, the remarkable way he had of completely rumpling any bed no matter how tightly she tucked everything in.

His lean, bony body filled the bed.

Almost.

It didn't look quite as big as it should.

She saw the outline of the moon from behind the filmy curtains.

She took a step into the room.

The wooden floorboards creaked. Another sound out of her past.

She wanted to unravel her son a bit. Look at his face, always a beautiful thing when he slept, so peaceful, free of trouble.

But not if her motherly interests would be trumpeted by the ancient wood floor.

So she turned away and went back to her room.

When Tom Smith looked up from his coffee, his first thought was, *Oh, shit, I blew it. Now this Ward fellow subject knows he's under surveillance. And Watson is going to burn my butt.*

Then he realized that he could come up with a story to explain why he stopped here.

Oh, hi, sir, just wanted to have a gulp of coffee, warm myself up. Beautiful night, eh? And isn't that one hell of a moon?

But the surprising thing—even as he thought of that quite plausible story—was that Alan Ward wasn't coming out alone.

No, his mother—at least, Smith *guessed* it was his mother—was following him.

A regular welcoming committee.

Smith put down his cup on the passenger's seat, and got out of the car to meet Ward and his dear old mom. He put his hand on his hip, right above his gun. Gives you confidence, wearing a gun. Makes you kinda feel comfortable in almost any social situation.

"Hi, there," Smith called to them.

Smith smiled, ready to lay out his bullshit story. *What a night. . . . stopped for some java . . . Say, ain't your mom getting a bit of a chill out here?*

He didn't really see what happened next. The moon was in

his face, big and goofy bright, and Ward looked like he was wearing a Halloween mask, for all Smith knew.

It happened fast.

And Smith knew that everything he had planned—for the next few minutes—and for the rest of his life—had just gone down the toilet.

He knew that as Ward's head exploded, sending ribbony white streamers flying at him.

And they all landed—heh, heh—on Smith's face and throat.

The cop thought he said something. Like "Hey, stop that would you? Now just cut that out!" But his mouth was covered. Filled with the things. He knew that, because when he tried to talk there was nothing.

He chewed down on the ribbony things, trying to bite them away. But they were too tough. His jaw ached. He felt them worming their way down his gullet.

(No. Not all of them. Some were going up, up into his head.)

He screamed.

He heard himself scream!

There was only one problem.

The sound, all wet and hollow, came from a great flapping hole in his throat.

He got off one more scream before the hole was too clogged for anything to get in—or out.

He felt things grabbing his legs, wrapping around his calves, burrowing through his pants legs and socks. Wondering . . . *What the hell is that?*

Oh, he thought dully, *I forgot all about his mother.*

How silly of me . . .

"Hey, I do hear something," Clara said, cocking her head this way and that, standing on the very top of the hill.

"It's coming from—" She looked around once again.

Josh heard another scream cut through the still air. *God*, he thought. *It's horrible, the way it echoes off the hill . . . disappearing.*

All those summer sounds, those creepy summer sounds, stopped.

Josh stood up, feeling cold and still.

"Over there," Clara said, pointing.

She pointed just where Josh knew she would. Sure, right over there. Over there. By the cottage. By the black pickup.

Then Clara took some steps in that direction.

"Where are you going?" he snapped.

"I'm going to see if anyone needs help. *Duh*. Come on."

He felt her watching him. Waiting for him to move.

"I . . . I don't think we should. . . ."

"Josh!" she said, her voice loud, accusing him. "Somebody might be in trouble. They might need help, for Pete's sake. Now, are you coming, or not?"

No, he wanted to say. *I'm not going. This is just what I thought would happen. Yessirree! Something bad*. Like there was no way to stop it, no way to throw the brakes on this train. No way to stop this stupid movie.

The moon lit her full face, confused, wondering, *Why won't he help? What is wrong with this kid?*

Until, under the force of her super-powered blue eyes, he knew that there was only one thing he could do.

"Okay," he nodded slowly, taking a step. "Let's go."

She turned and bolted down the hill.

Josh couldn't see the cottage. It was still hidden by another hill. But he knew it wasn't far. Clara was well ahead of him, running like a deer, jumping over rocks, calling back to him to hurry.

And Josh ran. The last thing in the world that he wanted to do.

But he did it.

Clara stopped at the crest of the other hill. And he came running up to her, panting, warm now.

And he saw who was screaming.

The bear prowling the Stoneywood dump had no idea what it was looking for. He learned long ago that some things here could hurt if he just bit into them. There were sharp things here, things that made his tongue open, filling his maw with blood while he swiped at his snout trying to knock the pain away.

Still, the bear knew that there were new, wonderful tastes hidden here, under the metal, under the paper, inside all the green and white and black things.

And there was plenty for all.

Other bears claimed different parts of the dump, climbing up to their own mountain of garbage, perching there before ripping into the day's fresh deliveries.

But tonight it wasn't very crowded.

Just a few older bears with tattered pelts, none of them very near. Grunting to each other, licking at the funny tastes that collected on their snouts.

None as young and hungry as he was.

And there was something really good here. Deep though, well-down in the pile.

He started clawing his way through the topmost bag. There was nothing in it, mostly hard things that weren't any good to eat. But the smell was stronger when the bear whacked that bag out of the way.

So strong, the young bear rose up on his rear legs and honked out a warning to any others that might pick up the scent.

This is mine. *I found it*!

Whatever it was.

Then, casting one long, slow look around, the bear went down, back to his work. He opened another bag, discovering immediately that there was nothing of interest there. Then another.

Until the scent was overpowering. Wonderful.

The bear looked around. But none of the older bears were coming over to inspect this treasure. The bear sniffed the wind, unable to believe his good fortune. Then he dug deeper, until he came to a large black bag. The bear put his snout right up against it.

He sniffed deep.

That was it.

He opened his maw wide and pushed roughly against the bag, feeling something soft and mushy and wonderful inside.

He chomped down on the plastic, and tore a chunk away. The bear rolled backwards with the force of his tug.

And one of the older bears, from across the dump roared.

The smell was everywhere.

The young bear licked, tasting the wonderful wet taste, the scraps of delicious meat, the gleaming white chunks of bone just there, ready to be snapped in two.

The bear ate.

* * *

Clara grabbed Josh's hand. She squeezed it.

At first it was impossible to see what was happening. Josh saw the police car all right, and some people. But that was all.

But then he made out the policeman's uniform, his gun, and then a bit of color on his hat caught the light.

The policeman was on his knees. Writhing around like a—like a—

Like a bluefish dragged onto shore, snagged by a surfcaster. Kicking and flapping. Knowing that every second could be its last chance to get away, back to the water.

"Josh . . . Oh, God. Josh, what's happening? What's—"

The policeman was on the ground. And there were all these lines on him. Like he was playing with a ball of yarn. Lines leading to the other two people.

And Josh knew where he had seen it before . . . just a little while ago. In his sketch.

I drew it, he thought, sickened by the idea. Sickened, and frightened.

He saw the policeman's body kick a bit, and then it was still. The lines fell from him.

The two people turned. It was hard to see what happened next, too dark, too—

But it looked like the lines disappeared right into their bodies.

"Oh, shit," he said.

"Josh," she whispered. "We gotta go. We gotta—"

He nodded. Took a step backwards.

And then . . .

Just a few feet from the protective cover of the crest of the hill . . .

The two people turned away from the policeman and looked up at Clara and Josh. And the moon caught their faces. Changing. Like open sores, all wet and pulpy. Changing. Into a mouth. Nose.

And eyes.

"Oh, no," Clara moaned.

She pulled Josh back.

The people looked up at them. And started moving towards them.

"Run!" Clara screamed, turning, pulling Josh with her. "*Run!*"

And he ran as hard as he could, pumping up the hill, running right towards the moon.

He stumbled once on the way up, twisting his ankle, but he scrambled up and hobbled a few steps until the stinging stopped.

Still, Clara held on. Pulling at him. Begging him to, *please, hurry.*

Let me wake up, he thought. *Let me wake up and have this a dream so I can smile and say,* "Boy, I'm glad that's over. I'm glad *that* was only a dream."

He heard a truck engine start.

"The pickup!" he said, just as they reached the hill.

"What?"

"The pickup. The truck. They're *coming* for us in the truck."

And he watched Clara's face as she too heard the rumble of the engine in the perfect quiet of the hill.

The bear growled, a piece of the meat still dangling from his teeth. He would eat all of this, he had decided.

All of it.

And he would kill whatever came near and tried to get some.

He chewed a particularly tough piece. Some small bones crunched. Too many bones, and the bear spit the piece out.

Off to the side.

Where something was watching him.

The bear roared and spun around. He was ready to attack. He raised one paw, claws extended, ready to slash at a belly or a throat.

But it was just a small animal staring at the bear. Watching the bear eat. Small. With berry eyes and a great curl of fur behind it. A small animal.

The bear gave a chew.

Confused by this small animal.

The bear roared.

But the animal sat there. It hopped closer, blinking its berry eyes.

The bear sensed something wrong. He'd never seen such a small animal come close like this. The bear licked his maw, the taste now, somehow, not as sweet.

Another hop, and the animal with the bushy tail and small pointy ears was right next to the bear.

Something in its eyes warned the bear.

Too late.

The small animal popped, like some of the cans the bear would bite into. Stringy pieces of the animal erupted at the bear, holding onto him. The bear howled and then honked out a great roaring moan.

And the other bears answered it.

But when the bear tried to pull away, he found himself pinned to the bag of meat, writhing around.

While something terrible happened.

The bear blinked his eyes. They watered from the pain.

(And the other bears stopped their eating and slowly backed away into the woods, grunting low to the ground. Knowing that for tonight, at least, they'd best stop searching for food.)

Clara tripped over a rock.

"Damn," she said, tumbling down hard.

Josh heard her leg smack into the ground. "You okay?" he asked, helping her up.

She nodded.

"Do you still hear the truck?"

He nodded.

Now, Clara—brave, fearless Clara—looked scared.

"What are we going to do?"

Josh looked around. He said, "Where does that road go? The one by the cottage?"

"Mountain Road? Down towards Route 133."

"And 133?"

"It goes to town and—"

"Does it come up this way?"

"No . . ." she said. "Not unless—"

She stopped, biting her lip.

"Not unless what?"

She turned away. "Not unless you take the road up to your grandmother's."

Josh looked over his shoulder.

If someone was following them, clambering up hill behind them, they'd appear soon.

He kept watching the hill, waiting for the outline of a body to appear. Praying that nothing would happen.

He counted to ten.

One. Two. Three . . .

Eighteen

. . . TEN!

Josh took a breath. "I don't think they're following us."

Clara nodded and said, "What are we going to do?"

"We're going to run back to my house. And watch that no one drives up here."

He tore off, and Clara jogged alongside. His right ankle still felt wobbly. Each step threatened to send him flying to the ground. But as they came to Barrow's Hill he found the trail they had blazed through the tall grass.

In the farmhouse, the living room light was still on. And for a moment his only fear was that they might have discovered he was missing. He started up the hill.

Clara grabbed his arm, stopping him. "Hey, what are you doing?"

"I'm going to wake up my mother and tell her what happened. What do you think I'm going to do?"

Clara shook her head.

"You can't do that. Do you know what kind of trouble you'll get into? And me? Christ, I'll be grounded forever. You just can't do it."

Josh looked over his shoulder. The wind blew his hair.

"I gotta, Clara. What if that cop's hurt? What if he needs help?"

"But, God, Josh. Don't you know what will happen to me? My old man is just looking for some excuse to lock me up inside that house."

She turned away from him.

He heard her crying. "For Pete's sake, Clara, don't—"

"You don't know. Oh, it's easy for you, easy—"

He touched her arm. And let his hand rest there.

"I'll tell them I was alone. I'll say I was out by myself. And I saw what happened. Alone."

Slowly, she turned back to him. "But then you'll get into trouble. You'll—"

"Hey, don't worry about me. I'm new at this. I have a ways to go before my mom starts thinking about reform school. But what are you going to do?"

"I-I'll go home."

And Josh thought of the pickup. The quiet, sleeping streets of Stoneywood. The stoplight where no one stops. From down in the barn he heard the horse snort and whinny, the sound clear and close.

"Do you want me to come with you?" he asked slowly.

Clara shook her head. "You'd better tell them now."

"Stay off the roads," he said. "And stay out of sight. If anything happens—*anything*—go to someone's house and get help. You hear me?"

She nodded.

"I'll meet you tomorrow morning," she said. "If you can get out. In front of the library."

And then—completely unexpected—Clara leaned forward and kissed him on the cheek. Then she turned and ran down the hill.

Josh reached up and touched the small wet spot made by her kiss.

The wind blew the grass around his feet.

He looked over his shoulder one more time.

And then he walked up to the farmhouse.

Johnson flipped down the heavy wood cover, latching it tight. His Knock 'em Down cats, little clownish guys that couldn't get knocked down unless you caught them just so, were all fluffed up and ready to trap the suckers of Stoneywood. The gag never failed to work.

"Looks pretty easy to me," the rubes would say, strolling past the game. They always figured that something had to be wrong with everyone else who played it. No matter how many times they'd watch people blow it, they figured that *they* had the answer.

Sure.

And as long as the stooges went on thinking that way, carny gags would always work.

He turned around.

And he saw Jim. Walking around in the darkness.

The days of the carnival freak—the two-headed boys, the lady who eats glass, the pin-headed man—were over. No more disturbing monsters for the normal folk to gawk at, reassuring them that they were okay. *Hey, I'm not like him. I've only got one head. I'm not a half-man, half-woman. I've got legs. I've got fingers!*

I don't have four tits! I'm not three feet tall!

Yeah, those days were pretty much all gone.

Johnson had read up on the whole thing, the whole history of sideshows and midways. And he'd heard about some sideshows that still toured. In the small towns down South. In the mountain towns and the dust bowl shitcans. Where you could still find people ready to come out and see a nice collection of freaks.

Johnson tugged on the wood cover one more time. Like most carny games, it was his gag. He owned it. And if anything happened to it, it was out of his pocket.

He kept an eye on Jim.

No freaks here. No, the closest to a freak was Jim, the Pardone Brothers' Bozo. A buck for three balls, and a chance to knock the cretin into a tub of water.

Johnson leaned against his stall and lit a cigarette. It was late—too fucking late—but Jim's little show was worth a few minutes of his time.

As a student of the thing.

Jim's setup was one complicated chunk of metal. Heavy, a real bitch to get together, all those metal mesh flaps. But Jim did it by himself. Setting up his cage, then positioning the drop chair over the water basin. (He'd fill that tomorrow and let it go smelly and stale for three days until it was disgusting.) And then he checked the ladder leading to the chair.

All so he could taunt the locals into paying for the privilege of knocking his ass into the water.

Johnson had watched him set up dozens of times. That was no big deal.

But he never tired of watching old Jim walk around, prowl really, all around his setup, muttering to himself—practicing his routine—with a quiet little voice that sounded like it was ready to scream right out of control.

"Hey, *rube*! What's the matter, hay-brain?" he whispered, talking to himself. "Afraid you can't hit me? I'm *right* here, four-eyes! And how'd an ugly thing like you get such a nice-looking honey?"

The weirdest part had to be seeing old Jim leer in the dark. Leering at nobody.

Back and forth, walking around outside his Rube Goldberg torture machine. In the middle of the night. Talking to himself.

A modern-day geek . . .

He might as well be biting the heads of chickens.

Christ, what a sicko.

Of course, I'm a paragon of respectability, Johnson thought. *Sure. The Master of the Knock 'em Down.*

"Ain't you tired, big guy?"

"Huh," Johnson said, startled, turning around.

Jim looked over at him then, aware that someone had been eavesdropping on him, and hurried away.

"What are you doing out here, all by your lonesome, Johnson?" Pat asked.

Johnson smiled at her. She was new, and Johnson was aware that she'd had her eyes on him for the past three towns. And though she wasn't exactly unappetizing, with blond hair—of a sort—and a face that didn't look too bad with a solid coating of makeup, Johnson was being cautious.

Women were bad news in a traveling show. People fell in and out of lust all the time, and mostly everyone grabbed as much ass inside and outside the carnival as possible. Except it could make for some real problems. Guys got their balls cut off by jealous bitches. And some people didn't appreciate it when you slept with their floozy of the month.

So he'd learned a long time ago—about the time he realized that he'd found his niche, his home, in carnivals—to just take his time. See which way the wind was blowing.

She came closer to him.

"What'sa matter? Cat got your tongue?"

This one certainly knew how to turn a phrase.

"No, just finished setting up."

Pat looked at his stall. "Got all your kitties sitting up nice and straight, huh?" She looked up at him. "All done for the night?"

Johnson nodded.

She winked at him, and licked her lips. Nice and subtle. "Me, too. Now, how about you . . . and I . . . go for a little walk?" She touched a hand to his cheek.

He smiled back. It was fun watching her attempts at coyness. "Well, I don't know. I'm kinda tired . . . for a walk."

Pat's eyes took on a desperate look. Hungry. She let her hand trail down from his cheek, down his sweaty denim shirt. "You know, Johnson, I think I've been real patient with you." Her hand kept trailing down, past his belt.

Real coy . . .

"And I don't think I should have to wait anymore."

She squeezed him then. And even though he had on heavy denim jeans, real tough Levis that he could wear day after day until they had a life of their own, he had to admit that her hand felt nice, grabbing him there.

He grinned.

He touched her cheek. Brought a finger to her lips.

What the hell, he thought, pulling her close.

It would be a shame to let this great moonlight go to waste.

And he kissed her. Her mouth was sloppy, wet, and all over him.

While out of the corner of an eye he saw Jim, across the carnival grounds, walking around, still talking to himself, watching them.

Crazy as a loon . . .

It wasn't too hard staying off the streets.

That was easy, Clara thought. She knew all the yards and secret paths that led to the mountain, or cut over to the lake, or, at Halloween, snaked up to the back of the graveyard.

Except that after fifteen minutes of walking, and looking over her shoulder, and walking some more with her heart thumping so loud, Clara knew she had to go on the street.

Just for a bit.

There was nothing else she could do. She *had* to cross Faith Avenue.

Then she could work her way past Grant's Market, past the dumpsters (where she knew there had to be rats), into people's backyards . . . and *damn*!

She didn't think she could do it.

It would be simpler, she told herself, to just cross the one block and walk—

(No, run—)

Just as fast as she could to her house. Staying on the sidewalk.

(*And I'll worry about my father when I get home.*)

Yes, she thought. *That's what I'll do. Nobody is around.*

She ran down to the road, leaving the sprawling field at the bottom of Barrow's Hill.

It was quiet.

There's nothing, she thought. No cars. No trucks. Nothing. She hurried to Faith Avenue.

Something clicked.

The stoplight down by the bank changed from green to yellow then red.

Clara saw that everything was closed.

Even her father's favorite place.

Sheehan's.

She ran across the street.

(The sound of her sneakers so loud, too loud. Flapping so noisily on the pavement. *Damn, why am I so lead-footed?*)

She tried landing on the balls of her feet, but it felt so awkward.

Another click. The light changed again.

She kept on running.

Down her block.

Then there was another sound, even as the darkness of the old trees swallowed her.

A car, she hoped. Zooming out to the diner, or to the 7-Eleven out on 133. *Gimme a slurpee. And some nachos with cheese.*

But it wasn't a car.

Too deep. Too low.

She walked faster.

A few houses still had their lights on, and she remembered what Josh had said. If anything happened, go to someone's house.

The sound was closer. Was it coming up Faith Avenue?

It was a truck sound. She knew that now. No doubt about it. It was a truck.

"Oh, God," she whispered. Not that she believed in any god. Not really. She gave that up a long time ago, with Santa

Claus, and the Tooth Fairy. She knew that if she was going to get through all this, it wasn't God's doing.

Still, it was better to be talking to someone.

The truck sound stopped.

Was it at the light?

Then the engine revved up, and was coming towards her.

She ran the rest of the way to her house, not caring what it sounded like or if anyone looked out their window at her. And then around to the back, trailing along the fence that was ready to slip to the ground. Stepping on dry, overgrown grass that needed cutting weeks ago. Around to the back door. Opening it. Expecting to hear the TV.

She went in fast. Breathing hard. Her heart thumping even louder.

It was quiet.

She looked at the clock: 12:45.

Her mother wouldn't be home. Not yet.

Why was the TV off? Her father never shut it off. Never. He just fell asleep there, plopped in front of it, a beery beached whale. A drunken couch potato.

(*And I know what you want, Dad. I know.* . . .)

Where was he?

She stopped gently now, tiptoeing through the tiny kitchen. To the hall.

She edged herself forward so as to just peek in at the king's seat, the big tattered easy chair, its cracks and furrows filled with bits of pretzel and sandwiches and cigarette butts.

She stepped closer to the shadowy living room.

And she saw the empty chair.

When Walt Johnson finished with the woman, he fought, unsuccessfully, the urge to get up off the cold ground and get away from her as fast as he could.

She had no trouble reading his sudden lack of interest.

"I've got to check the booths," Johnson half-mumbled, hoping to hell she didn't say, "check them for what?" It was not easy, this bedding down with carny bimbos. As much as they always protested that they didn't want anything more than a roll in the hay, or on the ground, somehow they tried to stick their meat hooks into your life.

And that, Johnson knew, was something he couldn't allow.

She got up and knelt on the ground, and dug out a cigarette.

He saw that she was waiting for him to give her a light. Whic
he didn't do. Best, he thought, to do nothing than to give he
any false encouragement. When she finally lit her ow
cigarette, he nodded, and said, "See you around."

"Sure," she said.

And he was away, free.

He was going to go straight to his trailer, and take
lukewarm shower. And then have a nightcap before anothe
day, like all the other days, of tempting the rubes to throw thei
money away.

But he felt edgy, unsettled. He thought he'd walk around the
grounds a bit, get some air, clear his head . . . try to forge
the unpleasant drained feeling in his pecker.

He walked past his own booth and then past the blonde'
Spot the Spot booth. Then he walked towards the right, nea
old Jimbo's shop, the Bozo stand.

He heard something. Soft, wet sounds, just on the other sid
of the booth.

More midnight fucking? he wondered, grinning a bit
Johnson stepped closer, curious about what other emotiona
freaks were getting it on tonight.

The sounds were steady, rhythmic.

He came to the corner of the great metal cage. And sur
enough, there was Jim. Standing there, rocking back and forth
like tall, reedy grass blowing in the breeze. And a man wa
kneeling in front of him.

Well, I'll be damned, Johnson thought. *Crazy Jimbo is gay
Sonovabitch* . . .

He couldn't see the man servicing Jimbo. So Johnson took a
few more steps, moving away from the corner of the cage
catching a bit of light.

And he saw who the other guy was.

Ed Stein. The carny's advance man.

Jesus, now that was incredible. Ed always talked such a
damn good story about broads. Always calling them broads
buying the town barflies drinks, bragging about his cocksman-
ship.

And now, he was kneeling there with Jim—chomping on
Jim. . . .

The sounds grew louder. Wet, sloppy, hungry.

Johnson felt a little sick to his stomach, and his head was
beginning to ache.

What the fuck, he thought. *The world's going to hell in a handcart.*

And he crept backwards, back to the shadows, back to his trailer.

"Can I get up now?" Josh asked her peevishly.

Erica shook her head.

"I've *got* to go to the bathroom," he groaned.

"Okay, go. But you get yourself right back here."

Josh got up noisily, scraping the kitchen chair across the linoleum.

What is this? Erica thought. *My husband dies, and all of a sudden I'm in the middle of* Rebel Without A Cause. *What did I do to deserve all this—?*

Shit.

She took a sip of orange juice. It tasted bitter, biting. Gone to acid.

Josh returned to the kitchen and sat down.

And they waited.

She heard a car. "There he is," Erica said. She got up and went to the window. "Thank God." The police car pulled right up to the back of the house. She quickly opened the door.

"Thank you for coming, Captain—"

"Torey Watson, Mrs. Tyler. No problem. Things tend to get a bit sleepy here. Is this Josh?"

Erica nodded.

Watson walked over, took a chair, and sat down facing Josh. *He has a nice, calm face*, Erica thought. *Peaceful and unruffled. Perfect for this town.*

The policeman said, "Well, Josh, why don't you tell me what happened."

Josh cleared his throat. "I-I, er, wanted to go out and see the full moon. Go up on the hill."

She saw Josh's face light up, like he'd just gotten an idea.

"That way I could see the town and the mountain, in the moonlight."

Watson nodded.

"And when did you get this idea?"

"I guess after the movie on TV . . . I couldn't sleep. So I thought I'd take a walk."

The Captain looked over to Erica and she shrugged. All of this was news to her.

"So what did you see?"

"Well, I heard something first. Someone calling. At least, I think that's what it was. But then it sounded more like a scream."

"And where did that sound come from?"

"Behind me, past the hill that leads to Mountain Road. Near that cottage—"

"The Ward place—" The Captain added.

Josh nodded. "That's where I saw what was going on. . . ."

"Which was?"

Erica watched her son lick his lips.

Please, she thought. *Don't let this be some story that Josh made up. Something to get attention. Please.*

Because then I got a big problem.

"I saw a police car. And three people. Someone, it was a policeman, was on the ground. He was making sounds—I dunno—like he was in pain. The other two people stood over him, like they were doing something to him."

Watson nodded again, then squinted at Josh, not understanding.

"Doing something? Like what, Josh?"

Josh clenched his fists. He looked at Erica.

"I couldn't tell. It was too dark. He looked tied up. But when they were done, the man on the ground didn't move anymore . . . and they looked up at—"

His voice caught for a second.

Erica detected his attempt to catch a word on his lips.

"At me. Then I ran away . . . I woke my mom. . . ."

She saw Watson jotting things down in a small notebook, grunting, "Uh-huh . . ." The Captain stared at the small spiral pad for a long time. Then he looked hard at her son. "Josh, I've no doubt you think you saw something out there tonight. Something . . . But even you said it was hard to see and—"

Josh shook his head. He raised his voice. "But I *heard* things too, screams and—"

"Okay, you heard sounds. But who knows what you heard, Josh? It could have been crows or people talking or—"

Josh stood up. "It was someone being killed," he said. "I know it was. Why won't you believe me?"

Erica heard another car pull up outside. A car door opened.

"You see, Josh, I know . . . because I had one of my men there all night. He was there all night. . . ."

"Then that's who it was!" Josh said, his voice rising. "That's who was attacked. It had to be—"

"Captain," Erica asked, "Could it have been—"

But Watson was shaking his head. "No, Mrs. Tyler. That's just not possible at all."

There was a knock at the kitchen door, and Erica went to answer it. A young cop walked into the small room.

"You see Tom Smith was there all night. It was his car you saw, Josh. And he saw nothing. Absolutely nothing." Watson paused, looking from Erica to Josh.

And then Watson looked at the cop.

"Isn't that right, Tom?"

Where was he?

Why wasn't he passed out in front of the tube?

She thought of calling for him then. Better to know where he was. Instead of guessing.

Dad. Where are you? Don't fool around with me, Daddy. Not now. Not when it's dark and I'm scared and—

(I can't get my knife.)

She walked down the tiny hall to the stairs, looking all around.

All empty and quiet.

Clara backed up.

Almost to the stairs.

Almost.

She backed up another step.

And bumped into someone.

Clara spun around.

Ready to say, O*h, Daddy. I didn't see you, didn't hear you. Why aren't you watching TV? What are you doing?*

(In the dark. Standing there. Watching me.)

Except, when her mouth fell open, she saw it wasn't her father.

It was her mother.

"Mom," she said, relief rushing out of her like a balloon losing air.

"Mom, I didn't know where Dad was. . . . I—"

Her mother took the last step down.

None too steadily.

And Clara wondered . . .

What is she doing here? She shouldn't be home, not this early, not yet.

Clara backed up.

"Wh-where's Daddy?"

"Your father . . ." her mother said slowly, "is . . . resting." She tilted her head. "Upstairs."

Clara nodded.

What's wrong? she wondered. *Why is she home? And why does she seem sort of sick? Her voice so low. Like she has a sore throat. A cold. Something.*

Her mother took another step, and she landed on the floor unsteadily. She brought a hand up to the wall, steadying herself.

She's drunk, Clara thought. *She's home early and drunk.*

Her mother looked at her, blinking. In the half-light, with ugly long slices of the reflected moon cutting into the hallway.

Clara saw her mother swallow. As though something were wrong with her throat. Her mother opened her mouth.

Clara shook her head.

"Mama . . . what's wrong . . . ? What's . . ."

Her mother leaned against the wall, palms flat against the dingy brown wallpaper. Her eyes closed.

"I'm going to bed, Mama," Clara said. She took a step on the stairs. Another. "Maybe you should rest too. Maybe you're tired. . . ."

Clara turned and walked up the stairs, thinking, over and over—

I have to get out of here.

She went to her door.

(Stopping just a fraction of a second, to listen if her father was there, crouching like a monkey in the dark, ready to spring at her.)

She went into her room and shut the door.

She went to her dresser and picked up the key. She took it to the lock, stuck it in the keyhole, and turned it.

("Never lock your door!" her father had screamed. "Never! You hear me?")

She tested it.

Then Clara went back to her bureau.

And took out the knife. Gleaming, clean. But heavy in her hands. Especially now, especially after tonight. She was so tired. Her whole body hurt. And Clara took the knife over to her bed. She sat on her bed and wedged it into the space between the frame and the mattress.

Then she lay back and tested whether she could easily grab the knife.

She reached down. Felt for it, the ribbed handle all bumpy and large.

Then she reached to the other side of her bed. A faded doll sat there, once pretty but now just warm and familiar. *But I love that doll*, Clara thought. *I'll never let her go.*

She pulled her blanket around her.

Staying dressed. Keeping the light on.

Listening to the sounds.

In the streets. In her house.

"Thanks, Tom. I guess you can go home now. Won't be much to see there tonight."

The young cop made a coughing noise.

"You okay? This night work giving you a cold?"

Smith nodded. His voice had sounded strained and hoarse on the radio. And now Watson saw that his deputy wasn't saying much. Pretty damn quiet.

He even walked a little sluggishly.

"Get home, Thomas, and let that new wife of yours take care of you."

"Yes, Captain," Smith said, turning back to his car.

And as Watson saw him pull away, he thought of the odd story the boy told. Very odd. But it might be of some interest to that Navy fellow, McShane.

Even if nothing did happen.

Too late now to call him, of course.

But first thing in the A.M.

He got into his patrol car.

Yes, after he got some good shut-eye . . .

It was a dream.

She knew that.

Knew it!

But it didn't help.

Her parents sat in two straight chairs, sitting stock-still, looking at her, lying in bed.

And in the dream Clara tried to get up, to ask them, *Hey, guys? What are you doing? What's going on?*

And, as she tried to move, she felt them.

The tiny threads that crisscrossed her bed, over and over, thousands and thousands of them. Holding her fast to the mattress.

Everything, except her head.

That, she could move, and turn around . . . twist this way and that.

(Now she tried to wake up. Telling herself, *It's just a nightmare. Just a dumb nightmare. That's all.*)

But the dream paid her no mind.

The threads tightened, pulling the thin sheet tight against her body.

Her father stood up.

Her mother stood up.

She screamed: *No. Go away! What are you going to do?*

But they just stood there and did nothing.

She heard a skittering on the floor. Tiny scraping sounds. She strained to look over the cliff of the mattress. To see what was making all those sounds, all those little tapping sounds.

She felt movement.

The things making the funny sounds were climbing onto the bed—

(Her parents smiled at her.)

—Climbing higher, until the first one was on top of the bed. It was a spider. Not so big. Not so different from the hundreds of other spiders she'd seen and been terrified of.

"I hate spiders," she explained to everyone. "Just hate 'em."

And of course everyone teased her about them.

But this lone spider paused. Its forelegs twitched in the air. As if sensing her.

Then the rest of them were there.

Row after row of spiders, pushing each other out of the way, climbing over each other, streaming on top of her trapped body, spreading along the web of lines, moving onto her face. Grabbing at a lock of hair. Jumping at her cheek. Creeping close to her eyeball.

Her parents laughed.

She screamed. Wondering . . .

Maybe it isn't a dream. Maybe—

* * *

She screamed.

Awake at last.

She breathed in and out, fast, over and over.

Her blanket was wrapped completely around her. Her legs were imprisoned and one arm was stuck.

How loud a sound had she made?

Had she really screamed? Or had it only been a tiny gasp?

She listened.

Kicking the blanket away.

Because immediately Clara wondered what had awakened her.

It couldn't have just been the dream.

She heard steps.

"No . . ." she whispered.

Two people.

"No . . . Please . . ."

She let go of her doll.

The steps stopped outside her door.

"No . . ."

Eyes locked on the door (so glad she'd left her light on!) she reached over the side of the bed. And she felt around for the bumpy blade. Her fingers crawled along the crack, probing, digging.

Finding nothing.

"No . . ." she whispered.

She thought . . . *What's wrong with my mother? Why is she letting him do this? Why?*

A sound. The click of the door handle being turned.

Slowly, then gaining speed, until—

It caught. Then it rattled back and forth angrily.

Open, goddammit! she could imagine her father saying. *Now you open up this fucking door, missy, or I'll just have to break it down.*

Now!

She flapped at the side of the bed, digging around. Had the knife fallen through, tumbling to the floor? And what would happen if her father found it?

"Oh . . . please . . ." she whispered.

Then, as if in a game of hide-and-seek, her fingers stumbled upon it—just a bit farther away than she thought.

She pulled it up, breathing in fast.

Ready.

The doorknob rattled again.

And there was quiet.

Come on, she thought. *I'm ready now. Come on. Better this than waiting every night—every night—for you to play your games again.*

Come on.

But the steps moved away. No talking. No cursing. No threats.

Just away.

And Clara lay there.

All night.

She listened. She waited. She saw the moon vanish.

And she saw the black sky lighten to a deep blue.

It was Friday.

Carnival Day.

Emperor Two

"Get the fuck out of here," Wilson muttered.

Aguerra snapped his gum, a staccato pop, and grinned at him. "You having some kind of problemo, Wilson?"

Wilson held the wall-strap tight. After climbing steadily for fifteen minutes, the pilots had the Sikorsky banking like they were going to strafe the fuckin' glacier.

"Jeezuz!" Wilson said. "What the hell are they doing?"

"Who knows, man? Just sit back and enjoy the ride."

Wilson shook his head. The snowcats, big Johnson Skee-Horses modified for the worst the Antarctic could throw at them, pulled against their chains. If one came loose, it would rip a hole right through the chopper.

Then the Sikorsky leveled out a bit, and Wilson felt his stomach plop back into place. *It's okay*, he thought. *We're doing fine, just fine.*

He knew what was happening. McMurdo was at sea level, while Ice Box Station, right near the pole, was nearly 10,000 feet above sea level. Almost two fucking miles! As if it wasn't cold enough.

The copter's cabin was warm now, two giant exhaust ports pumping out engine-heated hot air. But Wilson heard the pinging sound of the snow squalls outside. He couldn't see shit. It was pitch dark out there—the long southern night, and no moon due for another hour or so.

The Sikorsky started bumping around in the air, creaking noisily. Wilson grasped the strap even tighter. The engines—just past the metal bulkhead—whined even more urgently.

There were more bumps, and the snowcats pulled against their cables. But then the chopper started losing altitude.

Aguerra popped a bubble.

"We're going down," Aguerra grinned. "Don't lose your mittens."

The pilots were moving her fast. Wilson knew that there was just too much wind to chance a leisurely cruise across the Antarctic plateau. Somewhere around here they were crossing Scott's trail. Right over the place he and his party of four hauled heavy sleds to the pole and back.

Almost.

The chopper dropped some more altitude.

He plastered his face against the tiny cabin window and saw the brilliant tungsten lights of the chopper, pointed straight ahead and down. Picking up the waves of sastrugi, frozen icy breakers, a sea of crusty ice that could cut through your boots or split the tracks of a snowmobile. No such problem with the SkeeHorses. They had rubbery tracks made out of a polymer that even a chainsaw would have trouble cutting through. There were twin tracks—the machine could move with just one. And on the gleaming rows of metal cleats, every fifth one on the tracks was an ice cleat.

A three-inch pick that could chop into the ice and hold on.

The chopper turned sharply to the left.

"What the—?" Wilson said.

Aguerra shrugged.

The pilot's door opened.

Captain Finch staggered out, arms stretched to either wall, bracing himself as he lumbered back to them.

"We're near the spot," he yelled. "We're trying to find some place to put the chopper down." Finch smiled, as if this was good news. "Shouldn't be long now, guys."

Wilson nodded.

The chopper suddenly banked the other way, nosing around the icy plateau like a dog sniffing out a bone.

As Finch started back to the pilot's cabin the chopper did a complete turn, a maneuver possible only in a turbine-powered machine. Somehow the props and the rotor kept the thing in the air while it turned dead around. And Finch was thrown to the ground. He rolled hard into one of the snowcats.

Aguerra grinned.

Then they felt the chopper coming down fast.

(And damned if the ice pinging against the cabin didn't sound even louder. What was it doing out there?)

The chopper crunched down onto the ice, and tilted—just a bit. The pilots cut the engine. Wilson undid his seat belt and hurried over to Finch. "Okay, sir?" he said, extending a hand to the officer. Finch took his hand to get up, and rubbed the back of his head.

"Fine," he said. "Just knocked around a bit. Let's get moving."

Then they moved quickly. Wilson made sure that his parka and hood were fastened, with not even the tiniest crack open to the wind and ice. Aguerra was already unstrapping the snow-cats. They normally had tinted shields to give some relief from the icy glare, but these were fitted with clear Plexiglas.

Wilson didn't open the door until both SkeeHorses and their pallets were ready to be rolled outside. The two pilots showed up, dressed for a nice stroll on the Antarctic plateau.

"We left the control panel and automatic temperature switches on," one of the pilots said through a small opening in his parka. "She should be okay until we get back."

"Good," Finch said, looking at the two unwieldy snowcats, now free of their restraints. "Hope to hell someone gassed these up," he joked.

No one laughed.

"Okay," Finch said, gesturing first to Wilson and then to Aguerra. "Let's get them out of here."

The fatal moment arrived. Wilson reached over and opened the cabin door. Like a thousand tiny invaders, a miniature tornado, swirls of icy specks flew into the cabin. The whistling howl was even louder than the engines.

"Come on," Finch ordered. "Let's move it!"

The cat was dead weight until they could get it outside and start the engine. But after everyone started pulling and pushing on it, it started sliding across the metal floor to the open cabin door. A flat ramp led down to the ground. As the cat popped its nose out of the chopper Wilson hopped outside, into the maelstrom, ready to guide it out. The snow crunched dryly under his feet.

"Okay," he yelled. "Come on! Ease her out. . . ."

And they did. But much too fast. The snowcat came out at an angle, then picked up momentum. It was sliding down the ramp sideways, heading right towards Wilson.

He pushed back at it, nearly half a ton of metal sliding on top of him.

"Shit!" he screamed. "Grab it! Grab the fuck—"

They must have done just that. The cat slid a bit more towards him, then stopped. When Wilson finally peered over the precariously balanced cat he saw Captain Finch and the rest holding onto it for dear life.

"Would you mind straightening . . . out . . . her nose . . . a bit?" Aguerra grunted, obviously bearing the brunt of the cat's weight. Wilson snapped out of it and pushed at the snub-nosed vehicle, getting it pointed straight down the ramp.

"Okay!" he yelled. And they lowered the SkeeHorse onto the snow. They all hopped out of the chopper to move it to the side. They quickly got the other snowcat out. Then came the moment of truth.

"Ready when you are," Aguerra said to Wilson. Aguerra was sitting behind the wheel of his cat, like it was a Kawasaki 750. One of the pilots got on behind him. Wilson got behind the controls of his snowcat followed by Finch and the other pilot.

Finch looked at a digital compass and checked the laminated charts of their position. "Due east," he yelled. Then he signaled the direction to Aguerra. "Three miles."

Wilson nodded. *Where is Ice Box?* he wondered.

I thought we were going to Ice Box.

He looked at the chopper. It was the only point of light out here. There were clouds overhead—or maybe just the ever-present snow squalls. He turned on the twin headlights, powerful lights that you could see from five miles away.

Except here. With the lights pointed ahead, visibility was about fifteen feet.

And shit, Wilson thought, what kind of unknown crap were they going to plow over?

Finch tapped his shoulder, and Wilson turned around. The Captain signaled them to start their engines.

Wilson nodded. The dials were all lit, looking ready and eager to work no matter how fucking cold it was.

He turned the switch.

And, amazingly enough, the engine started.

This was crazy. Totally crackers.

He couldn't see anything coming at him until it was already there. He ploughed into a couple of icy walls, stopping the cat dead before the tracks finally clawed their way over the hummocks. There were pits covered with crusted snow, thin caps that gave way just as soon as the cat hit them. Most of them—so far—had been small, small enough that the cat flew over them before being gulped down.

But all the icy hills played hell with the SkeeHorse's control. The center of gravity went haywire, and there were times Wilson thought the cat was going to flip right over.

He tried to take it slow. But Finch yelled in his ear to keep hauling ass. An order is an order, and Wilson obeyed by reaching down to the throttle on the right and opening it up. He pressed his feet against the ribbed running board.

Let Finch worry about hanging on.

Finch, in the classic gaffe of the inexperienced passenger, bumped his head against Wilson's back—a nasty bang.

Aguerra was ahead of him. An ice cowboy.

Gonna lose his ass if he ain't careful.

Finch tapped his shoulder again.

"It's close . . . real close!"

Wilson nodded. The engine sounded okay, coping with what? Thirty below? Forty below? Thank God it was so fucking dry.

He hit a pile of loose snow, rare on the plateau, and the cat churned it into the air, adding to the flurry. It got deeper.

And Finch signaled him to stop.

As prearranged, Wilson blinked his lights, telling Aguerra to cool it.

The loose deep snow was the clue. It had to be done by digging, excavating through the mile-deep ice floor.

They were here.

Wherever . . .

"Should I kill the engine, sir?"

Finch nodded. The lights were left on. Wilson watched the Captain look all around, then back at his chart. "It's got to be right here," he yelled. "Got to be."

What? Wilson wanted to say.

Aguerra walked up to them, his moustache coated in white. His mouth still moving up and down, chewing gum.

Finch asked, "Can we use these—" The wind bellowed,

swallowing his question. He waited until it quieted a bit. Then, again—

"Can we move these lights?" he asked, tapping the twin headlights.

Wilson nodded and tilted the lights right and left.

Finch took them and began a slow crawl, sweeping from the left of the snowcat.

We can't see shit, thought Wilson. He looked at the warm glow of the instrument panel on the SkeeHorse. *Let's bag it*, he thought. *Let's call it a day for this fucking expedition. No luck. Too bad. Now, let's hustle back to McMurdo and catch a few baseball games on tape.*

Ain't nothing like watching three Dodger games in a row, zapping through the commercials.

But Finch completed one arc. He started another, and then stopped. "There it is!" he yelled. "Over there." He pointed. "See it?"

All Wilson could see was a great chunk of upended ice and a wall of swirling snow. But then, looking down, he saw something darker. An opening in the plateau.

And only about twenty feet away.

Lucky us.

Finch was already unpacking rope, ice hammers, and tungsten lamps for their belts. Behind each SkeeHorse was a pallet.

Filled with empty body bags.

Wilson took the rope from Finch and strung it through his belt. He also took one of the lamps, switched it on. He swung it left and right, jiggling it. The beam was nice and strong . . . wouldn't want it to give out somewhere out there. No way. He strapped the lamp to his belt.

Finch handed him an ice pick, which he also strapped to his belt. Then, after checking everyone, the Captain took the lead and marched them away from the snowcats.

The ground was jagged, and Wilson felt like an ant walking over the teeth of a saw. Up and down, not too fast. A tumble here could rip his parka or the thermal leggings.

The Captain reached the hole first and signaled everyone to surround it, pooling their light. Damn, all Wilson wanted to do was get the hell out of there. He reached the lip, stomped down to make sure of his perch, and then took a look-see.

Under the lamps, the dark red stains showed brightly.

"Shit," he said.

What was fucking blood doing here? And where were the bodies? How many were down there, and where the fuck were they?

Then Finch gave them the bad news.

He pointed down.

They were going into the hole.

"Goddam it," Wilson muttered to the wind, knowing that the officer wouldn't hear.

Finch took the first step, real tentative, checking the ice. The hole was about twelve feet in diameter, and a lip ran inside it, an icy walkway made by the poor bastards who came before them.

But where the hell did it lead to?

The icy lip held. Finch took out his ice hammer, waved it for everyone else to get the idea. Then he took another step, deeper into the pit.

The deeper they went, the more it narrowed.

Wilson looked at the walls, clear, opalescent, with a bluish tinge. Here and there were more streaks and dabs of red. Whose blood? Wilson wondered. Preserved. Forever. *With every step, we're looking at ice that's another thousand years old*. Step. *It's the time of Christ*. Step. *King Tut*. Step. *Party time in Ancient Sumer*. Step. Step. Step.

And always the ice looked the same. As hard as any stone on the planet. Had someone blasted their way down? or cut through the ice with chainsaws? Whatever had been done, they must've had a bitch of a time getting through this shit. And what were they looking for? What the hell could be this far down?

Finch stopped. He backed up a step, pushing against Wilson.

Wilson felt his balance go. He started to slip off the lip, tumbling into the hole. He pulled his ice hammer off his belt and swung it as hard as he could into the wall.

He kept tilting away.

The hammer hit the ice, a noisy thud. And it held.

Finch was still inching back a bit.

What the fuck is he doing? Why doesn't he just keep—

But then he could see over Finch's shoulder.

It was the bottom of the ice pit. A flat slab of stone.

And on top of the stone, just ahead—just a few feet in front of them—there were the bodies. . . .

Aguerra pressed against him, trying to see.

They were split open. Neatly, right down the middle. Their bellies were open, their entrails frozen into strange shapes, modern sculptures.

"Shit, man," Aguerra whispered, real close to Wilson's ear.

Finch went a bit closer.

Come on, man, Wilson thought. *Let's just get the hell out of here.* But Finch took another step and the line went taut. He felt Aguerra behind him, pulling back. Wilson had to follow the Captain.

And he saw their faces.

He had been too preoccupied with the sick display of their splayed bodies, all open down the middle, to look at their faces.

(*Oh, shit, man, come on. Get us the hell out of here!*)

Their faces!

Finch bent down, close to one of the bodies.

(*Get away, man. Just get—the hell—away!*)

The Captain pulled out a knife, and a zip-lock plastic bag.

He scraped at the frozen entrails of one of the bodies, flicking specks of the blood into the bag. Then he took out another bag and scraped a sample of the stone on the floor. How fucking old was it? 100,000 years? A million? More?

Wilson took a step closer to Finch.

All the time watching those bodies all jumbled together.

"Captain," he said in the stillness. His voice echoed strangely. Finch kept scraping. Then, louder—

"Captain!" The officer finally looked up at him. "Do you see them?" Wilson asked "Did you see their faces?"

Finch turned back.

"Oh, God . . . What the fuck are you—" Finch looked up again.

Forget the bodies, Wilson thought. *Forget your little bags and your samples and all that shit. Yeah. Look at the fucking faces.*

Each one was just a little bit different. Here the nose was a bit off. Here the eyes didn't quite form right. And there, the chin just sort of melted into the chest. *Look at the fucking faces, asshole.*

It was the same goddam face. Like someone was trying to

make copies over and over, learning a bit more with each try, until—

Finch stood up. His hands holding the baggies were shaking.

All of them saw the faces then, staring at them, fun-house pictures of the same one face, with a scrambled surprised look. Each one just a little fucked up.

Finch stepped back from them. The wind gusted a bit differently and the pit vibrated like an organ pipe.

Finch stepped back some more.

And dropped his knife.

Nineteen

JOSH SAW HER waiting for him, alone, outside the red-brick library. She looked all around and when she finally spotted him, there was no smile. He ran up to her.

"Where were you?" she asked him.

She looked terrible. Her hair was plastered down in a funny way on her head, and her eyes were all puffy, with deep, baggy shadows hanging under them.

"What do you mean?" he said. "I came right after breakfast."

She chewed her lip—a habit of hers, Josh knew by now. She worked at her mouth like it was a piece of hamburger. "You okay?" he asked.

She looked away as if she could feel his eyes studying her.

"Sure. I just was worried about what happened. With the police and everything."

He shook his head. "Well, that was a big screw-up. You know that cop, the one we saw on the ground—or thought we saw. Well, he showed up in my house last night, looking perfectly fine."

"What?"

"I don't know what we *thought* we saw, but the cop was okay. I don't know, Clara. Maybe they were doing some drugs or something. I felt like a real a-hole."

But Clara shook her head. "No. Josh, we saw something. That guy was in trouble, he was on the ground!" She grabbed his arm.

(*She's always touching me, trying to hold on or something.*)

"He screamed. We heard him scream."

The wind gusted a bit and the enormous Carnival street sign flapped in the air. The hardware store, Gelson's, was across the street. Josh watched people go up to the door, try it, peer into the shop and then move on.

It was closed. And that was kind of funny.

Like last night.

He shrugged. "It was dark. Who knows what we saw? There was only one cop there last night, and nothing happened to him."

"Something weird is going on, I know it . . ."

Clara blinked in the bright morning sunlight. And he looked right at her. "You sure there's nothing wrong with *you*?" he said.

She tossed her head. "No!" Her eyes widened, warning him away. "Did you bring your drawing?"

Josh dug the folded piece of paper out of his pocket. He unfolded it, revealing his sketch of the fossil.

"Let's go see what it is," Clara said. *She wants to stop talking*, Josh thought.

She ran up the steps, into the small town library.

Bob O stood beside his white Lincoln Town Car . . .

Thinking.

Where the hell is everybody? Only half my damn crew shows up, and the ones that do, act like it's a freakin' holiday. Already they were at the coffee wagon, scarfing down danish and sticky buns, looking up at O'Connor.

At least we're here, their looks said. *So maybe we're not doing too much fucking work, but we're here, boss-man.*

Where the hell were the rest?

But there was one person he wondered about more than the others.

Ed Skye. Yes, good old Ed was set to help him with his special project this morning, and where the fuck was he? O'Connor called him on the car phone, ready to say, *Hey, pal, remember the five C notes I gave you? Now get your ass down to the quarry* prontissimo.

But there was no one home at Chez Skye.

Of course, I could do it myself, O'Connor thought. *Sure I could.* And as that prospect loomed more likely, he opened the trunk and hoisted out the heavy burlap satchel.

It wasn't *that* heavy, he thought. No, he could manage hauling this down the road, and then up the north face of Mount Shadow. No problem.

Except that he was just a tad nervous handling explosives on the mountainside. It wouldn't be good to slip, with all that plastic whammo dangling from his back.

No sirree, Bob.

But his plan was too brilliant to let it get hung up just because drunken Ed Skye didn't show up.

O'Connor yelled down to the foreman, a burly bulldog whom he suspected of being the workers' pal. He was too damn easy on the men.

"Yes, Mr. O'Connor," the foreman said when he'd climbed up to the Lincoln.

"Tell everyone to go home," O'Connor said. "No point in trying to get any shit done today. Any idea where everyone is?"

The foreman scratched his head.

"No sir. Could be a summer cold . . . or something."

Right. O'Connor nodded. *Thanks for the expert analysis.*

And he stood by the open car door, the large satchel at his feet, waiting for everyone to leave.

A knock on his door was the last thing Brian expected. He sat up in bed, wondering for a second, *Where am I? What am I doing here? What day is it? And why do I feel so crummy?*

All the answers fell sluggishly into place—the last one answered by the empty wine bottle. Brian got out of bed and padded over to the door. What was that nice Mrs. Simpson waking him up for? *What did I ever do to her? The rent's paid. Why can't I sleep until noon?*

He opened the door.

"Morning, Brian. Sorry if I woke you."

Captain Torey Watson looked, if anything, much too awake.

"No problem," Brian smiled. "I guess I should be getting up anyway. Come in. Have a seat," he said. The one wooden chair was acting as a drunken valet. Brian tipped the chair, sliding his clothes onto the floor.

"No, I can't stay long. Just thought that I should tell you something."

Brian's heavy eyelids opened. "Huh, what do you mean?"

Watson rubbed his chin. "I sent Tom Smith over to the Ward house."

Brian sat down on the bed. "And something happened?"

"No. At least I don't think so. But a kid, Josh Tyler, claimed he saw something."

At the mention of Josh's name, Brian came a bit more awake.

"Saw what?"

Watson walked over to Brian's window and looked outside. "The boy said he saw someone attacked, lying on the ground." He turned back to Brian. "Someone in a policeman's uniform."

"Seems like Josh Tyler is having his difficulties these days." Brian told Watson briefly about the cave incident. "Was he alone?"

"Said he was, Brian. But I don't know. . . . Anyway, Tom Smith is fine. He said nothing happened—that the Ward house was quiet as a church."

Brian looked up at the Captain. Cops can smell things, he thought. They have an instinct for when things aren't right.

Watson was not happy.

"So why are you here, Captain?"

Watson walked over to the end table, and tilted the empty bottle of wine to read the label. "How's the head?"

Brian grinned. "It's been better."

"I thought you should know, I mean since you're here to watch Alan Ward. I thought that—"

Come on, thought Brian, *out with it*.

"And I thought I'd take a run over to the Ward cottage. Take a look around. I'd feel better." Watson grabbed the doorknob. "And, I just thought I'd see if you'd like to come. . . ."

Goddammit, this was a bitch!

Hiking through the brambles and the scraggly pines at the bottom of the mountain was no problem, but carrying this sack—oh, so carefully—up the northeast slope of Mount Shadow was an absolute bitch.

But finally O'Connor reached the great stone wall.

He looked up. There was a 45-degree slope, filled with loose rubble and boulders, before the mountain veered almost straight up, a sheer wall of rock. His plan was simple. Set up a ring of explosives just at the point where the wall met the

rubble. Do enough damage to crack the wall. And then, *bango!*
*Oh, too bad. Now we've got this gigantic chunk of grade A
granite stuck out in the middle of nowhere. Now what are we
going to do with it?*

He had no doubt the Inn's board of directors would call him.
*Say, Bob? You know that plan you had? To mine the northeast
prong of the mountain? Well, there's been a nasty rockslide.
An earthquake. A real bad tremor. Can you believe it?*

(Yeah. I believe it.)

Give them a *fait accompli*. Fuck waiting for Wallace Porter
and his board. And even if the stone wall didn't crack, there
still would be a tremendous amount of loose rubble he could
pick up.

He shifted the heavy bag on his shoulder, the dead weight
slipping down. And he gingerly started climbing over the
boulders and rubble at the base of the mountain.

Steady, boy, he thought. *Nice and steady.*

The librarian, Mr. Pennyfield, didn't seem very pleased to see
Clara. He looked up at her through very thick glasses, his black
wavy hair like something out of a *Little Rascals* short. His
rubbery lips worked overtime when he talked.

"Yes," he said, some of the words honking out of his nose,
"can I help you youngsters?"

Josh grinned. *Youngsters! So that's what we are.*

Clara moved back and forth, all fidgety, like she was trapped
in the principal's office. The librarian looked as though he were
expecting a pie in his face.

Clara nudged Josh.

"Oh, yeah. I found this. I mean, this is a sketch of a fossil
I found." He handed the librarian his drawing.

"What is it?" the librarian wheezed.

Josh rolled his eyes at Clara. This guy wasn't going to be any
help. "It's a fossil. I found it out in the gorge. Do you have any
books that might tell me what it is?"

Pennyfield, looking a bit interested, handed the paper back.
"Maybe." He stood up and led them back, towards some
narrow corridors filled with the wonderful smell of books,
pressed together, the glue and paper aging, filling the small
library with their scent. Pennyfield's hands flew around,
emphasizing his every word.

"Now, this is not a *big* library," he said, looking over his glasses at Josh. "But"—he brightened—"it does have some marvelous collections. And our wonderful Natural History shelves, the Mrs. Henry C. Farp Collection." Pennyfield paused. He snorted and his nose made a fart sound, and Josh had to keep his lips tight to keep from laughing.

"Our Ornithology shelves are better than the Saratoga Library. So"—he swung back, marching to the rear of the building—"we have some fine books on fossils."

The librarian stopped in front of some dark wood shelves in a dimly lit corner. The wood was aged to a blackish-brown, with hairline cracks and open pores. Josh was sure it would be sticky to the touch.

What a great creepy joint!

There was a small table just to the left, at the place where Modern History met the Natural Sciences.

"Fossils," Pennyfield said to himself, running a practiced finger/roadster along the spines of the plastic-covered books. "Ah, here we are. From here . . . down to . . . here." He pointed to the very bottom of the shelf.

Josh nodded. "Thank you."

"Good hunting," Pennyfield said, and he disappeared down one of the narrow corridors.

"Damn!" Bob O caught himself just as his foothold slipped, rolling behind him. It was all loose rock and rubble here, the work of years of frost heaves and aging.

He caught himself with one hand, holding his bag of goodies high in the air. He took a deep breath. *I shouldn't hurry so much*, he thought. *Take my time. Wouldn't want to blow myself up, now would I, heh-heh?*

Puffing away, he looked around. This would do for the first blast. His idea was to ring the northeast base of the mountain with explosives, all timed to go off when just about the whole town would be—

Something hit his back.

"What the—"

He turned around, his heart beating like crazy. And he saw a sparrow, dazed and unconscious, lying in a crack between two rocks. *Well, I'll be!* he thought. *The stupid bird flew right into me.*

He reached down and picked up the quivering bird. Its

eyelids were slits, half-closed. Its chest was going up and down real fast.

"Well," he said, talking to the bird. "You'd better get your ass out of here soon, little guy." He put the bird off to the side. Then he unslung his pack and dug out one of the square packages of plastic explosives—in the *convenient family size*, he said to himself, grinning. He wedged it between two boulders. The timer was a simple clock mechanism attached to two brand new AA Duracells.

("For my kid's Lazer Tag gun," he'd told Al Gelson at the hardware store.)

Two copper-edged prongs were stuck into the explosives and, after he checked the timer against his watch, he pulled up the small igniter on top of the clock.

There, he thought, standing up.

Numero uno. All set and ready to blow.

Just as the good folks of Stoneywood are enjoying the carnival.

And Bob O trudged on, whistling as he walked.

The Happy Demo Man.

The books were big, heavy and intimidating.

I'm too used to my computer, Josh thought. Punch in a few words and a couple megabytes of RAM did whatever you asked. But these books expected you to come with some knowledge, some plan of attack. And though Josh knew a bit about prehistoric life and fossils, these ancient books were from another world completely.

So he did the only thing he thought he could do.

He flipped through the pages, looking at pictures.

Through *Alcott's History of the Natural World*, and *The Encyclopedia of Paleontology*, and a two-inch brick of a book called *The Fossil Guide*.

He groaned. It was going to be a long day.

And Clara still seemed fidgety. At first she looked over his shoulder, looking at the pictures, declaring this one to be "gross," and this one "weird," but then she drifted away in search of more interesting stacks. Mr. Pennyfield breezed by on a tour of inspection, acting surprised to see Josh actually bent over a book.

And Josh flipped the pages, passing chapters about prehistoric cetaceans and cockroaches up to trilobites and other overgrown invertebrates. Not for the first time, he wished he had a time machine.

From time to time, he glanced at his sketch.

Sitting right next to his book.

And he thought . . .

Something's wrong with it. It looks like the fossil, sure enough, but still, something isn't quite right.

But what?

He flipped the page.

It was a chart of the Devonian period, early dinosaurs, wacked-out plants, and dragonflies the size of eagles. Must have been fun.

He looked at his sketch.

(*Earlier. Yeah, it's got to be earlier than that.*)

He nodded. Yes, of course it was. It was something primitive, something sluglike, maybe one of those things that crawled along the bottom of the ancient sea floor, snorkeling up weird shellfish.

He touched his picture.

It's old, he thought. *Real old.*

He flipped another page.

God, there were limits to how much she'd put up with for her new friend.

Clara didn't like the library. Not at all. Pennyfield was a duck-faced creep. Even if she did feel a bit guilty about the times she and Bobby Tamm came running up the steps, pushed open the door and yelled at the librarian.

Calling him "Pennyfart."

"Hey, Pennyfart! Can you blow it out your mouth?"

And then dashing away, nearly rolling down the steps at the absolute hilarity of it all.

She grinned now, remembering how hard they laughed. It was cruel. So what?

There were a lot of cruel things in the world.

Lots.

And she thought about her plan as her eyes idly followed the line of books. . . . Ghosts, Magic, ESP . . .

She was going to run away.

(*No turning back*, she told herself. *It's . . . decided.*)

She wasn't sure where. Not yet. She knew that it wouldn't be

New York. She wasn't *that* stupid. But she wouldn't stay in that house anymore.

Something had always been screwy with her father.

(*I know what you want*, she thought every time she looked at him.)

But now her mother was acting funny.

She crossed over to the next shelf of books. Monsters. . . . Big Foot . . . Loch Ness . . .

She was going to ask Josh to hide her for a bit. If she tried to leave town she knew the cops or somebody would pick her up the same day. So, she'd ask Josh's help. To hide her, bring her some food. Maybe in his barn.

Then she'd leave. Find some kid's shelter or something. And tell them that she'd never, ever, go back to Stoneywood. She'd never go back to her parents.

She skipped over to another shelf.

And stopped.

There was book there, at the end of a stack, facing out so she could read its name and see the cover.

The Drawings of Nostradamus. She picked it up, flipped through it. And in a few minutes, she knew it wasn't about Nostradamus at all, whoever he was.

It was about people who drew pictures of things . . . before they happened.

She clutched the book in her hand and ran back to Josh.

"I'll just tell Ward that you're a visiting cop from some other town. Don't worry about it, Brian," Watson said, getting out of his car.

Brian followed the Captain, and the slam of the patrol car's doors sounded like two gunshots in the still morning.

It felt strange to be cavalierly walking up to Ward's cottage. He looked up to see if Alan and his mum were peeking out the window at them.

"Though I'll tell you," Watson added, "I can't imagine Alan doing anything odd. His father was a wonderful man, and so was his mother. Very nice, quiet people. Alan spent his summers here, went swimming in the lake with my kids." Watson looked over at Brian. "Nothing could change someone that much."

Brian nodded.

They climbed up the gravelly path to Ward's door. The black

pickup was parked along the side of the cottage, so Brian guessed that they'd be home. "You'll see," Watson said at the door. "Everything will be fine."

Watson knocked on the door.

Once. Twice.

He looked at Brian, and made a confused face.

And then he knocked again.

"Hi-ho, hi-ho, it's off to work I go. Dee dee dee deeee! Duh-dee dee dee deeee! Hi-ho, hi-hooo."

Bob O hummed and sang. *I'm like a modern Johnny Appleseed*, he thought, *planting my seeds for a new Stoneywood. A new year-round resort, with condos by O'Connor.*

Hell, it would be great for everyone. Everyone would make out like bandits.

He grinned. *Though no one will make out quite as well as me. Some of us get to be papa bears, and some of us have to be baby bears. And some of us don't even get a pot to piss in.*

He stopped, puffing from the climb. *Got to start running again*, he thought. *Maybe play some tennis. Lay off the booze and the smokes. Take care of myself so I can enjoy my new estate in life.*

He looked up at the mountain. It rose nearly straight up from here—a dark, pure granite, jutting angrily up to the sky. *Natural beauty*, he thought. *Great stuff, but it don't pay the bills, Bosco. Besides this is the new age, when everyone realizes that the planet is here for us to use, damn it. So it won't last forever.*

So what?

He turned to look the other way.

He could see part of Miller Lake, leading from Dewey State Park in the east down to the town beach. He saw some kids swimming around, enjoying the warm water. *Hey*, he thought, *I'm keeping the lake. Sure. Might get a tad overcrowded with all the new residents, but*, he thought proudly, *the lake stays.*

At least I think so.

Well, time to plant the last package, he thought. He moved two heavy rocks aside to make a depression to hold the plastic explosive. He set the timer and stepped back from it.

He took another step back.

And slipped again.

At least he thought he slipped. The rocks under his feet just gave way, and he tilted forward, sliding down the mountain face. Like tumbling dominos, other rocks below him started moving, gathering momentum. His hands slapped forward and he supported himself on all fours, sliding down doggie style.

The empty bag dangled from his back.

And all the time he kept wondering, *Is my little bomb moving? Just how volatile is that stuff? How easy can it go—ha, ha—bang?*

One foot dug into a hole while his other leg slid a few more feet. His right ankle caught in the hole and then it twisted. Harder, and harder, until . . .

(*Oh, shit, the pain! The fucking pain, going right into my foot and up my leg and, oh, damn I can't take it. I can't—*)

He felt something snap. And then he felt nothing.

Small rocks and bits of rubble kept rolling past him, some of it covering his right leg.

Where's my leg? he wondered. *Oh, Jesus!* He reached down, and touched it. *Still there. Great, it's still there!*

But why can't I feel it?

He tried moving his other leg. He shook off some of the collected rubble and dust on it. It seemed okay.

He twisted around, grunting, trying to see just where his other leg could be hiding.

(*Come out, come out wherever you are—*)

He saw it. Twisted in such a sick way that it looked like it was part of the mountain, like it belonged to someone else. It was covered by rock. He felt nothing below his thigh.

He peed then. A great wet splotch bloomed in his pants. Thinking: *Plumbing's okay. Thank God, the plumbing's okay.*

And he looked up . . .

At the small packet of explosive, sitting right where he put it. The clock ticking away.

Tick. Tick. Tick.

III

The
Mountain

Twenty

HE FOUND IT.

There was no doubt about it. Josh flipped back and forth, checking the other pages to see if there was anything else that looked even remotely like the bumpy fossil he had found and lost.

The photograph in the book was almost an exact duplicate of his sketch.

He read the description.

Stenolaemata.

Then he said the name aloud, reading the phonetic spelling. "Stee-no-lay-mata." The caption said that it was actually a colony of creatures, like modern-day bryozoans. Except that this specimen dated back to 500 million years ago.

Five hundred million years? How could a fossil that old just lie in a gorge, waiting to be found?

He jumped to the text to see what else it had to say about his find.

(Feeling . . . *Something's wrong here. Very*—)

It was a primitive invertebrate that formed bulbous colonies, colonies that worked together, filling the prehistoric ground with clusters of the strange-looking creatures.

(*Something's*—)

And as each part joined together, it became subservient to the whole colony, growing, expanding, processing food, acting as one creature and not thousands.

He picked up his sketch.

It wasn't an exact duplicate. But it was darned close. It had to be in the same family . . . had to be. It looked just like it. Except for bumps that covered the colony, bumps that looked like they were once sharp but were dulled by millions of years of erosion.

And now Josh looked back at the photograph.

"Josh . . . Josh!" Clara's high-pitched voice cut through the musty air. He felt cold, though the air was as dead and warm as an attic in summer. "Look at this," she said. "Look at this book."

She plopped it down in front of him, right on top of his fossil book, covering the photograph.

"See, it's about these people who sort of drew things before they happened." She turned some pages. "Here, *look* at this. This lady drew a picture of her son in a car crash *before* it happened. And here"—she flipped again—"there's this man who painted this picture. See, it's the *Titanic* going down. Only it hadn't even sailed yet. It hadn't sailed, Josh. . . . Josh?"

He nodded at her find.

Thinking.

Tell me something I don't know.

He pushed her book away.

"What's wrong?" she asked, sounding annoyed. But then she noticed the photograph of the fossil. "Hey, you found it! Way to go!"

But he said, "It's not the same. Not exactly."

And he pointed to something printed under the caption, something in parentheses that he had missed at first.

The photograph was enlarged over one hundred times. *One hundred times* . . . A colony of Stenolaemata was tiny, microscopic. Just about invisible to the naked eye.

Not something the size of a football or—

He picked up his pencil. His fossil had been only a small part, a very small part of something larger—a parasitic colony. He started drawing, making the fossil curl around on itself, spiraling off the page, larger and larger, until he had some idea just how big it really was.

"Hey, what in the world are you doing?" Clara asked him. He kept on sketching.

"What are you—" He heard fear in her voice. But it didn't matter. All that counted was drawing now, capturing his vision.

Pennyfield came bustling down one of the aisles.

The librarian stopped at Josh's elbow. "Now, just what's going on here? What is all this talking—"

But Josh ignored him, and Clara with her book about people who drew the future.

And he worked to finish his drawing. Letting the raised bumps taper to points, sharp, needle-like points. Sharper, tinier, until he could imagine how painful it would be to touch one.

Or to have it touch you.

And then—with Pennyfield jabbering in his ear—Josh started sticking other things in. A small merry-go-round. A ferris wheel—the carnival. His pencil moved like lightning across the page, filling every inch of white space. The church tower. A street. Buildings. Then small lines, squiggles, that slowly—

"Josh," Clara said, crying now, grabbing him.

"Look here," Pennyfield tried to bark.

He made little lines now, on the paper, all of them touching the curls of the things. Lines with tiny dots for heads. Squiggles for feet and hands. Josh couldn't draw them fast enough.

People. Hundreds. Thousands. Filling the page.

The point of the pencil snapped.

The pad slipped to the floor.

And Josh sobbed. Shaking. Heaving. As Clara—scared, tentative—put an arm around him.

In the musty half-light of the library . . .

Commander Charlie Alexander waited by his fax machine, doing nothing else except sit there, drinking black coffee, and smoking cigarettes.

His secretary popped in the door.

"Want a refill?" he said.

He shook his head.

He didn't need any caffeine to stay awake another twenty-four hours.

Come on, he thought. *Send something!*

And though he'd made the same plea dozens of times already, this time the machine came to life. The compact Panasonic fax machine gave out a small beep, and immediately started spewing forth a piece of paper.

Alexander didn't wait until it was completely out before pulling the page up to read.

"Ice Box full," read one line.

Then, just below it.

"Heading north."

He looked at the map of Antarctica on his desk. How long would it take them to get back to McMurdo? Three, maybe four hours?

And then everyone's worst fears would be put to rest.

Or maybe not.

"No answer." Watson said shrugging.

Brian shifted uneasily on his feet. He wasn't too crazy about meeting Ward in the first place. "Maybe we should call some other time."

Watson shook his head.

"No, I've got a report of an incident. And it's my job to look into it."

Watson grabbed the doorknob.

"But your deputy said everything—"

"Sure, and I believe him. Still, I've always liked seeing things with my own eyes."

Watson opened the door.

The cottage was dark.

"Alan!" the Captain called. "Mrs. Ward? It's Torey Watson."

The Captain took a step inside.

(And Brian felt like Lou Costello, ready to let Abbott face Bela Lugosi by himself. *I'm not goin' in there, Abbott. I'm not—*)

He followed the Captain.

(Noticing that Watson had his hand on his gun.)

"Alan? Are you here? I'm—"

Watson stopped walking.

"What is it?" Brian asked. "Is there somebody—"

It took a few seconds for Brian's eyes to adjust to the gloom, the pupils widening, letting more light in. It had been so brilliant outside. But this was like a tomb.

(*Like my grandmother's place, her basement apartment in Brooklyn where she sipped her glass of Rheingold and perpetually mourned her dead husband. A living dead woman. Her hands like leather caressing my skin. And I could never wait to get away from her.)*

He saw them.

"Oh, my God," Watson said.

And then they both immediately looked around, away from the bodies, checking the tiny hallway leading to the single bedroom. The kitchenette, cut by a trio of thin sunbeams. Incongruous. Stagey.

Then they looked at the bodies.

They looked the same, both split from the throat down to midsection, neatly filleted, their skin peeled back, like lobster tails stuffed with crabmeat.

With the crabmeat scooped out.

Brian coughed, gagging on the foul smell. A glob of phlegm collected at the back of his throat.

"Jesus," Watson said, taking a step closer.

"No," Brian choked out.

(Not knowing just *what* he was warning Watson against.)

"Don't touch anything, Captain. Not until you get some—"

(Who? Experts? People who know about . . . *this*? There were no such people.)

"They're dead," Watson said. "That's for sure."

Brian thought of Josh then.

"Didn't the boy say that they attacked your deputy?"

Watson nodded. "That's what he said. But it was night. Who knows what—"

"You'd better talk to your deputy again," Brian said, staring at the two exploded bodies.

(He searched for the right word, the perfect word to describe them. He kept staring. And the word came.)

Eviscerated.

Brian grabbed Watson's arm, pulling him back from the bodies.

"And I'll talk with Josh Tyler," Brian said.

It was afternoon.

Bob O knew that from the way the sun was not directly overhead anymore. He licked his lips. And once again, he yelled.

"Help!" It was a croak. Nothing more. Halfhearted and hopeless. "Anybody. Help. Please!"

A few times he turned, thinking he heard somebody or

something just behind him, creeping up behind him at an angle he couldn't reach.

But it always disappeared. A phantom.

He tried hard not to think about the ticking. It was always there, so close, mocking him. *Here I am*, it said. Tick. *Why don't you come up here and just push the button? Save your ass.*

He scraped his leg raw, pulling at it. He saw white and pink strands hanging off the leg. Was that muscle or flakes of bone? *How much blood can I lose?* he wondered. *How long can I twist and rub my leg, pulling at the open wound, sending fresh blood splattering onto the rocks? How much, before I cross some point of no return?*

He tried tasting his blood.

It was wet. It had taste. He touched the small red pools on the rocks and brought his fingertips up to his lips.

Too salty. And though his tongue snaked out to savor the red liquid, he realized something:

This is crazy. Ha, ha, I'm lying here tasting my own blood. What the hell is wrong with me? What the hell—

Tick. Tick. Tick.

He didn't think about what it would be like when the explosion went off. No, that wasn't a real possibility. Somehow, he'd see or hear somebody. He'd call them, and they'd hurry over, dig him out. Sure. And they'd say, "Hey, what happened to you, buddy?"

What in the world happened to you?

And maybe he'd get rescued and no one would see the goddam explosives. Sure, he could get the hell out of here with his plan intact. Except for one problem. The longer he thought about it—and the more the sun started dipping towards the west—the more another possibility began to loom as more realistic.

I could still be stuck here tonight. When the explosives go off.

(And what would he do then to get away? How much pain and blood would he be willing to see to get his leg out?)

He turned and looked at the lake.

There were people swimming there. Kids probably. He could see them, wave to them as they swam back and forth. But they couldn't see him. No, he was just a dot on the hillside.

He watched someone swimming to the center of the lake.

A kid.

Tonight. *Stroke*. He'd find her and that geek. *Stroke*. And have it out. *Stroke*. With Clara.

Bobby Tamm was swimming full out. *Just what the hell is her problem*? he wondered. Here he thought he was going to get laid this summer. He'd already felt her up, already worked his hand under her shirt. Felt her little titties.

Clara was going to be the first.

Now, she was spending all her time with the wimp from New York.

Stroke. He kicked and flipped around on his back, doing a lazy backstroke, catching rays. Though he was on the Stoney-wood swim team, right now his timing was off. He grinned. *I guess that's what three beers will do to you.* His bladder was full. It felt like he was going to pop.

"What the fuck," he said. And he let go, pissing right in the fucking lake.

Ahh, that was better. He kicked around and started swimming some more. He wanted to swim all the way to the other side, over to the Inn's boat dock—though the boat boy, some college asshole, always screamed at him when he did that. "Fucking townie!" he yelled at Bobby.

"Fuck you," Bobby yelled back.

But he felt tired now. So, he kicked around, and started back to the beach. *Yeah, I'll creep into the woods for another beer. Then just hang out until the carnival opens.*

He dove under the water.

He kicked hard, digging into the water with his arms, pulling at it. Then he surfaced, gulping the air. It was so quiet under there. Quiet and dark, like you could get lost if you didn't know which way was up. He kicked back, and again dove under the water.

He opened his eyes. The lake was a murky brown, filled with tiny specks of who knew what.

He saw an eel.

Not the first time. The lake was filled with the long black suckers. It was fun to dig them out of the bottom of the lake and swing them around like a piece of rope, smash their heads against some rocks. Lots of fun.

The eel swam past him. It was a spaz, jigging up and down as though it was trying to write a fucking S with its body.

Bobby started up for the surface.

The eel touched his feet.

Slimy sick bastard.

His arms reached up for the surface, grabbing at it. Just a few feet more.

He felt something close around his ankles. And pain. *A fucking charley horse!* he thought. But then he was stopped, jerked backwards. *What the*—? His hands clawed uselessly at the water above him.

(His bulging cheeks begged to open, to gulp in fresh air.)

He was being pulled down.

He brought his legs up, trying to brush away whatever the hell was holding him.

(*I'm still going down*, he thought. *I'm still going the fuck* DOWN!)

He felt something. Like prickers. Like thorns wrapped around his ankles, oozing over his calves, digging in.

It stuck his hand, pricking it.

There was a crunching pain inside his head, pushing against his eyeballs. He screamed.

A flurry of bubbles escaped his mouth and flew up to the surface.

(So far away now.)

He opened his mouth and breathed in the water.

"Where the hell is your brother, little Ricky?" Jack Power asked, looking out over the lake.

"Search me," Ricky answered, looking up.

Jack wiped his mouth, tasting the last few drops of beer from the Genny he'd just chugged.

"Probably got tossed out by the boat boy, the dumb fuck." Power laughed.

Ricky shrugged.

"Probably."

Jack looked across the lake to the Miller Inn boat docks. He didn't see anybody there.

Nothing to worry about. Not with Bobby. If there was one thing that shithead could do, it was swim.

Power knelt on the blanket and collapsed forward, ready to be baked by the hot sun.

* * *

"You're going to what?"

"Don't try to talk me out of it," Clara said, walking straight ahead.

Josh shook his head. "I think you're crazy."

"Are you going to help me or not?"

"You've gotten me in more trouble in one week than I've ever been in my whole life."

Clara stopped walking.

"Say *yes*, or *no*."

Josh shook his head. "I've got to be crazy. But okay. What do you want me to do?"

She grabbed his arm. "Call your mother. Tell her you're eating at my house. Tell her you'll meet her at the carnival later."

"And what will I really be doing?"

"Coming with me. I'm going to get some stuff out of my house. Then I'll hide for a few days while everyone is looking for me."

"Where?"

"In your barn."

"Oh, great. You and the horse and—"

"No one will know I'm there. Then, after a few days, I'll hike to Bradford and take the bus to Albany."

They were at the Methodist Church, so white and gleaming, the tallest thing in the town.

But not as high as the mountain behind it.

"You'll help?" she asked.

And he thought then of the first day they went biking together, to the gorge. And he saw her arm, all mottled with black and blue splotches, ugly bruises covering her thin arm. He worried about her then. And he worried now.

"Yes," he said finally. "I'll help." He looked around. "Where do they keep the pay phones in this one-horse town?"

Brian knocked on the back door of the house. And Josh's grandmother opened it up.

"Hello, Mrs. Stoller."

"Mr. McShane!" She opened the door wider. "Come in. It's nice of you to stop by. We were just talking about you, how nice—"

Brian smiled. "Yes, but I—"

"Who is it, Mom?" Erica said. She came out to the kitchen, with wet hair, wrapped in a white robe, fresh from the shower. "Oh," she said.

"Torey Watson told me about your son, and what he saw last night."

"What he *thought* he saw," Erica said, scrubbing at her long black hair. "You're not a policeman, are you, Brian?"

"Not really," he said. "I'm actually with the Navy."

"I hadn't noticed any battleships in town."

"Coffee?" Mrs. Stoller asked, filling the kettle.

"So what are you doing here?"

"I'm with the Judicial Branch. And I was here to watch Alan Ward."

"Oh, did he need watching?"

"That's what I was supposed to find out."

Her mother put down three cups and spoons on the simple wooden table. "But there's no problem, Brian. Captain Watson's deputy said that everything was fine . . . that nothing happened."

Brian nodded. "That's what he said. But I'm afraid there is something wrong."

Erica stopped toweling her hair. She stepped to the table, sat down. The kettle started a slow, wheezing whistle.

"What do you mean?"

"Ward and his mother are dead."

Elizabeth Stoller was carrying the sugar bowl to the table. And she dropped it.

"Dear God," Mrs. Stoller said. "The poor woman. What happened?"

Brian stooped to pick up the pieces of the bowl from the floor. "I don't know. Captain Watson is going to talk with Tom Smith some more. And I'd like to speak with Josh."

Erica looked at her mother, her face suddenly pale.

"Josh . . . isn't here. He . . . he just called. He said he's having dinner with that girl, that—"

"Clara."

"Yes. And he said he'd meet me at the carnival."

Brian rubbed his chin. "I need to find him. Would you mind coming with me? I don't want to scare the boy or—"

"Certainly," she said. "Just let me throw something on."

Erica hurried out, and Elizabeth Stoller poured a cup of hot water into Brian's cup. She put the jar of Instant Maxwell House next to him.

"Thank you."

He smiled and idly read the label.

"Good to the last drop."

Watson Torey didn't know where the hell Tom Smith could be.

He didn't answer when he was called over the radio. That was odd. If Tom was in his car or carrying his radio—strictly S.O.P.—he'd have to hear him.

But there was nothing.

He phoned Smith's home, hoping to speak with his wife. He let the phone ring a dozen times before he finally hung up.

Okay, he thought. Could mean nothing. Absolutely nothing. *I sure as hell hope it does.*

And he decided to drive out to Tom Smith's trailer.

Twenty-One

A FEW PAGES streamed off the fax. And the first one, direct from McMurdo via Comsat III, contained three short paragraphs signed by Captain Finch.

Alexander read the material twice. Then, rudely snapping his attention back, more pages followed. Chemical analyses, blood types, all the information that Alexander would need if he ever had to explain what had happened . . . and what was going to happen.

But that didn't matter.

Not now.

He picked up the phone. Lines were open and waiting—to the Pentagon, the White House, the New York State Police, and the major hospitals within a 200-mile radius of Stoneywood.

But before he called them, he called Brian.

"Now, you wait here," Clara said. "No one's home. I'm just going to go get some stuff and come right out, okay?"

"Sure. And what if someone *is* home?" he asked. Clara's house looked even grimmer than he'd imagined.

She took a nibble at her lip and shrugged. "Then I'll throw my backpack out the window and just run out."

He smiled. Nothing was going to stop her from getting away. Nothing.

"Wish me luck." She turned and grinned at him, then darted up the cracked cement path to the front door of her house. He watched her pause at the door and turn to look at him one last time.

Then she opened the door and went in.

Someone was home.

Clara knew that immediately. Even though she couldn't hear anybody or see anyone, she knew it. She closed the door gently behind her and walked to the stairs.

Then she heard a sound.

A hissing sound. A bubbling. Coming from the kitchen.

Like spaghetti cooking. Boiling, bubbling water.

She started up the stairs, very quietly.

Someone was cooking. Yeah, that was it. Someone was cooking something.

But the smell in the air wasn't like any food she'd ever eaten—certainly not macaroni and cheese.

She took each step softly, afraid that the wooden stairs would shriek out an alarm.

She reached the top of the stairs.

And went into her room.

She looked around, quickly—one last time at her bed with its tattered pink spread. Once it was new, and she was little, and things were different.

She packed a pair of jeans. A sweater. Two T-shirts, including one from the Middle School with a Stoneywood Eagle. 'None Soar Higher.'

And her knife.

She had over thirty dollars, in crumpled bills and coins. A lot of money to her. But it wouldn't mean much out there, she knew. The bag was nearly full.

She looked at her bed.

She saw her doll. Its wide-eyed, dazed expression never changing. She shook her head. She wouldn't bring it.

But then she walked over, picked it up and stuck it in the top of her backpack. She pulled the zipper closed. One of the doll's arms stuck out.

And she heard the sound.

Hissing. Bubbling.

Closer. On the steps.

Here's some hot lunch for you, Clara. Something to take the chill off.

She thought of opening the door and seeing who was there.

Oh, I'm just hanging out, she could say. *Yeah, and now I'm going out for a while.*

See you.

She grabbed the doorknob.

Her nose twitched.

(What was that smell?)

She backed away from it.

And ran to the window. The screen was pitted with holes and gouges, tiny twisted barbs. She tried to see how to get the screen off. There was an eye-hook at the top and two more on the side, holding the screen. But they had been painted over, sealed tight. She looked down and saw Josh watching her.

"Fuck." She said the magic word. The all-powerful F word. She took the bag, heaved it backwards and forced it through the screen. For a moment, the metal mesh wouldn't budge. But then the whole screen popped limply out of its frame. She tossed her pack down.

She heard it rustle as it landed in a bush.

And she heard the hissing. The bubbling. Right by the door.

She could just walk past them, walk past her mother and father. *Don't stop, don't talk*, she told herself, *just keep moving and get out of this hell-house.*

She thought of Josh's picture. The ugly, barbed spirals. The screams they'd heard last night. Everything seemed to be coming together. *There's no way I'll stay here*, she told herself. She went to the window and looked out.

A splintery lattice was nailed to the side of the house, something on which the vines—now long dead—had once climbed up to her window.

Could it hold her weight?

She stepped out.

Josh called to her, warning her. "Clara!"

First one foot then the other, resting on the thin wood slats at the top of the lattice. She stepped down.

(Not looking up. Not seeing her door open.)

One foot after the other, nice and steady. As if it were something she did every day of her life.

Now her hands grasped the wood and she felt how old and splintery it was. But it held her weight so far.

"Clara!" Josh yelled.

She heard the bubbling above her.

She took another step down.

And the wood snapped in two, like paper. She lost one foothold and started kicking at the side of the house, scrambling for another. Then the other foot fell through, and she was dangling above the ground, hanging on with just her hands. The splinters dug into her palms.

Please, she thought. *Don't let me fall. If there's a God, you won't let me fall. Please.*

Her feet kept finding other wood struts and chewing right through them. One of her handholds started to loosen. She watched the small nails pop out.

Until she flew backwards, into space.

There was nothing he could do, Josh knew. Just watch her try to climb down. And then watch her fall.

But Clara landed just where her pack did, right on top of an overgrown bush that hadn't been trimmed for years. She groaned, and he heard the thud of her body, finally landing against the ground. But her fall had been broken.

He helped her out of the bush. Her face was scratched, thin lines of red on her cheeks.

"Come on," she said, popping up, her eyes wild, crazy. "We got to get away from here." She stooped down to pick up her pack.

"What happened? Did they see you, did they—"

He happened to look up then.

And he thought he saw a hand at her window.

A hand, he told himself. *That's what it was.*

Except, as he thought about it later, (not telling Clara) it didn't look anything at all like a hand.

Watson knocked on the door of Tom Smith's trailer. Smith's patrol car was parked outside.

He's probably enjoying some afternoon delight, Watson thought with a grin. But this was serious business, with the Wards dead and Smith's report beginning to look a bit funny.

He rang the bell.

"Tom, Watson here. I've got to talk with you," he barked through the chintzy aluminum door.

And sorry for the coitus interruptus, pal.

But the door opened surprisingly fast.

And he discovered that Tom Smith and his Poopsie hadn't been fucking at all.

* * *

Alexander reached everyone.

Everyone, except Brian.

"Keep trying that damn boarding house," he told his secretary. And the damndest thing was he couldn't send anyone in there to get him out. *Hell*, he thought, *I shouldn't even bring McShane out. But I owe that to him. Give him a chance to get out of the town.*

Before it was too late.

By now, the fax machine was running constantly, pumping out reports from a dozen different places.

Reserve troops activated. The Pentagon informed. Medical teams. Even the goddam National Security Council.

God, he thought. *I hope we're on time.*

Because if we're not, it's all over.

The whole shooting match.

Gone—

Josh crouched close to Clara, just at the edge of his grandmother's cornfield.

"Great," he said. "I don't see my mom around. And I bet my grandmother is napping. Come on."

He scrambled over to the barn, bent over, feeling like GI Jerk, while Clara followed. He looked into the barn.

The horse was gone.

"Where's Mister?" he said.

Clara looked around. "Your horse? Is he out in the fields someplace?"

Josh shrugged. "Could be. But he's such a beat-up old nag, Grandma likes to keep him in the barn, or just outside."

Then he noticed that the sheep were also gone.

"Looks like you'll have the place to yourself, Clara."

"Great!" She ran to the darkest corner of the barn, back to one of the empty stalls. "Hey, this will do fine. I'll just stay here until night."

"And what should I do?"

"Go to the carnival. Meet your mom there. And I'll meet you here later."

"And if my grandmother brings the animals in?"

"Don't worry. I know how to hide."

He nodded.

"Well, good luck then."

"Yeah," she said. "And I'll see you later."

He went to the barn door and checked that no one was watching from the porch. Satisfied, he ran out to the cover of the cornfield.

Erica watched Brian rap one more time on the door. A peeling piece of tape held the occupants' names under a doorbell that didn't work.

Ed and Nancy Skye.

"No one home," he said, raising his eyebrows.

Erica looked at her watch. "It's getting near five."

"You sure he said Clara's house?" he asked.

She nodded. "Where could he be?"

"I don't know. But he also said he'd meet you at the carnival, right? So, why don't you just do that. And I'll find you there later."

She turned away from the door, tasting that terrible fear when you don't know exactly where your kid is. He could be anywhere. In a ditch. In the back of someone's trunk. Anywhere.

She looked at Brian, glad that he was with her. "You know," she said, "I should apologize. I haven't been too polite . . . too nice. Bad habit from the big city." She paused for a moment. "Consider this a formal apology. And thank you for your help."

"Don't worry about it. It looks like we have some time to kill. Let me buy you a cup of coffee." He took her arm. "And then you can tell me exactly what Josh said he saw last night. . . ."

Alexander organized the sheets in something resembling chronological order. *Got to be organized*, he thought. *Yeah, real organized for when they ask me what the fuck happened.*

At the top the pages were labeled, 'Gaia Prime.'

The beginning was perhaps the easiest part to understand. Antarctica was a giant icebox, with chunks of the prehistoric past frozen beneath miles of ice. Lots of buried stuff there, dating back to when it split off from the megacontinent Pangaea and drifted south.

But no one expected something like the Gaia Prime find to show up.

First, there was the geological anomaly. The Antarctic plateau was flat, at least until the Queen Maud Mountain Range. Flat, and shaved to a uniform height by the force and weight of millennia of glaciers. But then subsonic mapping, courtesy of the new spy satellite released by the space shuttle Atlantis picked up a strange formation, a 'prong.' A column of stone, nearly a mile tall. Like Devils Tower in Wyoming. But narrower.

There was nothing like it anywhere in Antarctica. And it blew the geologists of the NSF away.

Of course, Navy secrecy kicked in right away. It was given a code name: Emperor Two. And the Ice Box Research Station was used to field an expedition.

(Alexander lit a cigarette. The air conditioner sent a steady stream of cool air across his desk, swirling the smoke away. He flipped a page, and pulled out the summary of Wynan's first report to the National Science Foundation.)

The prong, the great column of stone, turned out to be a recent feature—geologically speaking. But the stuff sitting on top of it was dragged from the very center of the continent. And it turned out to be incredibly ancient. First estimates put it at least 500 million years old. Some of the scientists thought that it could be even older.

Which meant that whatever sat on top of the prong dated back to the first living things to develop from single-celled organisms.

(*And shit, this is where the surprises started showing up.* . . .)

Gaia Prime is what Wynan called this fantastic find dating from the first explosion of plant and animal species. And, prophetically, he used 'Gaia,' the geologists' new name for Earth, a name that treated the planet as a living entity.

He reread the first paragraph from Wynan's preliminary report . . .

For over three billion years life on Gaia never developed past the stage of simple single-cell organisms. Then, with amazing speed, evolution and natural selection suddenly began to create a multitude of species. The impetus for that incredible development remains unknown.

The first lab reports from the exposed layers on top of Gaia Prime were unexciting. Ordinary basalt and granite rock, carbon-dating well up to half a billion years ago. But nothing else of interest. Until Wynan blasted through the top of the prong.

At first Wynan thought he had simply exposed a wonderful fossil record, great clumps of Devonian material somehow mixed in with more ancient stone. Except that what he uncovered was unique—great, coral-like creatures of an incredible and unimagined size.

They resembled other simple creatures that lived in colonies, like simple corals and bryozoan. They were near the very bottom of the evolutionary pyramid. But the swirling curls of the Gaia Prime creatures went on for a dozen feet or more. And the colony was covered with scaly, razor-sharp shell.

It looked armored. Dangerous.

There was one thing that nobody could understand about the new creature. It didn't seem to have any means of reproducing, asexually (like other such creatures) or otherwise.

The history of paleontology, Wynan suggested, would have to be rewritten. Never was it thought that such creatures could grow to the incredible size found at Gaia Prime. And having grown so large, what caused their extinction?

But then the first disturbing field reports trickled in from the Ice Box Station. . . .

The calcite shells of the creatures dated out to the same age as the stone.

Which was impossible. Where was the fossil record of the incredibly early appearance of this heretofore never seen specimen? Did it just appear in this one place, from nowhere? All of a sudden? Evolution just didn't work that way . . .

Then Wynan's resident biologist told him that he was picking up bizarre readings from the find. Impossible readings. There were very slight electromagnetic pulses . . . barely measurable. But they were undeniably an indication of some kind of activity within the find.

Nobody said the word 'life.'

Nobody said the word 'quarantine.'

Nobody thought about any danger.

But the next thing the Navy knew, it had a dead expedition. Except for one man . . .

Who had never even been near Emperor Two. Never even near the find.

Had they all picked up an infection from the sample, something that made them go crazy, killing each other? And did Alan Ward escape it? That was one popular theory. Or did Ward, who tested negative for every virus known to science, bring back whatever it was inside Gaia Prime?

There were those who said that Wynan, and maybe Ward too, had simply gone amuck under the pressure. Cabin fever could become a serious problem during the long Antarctic night. Psychotic behavior at the poles wasn't exactly unknown.

That's where Brian McShane came in. If Ward had gone psychotic—even temporarily—McShane was going to push Ward's buttons again. A little pressure. Some obvious surveillance.

Only Brian didn't know that's what it was all about.

Alexander stubbed out his cigarette. And looked at the clock. He picked up the phone to call Brian again. *I like him*, he thought. *He's a talented prosecutor. Unlucky, but talented.*

How much time was left? An hour? Less?

Alexander pushed some pages away until he was looking at the last report.

There were no oversized bryozoans at the Ice Box twenty-four hours ago. No, just the bodies of the scientists and the Navy men. All looking like bad copies of the same leering face.

(The faxed photos had just enough detail to make him sick. The bodies ripped apart. The faces almost making it, just about finished before melting into some undefinable clump.)

No, Wynan's find was gone, off the prong.

And now they all knew where.

It was in Stoneywood, alive—if the word was appropriate—after half a billion years.

(Oh, and Alexander could imagine explaining this to the Select Committee in the Senate. Explaining about dormancy, hibernation, and a form of existence that could not be called 'life' . . . something that would need a new name.)

And bit by bit, fellows, he could tell them, *it is growing.*

He heard the phone ring. Once. Twice.

And somebody answered.

Clara heard the car slowly pull up the hill to Josh's house. Something about the sound of the engine bothered her. Maybe it was the tentative way it turned into the small driveway, or the deep rumble of its engine.

It sounded like it didn't belong here.

And she decided to steal a look at who it was.

She crept out of the stall, not so dark now that her eyes were used to the blackness. The barn door was open just a crack, just enough to let in a thin shaft of late afternoon sun.

She stepped slowly, the dry hay crunching under her feet. She looked out the door.

It was a police car. And two policemen, their backs to her. She couldn't see who they were. She watched them, breathing heavily, afraid that at any moment they'd spin around and say, *Aha! There you are, young lady. Missy!*

You're going home now.

Your parents have missed you. And boy, do they ever have a nice surprise for you.

The policemen knocked and waited at the door. It opened, and Josh's grandmother came out to talk with them.

They're looking for me, she thought. *I just know that they're looking for me.*

One of the policemen—it was old Captain Watson—turned slowly and gestured out toward the hills. Clara ducked into the barn. She was breathing so hard, and so loud!

They know I'm here. They're going to come right over here.

She chanced another look out the door. Josh's grandmother had let the policemen into her house and closed the door.

Clara knew she had to get out. She decided to leave her pack there. Maybe it would be safe to come back later. She waited a few minutes to make sure that everyone was still inside.

And then she pushed open the door and darted down the hill, past the cornfield, past the house.

Down towards Stoneywood.

"Live fucking ammo! Will you tell me what in the world we're supposed to be doing with live ammo?" Dwayne Gaffney was looking around the barracks, at all the other dopey faces who knew as little as he did.

Charlie North shrugged. "Hey, how should I know? Maybe we're going to be doing some night target practice."

And Dwayne—a good ole Southern boy who had no qualms about bunking in the new Army with a black kid from Bed-Stuy—shook his head. "No way, jay. Not with these mother shells," he said, holding up a handful of the M-16 cartridges. "These are for elephant hunting, not target practice. And they got us hauling full packs too. Damn! I'll tell you, Charlie-boy," he said coming close to North. "Some real heavy shit is coming down. Mark my words. Real heavy."

North nodded, thinking: *This is all mighty peculiar. I was just getting to the point where I was starting to think about a career in the Army. Being all I can be, and all that shit—as long as there were no wars, or police actions, and we were close to a PX.*

But this was looking bad.

Live fucking ammo!

Westfield Army Corps Headquarters was considered the country club of military bases. Stuck in the mountains, it was like going to a fucking mountain resort. Lots of good R&R in Albany, chasing State College cooze in Albany. Clean air, lots of exercise, and target practice up near the mountain markers.

North heard the trucks pull up outside.

"See?" Gaffney said, pushing at North's shoulder. "You hear that, asshole? Trucks. Taking us somewhere."

Their beefy sergeant, whom they called 'Doughboy,' came into the barracks.

The men fell to attention.

And they gave each other the strangest look when they heard just what they were going to be doing.

"Thanks for the coffee. . . ." Erica said.

"Sorry we couldn't stay for a refill. It looked liked they could have used the business." Brian said.

The diner had been deserted. Too deserted, she thought.

She smiled at Brian, undecided as to whether she appreciated his interest. Not a bad face on him, she thought. Open, warm. Easy on the eyes. And a smile that said 'trust me.' But his blue eyes were always darting away, as if he were checking for the nearest exit.

"I'll find you later, at the carny," he said. "Tell Josh I want to talk with him. But I have to find Watson before I file a report with my exec."

She looked out the car window. It wasn't dark yet, but already the carnival booths were open and a few young parents were taking the squealing small kids on the mini-carousel (where the horses didn't go up and down) and the ever-popular metal boats with bells.

"We'll be here. You'll find us," she said. She opened the door. "And thanks again."

She got out and smelled the air laced with the ancient scent of cotton candy, hot dogs, and overpopped popcorn. She made a loud sniff. "Smells good out here," she said.

"I'll buy the wieners when I come back." Brian grinned.

"You're on." She shut the door.

And she watched Brian drive away.

"I told you . . . I don't know where Mr. McShane is. Now, I put a note under his door so that when he *does* come home he will call you. Now, what *else* do you want me to do?"

Agnes Simpson listened to this crazy man calling from Washington asking her to go actually run out and find McShane. "Life and death," he said.

(*Sure. I can just bet it's life and death.*)

"Well, I can't do that because I'm going to choir rehearsal. So you'll have to be patient. He'll be back sooner or later. Now, I have to go."

She hung up, cutting the fool off in midsentence, some gobbledygook about a 'national emergency.'

What does he think? That I was born yesterday?

And she hurried out the door, thinking:

I haven't missed a rehearsal in five years.

And, praise the Lord, I don't plan on missing one tonight.

The police station had been deserted when Brian checked it. He went back to the guest house, thinking . . . *I should try calling the police station again.*

There was no answer.

Then he got an idea. He picked up the local directory, which was sitting on the linoleum floor by the pay phone. He thumbed through the pages until he found Watson's home number.

He dialed.

No answer.

He hung up and held the phone a second. *Maybe I should call Alexander. Give him the bad news.*

("Er, Commander, Ward and his mom had a little accident.")

But he wanted to speak with Watson first. See if there were any ideas about what had happened to them. Suicide? Murder? Indigestion? *Yeah,* he thought. *That's what I better do. Get some facts first.* He hung up the phone and walked up to his room.

Some old geezer down the hall opened his door. He popped out of his room, a toothless spook.

"Edna was looking for you, mister. She was *looking* for you." The man squinted with the earthshaking import of his words.

"Oh," Brian said, smiling at the ghostly figure. "I'll go talk to her."

He turned on his heel. But the man grabbed him, a skeletal hand, more bird than human. "She's ain't here now, mister." The man grinned. "She's at choir practice."

So great, thought Brian. *I'll go have my shower.*

"Thanks," he said. He opened his door and walked into the small room. He hit the wall switch that worked the small lamp on the bureau, but nothing happened. Probably he'd used the lamp button when he'd turned off the light. Now the stupid wall switch didn't work.

So he went on into the tiny bathroom in the dark, just wanting to let the hot water stream off him.

He walked right over the small piece of paper on the floor.

And when the phone rang again downstairs, he was in the shower, blowing bubbles into the lukewarm stream rolling off his face.

It rang and rang and rang, and nobody answered it.

Twenty-Two

"IT'S REALLY VERY easy, sweetie. Why not give it a try?"

Erica had already shaken off the siren call of the barker, or, in this case, the barkerette. But to no avail. The persistent woman kept encouraging Erica to step over and just have a look at the game.

And though all she wanted to do was just stand there and let the sights and sounds of the carnival wash over her, she let herself walk over to the blowsy blonde's game of skill.

Spot the Spot.

Fuzzy pink and purple creatures of an unknown species were lashed to the stall, waiting patiently for freedom.

"It's very easy," the blonde repeated. Erica looked down at the counter. There was a big red circle and five small metal circles. The blonde scooped up the metal discs. "The object, honey, is to drop the metal circles and completely cover the"—drop—"big"—drop—"red"—drop—"circle. Now," she said, having completely blotted out the red. "Isn't that easy?" The barkerette scooped up the circles and offered them to Erica.

She looked around for Josh. Slowly, the lights of the carnival, from the rows of colored bulbs on the ferris wheel to the big glaring flood lights on the food booths, were growing brighter as the sun went down.

Where was Josh?

"Give it a try?"

She shook her head. "No, I—"

"Go ahead, Mom. Try it."

And there was Josh, right at her elbow. "Josh! You startled me," she said. She put her arm around his shoulders and gave him a squeeze. So big . . . he was more like a man than a boy.

Then she studied his eyes. "Is something wrong, Josh? You look like you haven't had any sleep or—"

He smiled, a forced smile, she thought. *What is wrong with you, sweetheart? What is going on in your life?*

And is it my fault?

"Give it a try," the blonde chirped happily, trying to call her back to the game.

"Go ahead," Josh said, eager to shake off her attention.

Reluctantly giving in, Erica dug out a dollar from her purse, gave it to the woman, and picked up one of the discs. She hovered over the red circle and then let it fall.

But with the first disc, she knew she couldn't do it. It had landed much too near the center. She'd have to drop the other discs close to the outside of the circle.

"Oh, no," she said when the second disc landed, confirming the impossibility. She hurried through the other three.

"Hey," the girl said. "You were close. Try it again."

Erica shook her head.

"Go ahead, Mom."

The girl again demonstrated just how it was done. The metal circles landed perfectly, plopping down with an effortless smoothness while Erica watched.

What's the trick? she wondered. There had to be a trick, some gimmick.

She gave the girl another dollar.

She tried it again, and this time she completely covered the big red circle . . . except for a tiny dot in the center.

"Aw," the girl groaned. "You were very close. Real close. Now—"

Erica grinned and pulled Josh away.

"Come on, let's see what other money-magnets the carnival has to offer." She walked past a food booth offering, in big, bright letters: 'Ice Cream! Soda! Beer! Hot Dogs! Sausages!' She asked Josh if he wanted something, but he shook his head. They kept on walking.

"Josh, Brian stopped by this afternoon. . . ."

Josh nodded.

"He wants to talk with you about last night."

He turned to her. "I know what I saw, Mom!"

"Yes . . . well, that's what he wants to see you about. Something did happen there last night. Something—"

They were behind a metal cage, one of the attractions. Erica heard someone yelling, a high-pitched voice that cut through the noise of the rides and the canned music and the clamor of the games.

"What's that?" Josh asked.

"I don't—" she started to say. And Josh pulled ahead of her to look. . . .

The voice was shrill, horrible. There was a crowd of people standing on the other side.

"Hey, four-eyes! Can't you see me, dumbo? I'm up here. Yoo-hoo, dimwit? *Over here.*"

"What in the world is it?" Josh asked, when his mother caught up with him. He read the sign.

'Dunk the Bozo.'

The screamer was dressed as a clown. Sort of. He wore oversized jeans and a puffy plaid shirt. He had a big red nose and rubbery lips. A small porkpie hat sat on his head.

But he was a perverted clown, demented, yelling at everyone, challenging them to throw a hardball at a small bull's-eye and knock him off his chair.

"Hey, rubes, what's-a-matter? No men in Stoneywood? Need your women to take care of you? Hey you, you there, Mr. Baldy."

The Bozo stood up in his chair, screaming at a bald man near the back of the crowd. The bald man stood with his arms folded.

"Yeah, you dome-head. I see you watching me. And if you don't like what you're hearing, then why don't you try and knock me off of here?"

Erica shrugged. "Let's go. I've heard enough. . . ."

But Josh held her arm. "No, Mom. I want to see what happens."

The bald man unfolded his arms and started walking through the crowd. It was a dollar for three balls. The man paid, and took aim.

"Fat chance, pal. Hey, who makes your clothes? Woolworth's? *Nice shirt.* Does it come in human sizes?" The man threw his first ball, missing. Then another. And another. The man forked over another dollar.

"Hey, there goes your week's pay!" the Bozo screamed out. "No more Slim Jims for you this week, hey rube? Hey! Popeye! I'm over here, over here! See me?"

The Bozo was standing on his platform, out of his chair, wildly waving at the man. But then the man's last ball hit the bull's-eye. A bell rang and a siren shrieked. The trap door was sprung and the Bozo tumbled into a vat of water.

Everyone started clapping and laughing. And Josh laughed too.

The Bozo crawled out of the water.

"My cigar's still lit, rube!" he shouted, holding up his stogie. "Still lit!" He climbed back into his chair.

The Bozo turned, glaring at the crowd.

And he looked right at Josh, and then his mother.

"Hey, Momma," he called at her. "Looking *goood*. Ain't he a little young for you?"

"Come on, Josh," she said. She pulled at his arm.

"Oh, is that your mommy, sonny?" The Bozo started whining. "Then you'd better run off with her, little baby."

The crowd was still laughing, only now they were laughing at Josh.

"Come *on*, Josh!"

"Dat's right. Momma's got a hot date later and wants widdle sonny in bed."

She tugged at him, but he pulled away.

He ran over to the man with the baseballs and gave him a dollar.

The crowd cheered.

Josh's first ball wasn't even close.

Everyone's watching me, he thought, *and I'm spazing out.* He knew his face was red . . . with anger.

Or maybe just embarrassment.

"You don't got the arm, sonny!" the Bozo yelled, his voice snapping now. "Take a hike, kid—you'll never hit it!"

The second ball came closer.

He got ready to throw his third ball.

"Aim a little high," someone whispered.

He turned. It was Clara, standing right by his elbow.

"Oh, you got a girlfriend. Well, nerd, you're gonna—"

And Josh threw the ball toward the top of the target. As hard as he could. It hit, ringing the great bell and cutting the Bozo off in midsentence.

Then he turned to Clara.

"What's wrong?" he asked—seeing his mother walk over to them. "Why aren't you—"

And Clara told him why she was there, told him about the police coming to see his grandmother.

When his mother came up beside them, Josh tried to give her his best reassuring smile. *Everything's okay*, he wanted his face to say. But he kept thinking about his sketch—the rides, the people, and the coiling thing that encircled everyone . . . everything.

Josh kept smiling, and said, "Mom, Clara wants to show me something back by the rides."

"But Brian wants to talk with you, Josh. I told him we'd meet him—"

Clara came close to his mother, smiled at her.

"It will just be a few minutes, Mrs. Tyler. I want to show Josh—"

She paused, and Josh knew that she was trying to think of something.

"Mirror Madness. It's real close. Then we'll come right back."

His mother looked around.

"Five minutes, Mom," Josh pleaded. "Then we'll meet you here." He looked over his shoulder. "By the hot dog stand."

"Okay," she sighed. "But don't get lost."

Josh smiled, and let Clara lead him away.

They were in the shadows, by the rides. A safe place to talk, Josh guessed.

"How do you know the police were looking for you?" he asked. "Maybe," he continued, "it's not such a good idea for you to run away."

"I'm leaving," she snapped, eyes narrowing.

"Okay, okay, but—"

They were right near the ferris wheel. A creaky rusty ferris wheel that groaned with each turn, louder than the rap music that thumped out of megaphone speakers. Around and around, all the time while they talked.

"They *had* to be looking for me. They know you and I have

been hanging out. But they won't come back. I'll just go back to your barn tonight, after the carnival closes."

He nodded. The ferris wheel went around and around. People were laughing. Calling. Squealing.

Someone was crying.

A little kid. Yes, Josh saw a man lean out of the seat, yelling that it was time to stop. His kid was screaming.

Time—to—stop.

The little kid was crying real loud. Almost as loud as the weird sounds made by the ferris wheel.

"So let's go back now," Clara said. "Maybe you can get Brian to believe—"

She stopped.

Josh was watching the wheel. Around and around and—

"It's not stopping."

Clara screwed up her face. "What do you mean?"

He grabbed her and turned her to face the ride. "The ferris wheel. It's not stopping. It's been going since we started talking and it's *still* going. The people are getting scared, they—"

He thought that the ride operator had taken a hike. Out to the porto-potties, leaving the locals for a long ride. Or maybe he wanted to quit the carnival and this was his way to get even.

But Josh saw him. Right there. Right by the controls.

And the guy was looking right back at Josh.

Brian was toweling himself when he saw the note. Sitting right on the floor where he must have walked over it when he came in.

He picked it up and read it.

"Shit," he said. The woman had written, "Natural Emergency, call Captain Alex . . ."

It was doubtful that Alexander had been promoted. And it was equally doubtful that the emergency was natural.

He threw on some clothes and ran down the stairs.

He dialed Alexander's switchboard, hoping that his boss was still working, still in his office.

His call was answered in the middle of the first ring.

"Commander, Brian here. I just got—"

"Get the hell out of there, McShane. Move it. Now."

Brian scratched his still-wet hair. What the hell was Alexander talking about? "What, sir? What do you mean?"

"You heard me, McShane. Get out of that town immedi-
tely. You have forty, maybe forty-five minutes before it will
ve too late."

"What are you talking about?" Brian said loudly.

A door opened upstairs—Brian's elderly neighbor. He
veered down the stairs at Brian, looking like an angry rooster.

Brian heard his boss take a breath, frustrated. "Ward
vrought something back from Antarctica, something—"

"Ward's dead," Brian said.

And Alexander said, "He was dead six months ago."

"What?"

"Brian, there are soldiers sealing off the town. If I'm not
wrong, all hell is going to break loose." He paused. "You
might not get out."

What is this shit? Brian thought. *Soldiers?* He looked at his
watch. He didn't understand a thing Alexander was saying to
him.

But he thought of the bodies. And he thought of Erica and
her son Josh. *Is this another McShane fuck-up?* he wondered.

"Brian," Alexander said, snapping his attention back. "Get
your ass out now, you hear me? Now!"

"Right," Brian muttered.

And he hung up the phone.

And he looked at his watch again.

Where were Josh and Clara?

And where was Brian? thought Erica. She stood next to the
hot dog stand, getting sick from the smell.

Maybe I should go find them? She looked at her watch. How
long had it been? Seven, maybe eight minutes. No need to go
crazy.

Relax a bit, she thought.

She looked over at a nearby game booth. 'Knock 'em
Down,' it said, offering still more puffy animals that were
impossible to win.

She walked over to it.

It was completely dark now.

Yes, thought Bob O. *Just the stars and me.* Even the moon
wasn't up yet. *Just me and my explosives. Ticking away. No
one came to save me after all. Well, that's a surprise. Guessed
wrong on that one.*

He looked down at his leg. The bleeding had stopped, but not before it had covered his leg with a red, crusty patch.

I must smell to high heaven, he thought. *All that blood, and my sweat and piss. It must really stink.*

He looked at his Rolex, the crystal all scratched now. *So how long before I can't wait any longer? Oh, about thirty minutes . . . maybe a bit more.*

His leg was still hopelessly pinned.

There seemed to be only one option left.

Somehow, I have to separate the lower part of my leg from the rest of me. Yeah, that's all I have to do.

Piece of cake.

He said it aloud.

"Piece of cake."

And he laughed, letting the hysterical laughing turn into crying, screaming . . . demanding help.

And this time . . .

Oh, God, thank you, thank you! You really exist, you really do—

He heard someone walking up the trail.

"Hey," he yelled. "Shake a leg will you? I've got, er, a big problem here."

(*And if you don't move your ass we'll both get blown to bits.*)

But whoever was coming didn't seem to hurry. He heard the heavy, plodding steps. "Hey, come on, get a move on. What's the problem? What's—"

But whoever it was didn't answer. And didn't hurry.

Bob O heard the steps behind him as they reached the rubble, leaving the woods. *Good*, he thought, *they're climbing up to me. Keep coming, baby, keep on coming!*

(Meanwhile, part of his mind was engaged in testing reasons why the person wasn't answering . . . or hurrying. Maybe, he thought, they were deaf and dumb. Some old mute mountain man. Yeah, maybe that was it.)

Or maybe—

(And he swore his heart stopped.)

Maybe it's not anyone at all.

A mirage. Right. Sure, he had seen it in the movies, crazy guys, all hungry and thirsty, imagining stuff. A mirage, it was called.

But the steps were just behind his head.

As real as anything he ever heard.

"Oh, man," he said, twisting his head this way and that, wishing he could turn just another few inches and see who it was. "Man, am I ever glad to see—"

Another step.

And Bob O smelled something . . . something like his German shepherd when it had been out in the rain. That stinky smell the dog gave off, as if the stench of everything it ever chased or ate came to life on its pelt just as soon as it became soaked.

Something wet touched his ear.

Then it grunted.

And when the bear—

(*A fucking bear! Am I lucky or what?*)

—took another step forward, studying Bob O, all of a sudden the explosives didn't seem all that important.

Twenty-Three

"KEEP WALKING," JOSH barked at her. "Don't look behind us. Just keep walking."

What's his problem? Clara thought.

He pulled her roughly, holding her wrist tightly, pinching it.

"Hey, Josh, don't you go get weird on me."

Still he jerked her along, past the pool of kiddie boats with their clanging bells, past an inflatable castle, past the balloon stand with its big red tanks of helium.

"Will you tell me what you're doing?"

He shook his head. "Something's not right here. Those people are trapped on that ferris wheel—"

"What?"

He squeezed her hard. "They can't get off, Clara. *They aren't being let off.*"

She looked behind them, back to the wheel. Her mouth opened, ready to laugh the whole thing off.

But she heard the screaming, the crying, coming from the wheel.

"Don't look!" Josh hissed. "The guy running it saw me . . . saw me looking at him. I think he's following us."

Clara snapped her head forward.

Then he saw something. Just ahead. And now she pulled back at Josh—

"Stop," she said.

Almost a whisper.

"Come on, Clara. We gotta—"

"Look," she said quietly, pointing at some people in the

darkness ahead. They were looking around as if they hadn't seen her yet. Checking the games, staring at the rides, their necks craning all around.

"My parents," she said.

"What?"

"They're looking for me," she said.

Josh shook his head. "They probably just came to the carnival, that's all, probably—"

"No! They never come to the carnival." She turned to him. And he thought of her window, and what he saw there . . . reaching out. "My mother is supposed to be working. She's supposed to be at work!"

She looked back. Her parents were still nosing around. Then slowly, her mother turned.

And saw her.

"Oh, God, Josh, you gotta do something. They see me."

He looked around.

"There," he said, pulling her out of the main path. "Over there."

She turned around.

Mirror Madness.

He took her hand and pulled her along quickly. "Can we lose them in there?"

"I—I—"

"Clara! Is it a maze? Can we lose them?"

"Yes." She ran beside him. And when they got to Mirror Madness, there was no one outside taking tickets.

So they just ran in.

"Try your luck, miss?" the man said.

Erica smiled. "No, I never could throw a baseball."

Then, to demonstrate just how easy the game was, the barker gave one of the balls a gentle, underhand toss. It spiraled towards the row of targets and knocked one of the fluffy kittens backwards.

Where were they? she wondered. She checked her watch again. It was over ten minutes now. She shouldn't have let Josh out of her sight. What in the world was wrong with her son?

She thought, *Maybe I should go look for him.*

But she shook her head. Then she'd miss Brian. And it was important that he talk to Josh. Find out what really happened.

"So what do you say? I'll even give you a practice ball on the house."

The barker stuck out his hand holding one ball.

"No," she said, quietly, backing away from the Knock'em Down.

She took a few steps towards the ride area.

I got my first real kiss here, she thought. And had *my teen-age titties squeezed*. The memory was so vivid—the excitement of it all, sitting in the ferris wheel, going around and around, above everything, above the noise, the lights, the town. Everything. And Tommy Davis had kissed her, a long gentle kiss that belied the relentless maulings to come.

Then, while she was still savoring the warm feeling, his hand had slipped off her shoulder, smoothly, down to her breast. He touched her there, again gently. And though it felt wonderful, she pried his hand away and smiled.

She took a breath. The carnival felt the same. The smells, the sounds. All the same rides.

Only I'm different. That moment—sweet and naive—is gone forever.

She drifted away from the game area, away from the food stand, her memory alive now, guiding her.

By the end of that summer, she was no longer a virgin. And she eventually saw Tommy for the practiced seducer that he was. Still, she imagined that there were worse people to lose one's cherry to.

She checked her watch again. Where was Josh and that girlfriend of his? This was getting ridiculous.

She walked behind a family. A man, big and sturdy, dressed in a plaid shirt. His wife in a simple blue dress—country generic. A young daughter. And a baby in a stroller. Looking at them, she felt bitter. Happy families. Was there anything more irritating, more annoying?

More unfair?

An old woman walked towards the family, brightening as she recognized them. She stopped, clasping her hands together.

"Oh, you've brought little Suzy!" Erica heard her gush. The family stopped, and Erica idly watched the scene. "Little Suzy Hammer!" The woman bent down. "Why, if she doesn't look as cute as a button . . . Just as cute as a button."

The woman looked up at the parents. "Now, how old is she?" Then, to the baby: "How old are you, widdle Suzy. Such a beautiful little lady. I just have to—"

Erica smiled, watching it out of the corner of her eye. A jealous voyeur.

The woman bent down closer.

Her gushing stopped.

The woman was bent over the baby.

Erica took a step forward. Curious. *Well*, she thought, *let me see this little darling*.

Then there was another sound. A gurgling noise. Except it was real loud. Too loud.

Another step. And she was ready to pass the family. She looked down to the stroller, wondering how such a small baby could make so much noise gurgling like that. What a pair of lungs, what a—

She looked at the baby.

And she saw that it wasn't the baby that was gurgling.

No.

It was the woman.

"Which way?" Josh asked. The maze split into three narrow corridors, all lined with cheap smudgy mirrors that merely distorted their images.

"I don't know," she said. "I don't remember where any of these lead. We just used to wander around and—"

Josh heard someone push through the turnstile.

He grabbed her. "Someone's coming. Go left. . . ." he whispered.

Somewhere he'd read something about mazes . . . something about how to get out of them. *If that's what we want to do*, he thought. It might be better if they just stayed lost in there for a while. At least until Clara's parents got bored and went home and the crazy ferris wheel man went back to his ride.

The corridor turned into a dead end.

There was message, scrawled with red lipstick.

"Fuck this," it said.

"This is no good," Clara said. "We have to go some other way."

Clara started back the way they came, and he had to hurry to keep up with her. But then, instead of taking the turn that led back to the beginning of the maze—

(At least, he thought that was the turn that led back to the maze. . . .)

—she went to her right, heading deeper into the cheap-jack maze.

"Where are you going?" he hissed at her.

But she just kept moving.

"Wait a sec—"

He called to her.

She took another turn. He followed. And he quickly came to another turn. He thought he heard her walking down to the left. He went that way.

And then he didn't see or hear her at all.

"Clara!" he yelled in a hoarse, whispery voice. Then louder, "Clara!"

He waited. A half-dozen Joshes looked back at him, all blurry and disheveled.

And he was alone.

The woman's head was held fast to the baby by strings. And the woman's muffled gurgling and groaning was barely audible now, with her face buried in the baby's blanket.

"Oh, God," Erica whispered. The woman's legs kicked and pulled at the dirt like a skittish horse. Like Mister when he saw a copperhead. "Oh, no," Erica moaned.

She looked away from the baby, away from its bright blue eyes and tiny hands swimming around the old woman's bobbing head. The old woman's sounds stopped.

And the family looked at Erica.

She stepped back from them.

The family hesitated. The father took a step.

They looked at each other, as if Erica had interrupted some intimate, private moment.

"I'm—" she mumbled.

She backed away.

(*I've got to get out of here*, she thought, trying to calm herself. *Yes, just turn and run. Before they take me, before they have me look at their baby too.*)

She took a breath.

And she spun around—

Running right into someone.

* * *

Josh walked a few paces down one corridor. It didn't matter. At this point they all looked the same. He tapped the mirror walls, hoping that if Clara was on the other side she'd tap back.

He came to another dead end, and turned around.

If I'm going to get out of here, he thought, *I have to use a plan. I'll just follow the right wall. All the way. Wherever it leads—*

(Eventually it would have to lead out.)

—and hope that Clara can find a way out too.

He pressed his palm against a wall, and he felt the mirror wobble a bit. They weren't very strong or secure. Probably the panels of the maze could be put together in hundreds of different arrangements. He walked quickly now, his fingers gliding along the wall.

(*So old, and filmy*, he thought. *Like it's never been cleaned after years and years of people walking through it*.)

He came to a T, and he turned, following the right wall. Then another T, and again he headed right.

He heard some voices. Low, mumbling. A laugh. Then nothing.

It was cold in here.

(*No, it's not. I'm sweating. How can it be cold?*)

He heard the voices again. Just on the other side of the wall. And Josh walked more slowly.

But he kept on going.

"No!" Erica screamed, running into him.

And she shot a glance over her shoulder, her eyes wild, terrified.

"Erica . . . Erica! Take it easy. It's me. Brian."

She looked up at him. "Brian!" Then she pulled him down the alleyway between two games.

"I just saw"—she stopped, catching her breath—"a baby. It was feeding, attached to someone. . . ."

He took her by the shoulders. "We have to get out of here."

"It was on this lady, wrapped around . . . I don't—"

She was losing it. Brian looked around. There was a queer stillness here. The music played, the rides clanked and screeched. But there was this strange quiet.

The voices. The happy, squealing voices. The laughing. The chatter. He heard none of those sounds.

He shook her. "Erica. You have to leave the town. Now. With me."

She nodded. Then she shook her head. "But Josh . . . and—"

"Where is he?"

"He went with that girl, over to the Mirror Maze. He said he'd be right—"

Oh, Jesus, he thought . . . how much time was left? Ten, fifteen minutes?

"I'll find them. But you go wait in the car." He led her out of the alley. "But don't open the door. No matter what. Don't let anyone in."

His car was parked under an oak tree, at the far end of the town square. There was nobody around the car.

"But what's going on?" she shrieked.

Damned if I know, he thought.

"It's something Alan Ward brought back," he said aloud, "something that's affecting everyone who came in contact with him." They reached the car. He unlocked it, checked that the backseat was still empty. Erica got in.

"Don't open the car for anyone. I'll go get Josh." He started shutting the door. "Where the hell is this maze?"

"Over by the gazebo," she said.

And he turned and ran off.

Clara stopped at the dead end.

And turned around.

"Clara."

It was her mother.

She waited for her father to appear, right next to her. His hands grabbing her.

(She chewed her lip, begging whoever was running her life to keep the old drunk away.)

"Clara," her mother repeated. "What are you doing?" Her voice was concerned, calm.

Her mother took a step closer to her.

Clara smiled. Tried to smile. "I, er, just came here with my friend. You know—"

Her mother took a step closer.

"Just hanging—"

Another step.

My knife, she thought. *Where's my knife?*

It's in my pack. Back at the barn.
Now her mother smiled. Wide, wider—
And Clara started crying.

Right. Right. Right. Always right. Until Josh heard the sound of the rides. The tiny speakers pounding out thumping music. Then there was darkness.

He was outside.

And Brian grabbed him.

"Come on, Josh. We have to get out of here. Your mother's waiting for us." He pulled the boy away.

"No. Clara's still inside."

"What?"

Josh grabbed Brian, and yelled. "*Clara's still in there*! Her parents were following her. Only, only——"

(Only they weren't her parents. He saw them in his mind, he saw everything in his mind, so clearly now. Why, damn, he could draw them as if they were standing in front of him. Perfect in every detail. Except he knew what would happen. Things would be twisting around them, disgusting, fat, shiny things, hungry things, touching them. He could see it all, then.)

He didn't need to draw it anymore.

I can just see it, Josh thought.

I think about it, and it's there. A picture . . .

Of what will happen.

Or is it just what might happen?

"They're not really her parents," he said dully. "Not anymore." He looked around. "Nearly everyone here isn't——"

Brian grabbed him by the shoulders, and shook him hard. "Josh . . . Josh! Go to my car. Wait for——"

Josh shook his head. "I'm coming with you."

"No," Brian said. "You——"

"I'm coming with you."

And Brian shrugged. He turned to the sign. 'Mirror Madness.' *Just what we need tonight*, he thought. The bulbs flickered around the sign, around garishly painted bleary-eyed ghouls. Off in the distance, Josh heard screaming. Growing louder and louder.

"Come on," Brian said.

And they went in.

* * *

"This is no good," Brian said to Josh.

(The girl could be anywhere. Including outside the fucking maze. A line of sickly bulbs on the ceiling lit the shiny walls.)

"We went left here," Josh said, standing at a T. "Then I lost her."

"Don't you get ahead of me. We've lost enough people for one day."

He looked at his watch. How much time left now?

Five minutes?

No minutes?

"Goddam, this is no good," he said.

He heard someone cry out.

Josh's face lit up. "That's her! That's Clara!"

It came from the other side of the wall.

"Clara!" Josh yelled.

"Stay there, Clara," Brian said, yelling at the wall. "We'll get to you."

"Hurry!" her muffled voice begged.

Brian looked ahead. Another fork. How the hell could he get to her? He'd just end up wandering around, chewing up minutes, wasting time.

He looked back at the wall.

"Here goes nothing," he said.

He pushed against the wall. It bent in. Then more, with his whole weight against it. And all the time Clara was still calling to them.

"Back away from the wall!" he told her. "Get back!" he yelled.

Then Brian pulled back as far as he could, and ran full out into the wall. It buckled, bending under his weight. But then it snapped back into position. "Shit," he said. It was stronger than he thought. He didn't hear Clara screaming anymore.

He tried it again.

And this time his 205 pounds popped the shiny frame out of its holder, and it wiggled violently away, smashing into the ground. Brian fell into another wall.

And Clara was there.

He grabbed her hand and pulled her back to his corridor. Without looking back.

He turned to Josh. "Do you think you can get us out of here?"

Josh nodded and led them back to the opening.

They ran.

Past the ferris wheel filled with screaming people, the smell of vomit filling the air. Past the games where people were sprawled on the counter, bent over like pieces of meat. Past the food booth, where nobody was eating the wieners.

Josh held Clara's hand.

People turned and looked at them. And Josh heard things snaking behind them, snapping at their feet. But there were too many people, too many for the writhing, snapping things to eat or whatever it was they were doing. Too many for them to worry about the three of them running away.

He held Clara's hand. And he asked her what happened.

"My mother . . ." she gasped. "She trapped me. In a dead end."

"It wasn't your mother," Josh said. "Not really."

"This way!" Brian said, leading them away from the carnival grounds, avoiding the entrance. The entrance, where the yelling and screaming drowned out the music, the rides, everything.

Josh looked at Clara running beside him. She had her eyes straight ahead. Her hand felt like ice in his.

And he felt scared.

"What did you do?"

"These things," she said, still looking ahead. "They came out of her mouth. Reached out for me."

"Hurry!" Brian yelled. "Get a move on!"

"And what?" Josh asked.

"I, I—don't know what happened. I guess I ducked under her, pushed past her." She was panting hard in the darkness. And Josh saw a lone car parked at the edge of the park.

"Is that my mom?" Josh asked.

Brian stopped.

"Yes!" Brian said.

Josh saw that his mom wasn't alone.

Captain Watson was beside the car, talking to her, and looking at them.

And in the distance, there were popping sounds, like fireworks, like—

Gunshots . . .

Twenty-Four

"HEY, MAN! WATCH what the fuck you're doing—"

Charlie North pulled his gun butt away from Dwayne's arm. "Chill out, Gaffney. Just *chill . . . out!*"

They were spread across the road, across Route 133, in a ragged line. And every dozen feet or so there was a point man armed with a flame thrower.

Industrial strength size. A big mother that could torch a jeep in one gulp.

"Shit," Gaffney muttered. "I don't like this crap at all, man. What the fuck is going on here anyway?"

Charlie heard some shouts over by the diner, confused voices and some yelling. A ring of soldiers covered the front and side entrances. A few people were forcibly led from the diner into one of the three waiting trucks, a dozen guns trained on them.

Then someone came out of the side door, the kitchen door. A short fellow, dark hair. Dressed in a stained cook's uniform. He was raising his hands, and yelling at the soldiers.

A lieutenant barked at the cook to get down from the steps. And again. He repeated the order, but the cook kept on yelling.

"What the fuck is going on, Charlie?" Gaffney said again.

"Probably has no green card, man."

Then the cook froze.

The lieutenant ordered his soldiers to raise their weapons.

"Oh, shit, man, what the hell is this?" Charlie said.

Then the cook walked down the steps, slowly. The soldiers backed away. The poor bastard looked scared out of his mind.

Why the hell is he moving so slowly? Charlie thought.

Two of the flame-thrower monkeys stood at either end of the ring of soldiers. The cook reached the bottom of the steps. And he stopped there. The lieutenant yelled at him to fall to the ground.

But he didn't. The order was repeated. Louder. There was nervous screaming, yelling—the soldiers screamed at the cook, freaking.

"What the—" Charlie said. The cook bolted. One second he was standing there, and the next he tore off towards the back of the diner. The rifles flew to the soldiers' shoulders. They fired. Blowing a dozen holes in his porky little body.

And the cook fell to the ground.

"Poor—"

But his body didn't stop moving. It bubbled and oozed, like something he might have cooked up for breakfast. A human egg frying right next to the dumpster. Tiny popping sounds filled the air.

Then something started screwing its way out of the chunky little man.

"Oh, shit, man!" Gaffney said. North felt him smack at his arm. "Will you look at that!"

The soldiers stepped back.

A dozen tubelike things suddenly popped out of the body. Curling in on each other. Separating. Coming together. It inched away from the body.

And Charlie saw the glistening needles that covered the tubes.

"Get me the fuck out of here," Gaffney muttered. "Drop me in a goddam rice paddy, but I want *out of here.*"

The thing reared up. And leaped at the nearby soldiers.

And in mid-leap the pair of flame throwers caught it, bathing it in fire. Charlie couldn't see anything except the brilliant flashes of yellow and blue.

Then it was over. The lieutenant walked up gingerly to the black pile of gummy ashes. He kicked at the shit with his boot. And then he turned around.

And after a few soldiers came out of the diner and said that it was empty, they were ordered to start walking down the road, towards Stoneywood.

Gaffney leaned close to Charlie North.

"At least we know what we're here for, eh, home-boy? And if you can figure out what the hell that was, don't tell me. Don't tell me, man. I don't wanna know."

Charlie nodded.

Wishing he held a flame thrower rather than his M-16.

Shit!

Brian saw Watson, standing by the car. The policeman waved to him, a big smile on his face.

Then he heard Josh moan.

"What's wrong?" Brian asked him. The boy turned and looked at him. The boy's face was pale, sick, as if he'd gone on the roller coaster one too many times. He was breathing hard.

"You okay, Josh?"

But Josh started shaking his head, as if he saw something, just there, over Brian's shoulder, out where Watson was standing. . . .

"Easy, Josh," Brian whispered.

Brian put an arm on the boy's shoulder. From behind them he heard the carnival sounds twisted into a nightmare, the delighted squeals transformed into gruesome screams and howls.

Except, with every step, the screaming was slackening.

There was less of it, Brian thought. Sure. Not as many people left . . .

He saw Watson smile again. Then the police chief called to them.

"Brian! Hurry . . . I'm going to help you folks get out."

Great, he thought. Watson had to know some back ways out of the town.

Erica got out of the car, hurrying to her son. "Where were you?" she asked, angry. "You said five minutes—"

"My parents found us," Clara said quietly, answering her question. "They chased us inside the maze."

"Well, come on everyone let's—" Brian said.

He started herding everyone inside the car. But Josh just stood there. Not looking at his mother. Not moving. "No," he said, quietly, then louder—"No!"

Staring right at—

* * *

—The policeman.

Watson smiled. And said, "You folks get in and I'll—"

You'll what? Josh thought. The Captain's Adam's apple bobbled in his throat. He smiled some more. The screams were fading. As the town of Stoneywood melted away.

"No," Josh said quietly, firmly, when Brian urged him towards the car. Now he looked at his mother. She had been there, standing with Watson, waiting for them. He looked at her hard.

Please God, he thought. *Not my mother.*

He looked at her, trying to see through her, to make the image appear in his mind.

And Watson moved. . . .

Brian gave the boy a gentle push.

"Come on, Josh. Get in . . . we don't have any time to—"

There was movement near Brian, slight . . . just a step. And then Watson was next to him. But Brian's nerves were raw, reacting to every little thing that happened. "Huh," he said, turning away from Josh and his mother.

Watson was opening his mouth. Like a circus lion.

"Watch out!" Josh screamed at him. "He's—"

But Brian was already ducking when Watson's head exploded.

Ribbony streamers, waxy party favors, lashed out of Watson's mouth.

(Surprise, surprise . . .)

And flailed at Brian.

And he thought—

Where the fuck is my gun?

Shit. It's in the car. In the glove compartment.

Way to go. And if I get out of this I won't make the same mistake again. Now he looked at Erica. Thinking . . .

Are you one too?

She pulled her son away, away from the streamers.

They missed their swipe, and Watson gulped back the streamers, ready to try again.

The fuck you will, thought Brian.

He charged the cop's midsection, catching him square in his overstuffed belly. Watson flew backwards, roly-poly style. And Brian turned and yelled at everyone.

"Into the car. Quick!"

And by the time he was behind the wheel, fishing the keys out of his pocket—

("Come on, come on," he said, working his fingers into the tight pocket.)

—Watson was up, his mouth a moving anemone, a medusa.

The keys slid out. He put them in the ignition. Turned it on. The car coughed.

Not now, he begged. *For Christ's sake, don't die now!*

Watson fell on the hood, and started crawling on top of the car, a blubbery human spider.

Erica pushed all the locks down.

Brian hit the ignition again.

It started.

"Thank you, God," he said. He jammed the car into reverse, and wheeled backwards, faster, faster, watching the Watson-thing slip from the hood, then claw at it, trying to hold on.

Until finally it flew off.

"How do we get out of here?" Brian yelled at Erica. "What's the fastest way?"

She shook her head. "We're not leaving," Erica said.

Brian turned and looked at her.

"What the hell do you mean?"

He saw Josh stiffen against her. Clara was lost, dazed. They were in shock, the two of them. "What do you mean 'we're not'?"

"My mother," Erica said. "We *have* to get my mother."

Brian looked through the windshield. People were streaming out of the carnival. Except, he very much doubted they were people anymore.

"Great," he said. "Just great . . ." He glanced at the rearview mirror. He saw flashes of light. And he heard tiny pops, like distant fireworks. Perhaps it was too late to get out.

Because, if I was running things, I sure as hell wouldn't let anyone out of here. No fucking way . . .

They'll probably just nuke the whole town.

"We have to go get her," Erica said.

"Right . . . sure."

And Brian put the car in forward. The carnival freaks emptied onto Faith Avenue, filling it. "Is there a back way? Because if there isn't . . ."

"Make a left here," she said quickly.

And while the carnival filled Stoneywood's Faith Avenue, Brian drove deeper into the town.

I'm the last, Johnson thought, crouching under his Knock 'em Down counter.

And they're gone. They've all left. They're gone!

Out to the streets to do God knows what. *They'll go get everyone who wasn't at the carnival*, he thought. *The old ladies. The sick ones. Maybe even the animals.*

Anything alive.

But I'm okay. He grinned, feeling mad, insane, giddy with his luck. *They didn't get me. No, sir. I'm alive. Shit, alive! I'm okay.*

And I'm going to get the hell out of here.

He risked a peek at counter-level. The carnival was completely deserted. Everyone had wandered away, out to the streets, into the town. He let himself come up a bit more. Not too fast. *Best to be careful*, he told himself. *Real slow, and—*

He saw Jim.

Inside his Bozo cage. Slumped over, sitting on his dunking chair.

Johnson looked left and right, imagining the things—

(*What the hell are they?*)

—ready to jump on him, and feed on him like they fed on everyone else. No, man, that wasn't going to happen.

He crept over to Jim, staying low to the ground. *I'm going to beat this*, he thought. *Like I've beaten other things.*

The Bozo looked like a caged animal. A museum display.

Bozo Americanus.

Hey, rube.

But then he saw Jim's chest rising and falling, ever so slightly. Rising and falling.

He's alive, Johnson thought. *Jeezus, someone else is alive, alive . . . and normal.*

Just too damn bad it had to be Jim.

He called to him. "Jim . . ." A whisper at first. Then louder, hissing the name. "Jim!"

There was no reaction. Then the eyelids fluttered open, sleepily, like sluggish elevator doors.

Jim's eyes opened, and he licked his lips. Like he was ready to jump into his routine. "Jim? Hey man, you okay? Everyone else is gone. They're all—"

Jim's eyes opened wider. "Yeah . . . I'm fine. Just—"

Johnson smiled at his comrade, the other survivor, once scorned but now so tremendously precious. Even though he was queer. So what? Johnson grinned in the dark. No one's perfect.

"That's great, Jimbo. Gr—"

But then Jim smiled at him, and Johnson groaned.

Jim gulped a few times, like something was stuck in his throat.

Johnson's smile faded. It went stale, rigid on his face. A mistaken smile.

He backed away.

Not nearly fast enough.

Jim roared, shooting the things at Johnson, right through the mesh, cleverly curling around Johnson's neck, his ankles, his hands, pulling him tight, tighter against the heavy mesh of Jim's cage.

Johnson screamed.

You fuck! he thought. *You were waiting for me, damn it. Aw, shit, it's not fair.* He'd been alone all along. The last one left.

All alone. And now the needles drilled into his skin.

He watched it happen. Thinking:

It's not eating me. No. I understand now. It's doing something else.

The pain traveled along his skin, like dominoes, trailing up his body, into the tiny place inside his head, the place he called me.

And then the real pain, the real horror began. . . .

"I have to get my pack," Clara said, opening the door and hopping out of the car, away from the Stoller house.

"Wait!" Brian said, hurrying after her. "Clara!" he yelled. "Hold on . . . I don't want you going anywhere alone."

She backed away from him. The moon was just at the crest of the mountain. He couldn't see her face. But he could easily know how sick and crazy it must look.

"You can't go," Brian said. "Get back in the car."

She backed up. Not listening to him.

She was used to doing what she wanted.

Then Josh was beside her. "I'll go with her."

Erica hurried to the kitchen, hustling to get her mother out. Trapped, Brian shook his head. "Okay, but if you see anyone, or anything, get the hell back to the house."

They dashed away. And after making sure that they got into the barn, Brian followed Erica into the kitchen.

"What?" The woman laughed, looking incredulously at the two of them. "Leave? What on earth for?"

Brian watched Erica go to her mother. "Mom . . . please . . . We're all in danger here. Everyone in town is gone. They're sick or—Mom, we have to get out."

"Danger?" The woman looked over at Brian, her eyes wide with disbelief. "Can't you two even tell me what kind of danger?"

Erica looked at Brian for help.

He took a step farther into the kitchen.

"It's some kind of creature," he said. "A parasite, something living. It gets inside of people, controls them—"

The woman laughed. "Ho, come *on*, you two. What a crazy idea. Absolutely the silliest thing I ever heard. Now will you just—"

"Mom! Please . . . we have to leave!" Erica was crying, holding the sleeve of her mother's dress.

Then Brian noticed something . . .

While they talked to the woman . . .

Trying to convince her that they had to get out—right now. The old woman had moved to the windows . . . then over to the door.

As if she was cutting us off, Brian thought.

Cutting us the fuck off . . .

Clara snatched up the pack and dangled it in front of Josh. "It's still here," she squealed.

It was pitch-dark in the barn, still heavy with the smell of the animals and the hay. A thin slice of light was visible at the open door.

"What did you think it would do?" Josh asked. "Get up and walk away?" He looked around. "Come on, let's go."

She grabbed him. "Josh . . . you came and got me out. Out of the maze. You could have kept going."

He nodded. "Sure. I'm a real hero. C'mon."

She held onto him. "But Josh . . . your mom was waiting there . . . with Watson. Do you think—"

He looked right at her. And he shook his head and pulled away from her. There was no doubt in his voice.

"No, I don't think—"

And then he stopped talking.

The barn door creaked open.

A small wind sent swirls of hay flying into the air. Swirling, flying, in a small tornado-like funnel. Up into the air, and then down. Josh sniffed at the air.

He saw it then, the police car in front of the house, Watson, the deputy. His grandmother opening the door. The screams, the screams!

He fell to his knees, crying, moaning.

No. It wasn't his mom. It was—

"Oh, God," he groaned, wiping at his eyes.

Then he stood up and ran out of the barn.

"Now, why don't you two just sit down and tell me all about it—"

Erica took a step toward her mother. "Mom," she started. But Brian grabbed Erica's arm, pulling her back. She shot him a look, confused.

I don't want to tip her off that I know, Brian thought. *Got to just stay calm, and think—*

The old woman had positioned herself neatly in front of the door. Smiling as if she were ready to surprise them with a nice homemade apple pie, ummm, hot out of the oven, topped with a big dollop of vanilla ice cream.

But that wasn't the surprise she had planned.

Brian took another step backwards. Wondering . . .

Is the other door locked?

He pulled Erica along. She looked at him. "Brian, what on earth are you doing—?"

But his face said more than any explanation. She turned slowly back to her mother, really seeing her now for the first time. The slight disarray of her dress. The small reddish-brown flecks on her chin.

Erica moaned.

"Erica, sweetie. Please sit down. And where is Josh? Out in the car?"

The old woman's eyes were watery, filmy, as if she were

lind, seeing nothing. Her head turned to them. But her eyes loated, unfocused . . . as if they didn't do a thing. Her voice racked a couple of times. Just the tiniest flaw, Brian thought.

Erica groaned. Mumbled. Inside the bright, old-fashioned itchen. "Mom—Mom."

"It's not your mother." Brian said, holding Erica tightly. "Do you hear me? She's gone. Gone. It's *not her!*"

This time he had his gun.

And he fired when the first tendrils snaked their way over the woman's dry lips. Right at her head. Blood and bone sprayed against the kitchen door, dotting the blue gingham curtains with big red splotches. And again. And again.

But the woman stood there. Half a grin on her cratered face.

Until she started splitting right down the middle, as if she were a crustacean shedding its shell. The room was filled with the sound of ripping skin and breaking bones, snapping loud and clear. Erica and Brian were sprayed by the blood shooting around the room.

And what was finally left, standing by the door, were tiny filaments from the woman's body, as if her nervous system had been replaced by the needle-sharp threads from the creature. What was left of her body collapsed behind it.

And now the writhing filaments snaked towards them.

Brian pushed against the back door leading out to the hall.

He tried the doorknob. *Open, goddamit!*

It was locked.

He started ramming his body against it, but it was a solid piece of wood. It wasn't going anywhere.

He fired more shots at the creature. But the bullets were absorbed by the scaly surface, almost gulped, leaving no damage, not even a mark—

The glistening needles that surrounded it quivered, sensing them . . .

Excited.

And then the kitchen door opened behind the creature.

Josh knew it. He knew his grandmother was gone.

And just as he knew that, he knew how to stop the thing inside her. He knew that Brian's gun wouldn't do anything.

Standing in the barn, he saw a picture of his mother and Brian cowering before this ancient thing, watching it crawl towards them, the kitchen bathed in blood, filled with his mother's screaming.

He grabbed the bucket by Mister's stall.

He ran to the tank where the gas was stored for the tractor. He began pouring gasoline into the bucket.

"Josh! What are you doing?" Clara asked.

He kept on pouring, just half a bucket. It wouldn't take much, he thought. Then he ran out to the house, the gasoline sloshing onto his pants, onto his sneakers.

"What are you *doing*?" Clara yelled, running behind him.

And he opened the door, and he saw his grandmother's body, crumpled, empty—just as he knew he would. And he thought:

That's not her. She's gone.

That's just—

Nothing.

His mother screamed for him to run away.

It was all in slow motion. Everything. He had all the time in the world.

The thing sensed him, and turned from his mother who was begging for Josh to turn and run away. "Run, Josh. Run as fast as you can. Run!"

Some more gasoline sloshed out of the bucket, spilling to the floor. Always waxed. Always so shiny. His grandmother worked so hard to keep it neat. So hard . . . and now—

It turned on him then. He was close to it. It could sense where he was.

Okay, he thought. *That's right. I'm here. Right this way.*

Clara clutched his shoulders, yelling at him to do it. "Just do it! Now, Josh, now."

It came closer. "Now," he said quietly.

He threw the gasoline on the creature, this white writhing serpent, a weave of tendrils. It twisted, stung by gas. It made no sound.

It had no mouth. No mouth of its own. Then it started moving again.

And Josh backed away when Brian fired.

It exploded into flame, burning crimson, and magenta—strange, weird colors that made the kitchen look like a vision of hell. The scaly whitish skin made a loud crackling noise as the fire covered it.

It burned quickly, filling the kitchen with a black smoke. He

eard his mother coughing. She called Brian's name, then
osh's. And then Josh saw Brian pull Erica through the smoke,
round the smoldering creature.

Not one creature, he thought. The colony . . .

Is it all there? Is it all burning?

He backed up, out into the yard. His mother was crying,
ugging him. Brian closed his arms around him.

And for a minute they didn't hear Clara behind them, crying,
hen screaming at them to stop, please stop, and turn, and look,
ook—

"Oh, God . . . *Look!*"

Twenty-Five

"LOOK . . ." CLARA'S VOICE was a whisper, but it made them all turn and look where she was pointing.

The people were streaming up the hill, Brian saw. All of them walking up the rutted mountain road. Some stumbling, some running ahead briskly, more sure-footed.

The people of Stoneywood. The old men, the children, the bank president, the druggist, the summer people. Everyone.

"Oh, shit," Brian muttered to himself. Erica grabbed his arm.

"What are we going to do?" she said.

"We can't go down that way." Brian shook his head. "We can't . . ."

Then something about the swarm struck him. It wasn't like the closing scene of Frankenstein, with the angry villagers, all noisy and out of control, carrying torches to the monster's hideout. No, these people—if they *were* people anymore——moved together. Like a tide. Or a line of ants.

"Is there another way off the hill?" he asked Erica. But she stood there, watching the swarm, not answering him. He grabbed her shoulders and shook her hard. "Erica! Is there any other way out of here?"

"No," she said dully. "There's just the road." Her hand dug into his.

"No," Clara said.

The girl stood by herself, just looking down the hill. Josh stood close to her.

"No," Clara repeated. Then she turned. The moon lit up her

face. So grim, so grown-up. "There's another way," she said quietly.

"No there isn't," Erica yelled, almost nastily. "There's no—"

"The gorge," Clara said quietly. "The gorge keeps on going . . . it runs, right around the mountain, and it comes out on a road . . . on the other side."

Brian went to the girl, grabbed her shoulders. "Are you sure?"

She nodded. "I've hiked it dozens of times . . . dozens. . . ."

Brian turned to Erica, looking for confirmation of Clara's idea. "She . . . she's right," Erica said. "But it's not an easy hike. And in the dark . . ."

"There's a moon," Josh said.

Brian looked down the hill. The human swarm moved slowly, but steadily. They had five, maybe ten minutes, to get away.

He said, "Besides . . . what other choice do we have?"

The people on the hill were getting closer. And strangely, there were no sounds. No talking and muttering as they climbed towards them. Probably no need for that, Brian thought. *And why are they coming? Are we the only ones left?*

"Let's go," he said.

"Wait," Josh said. "What if they catch up to us?"

"What?"

"There's more gasoline in the barn," Josh said.

"Right." He patted Josh on the back. "Good thinking." He turned to Erica. "Are there any empty bottles around?"

Erica shook her head. "I don't know . . . maybe—"

"Under the sink," Josh said. "There's some cleaning stuff. It's almost gone."

"I'll get the gas, Josh. You empty the bottles. Erica, get some sheets, and scissors." He went over to Clara. "And you watch out for them. If they start to hurry, scream as loud as you can."

Clara nodded.

"Steady," Erica said to him. "You're spilling some." Brian nodded. There wasn't a hell of a lot of gas left. Half a can, maybe three gallons. And Josh was only able to scrounge up four bottles.

Brian finished filling the bottle, and then Erica stuffed the piece of sheet into its neck. "Are you sure this will work?" she asked him.

"No, I'm *not* sure. I've never made Molotov cocktails before. But this is how I think it's done. Not too tight . . . there. I think we have to get the wick saturated."

She handed one finished grenade to Josh and then picked up the last bottle.

Brian filled it quickly, spilling some of the gas on the ground, onto his clothes. It was a sharp smell, and his eyes stung from the vapors.

The bottle was nearly full when they heard Clara scream.

"God almighty," Brian said, pulling Clara back from the road.

"What are they doing?" Erica asked, her voice cracking, screaming, demanding. "What are they *doing*?"

At first, it looked as though some of the crowd were engaged in a chicken fight, with one person climbing atop another's shoulders. But then a third one would leap atop the first two, making the column three persons high. Other people leaned into the pyramid, supporting it. A goddam circus act, Brian thought.

"Come on," he said, "we better—"

But he let himself look for another moment, disgusted, fascinated. He saw a face he recognized. The guy from the gas station. Right near the front of the crowd. And one by one the moonlight caught them, as their human shells rippled and burst, sliding off them like unwanted coats, peeling and bubbling to the ground. Layers of flesh fell to the side of the road, so much scrap. Then, great flakes of stomach and bones cascaded through the air, while their heads popped open like rotting pumpkins.

He heard Erica gag. She coughed and heaved.

While the colony came together.

Behind it, Brian saw fiery flashes of light from town.

Then Josh spoke.

"It's trying to get out . . . to escape," he said quietly. "It knows we're here and it wants to get out."

Brian looked at Josh. "What do you mean?" The boy's eyes glowed, fiery, strong—

Eyes that scared Brian.

"It wants to get out," Josh said, turning around, gesturing behind them, "past the mountain. There," Josh said.

There, Brian thought. *South.*

How far away from New York City? 120 miles? 100?

"Right," Brian said. "C'mon, let's move it." He herded them away from the road. "We'll worry about that after we're out of here." He touched Clara's shoulder. "It's up to you, Clara."

She nodded. "This way," she said quietly. And she started running past Barrow's Hill, up to the gorge.

Brian stumbled once, and the two bottles in his backpack rattled together. He reeked of gasoline, a living wick.

Erica asked, "Are you okay?"

He got up to his feet. "Where's Clara?" he called into the darkness. "Clara! Hold on . . . wait a minute."

She was as sure-footed as a mountain goat. Though the moonlight was blocked by the mountain, she navigated the gorge with ease.

He ran as best he could, trying to keep up with her, stepping into the water, catching his foot in the pits and ruts of the shallow stream.

Then they came to a wall.

Brian could only see Josh, about ten feet above him.

"Where's Clara?" he asked.

"She's already on top," he panted.

"Keep going then," Brian said.

Erica went next, and then Brian started climbing up behind her, the gasoline bottles still rattling noisily in his pack.

The small rocky ledges that had held the two kids crumbled and gave way under Brian's weight. His fingers ached from digging into the tiny crevices in the rock, holding on with just the tips of his fingers. His legs flailed around, kicking at the stone, searching for some kind of decent foothold.

"You okay?" Erica called down to him.

"Super. Just great."

Then he heard the sound.

Water. Splashing. Just below him.

Shit.

It's reached the gorge, he thought.

So fast . . . How did it—?

But he knew how it made such good time. It had thrown off

all those bodies, those useless bodies. There'd be plenty of new bodies on the other side. And then it could writhe its way right up the hill, and through the gorge.

He tried to hurry up the last few feet.

And he slipped.

His feet chewed through another stony perch, and his hands found nothing to stop his painful glide down to the bottom of the gorge. Dropping . . .

He imagined—oh, yes—falling right on top of it. *Plop*, watching it coil around him.

But he felt a gnarled, twisted branch that curled out of the wall. It whizzed past his legs, his waist. He had only one chance. He brought his hand out, ready to make a grab for it.

He felt the wood brush past his knuckles. His fingers— fumbling—tried to close on the branch. He felt the wood snapping past his hand, narrowing, slipping through his fingers.

He closed his hand—and his fingers locked on it.

"Thank you," he whispered, suspended above the stream.

Now he started back up. Taking his time, testing his handholds—despite the sounds—so fucking close now—of something large sloshing in the water beneath him.

I smell it, he thought. *God, what kind of smell is that?* Like nothing he'd ever smelled before.

"C'mon, McShane," he said to himself. "Move your ass, move it!" He just kept going, one hand over the other, inch by inch, not even letting himself think that maybe he wouldn't be able to do it. Until, at last, he reached the top.

And the thing was just below him.

He didn't look.

"Come on," he said, annoyed with himself for having held the others up.

And now they were running on a rough trail that curved around the base of the mountain. Nobody said anything. There were no night sounds, no crickets. No wind rustling the leaves. No birds screaming at them from the high mountain flight paths.

Nothing, but their single-minded panting.

Nothing until they curved around the northeast corner of the mountain, cutting off Stoneywood behind them.

When they all heard the voice.

"Help me," the voice cried. "Help meeeee!"

* * *

Charlie North's company marched double time up Faith Avenue, up to the bright lights of the carnival.

"Shit," he said. "Will you look at that, Gaffney? A goddam carnival."

Some garbled rap music boomed from loudspeakers.

"Yeah . . . Hey, Charlie-boy, where the hell is everybody?"

"Beats the fuck out of me, man. All I know—"

The line of soldiers stopped. Two lieutenants were having some kind of discussion.

"I jus' hope they don't split us up, man. You know what I mean, break us up into two squads."

"Yeah, me—"

North had been looking at the deserted carnival. A few of the rides—all deserted—were still running. The ferris wheel was going around and around, the metal girders making a repetitive creak. A small merry-go-round whirred. Another rap song came on, some bullshit antidrug rap by Ice-T.

Then Charlie saw something.

Two things.

"Hey man," he said to Gaffney, then louder, to everyone, "Hey, there's some dudes over there. Yeah, check it out, some—"

The two lieutenants stopped talking, turned and saw the two people coming out of the carnival grounds.

"Man," Gaffney said, "I'm sure glad to see someone alive, someone—"

But North tapped his buddy's arm hard. Tapped his arm, and raised his rifle up.

"Hey," Charlie said, looking at the two people walking over to the soldiers. Two people. Right. Except they were joined together, like they had been squashed together, *like some fucked-up road kill.*

"Oh, shit, man," Charlie said to Gaffney. "Will you look at that? Aw, hell, man, what the fuck is that?"

But Gaffney said nothing as he got his last glimpse at the thing before a pair of flame throwers filled the night air with the choking smoke of the burning bodies.

"Just keep frying those things, baby," Charlie North whispered.

"Fucking A," Gaffney agreed.

* * *

"Clara—wait!" Erica yelled.

"Come on," Brian said. "Keep going, Erica, keep—"

She shook her head. "Listen," she said, wondering if maybe he hadn't heard the cry for help. "Will you *listen*!"

He stood there, in the total quiet. And heard it.

"Help me . . . please . . . someone. Help!"

Brian imagined the creature behind them, grasping at the wall of rock using its skin and spiky needles to make its way up and out of the gorge. Out of Stoneywood.

"Erica, we've got to get the hell out of here, now!"

He held her arm. But she pulled away. "I know that voice, Brian. I know it. It's Bob O'Connor." She took a step off the trail, over piles of broken rock. "And if you're not going to help him, then I am."

She started running up the slope, towards the voice.

"Damn it," Brian said. He ran after her, slipping on the gravel, catching her. "Erica, damn it, come back."

"Help . . . please."

The voice came from above them. About twenty feet.

Brian reached her, grabbed her arm, holding her back. "*I'll* go get him," Brian said. "Please, go back down and stay with Josh and Clara." Erica's eyes glowed. "Go stay with them!"

She backed away.

And Brian climbed up to Bob O'Connor.

"What is it?" Clara asked him.

Josh turned and looked behind him.

It was so easy now. All he had to to do was think about it, and the picture was there.

He looked back into the darkness. His mom . . . he thought. No. Not his mom. Brian. "Oh, no," he said.

Clara grabbed his hand. "What is it, Josh? What's—"

But he ignored her.

Hoping that he'd be in time . . .

To save them both.

The man's leg was wedged, actually buried, Brian saw, under a pile of large rocks. Part of his leg looked chewed away, rubbed down to the bone by O'Connor's crazed attempt to get away. His blood had dried to a coppery pool on the surrounding rock.

"Steady, guy. You're okay now. I'm going to get you out. Just take it easy."

Brian took another step close to him. Even if Brian got him out, the guy's foot was likely to be a goner.

"I'm going to have to move some of these stones. It's going to hurt. So—"

Brian looked in the man's face, to see just how frightened he was.

And he saw that he wasn't frightened at all.

Josh stood beside his mother. "Mom . . . where's Brian . . . ? Where—"

"Up there," she said, pointing.

Josh turned, and he saw the shadowy figure of Brian kneeling down, closer to the man . . . whom they couldn't see.

And Josh knew what was going to happen. "No," he yelled. He started running up the hill, screaming at Brian, screaming for this man who had become so important to them. "NO!"

But it was like seeing an airplane drop into a swamp. An airplane with your father in it. Seeing it, because it had to happen. It was supposed to happen.

"No . . ." he said, panting, running up the hill, his mother scrambling behind him—

—Much too late.

"Let's just see how deep this leg—"

Brian tried to get one of the big stones off the man's leg. He wanted to dig him out as painlessly as possible.

He looked over his shoulder, listening for the sound of the creature. He heard Josh calling. Scared, probably. And Erica.

And was the creature up the cliff already? or was it having some trouble climbing?

He pushed the stone away from the foot. All bloody red, pulpy—but, there, inside the red mush—thin white lines, like muscle, like—

There was no sound. Nothing, except his own breathing. Steady, constant.

Precious.

He felt sad when he saw it. When he saw the white tendril slip out of the mashed foot and curl around his leg. More than anything, he felt sad. *There are things I'll never see*, he thought. *I never got married, never had children. How many other things are lost now?*

The tendril encircled his leg, this waxy ribbon crawling, sneaking out from inside O'Connor's body. And Brian was glad he had stopped Erica. Real glad.

I didn't fuck up, he thought.

This time I didn't fuck up.

He felt the needles drive through his pants legs, into his skin. The pain traveled up his leg. Sharp, then followed by an almost pleasant numbness.

He stood up.

How much time left? How many seconds?

The O'Connor creature started pulsating, excited by its ticket out.

That's what you think, fucker.

That's what you think.

He yelled to Erica.

"Get them the hell out of here—now!" he screamed. "For Christ's sake, get the hell out of here."

(The pain reached his groin, and he doubled up.)

"It's one of them . . ." he called out. Then, almost embarrassed—"It's got me. Get them away. Please!"

And Brian turned around to look at the creature.

A thin slice of moon broke the crest of the mountain.

And Brian saw something else. Sitting only ten feet away. A gray plastic package. He heard it tick.

Then he dug out the old ammonia bottle filled with gas and he grinned.

"Brian . . ." Josh heard his mother say, frozen, standing there, holding him back. "Oh, no . . . Brian."

Then Josh knew it was too late. Knew that Brian was already gone. He turned and started pulling his mother back down the mountain.

"Come on, Mom. We have to get out of here, Mom, *now*!"

He turned to look back at Clara. "Go on Clara . . . I'll get her to follow."

Clara nodded, and started moving away.

"I'm going, Mom." He stepped away from his mother. "I'm going . . . It's too late for Brian. But we can still get away. If we go now."

Then his mother slowly turned and looked at him. Her

cheeks were covered with splotchy streaks. She took his hand and they ran.

He saw the timer. Heard it ticking. And he saw the gray packet wedged into the slope. Now he understood what Bob O'Connor had been doing here.

It was close enough, Brian thought.

He tried to stand erect, even though it felt like there were all these barbed wires inside his chest, attached to every part of him, all of them pulling tighter and tighter. The wires licked at his throat, and dug up into his brain.

He held the bottle in front of him. One eye started to go blurry, then dark. Brian was crying from the pain, which was growing more and more intense.

Through the columns of pine trees he saw the creature working its way through the woods. Fast, then faster.

Hungry to find a way out.

Something at the back of his neck hurt, like a dentist's drill boring right into his skull.

He held his gun up to the bottle and fired.

"Keep going!" Josh said, when the first brilliant flare exploded behind them. He knew what that was, of course. He knew all along what Brian was going to do.

But then another explosion rocked the mountain. A huge blast that blew the wind at their backs. A flurry of branches and leaves and stones went flying at their backs.

Josh kept running, but through the stinging hail of flying dirt, he turned around.

And he watched the explosion break off great chunks of the mountain, ripping them right off the ancient cliffs, sending them smashing down.

Some smaller boulders smashed right behind them, plummeting through the trees. But though painful chunks of stone rained down, no large boulders hit them.

And when Josh risked turning around again, he saw the northeast face of Mount Shadow rear up, shudder, and then fall, sliding with a tremendous thundering sound.

Down, onto the gorge. Filling the gorge.

Burying everything behind them.

And he thought:

It wasn't just the explosion. The explosion hadn't been that big.

Clara ran down to the road, off the trail, and Josh grabbed his mother's hand, pulling her along, following. Branches scratched his face, as if trying to hold him. But he raced down the hill, grabbing at saplings, careening down, pulling his mother behind him.

Until he saw they were at a road.

A single lane road that led to the south.

Away from Stoneywood. Away from the gorge. Away from the mountain.

And when the rest of the explosions ringing the mountain went off, they stopped now and looked. A great cloud of dust ringed the mountain. Puffs of dust and stone flew out over the slope, a ghostly cloud. The rumble of the falling rock echoed back to them from the some distant mountain miles away, across the valley.

Josh thought about the fossil then. Trapped by the mountain. Trapped, until he found it.

And he knew.

This had happened before.

And he wondered if whatever was behind them, whatever was following them, was really buried.

There was the sound of a car engine in the distance. Then Josh saw two pinpricks of light. He grabbed his mother's hand, and then Clara's. He held them tight.

While the mountain went on rumbling behind him.

Epilogue

ERICA LEANED AGAINST the polished wood rail, watching the other skaters, and watching Clara and Josh.

Christmas in Manhattan . . .

In Rockefeller Center.

It was an unusually cold, frigid December day. No clouds marred the bright blue sky cut by the jutting skyscrapers.

She shifted on her skates, brand new and incredibly painful. It had been a long time since she last skated, a lifetime ago, and her wobbly ankles felt like they were ready to collapse. And even two pairs of wool socks from L.L. Bean did little to keep her toes from going completely numb.

A little boy went *splat* on the ice in front of her, and his father skated smoothly over to him—a giant crane—hoisting him up, and back on his feet. The boy was like Bambi risking the icy pond at Thumper's insistence.

She looked at Clara and Josh. The young girl—seeming a bit older almost every day—moved smoothly, gracefully on the ice, in direct contrast to her usual tomboyish awkwardness. It presaged the woman to come. Josh was clumsy and he kicked at the ice just to keep up with his friend.

Friend . . . I guess that's what she is, Erica thought. Except for when they went to school, Clara and her son were inseparable. Best friends. Sharers of secrets that she could only guess at. And it was okay for now, she guessed. Okay that the girl lived with them until some other arrangement popped up. Clara had no real relatives, none close by, and none that wanted to take her in.

Especially after what had happened.

And Erica couldn't resist Josh's pleading.

(Saying, "She saved us, Mom. *She saved our lives!*")

"Right," Erica said. Because she didn't know what else to say. So screw all her friends who said it wasn't healthy . . . a young boy, a teen-ager almost, and a young girl.

Screw them.

Because they needed each other. And she needed them.

She watched them skate past the small café that sat to the left of the skating rink. And they waved to her as they floated past.

"Come on, Mom!" Josh shouted.

She smiled. "I have to rest!" she called back, still smiling.

And as they skated by, she looked at the rest of the skaters. So happy, so lighthearted. An old-fashioned New York Christmas.

And her eyes trailed up to the golden sculpture that watched over the rink, a mammoth statue of Prometheus, all curling muscles and gilt. And, like so many things, the twisted limbs of the sculpture reminded her of the summer.

Always in her thoughts.

Always in her nightmares.

The representatives from the Government—CIA, FBI, or whoever the hell they were—couldn't have been more thoughtful . . . more concerned.

But, they told her, there were limits to how much they could explain. It was a question of security, they said. And panic. They needed her cooperation. Her pledge to keep quiet.

She mostly nodded.

Offered them tea. And Pepperidge Farm cookies.

And listened.

("You can explain it to the children," they said. "We're sure you can help them understand.")

She kept nodding. Wanting to say that the "children" already understood. *More than me. Maybe even more than you.*

The official version was simple. It began and ended at Stoneywood. A freak earthquake. A localized tremor of unusual force. There was nothing about Antarctica, nothing about some ancient creature that could merge into the nervous system, meld with another organism. That had to be kept quiet, they said.

Of course . . .

Already sections of the Antarctic plateau, exposed areas that had been opened up beneath the mile thick blanket of ice, had been quickly closed. Quarantined. The problem, they assured her, had been contained.

Until we're ready. They smiled. *Ready to study this thing.*

But the important thing to realize, they said, is that it's been stopped. At Stoneywood.

That's what they said.

Which she knew was bullshit.

Clara did a quick spin, circling right around Josh.

"Try lifting your feet up a bit. You move them like they're snowplows!" She laughed.

And Clara watched Josh, his face set, determined, trying to get his feet up off the ice.

Until he lost his balance, and his body did a few jerky twitches before crashing to the ice. She couldn't help laughing.

"Kindly keep your pointers to yourself, Clara."

"Oops!" She grinned. She skated smoothly over to him, and extended a hand to him. Pulling him up.

His hand closed around hers.

Strong, pulling her down, right on top of him.

And he scooted to his feet, laughing loudly. "I just had to see *you* on your bottom for once."

Then he came close to her and helped her up.

"Very funny," she said. But she wasn't angry. Not really. She loved Josh. She knew that, though she doubted she could ever say it, say those words. But he and his mother were her life now. They had saved her from her parents, from the town.

That was all buried.

And while she still had those dreams—of people she knew, people she grew up with, reaching out, grabbing for her— slowly it was fading. Becoming a memory.

Josh was grinning at her. Then he was looking over her shoulder, over to where his mother was.

And his face went pale and cold. And he trudged past Clara.

The man was standing next to his mother. Dressed in a sleeveless down jacket, a bright crimson, and a green ski cap and puffy red scarf. He smiled and leaned close to her.

It's everyone, he thought. Everyone he looked at, he had the same thoughts, the same ridiculous fears—

Except he knew that they weren't ridiculous.

He started skating awkwardly towards his mother.

They didn't talk about it. That was agreed. They never mentioned Brian McShane's name, or Stoneywood. The summer had been blacked out.

But Josh looked carefully at everyone who came into their lives.

Everyone—like this man he didn't know.

Thinking . . .

Is he okay?

Or is it there, inside him?

Had it finally come to New York? The Big Apple.

Because he knew it had to happen.

No matter how many flame throwers they turned loose. No matter how many explosions went off that night. They couldn't have got it all.

(And maybe, he thought, lying in the dark apartment, listening to the hum of Third Avenue traffic . . . maybe it couldn't be stopped at all.)

And that's when he tried to think, tried to imagine one thing, hoping for some answer.

What stopped it before? What stopped it hundreds of millions of years ago when life started on the planet?

He thought he knew the answer. The clue was in that mountain, in the fossils buried under layers of rock.

Only one thing could have stopped it.

The planet itself.

And if that was true, could it do it again?

Or have we fucked up everything so much that it's too late?

This time, would it win?

He skated to a stop right in front of his mother.

"Oh," she said, turning to her son. "Josh, this is Tom, the art director at the agency."

She looked at her son, waiting for him to say, "Hi."

He nodded.

"*Josh?*" she said.

"Hello," Josh said, without enthusiasm.

She turned to Tom. Tom, who had ended up capturing the corporate prize she wanted, the prize she deserved. She just didn't put the time in anymore. It just didn't seem to matter. . . .

Tom smiled, and then skated away. "See you Monday," he said.

"Josh . . ." she began, but her son went back to Clara.

I should talk to him, she thought. *Tell him that he can't look at everyone he meets, every stranger, like they . . . like they—*

She smiled sadly.

But how could she do that?

He probably knew how she checked the newspapers. Marking down the names of towns. A fire in this one. A small earthquake here. A flood there.

A bad year for natural disasters in New York.

Except that she knew that they weren't too natural.

And so she marked their locations on a map, watching the small circles she made as they meandered closer to New York City. And though she didn't say a word to Clara and Josh, they'd be leaving soon.

And where? South, most likely. Maybe west, out to California. How much time would that buy them? she wondered. Enough for a life? For her, and Josh (and Clara—she'd come too).

And how much time was enough? How many years?

And was *it* learning too? Was this ancient thing growing more subtle in its ability to control its human hosts?

She shivered.

Perhaps it was here already.

Waiting.

That man, over there, sitting at a table watching her. Or the young woman skating by herself, spinning on the ice like a ballerina. The poor homeless drunk they had to step over to walk down the stairs to this beautiful rink.

On this beautiful early winter day.

When the air smelled clear, and the blue sky seemed filled with hope and wonder.

And Erica, chilled now throughout her entire body, pushed away from the rail, skating hard towards her son, and the girl who meant so much to him.